'[A] challenging and exciting novel . . . a grown-up story seasoned with politics, religion and the terrors of breakdown' *Sunday Times*

'This brilliantly murky novel describes a nightmarish ten days in the life of a famous, highly successful but deeply dysfunctional family' *Spectator*

'This novel crackles with energy . . . The quick-paced, unadorned writing almost makes it possible to miss the sharp connections being drawn between the strait-laced and the strait-jacketed in contemporary Britain'
Daily Telegraph

'Heartache, soul searching and finger pointing swirl around this complex tale of a dysfunctional, yet powerful family' *Daily Mirror*

'Billington's persuasive and intriguing portrait of a family . . . a complex human drama that also embraces questions not only of how we treat the mentally ill, but crime and punishment, the place of religion, and the purpose of parliamentary democracy' *The Independent*

One Summer

'Billington handles the tension well and her main characters are well-formed . . . intense, brooding and self-destructive' *Daily Telegraph*

'Heightened emotionalism worthy of Iris Murdoch . . . prose that is supple and lyrical but never self-indulgent' *Spectator*

'A heady literary cocktail that hurtles towards its tragic denouement with this author's characteristic flair' *Easy Living*

'This great romance reads like a thriller' *Bella*

The Space Between

'Billington's warm portrait of life at a crossroads will strike a chord with all those determined to forge their own path, no matter how unclear it may seem' *Red*

'This is a good story, told by a sympathetic, compassionate and wise writer . . . this book leaves one full of admiration for the author: she is in the front rank of those who write of women's lives' *The Tablet*

'Billington's perceptive portrait of the complications of modern life is a Jane Austen tale for the 21st century' *Good Book Guide*

Rachel Billington has published eighteen novels and nine books for children, as well as several non-fiction works. She is also a regular journalist, feature writer and reviewer. She is co-editor of *Inside Time*, the national newspaper for prisoners, and a Vice-President of English PEN. She has four children and five grandchildren and lives in London and Dorset. Visit her website at www.rachelbillington.com

By Rachel Billington

ALL THINGS NICE

THE BIG DIPPER

LILACS OUT OF THE DEAD LAND

COCK ROBIN

BEAUTIFUL

A PAINTED DEVIL

A WOMAN'S AGE

THE GARISH DAY

OCCASION OF SIN

LOVING ATTITUDES

THEO AND MATILDA

BODILY HARM

MAGIC AND FATE

TIGER SKY

A WOMAN'S LIFE

THE SPACE BETWEEN

ONE SUMMER

LIES & LOYALTIES

Non-Fiction

THE FAMILY YEAR

THE GREAT UMBILICAL:
MOTHER, DAUGHTER, MOTHER

CHAPTERS OF GOLD:
THE LIFE OF MARY IN MOSAICS

For Children

ROSANNA AND THE
WIZARD-ROBOT

THE FIRST CHRISTMAS

STAR TIME

THE FIRST EASTER

THE FIRST MIRACLE

THE LIFE OF JESUS

THE LIFE OF SAINT FRANCIS

FAR OUT!

THERE'S MORE TO LIFE

Rachel Billington

Lies & Loyalties

An Orion paperback

First published in Great Britain in 2008
by Orion
This paperback edition published in 2008
by Orion Books Ltd,
Orion House, 5 Upper St Martin's Lane,
London WC2H 9EA

An Hachette Livre UK company

1 3 5 7 9 10 8 6 4 2

A CIP catalogue record for this book is available
from the British Library.

ISBN 978-0-7528-9387-7

Typeset at The Spartan Press Ltd,
Lymington, Hants

Printed in Great Britain by
Clays Ltd, St Ives plc

The Orion Publishing Group's policy is to use papers that
are natural, renewable and recyclable products and
made from wood grown in sustainable forests. The logging
and manufacturing processes are expected to conform to
the environmental regulations of the country of origin.

www.orionbooks.co.uk

To Kevin

Our Lady, Star of the Sea
Pray for seafarers
Pray for us

O Mary, Star of the Sea, light of every ocean, guide seafarers across all dark and stormy seas that they may reach the haven of peace and light prepared in Him who calmed the sea. As we set forth upon the oceans of the world and across deserts of our time, pray that we will never fail on life's journey, that in heart and mind, word and deed, in days of turmoil and in days of calm, we will always look to Christ and say, Who is this that even the wind and sea obey Him? Our Lady of peace, pray for us! Bright Star of the Sea, guide us!

CHAPTER ONE

Found Hanging From a Tree

The two men were fighting on the floor. Although they tried hard to land a punch neither succeeded so that it was a kind of ineffectual pulling and kicking, wrestling and rolling, with arms and legs flying in all directions. Judging by their furious faces, equally red and sweating, they didn't intend to give up without drawing blood or at least gaining some advantage.

Jesmarie looked at them with amazement from the door. Roland Norrington Barr, head of chambers, had disappeared halfway under his large desk so that only his long legs, with the black hand-made lace-ups, slashed the air. She supposed that some might find the sight funny but she was horrified to see this usually dignified, powerful man, reduced to a scuffling schoolboy.

'Ugh!' Roland grunted painfully, as his head hit the underside of the desk.

'Serves you right!' shouted Leo, who was now half crouching and trying to pull Roland out. A shiny shoe made contact with his cheekbone. 'Bastard!' And they were back to rolling about the floor again.

Jesmarie began to feel she should take some action. Not that it was her place. She put down the cup of tea she was holding. They were brothers, of course, and brothers fought, but they were also grown men. As far as men did grow up. After thirty years in the chambers Jesmarie had her doubts. They were successful, all right: a QC and an MP – letters of honour. If they carried on long enough, they could do each other real damage and, worse still, it might even get into the papers. Maybe she should tell Mike – except he'd gone

1

out to lunch. Senior clerks should always be on tap in case of emergencies. From behind her she heard steps approaching.

It was Mike's nephew, Wayne. He'd just have to do. 'Take a look in there, would you?'

The boy, hardly more than that although dressed in the flashiest pinstripe she'd seen yet and hair greased like a basted joint, opened the door immediately.

'Shit, man.'

'Ssh.'

They both stared. Roland's jacket had been pulled off his shoulders revealing a thinly striped navy lining. Leo had retained his suit but the vent at the back had ripped showing a flash of pale blue satin. They were both big men, fit, in their forties and, although panting heavily, it was clear they could go on like this for some time. Now there was a mark with a little blood on Roland's cheek. Neither man showed any awareness that they were being watched.

Jesmarie gently pulled the door to.

'It's not our business, is it?' Wayne shrugged his narrow shoulders.

'Anything to do with the barristers is your business. How do you think you clerks earn your money?' He was no use. 'Where's Bert – or is Mike back?'

'He might be.'

'Get him then.'

Mike arrived remarkably quickly.

'Thank the Lord,' said Jesmarie at the sight of him. Only forty, but with twenty years of managing barristers. He got the point in a flash. Not that it was difficult with the noise still going on next door.

'What we need is someone to break it up.' Mike shook his head. 'Not like Mr Norrington Barr, this.'

'Rivalry?' suggested Jesmarie.

'He's got a big case Monday. Murder.'

Jesmarie shifted on her feet, which always hurt by lunchtime. She'd have to wear blasted trainers like everyone else.

'Get someone to call them. Wait.' They were all quiet. The scuffling, which had lessened, rose to a loud bang and a yelp. 'Another family member. We've got their numbers in case his mother passes away.' He sped off.

*

2

By the time the telephone rang on the large desk, the brothers were reduced to a kind of shadow fighting. They were still on the floor but more out of exhaustion than anything else. Occasionally one directed an elbow at the other, or a half-hearted kick or a punch, but their faces, although still red, were no longer enraged. They wore expressions more of shock and even sadness, as if this reality were worse than before.

Roland let the phone ring a few times, then stood up, tugging his jacket back on to his shoulders. He was even taller than he'd seemed on the ground, so tall that he had a slight, obviously habitual stoop.

'Hello.' His voice was hoarse. He cleared his throat and pronounced more decisively. 'Norrington Barr.' His fingers felt for his tie, which was not there since it had swivelled to the back of his neck. 'Portia!' His eyes turned to Leo, still sitting on the floor.

At Portia's name, Leo shuffled to his feet. He picked up a chair that had been knocked over and sat on it. He, too, was tall although an inch or so shorter than his brother and with broader shoulders. Both men were beginning to go bald and had neat well-trimmed hair, Leo's fairer and with a hint of curl.

Portia's voice was loud in the room, as if Roland had the loudspeaker on.

'Whatever's happening? Your clerk made it sound like murder.'

'Murder?' Leo stood up and took off his jacket. His shirt was patched with sweat. He found a handkerchief and wiped his face before sitting down again. He didn't meet Roland's eyes.

'It's not Imogen, then?' continued Portia, more hesitantly. 'He insisted I rang. Said it was an emergency.'

'Where are you?' Roland mumbled eventually. He, too, pulled out a handkerchief and wiped his face. It came back bloodied. He laid it on the desk.

'I'm on top of Monte Albán, an Aztec site near Oaxaca in central Mexico, trying to get publicity for a women's co-operative. I've brought a whole gang of them up here to be photographed and they're waiting patiently in ninety-five-degree heat. Anyway, I can't afford this call.' She sounded defensive.

Roland recaptured his tie and eased it round to the front. Once again he tried and failed to catch Leo's eye. When Portia stopped speaking, he said, 'Just hold on a minute.' He pressed a button on the phone and leaned forward to Leo. 'Shall I tell her?'

3

'It's up to you.'

'Oh, God.'

Leo shrugged. He smoothed the jacket across his knee.

'Bastard,' said Roland, without much energy.

'Who's the eldest here?' Leo's voice was mocking. 'With privilege comes responsibility.'

'Shut up!' Roland seemed on the verge of anger again.

'You'd better say something to her.'

Roland's fingers hovered over the phone. 'She'd much rather hear it from you.'

Leo relented. 'Turn it this way.'

'Thanks.' For the first time the two men looked at each other. It seemed to constitute a kind of truce.

Roland flicked the switch. Leo spoke with his eyes on the window beyond the desk. 'Portia, it's Leo. It's bad news, the worst news.' He hesitated. 'Charlie's dead.'

There was a discernible gasp from the other end. 'So that's why you were fighting.' Another gasp and a long pause.

'Porsh?'

'I'm just trying to breathe. There's a shortage of air up here. The women know about death. I'm sorry. I'm talking rubbish. I some-how never thought – despite everything. I can't believe it. I can't take it in. It's impossible.'

Now Roland spoke. 'I'm afraid it's tragically true. The hospital rang. He was found in the garden.'

'No—' Leo cut in abruptly.

Roland ran his hand across his forehead. 'When are you back?'

'Two days.' Portia's voice was breaking up, whether with emotion or a fault on the line it was hard to tell.

'What did you say?'

'I want to see him, and I'll come back as soon as I can get a flight.' Her voice was once more overwhelmed, perhaps by wind from the mountains, a sibilant wailing.

Both men looked down, embarrassed. It seemed like the sound of their sister's suffering.

Out of the airwaves came a thin voice of distress. 'I suppose he committed suicide.'

'What else could it have been?' Roland spoke and again his

brother's steely-eyed gaze stopped him telling her the details. 'I'm sorry.'

The line was cut, the silence in the office that, for a few minutes, had been filled with the presence of another, wider, world made it seem too enclosed, claustrophobic.

'I didn't think she needed the image of the tree,' said Leo.

'I expect you're right. I'm not so sensitive about these things as you.'

'You're a lawyer.' It sounded like an attack.

'Charlie's dead. He hanged himself in the hospital garden.'

'Can't you see how that could haunt her? What questions would she ask us? How did he do it? What with? What time of day? What was he wearing? Had he stopped taking his pills? Why did nobody spot him?' He added, as if to himself, 'Why ever would he commit suicide now?'

Roland ignored this, then mumbled as if he knew how Leo would take this comment, 'Most people would do it with pills.'

'You can't stop accusing him, can you, even when he's dead!' Leo's face was angry again. His fists, red and spongy, were clenched. He jumped to his feet.

Roland fingered his cut and sighed. 'I'm sorry. Don't let's start that . . .'

'No, you're not!' Leo looked ready to throw over the desk. 'You hate him because he breaks rules, makes trouble—' He sagged back again into the chair. 'Oh, what's the use. Forget it. I don't expect you made his life harder than he did himself.'

'No. I'm sorry.'

'Just don't say you're sorry!'

Barely stopping himself repeating the word once more, Roland pulled out a piece of paper from a desk drawer and laid it on his desk. Then he took up a pen from a narrow wooden tray. 'I'll make a list of things to be done.' He began to write, his hand shaking.

'A list. Yes, that should sort it out.' Leo sounded heavily ironic.

Roland laid down the pen. 'All right. I never saw the point of Charlie. Never understood why you all found him so lovable. Maybe that was my loss. But can we try to be a bit grown-up about this?'

'My eye hurts.' Leo felt his face gingerly. 'Is it going black? I've got a question down for tomorrow. PM's Question.'

'You should have thought about that before you thumped me.'

'You're bleeding, actually.'

Quite suddenly Leo laughed. 'God, think how Charlie would have enjoyed this. His big brothers fighting over his dead body.' He changed mood again. 'It just doesn't make sense.'

Roland remained sober. 'I must ring Maggie.'

'Don't forget Father Bill.'

'There'll be an inquest.' Roland was writing on his piece of paper.

'The police.' Leo buttoned up his jacket. 'That's what my question's about.'

'Critical?'

'Take a guess.'

Roland picked up the bloody handkerchief and pressed it to his cheek. 'It's stinging like shit.'

'You can call it a shaving accident.' Leo's tone was careless. He looked towards the window. 'I suppose a known bipolar suicide in hospital won't give the police much reason to hang about.' He gave a strangled gulp.

'You mean with doctors on hand to sign the death certificate?'

Leo stood up abruptly, just catching his chair before it fell. 'I know he was ill but he's been worse and he had so much going on. Things he'd never abandon.'

Roland's expression didn't change. Eventually he stood up, took off his coat and sat down again. 'We're both in shock.'

'Yes. Yes,' muttered Leo. He slumped and put his head into his hands. 'Who's going to tell Imogen?'

'What?'

Leo lifted his head. 'Our mother. The great umbilical. Who's going to tell her?'

'We always made Charlie messenger of bad news. As long as he was beside her she didn't care about anything else.'

'It'll probably kill her.'

'He should have thought about that.'

Leo leaned forward. 'Charlie was never suicidal. That was one of his charms – despite everything, a valiant survivor.'

'You always like to romanticise things. He tried to commit suicide two or three times, once at Christmas, causing maximum confusion for everyone.'

'But he wasn't *serious*. And he wasn't very ill any more. There were things going on—' He broke off. 'And Lizzie.'

'Lizzie, indeed. How do we tell Lizzie? Through the authorities, I suppose.'

'Oh, fuck. Fuck. Fuck.'

'His life's always been a tragic mess. Why don't you face up to it? Imogen spoiled him, literally. I could see it happening, even if you couldn't. By the age of seven he felt invincible, answerable to no one.'

'He had an illness, Roland. He was born that way. It's as if you'd been born with no legs.'

'He wasn't sick when he was a little boy. It was only when he had to tackle the big world with no mummy . . .'

'Do you know? I think jealousy is one of the most pernicious sins because it stops a person seeing straight. OK. Imogen loved Charlie best but that was because he was her youngest child, and he just happened to be better-looking, cleverer, wittier, brilliant at sport and—'

'Barking mad,' completed Roland.

Leo was out of his seat and heading for his brother when there was a knock on the door.

'Yes?' Roland was curt.

Wayne spoke before he was in the room as if to armour himself with words. 'Your sandwich, sir. Roast beef and horseradish, sir.' Under the surprised gaze of both men, he shifted uncomfortably. 'Hold it?'

'Do that.'

Once the door was closed, Leo turned and put on his jacket. He faced Roland before leaving. 'I'm going to the hospital.'

'You can do whatever you want. I can't think why he was allowed to wander round unsupervised,' he added petulantly.

'He'd been there for two months, Roland. Did you want him caged up like a prisoner? When did you last see him? I saw him two nights ago and he was nearly himself—'

'Himself!' snorted Roland.

'—speaking at a normal speed, able to sustain logical thought, sitting still most of the time. He would have been out in a week.'

'Bollocks!'

Leo didn't react as if he was concentrating. His thoughts of Charlie and Roland had become incidental. He went to the door. 'I'll keep in touch.'

Roland picked up his pen and wrote on his list. 'I'll go and see Imogen and contact the others.'

'Yes.' Finally, Leo's expression was sad and gentle. 'Whatever the truth, Charlie's death is a tragedy, as you said to Portia.'

CHAPTER TWO

Inside Out

Father Bill pushed his pass under the glass partition and followed it up with his mobile. The first came back, accompanied by a heavy bunch of keys, the second was put away by the lady in a white shirt with official epaulettes.

Bill had been a part-time prison chaplain for five years but he'd never lost the feeling of strangeness as he passed from the outer world to this barred and secret inner world. The corridors and sliding partitions of security led him into its depths. Powerful images of tragedy accompanied him on his visits to the lost souls in his care.

Not that they necessarily thought of him as caring for them. The Catholic foreign nationals, the Colombians and West Indians, tended to be more devout, crossing themselves or even kneeling in front of him, but more often he felt that they saw him as a slightly off-beam member of the prison staff, easier to bend to their will, maybe. It was a fact that most riots started in the chapel.

Sometimes Bill found this dispiriting but this afternoon he was on a real errand of mercy. He had prayed before he'd set out for the prison and now he prayed again as he circled the red-brick corridors, opening and closing one barred door after another. 'Lend me your light, O Lord, that I may find the words to bring hope, not merely suffering.' It was the fourth week of Lent. You expected, even looked for, suffering in Lent, but not this bad.

Lizzie Potts was sitting in her cell, staring into what space there was. Thank God her cellmate, who couldn't sit still or stop talking, had gone out to 'associate' with some other unlucky sod.

Lizzie had had a bad feeling when she'd received the message that Father Bill was on the way to see her. She'd needed a moment to get her head together. A few months ago that would have meant a spliff or a line. Now it meant a little time on her own before one of the officers came thumping along to lead her off to the interview room. Lizzie allowed herself to dwell for a moment on the substantiality of most of the officers, as if they were made of heavier fabric then her, stuffed with richer food. She had always been slight but the time in prison had stripped her further.

When she caught sight of herself now she saw a skinny girl, as unwomanly as a ten-year-old, her half-dyed blonde hair curling round the pallid face of a victim. Yet she was not a victim, she reminded herself, she was a survivor. Charlie had told her so, insisted she had a future. She'd be out soon. But why an out-of-turn visit from Father Bill?

Along the corridor came the weighty rubber-soled steps and the jangling keys.

Lizzie went and stood by the open door but her legs shook and her head hung. At the last moment she turned back and took a folded piece of paper from a drawer.

'Come along, Lizzie,' said the officer, not unkindly.

Lizzie stayed quiet but followed close behind her. The officer was called Pat, a head taller than her charge and twice as broad. She walked quickly, locking and unlocking doors with the same decisive gestures and each time stepping back the bare minimum to allow Lizzie past her. Lizzie hardly noted this small act of aggression. She was concentrating on keeping dread at bay.

At last they reached the room. Through the window in the door, she could see that Father Bill was already there, his broad shoulders, slightly thinning dark curly hair and reddish, regular-featured face, framed like a picture. He looked, Lizzie thought uneasily, very sad. The word 'distraught' came to mind.

The officer knocked and the priest's face changed immediately. He even smiled. His smile reminded Lizzie of Charlie, and she tried to cheer herself as she followed Pat into the room.

'Do you want me to stay, Father?'

'Oh, no. No need, thank you.' He seemed shocked at the officer's enquiry, although it was standard prison practice.

'Half an hour enough?'

'Fine. Good.'

Lizzie, watching him intently, caught another glimpse of that horrible sadness. She sat down opposite him and placed her hands on the table. They'd taught her to do that: in sight and out of trouble.

'How are you today, Lizzie?'

She hated his nervousness. Priests shouldn't be nervous. They should rest secure in the faith of Christ. 'OK.' She looked down. Although she was sitting with her back to it, she knew Pat had left the door open. She hated the lack of privacy.

'I'm afraid I'm bringing tragic news.'

Lizzie stared at him. She could feel what little blood there was in her body draining away.

'Perhaps we should pray first.' The priest's voice was almost pleading.

'I don't feel like praying.'

'What, Lizzie?'

She had muttered it. Why was he torturing her? 'No!' There were tears in father Bill's eyes. They were blue like Charlie's – not beautiful like Charlie's. 'Is it my mum?' He knew she hated her mum. Or, rather, her mum hated her. Came to the same thing. 'Bad news on my parole?' He wouldn't have said 'tragic' about that. There was only one thing that could be tragic in her life and she wasn't going there.

'I'm tougher than you think, Father. Go on, spit it out.'

Bill heard her brave voice above an inward gabble of prayer. For a moment he hated Charlie for putting him through this. But how much worse for her. Charlie was her knight in shining armour, her saviour. He had brought her back from the brink. It would have been better never to have rescued her at all if only to abandon her. She would never recover. Never. Perhaps he could avoid telling her the manner of his death. The huge eyes were fixed on him, like Mary Magdalene at the foot of the cross.

Bill felt his mind splintering with misery and fear. He was only a man after all and suffering himself. Dear God, give me strength.

'It's Charlie, isn't it.' Her voice was flat. 'What's happened to him?'

Bill realised he was shaking and sweat was prickling his scalp. He feared he might cry too. 'My brother,' his inward voice wailed. 'My brother! Did you have to go so soon after I found you?' Making a great effort, he stretched forward and put one of his large hands over Lizzie's pale, bitten fingers. 'Yes. He's at peace. He's passed away.'

He watched as the light went from the girl's eyes and they misted over as if she, too, was dying. After her earlier denial of prayer, he didn't feel he could make the offer again. Helpless, he waited for the inevitable questions. But she was silent. Only those terrible eyes.

'Roland rang and asked me to tell you. He was found this morning.' He stopped himself. No more information unless she asked.

Then he saw that a piece of paper was concealed under her hand. Her fingers were curling round it. He took his own hand away.

She brought out the paper, unfolded it, then pushed it across to him.

'You want me to read it?' She nodded.

He immediately recognised Charlie's writing. It was the mad form: smaller than usual, exceptionally regular as if he was trying to impose the order on his handwriting that he couldn't on his mind. Even so, every line or two a letter or whole word flew away from the regularity, making jagged excess.

He knew this concentration on the form was an avoidance of the content. 'Dearest Lizzie' – not 'darling', he noted, the appellation of a friend rather than a lover. Bill sighed and returned to the letter:

The blue bird sings with a red cloak and the sickle in the farmer's hand turns the corn to gold. What a big plum, says the little boy and when the crust is lifted, his thumb is found like a corpse in the bottom.

'Oh dear,' said Bill. Leo had told him about the impenetrable missives that Charlie composed when his brain was racing, sometimes in the form of puzzles or crosswords. Charlie had lost his reason, of course. Yet he was surprised by this one. Three days ago when Bill had visited him, he'd seemed quite calm. They'd walked in the garden – he'd commented on its tranquillity and they'd sat for quite a while on a bench. Charlie had convinced him that he was being very good about taking his pills and that the night before he'd had eight hours' sleep and that in the morning he'd played billiards with a fellow 'loony' and beaten him. His hands were shaking from the drugs, of course, but his mind was not racing, not enough to write this crazy letter.

'When did he write it?'

'This morning. I mean it arrived this morning.' Lizzie had a low, attractive voice – probably all the fags but, with her eyes, it was her most memorable feature.

Prisons didn't dispense letters quickly so three or four days was probably right. He looked again and saw it was dated three days ago.

'I was going to ask you what it meant but I suppose it doesn't matter any more.'

'Did he write to you often?' asked Bill. He saw tears were spilling out of Lizzie's eyes. Priests don't cry, he commanded himself. Mumbling that he would get tea, he stumbled from the room, forgetting till he was in the corridor that a prisoner mustn't be left alone.

When he returned, minus tea, Lizzie's head was on the table. Her skimpy fairish hair hardly spread beyond her scalp. He noticed a couple of coin-sized bare patches and remembered that she had a history of alopecia. It had been better recently. The letter was still on the table.

'I saw Charlie three days ago,' he said. 'He asked about you. He loved you very much.'

'He was sorry for me.' The words were muffled but not enough for Bill to pretend he hadn't heard them.

'I'm sure he was that too. But he was happy you were off drugs and going to education.' He recalled that when Lizzie had first come in she'd been on suicide watch and he thought dismally that before he left he'd better make sure she was put on it again.

'What's the point?' muttered Lizzie.

What indeed. Bill fought against a raging feeling of anger, definitely not against Charlie this time. Against madness, sickness, fate. Never against his God.

CHAPTER THREE

At the End of the Line

Imogen was enjoying the best hour of her day. As usual, she had consumed a quarter-bottle of champagne accompanied by a portion of smoked-salmon sandwich with lemon. Now she lay propped comfortably against the pillows and allowed her mind to wander freely through the more agreeable meadows of her life.

Beyond this languor and content, less charming aspects growled outside the gates. They would enter, of course, bringing eventually the worst hours of her day, or rather night. Then she lost her way in horrid shades that would not be dispelled by sleep until the nurse plunged her into an artificial Lethe.

It was hard being weak-minded and old but, for this little amount of time, she was happy.

Men. Boys. Little boys. Big men. Imogen remembered the first time she'd realised the difference between the sexes. She'd been three years old but she could picture the scene clearly. The male in question later became a friend and even later, for a brief moment, a lover – only for old times' sake. She had loved him most on that sunny afternoon by the lake. Harry had taken off his clothes and run down the grassy path to dive into the amber-coloured water. She'd watched delightedly, her hand held tightly by her nurse as he threw up fountains of glittering sunshine, followed by garlands of green weed and even sprays of flowers, yellow and cream.

Afterwards he had jumped out and run about to get warm and she had laughed, delighted.

She had learned everything about men then, their love of freedom, their simplicity, the waving willies that led them into unexpected places. At this she heard herself give a little chuckle. Harry must have been about ten, nearly eighty years ago and him dead too, but she would never forget him.

Men were boys. That was the point. So many women failed to gasp this. Look at Ophelia who drowned herself in watery weeds because she was too stupid to understand Hamlet. Boys had been Imogen's forte. And then she had had her own – so many that she'd given one away. Her finest hour, although some people thought her wicked but they were fools. Anyway, he'd come back.

Four sons. That was a lot for any mother. All handsome, brilliant, individual, large. It was wonderful to think she'd produced them. Briefly, she considered Esmond's part in this. In some ways, she'd been lucky with him. She could admit that now, grudgingly. When she'd come back from Paris, taking the night ferry over choppy waters – but she didn't want to think about those months. Oh, the pain of it, the humiliation. At the height of her beauty, Dior's favourite, dashed to the ground, craven and crawling. Such a mockery. The new look. Spurned. Abused. The only man she couldn't control. Stop. Stop. This was happy hour.

Esmond had been waiting for her. Esmond understood and he still wanted her. He adored her. He admired her. He allowed her to be special, called all the children his without asking awkward questions. Not that it had been necessary, as it turned out. He'd produced money, if not quite enough. He'd said she was the most brilliant and charming woman of her generation, and when she'd had enough of him, he'd retreated tactfully into Never Never Land.

Perhaps one of the boys would visit her. The tap on the door, the substantial form bending over her caressingly. She hoped it would be Charlie. Charlie was most like her – a rebel. So gifted. Too gifted to settle into a career like the others. Or perhaps journalism was a career. Too gifted for the world. How far from her he sailed sometimes. Bad times. Imogen felt her mind drifting further as she struggled once again to stop these bright moments passing into darkness.

'Imogen.'

She could never tell their voices apart. Strange that, utterly unlike in character, their intonation was exactly the same. Usually she needed a sentence to tell for sure.

'It's Roland.'

Of course they knew she was nearly blind. Would he see the disappointment in her face?

'Are you awake?' He was sitting by her bed. He must have pulled up a chair. 'You look beautiful. You're wearing the pashmina I bought you last Christmas.'

She took one hand from under the coverlet and felt the softness wrapped round her neck and shoulders. 'That was nice of you.' Did he think she still cared what she wore?

'You *are* awake.' His voice was strange, with a slight tremble.

'What is it, Roland?' He didn't answer her. But she knew something was wrong. It made her tremble too. She tried to pull herself up so she could make out his features from the swirling darkness.

He helped her. She put up a hand and felt his face. It was a little damp.

'What about one of your bottles of champagne?'

He wasn't much of a drinker. Charlie was the drinker. 'Yes. Yes.'

He left her to find the little fridge. She heard the cork pop and the fizz as he poured. At least she'd kept the use of her ears.

But her hands were weak and shaking. 'Put it on the table, darling.' It would do her no good to have another glass.

He was gulping.

'Is something wrong?'

Again, he didn't answer. She'd trained herself to be good at avoiding knowing the worst and often the worst went away, or turned out to be someone else's worst.

'My dearest.' He was bending forward now. Perhaps his head was in his hands. He had never been good at dealing with emotion. She'd always assumed that was the reason he had become a lawyer. Like his father. She put out her hand to touch his hair. She had forgotten he was partly bald. The feel of his scalp moved her with pity for both of them: he a middle-aged man, she an old woman.

'Charlie has killed himself.'

The words, released into the little room, danced mockingly around her oh-too-sensitive ears.

'Oh, no, Roland. Never that!' Her voice sounded to her like a little girl's: *Go away, you naughty boy. I've never really liked you. Go away.*

'I'm afraid so. This morning. In the hospital.' He was sitting up now. Was there triumph in his stance? He had always been jealous of Charlie. Could he have made up this story?

'You're cruel. Cruel!'

'I'm sorry.' But he didn't sound sorry.

She swung an arm at him, as if she was swatting an insect, smacking a child. Her outstretched fingers connected with the champagne glass. She heard the tinkle of breaking glass.

'Go away! Go away!' Her heart was burning. She mustn't believe him. Before he came, she'd been lying here, happily dreaming. 'You've always hated him. And now you're trying to kill him. Go away! Leave me alone! I only want to see Charlie. Tell Charlie to come and see me.' She shut her eyes tight and waved her arms like tentacles in a black sea.

'Lady Shillingstone.' Whispering, like ripples on a seashore. Someone else was in the room. A woman whispering to her son about unspeakable things.

'Go! Go! Murderer! Cain!' Losing control was a tiny release, water running from her eyes, from her insides, her poor withered, weak, old lady's insides. Oh, Charlie! The night. How could she bear the night? What would come in the night?

'Imogen, dearest, please.' So he hadn't gone. She couldn't be left alone.

'Here, love.' The nurse, of course, offering a little cup of something soothing.

'I can't.' How could she drink now? She was dead. Finished.

'Try. Just a little.'

But what dreams it might bring. Surely that was Roland grunting like a hog. Why was she coming back to herself? Esmond. Where are you? Why didn't you stop this? Could she not die?

CHAPTER FOUR

Suspended in Space

Leo knew the route to the hospital too well. He had always driven there with a heavy heart but never as heavy as today. Even at Charlie's sickest, when his brain was a jumble of crazy imaginings and his body a pill-sodden sack of despair, he was still Charlie, entertaining, infuriating, charming – and tragic, of course. Now there was only tragedy. Yet his head still pounded with questions.

The gates to the hospital were impressive, in a suburban street set back from one of the busy arteries leading from South London to the southern counties. The grounds were also surprisingly extensive, laid out, judging by the mature oaks, chestnuts and Wellingtonias, in another age and for a grander purpose than hosting the mentally ill, most of whom never ventured into them.

A police barricade with an officer in attendance was at the gates.

'Yes, sir?'

Leo showed his House of Commons pass. The man moved away the barricade without questioning further.

The buildings were nothing like as fine as the grounds, a fifties conglomeration of concrete and brick blocks. There were several police cars and other vehicles parked directly in front of the main building. As he drove up, an officer approached.

'Mr Barr.'

'You recognised me?'

'Yes.' He was tall, although not as tall as Leo, perhaps in his middle fifties. 'Chief Inspector Roger Burrows. We spoke earlier.' He waited while Leo parked and got out of his car. They stood together. It was a cool day in late March. Leo allowed his mind to wander and felt offended by a row of festive yellow daffodils.

'There has been a development. I've found a room for us to talk.' The chief inspector had small eyes that were fixed on Leo's face. The three silver squares on his shoulders glinted. He was the sort of man who would polish them and covet the superintendent's crown. Leo knew all about police grades and their badges of rank.

The chief inspector's look had made him uneasy in a new way and he felt unwilling to follow him inside. 'I would like to see . . .' Was this an inappropriate wish? He started again. 'I would like to see where it happened.' He took a breath. 'Where my brother died.'

'It is a crime scene, sir.'

'Surely not.' Leo stood his ground. He was used to doing that. It was no effort.

'Follow me, sir.'

Why had the man called it 'a crime scene'? Suicide hadn't been a crime for decades. He could come up with the date when the law changed, if he tried hard enough. Why was a chief inspector involved anyway?

They walked down an avenue of yews, straggly and very black. The sun, which had been so bright earlier, disappeared behind thick grey clouds.

'Across the grass to our left, sir.'

Leo saw the orange tape, the men from Forensics in white suits, the blue sheets disguising the specific area. The sheets, however, were not high enough to hide more than the lower portion of the chestnut tree, which burst upwards in a confident spread of branches. As they grew closer, he saw that they were adorned with fat, shiny buds, some of which were unfurling at the tip. This was where Charlie had chosen to end his life.

'There's nothing to see, sir.'

'Of course.' No body. No rope – or whatever he'd used. Leo wanted to touch the tree, a tree of death, not life, which yet continued to grow. But he could sense the policeman's impatience. He would return later.

They began the walk back to the hospital buildings. His suit was poor protection against the increasing cold and damp – the sadness. He put his hand to his eyes and felt a swelling at one side.

The room that he was led into was, by contrast, warm and stuffy. They sat, formally, on either side of a table. An interview room for those in mental breakdown?

'As I said, there's been a development.'

Leo resented the chief inspector's 'development'. Charlie was dead. Nothing could develop from that. He tried to give at least polite attention. 'Yes?'

'When we took your brother down . . .'

What a hideous expression! Or perhaps he could link it to Christ being taken down from the cross.

'. . . the doctor and pathologist found some unusual marks on his body. They found, in fact . . .' He paused and leaned closer to Leo. Those tiny eyes bored through him. 'I fear this may be painful to you.'

'Go on, Chief Inspector.' What could be more painful than death?

'They discovered that although he had died by strangulation he had not died by strangulation through hanging. In other words, he had been strangled by person unknown before he was hung on the tree.'

Leo struggled through the words confronting him. 'Are you saying he didn't commit suicide?'

'Correct, sir.'

'Are you saying, moreover, therefore, whatever, that my brother was murdered?'

'I'm afraid so, sir. We are conducting a murder inquiry. May I get you a cup of tea? If I can find one, that is.' He left the room speedily.

Alone, Leo found that he'd been wrong earlier. He'd thought that Charlie's death, his absence, was as bad and unchangeable as anything could be. But murdered? 'A development'. He felt for his mobile in his pocket, knowing he would ring no one. He supposed he would have to ask the chief inspector questions. Did they have a suspect? Another deranged man? Charlie had had friends inside the hospital. Had he argued with one? It had always surprised him that there was very little supervision of those patients who were allowed in the grounds. Or perhaps it had been careless supervision, a nurse who sat on a wall and enjoyed a cigarette. Over the years Charlie had boasted about what he got up to among the trees: drinking, smoking, even having sex. He was a natural rule-breaker and, perhaps, a liar. No. Never a liar. He merely enjoyed a good story.

There were stories and stories. Tomorrow, if things went his way, Leo would ask a question of the prime minister. A question about a story. Charlie's murder had to be part of it.

'From a machine, I'm afraid.' The chief inspector was back and offered Leo a polystyrene cup. Behind him a small, rotund man, in plain clothes, hovered. 'This is my colleague, Inspector Joseph Tring.'

'Good evening, sir.'

Evening? Was it already evening? They shook hands. Leo was surprised to see that he was wearing a wig, far too black for his skin colour and with a funny little fringe.

'I expect you'd like to see the deceased now.'

Leo looked at his grey tea. 'Like' hardly seemed the right word. Horrible images of a purple face with swollen tongue protruding. *Like* wasn't in it. Presumably they would *like* him to identify the body. 'Certainly. Now?'

'When you've finished your tea.'

Leo put down his full cup. The manner of the two detectives was so deferential as to border on obsequious. Another image came to his mind: the stone figure of *Melancholy Madness* chained naked and for ever to his palette. Carved in the seventeenth century, it was now housed in a small museum by the hospital's gates. He had formed the habit of visiting it on his trips to see Charlie. He'd decided it came under the heading of 'man's inhumanity to man'.

'You need formal identification?'

'If you would. As it happens, Mr Potts's doctor is unavailable till tomorrow. Of course, we had the contents of his pockets and the nurses had reported him missing.'

So Charlie had been wearing a jacket. Or did they mean trouser pockets?

'I'm ready.'

CHAPTER FIVE

Coming Down

Portia encouraged Charlie's death to float away. If only she could leave it on the top of Monte Alban where her group of Mexican women, so used to mourning, could take it to their villages and bury it with their other sorrows, the dead babies, mothers, lovers.

She had to carry the knowledge with her as she took the endless coach journey to Mexico City. She opened her blind, becoming unpopular with the other passengers who knew the blazing sun as an enemy. She recognised Charlie in the slabs of rocky mountain, in the sharp-toothed cacti that pierced the black crevices, in the sun itself. But she kept him from her heart. She would wait till she got home.

But the flight from Mexico City to London was so very long. She hadn't managed to get on a direct plane so had to make her way first to Miami where she had several hours to wait. It was there she'd tried to telephone Conor. His voicemail informed her he was out of contact in Scotland. Her boyfriends were never there when she needed them.

She was anxious, too, about the boxes of hand-embroidered blouses, the woven scarves, the tin jewellery – earrings made from bottle tops – theatrical little boxes. These she would sell on her market stall and, normally, she would have negotiated a good deal with Customs. It was, in effect, charity work because fifty per cent of the proceeds went back to the workers – hopefully to alleviate the poverty that made their lives miserable.

On this occasion, she had left too suddenly for any deal. So there were her large brown packages to be guarded, checked off one aeroplane and on to another because she didn't trust the airlines. She pictured herself, a small woman, hot pink cheeks, wild dark hair, layered in jackets, flustered, shrill. Oh, Charlie, how could you die? And to kill yourself – how cruel.

Portia squeezed on to a corner of a plastic seat and gave way to tears. Around her other travellers, Spanish speakers from Puerto Rico, Guatemala, Colombia or Mexico, showed little curiosity. Perhaps they sensed she cried for herself, not sympathy.

Then a young woman, black eyes, brown skin, reddened hair, crouched in front of her. She took one of Portia's hands. She looked into her face. 'I will sit with you.' She spoke softly in Spanish.

A man, on Portia's right, previously impervious to his surroundings, got up to leave a space. He stood in front of his wife who remained seated, staring straight ahead.

The young woman sat down. She opened a cheap plastic handbag, took out a small bottle, and a folded white handkerchief. She shook a few drops on to the cloth, releasing the faint scent of lavender water. Carefully, she pressed the handkerchief to Portia's wrists and then to her forehead.

Portia felt the cool freshness, the touch of the woman's hand, firm and steady.

'Thank you. *Gracias*.' She had stopped crying.

'*De nada*.'

They sat together in silence for some time. Gradually Portia felt the heat and noise of the airport again. She sighed.

The young woman stood up. 'We must carry on,' she said, in Spanish.

Did she mean they must go to catch their flights or something more philosophical? Portia watched her walk away. Her calves were rounded and strong, forced up by her stiletto heels. Portia was grateful there had been no questioning, that she had not had to say the word 'brother'.

Beside her, the dignified man who'd given up his seat sat down again. He still hadn't looked her way once but she felt protected all the same.

Charlie always used to say that strangers held the truth of the matter. That family, friends, lovers carried too much baggage. Perhaps that was why he'd married Lizzie, even changing his surname to hers.

It was often difficult to tell whether Charlie was acting out of some deep-held belief or a wish to shock – or entertain. She understood him so little that she didn't even know whether he'd had sex with Lizzie – before she went to prison. Before their marriage. After all, he'd had sex with most women he'd met. He used to boast, 'I'm irresistible.' The family view painted Lizzie as a pathetic, characterless creature but maybe Charlie had seen something different. He was good at seeing things no one else spotted.

He'd once asked her, 'Why do you always wear red, Portia?'

'It cheers me up,' she'd answered.

'But you're the most cheerful person I know.'

'Now you know the reason.' They'd both smiled but she'd understood seriousness. Why did she pretend to be someone else?

CHAPTER SIX

A Development

'Would you like a few minutes alone?' The bewigged inspector indicated a chair not far from where Charlie lay.

Taking Leo's silence as assent, he left the room.

The truth was that Leo had not yet managed to look at his brother. He just sensed distorted colour and features gone awry, brow lowered, nose shortened, mouth enlarged. Was he expected to sit beside this sad travesty? Perhaps hold its hand?

More because of a supposed duty than from any real desire to see Charlie closely, he took several steps forward.

He focused slowly on the face. The rest of the body was covered with a long grey sheet.

Could death disfigure so much? It was horrible that this person could seem such a stranger, all Charlie's strong personality negated by the manner of his death. Even his hair was different, bulkier but less golden, not curly but frizzy.

Leo stared, the unrecognisable features gradually making him feel rather sick and even dizzy. 'Oh, Fuck! Shit!' He swore loudly, took several steps back, found the chair and collapsed into it.

The inspector returned to find him there. 'Sir? Are you all right, sir?'

It took Leo a moment to speak. 'It's not him.'

'Sir?'

'It's not him. It's not my brother. The man here is a total stranger. I've never met him.' He spoke urgently, a little madly. He felt mad. Charlie wasn't dead! How could he have thought it was him for one second?

The policeman looked as stunned as Leo felt. 'Not Mr Potts? Not your brother?'

'Not at all. Nothing like.' He continued irritably. 'I can't think who identified him in the first place. It's a real cock-up.'

The man recovered himself. 'You're quite sure?'

'Are you suggesting I don't know what my own brother looks like?'

'I think we should go to the office.'

'Yes, yes. So do I.'

They hurried along corridors, back to the stuffy room. There, Chief Inspector Burrows looked up from the table. He had adopted the sympathetic expression suitable to receive a man who had just seen the murdered remains of his brother.

Leo's escort drew back a chair for him. He addressed his colleague. 'There has been another development.'

Leo was overwhelmed by anger. 'Development! What do you mean by development? This isn't a development. This is a matter of death! *Death*. My brother's death. At this moment my frail elderly mother is being told of her youngest son's death and you talk about development! You're supposed to be detectives but you can't get the first thing right. You cause anguish, anguish . . .' Through his rage, Leo became aware of a hand on his arm.

'Sir – please, sir. I understand your feelings . . .'

'You understand my feelings!' He was about to start shouting again. It felt justified and free until he noticed the amazed face of the chief inspector sitting behind the desk. Of course he didn't have a clue what Leo was going on about. Abruptly he sat down. Behind him, he heard the rotund colleague let out a gasp of relief.

'I'm so sorry,' said the chief inspector. 'I know it's a harrowing experience.'

Leo looked fully at him. The small hooded eyes and leathery, well-shaven cheeks gave him a reptilian look. Tomorrow he planned to ask a question in Parliament that would make him hated by the Metropolitan Police. 'The body you have, the man I went to identify, the hanged man,' he spoke slowly and deliberately, 'the man found hanging from the chestnut tree we visited earlier, that man is not my brother.'

As he said these words, the changed situation hit him fully for the first time. Charlie was not dead. The nightmare was over. Charlie was alive.

CHAPTER SEVEN

Maximum Distress

Roland walked slowly away from the nursing-home. He'd turned off his mobile phone on entering and he didn't switch it on again. The sight of his mother, desperate and witless until subdued by a needle in her arm, had offended and saddened him. Everything about it was wrong: her unreasonable love for Charlie was nothing new but he hated that it took away her dignity. Love did that, of course.

He picked up speed, shying away from the subject. He should ring Maggie, tell her about Charlie, but he needed a drink first. The fight with Leo had left him physically exhausted, and now this miserable interview with his mother. It was typical of Charlie to leave the world causing maximum distress to everyone. He signalled to a taxi.

Roland's club was within walking distance of Soho. As he mounted the wide run of stone steps, he wondered if this was really where he wanted to be.

He continued upwards. It wasn't the time for anything else.

'Good evening, Mr Norrington Barr, sir.'

He acknowledged the porter's welcome. He was a long-standing member.

Roland never felt richer than when he was sipping a glass of whisky in his club: the chair he sat in was made of thick, soft leather, the table of highly polished mahogany; around him, on crimson walls, hung oil paintings of famous actors and actresses, some even by famous painters – his favourite was a scene from *The Marriage of Figaro* by Zoffany. He stared at it now, sipping meditatively. All life was theatre, he thought, artificial like these bewigged and rouged figures, posing, pretending like that extraordinary policeman. He himself wore a wig in court. He posed. He defended the indefensible, he prosecuted the innocent.

Recently, sitting alone in the same chair, he'd overhead a conversation between two senior law lords. They were discussing attributes in barristers suitable to join them in the House of Lords. 'Criminal lawyers never do well,' the first had said. 'They've had too much experience of the bad side of human nature, probably of the law too.'

'Disillusioned and cynical,' the second law lord had agreed. 'Cynicism is the enemy of good law. Give me a commercial lawyer any day.' He'd smiled, which had reminded Roland that this particular law lord had been a very successful commercial lawyer.

He emptied his glass and called for more, but by the time the waiter returned, he'd changed his mind.

'Too late.' He hurried out, absentmindedly returning various friendly waves. In the street, he found a taxi. 'Waterloo.'

What were wives for, if not moments like this? He pictured Maggie's fair, curly hair, her wide blue eyes with their heavy lids, her robust figure, fattened since their marriage by three pregnancies. He looked at his watch: seven thirty. If he rang to say he was coming they could have a late supper together, his father in bed, his children, those who were at home, out of the way.

He pictured the kitchen, glowingly decorated in terracotta, yellow and blue or something similar. She would put candles on the table and bring hot food straight from the Aga – soup, pasta, accompanied by the bottle of red wine he'd choose from the cellar.

He flicked open his mobile, then shut it again, although not before he had seen the messages piled up. He wasn't ready for Maggie yet. He would take the train, arrive, talk to her then. After all, it was his home.

Maggie was on her second glass of red wine. She loved her father-in-law and gladly looked after him, but tonight had been disturbing. What was it he'd said over and over again? 'I am sailing, sailing over the open sea.' What had he meant? As far as she knew, he'd never had the faintest interest in the sea. He'd been a city lawyer, at home in heavily enclosed places, law courts, meeting rooms, special houses or hotels when he was a circuit judge, then the House of Lords for ten years, every day it was open. He hadn't even worked in Hong Kong as far as she knew – far too successful in England. But now he was sailing, sailing over the sea. A metaphor, she guessed, for his aloneness, his fear of drowning, the wide unknowingness of his horizons. He didn't have Alzheimer's as such, the doctor had informed her, repeating 'as such' meaningfully. He was just tired, tired body, tired mind losing its grip. Poor Esmond. It was unbearable, really, if you thought too much. Although his expression as he talked had been more exhilarated than unhappy.

Maggie put down her glass and got up to tell Jake and Tom it was time for bed. Mungo, her fat old Labrador, thumped his tail encouragingly. The boys were back from their boarding-school for the Easter holidays. In a few days Hettie, their daughter, would return from university.

She sat down again. When she had been the boys' age no one had policed her. Her mother had left such things to the au pair and the au pair had left them to Fate. But, then, she didn't want to be like her mother. She got up again, sat down again. She sighed. It had been sensible to have an armchair in the kitchen. She sat there when the vegetables were boiling, the sausages cooking, when she needed to be comfortable, to think or not to think.

It made up for Roland's hard uprightness – like a dining-room chair, the old sort with no upholstery. Perhaps that was why he'd married her – to provide the padding. She knew one of the reasons she'd married him; it was not a worthy reason.

She must resist a third glass of wine or she'd get fatter still, like one of those depressed country wives who sat waiting for their husband's return. That was one thing she'd never do. If Roland wanted to remain an enigma, that was good enough for her. Besides, she was an enigma too, although she was sure he'd never suspected it. She just didn't look like enigma material. In fact, she wasn't very fat. Occasionally she caught a glimpse of herself in the bathroom mirror and was surprised by her waist and the elegant curves of her body. She dressed badly, she supposed, heavy sweaters, thick skirts, boots. Underneath it all, she was rather lovely, if not in the modern skinny fashion.

She smiled at herself. Another glass of wine and she'd decide she was a raving beauty. But it was true she wore a disguise, even from herself: the competent mother of three, plus one ancient father-in-law. Not to mention the four rental houses she managed in town. And now the little gallery too. She was so busy. So busy. She stretched and her head sank back against the cushions.

Roland had to wait for a taxi at the almost deserted country station. He could smell the softness of wood fires and the sharpness of manure spread over the fields. When he heard a train announced for London, he nearly caught it. Why should he want to see Maggie at a time like this? It was all fantasy, all theatre.

Maggie opened her eyes – she had only drifted into sleep for a moment, she thought – and there was Roland, standing above her with a self-righteous expression. Why did he do that to her? Put her in the wrong, make her feel inadequate.

'When did you get here? Did I miss your call?'

Roland stared at her. 'Sorry to wake you.'

'I was tired.' She could have pointed out that it was *his* father who was the main reason for her tiredness, but why should she give him reasons?

'Yes. I'd kill for a glass of wine.'

Was this a criticism of her drinking habits? 'I'll pour you one.' She stood up as he sat down. She registered his weariness. The strength of her urge to care never ceased to amaze her. She poured out the wine and put it in front of him on the table. 'I can warm up some stew.'

'That would be great.' He picked up the glass but didn't drink from it. 'There's some very bad news. Family news.'

'Oh!' After all, Maggie gave herself a third glass of wine. It wasn't her children. 'Is it Imogen?'

'Imogen will never die.'

He seemed to have spoken bitterly. But did he mean that some-one else had died? She felt herself flush; her heart going too fast. 'Who?' From the far end of the kitchen, the telephone began to ring. It was playing a line from a pop song. 'The boys changed it,' she apologised. 'Shall we let the answering-machine get it?'

'Why do that?'

Obviously because you were about to tell me something important, thought Maggie, but she went obediently to the telephone. 'Hello.'

'Maggie?'

'Yes.'

'It's Leo.'

Of course she knew it was Leo. Not dead.

'Is Roland there? I've left a million messages in London and on his mobile.'

'He's just arrived.' She brought over the phone. 'It's Leo.' Roland took it and moved away.

Maggie sat down. She didn't try to listen to the brothers' conversation. Then Roland began to shout.

Hardly knowing what he was doing, Roland perched on some books piled on a window-ledge. This morning Charlie's suicide had seemed the most horrible news – so bad it had reduced him and Leo to childish habits. They had always fought over Charlie, always. Now he was being told some scarcely believable story about Charlie not being dead but another lunatic, causing the police to suggest that Charlie had murdered this lunatic and done a runner.

'*We* know it's out of the question,' said Leo, in absurdly reasonable tones. 'It's just not in Charlie's nature. But the police have a point. First of all, they're faced with a suicide, then they discover it's not suicide but murder made to look like suicide. At which I come along and point out that the man they found hanging from a tree is quite unknown to me and certainly not my brother, Charlie Potts – I feel pretty glad about this, incidentally. They follow this up with the hospital records – which are clearly in a mess – and discover there is another poor chap missing, a Horace Silver – at least, that was his adopted name, after the jazz singer. Horace was a known suicide risk, occasionally aggressive and should never have been in the garden. Whether or not Charlie should have been there seems like a grey area.'

'Like so much of Charlie's life.' The books shifted uncomfortably under Roland's buttocks but he was too tired to stand.

'I see him in bolder colours,' said Leo, still sounding calm. 'The police are not exactly keeping me informed of their thinking but their questions to me suggest they picture a scenario in which these two crazy men had a fight, Charlie killed Horace, made it look like suicide, then dressed him in his own jacket so he'd time to get away. They asked me about Charlie's passport.'

'But you're not at the police station?'

'Not now. I had to go to the House. There was a division on yet another education bill and I don't like to antagonise the whips more than I have to.'

'You could have fooled me.'

Maggie put down her glass and came towards him. Behind her, the dog heaved himself up and watched her progress. She stood in front of him, eyes big and blue, but now he could see the dark shadows, the lines of anxiety or age.

'I must explain to Maggie,' he said into the phone. 'I'll ring you back.'

'Just a minute. What about Portia, Bill, Lizzie? They all think Charlie's dead. And Imogen, did you tell her?'

'Yes. She hated me for it. She'd like to die for love of Charlie. In the end the nurse gave her a sedative.'

'Please don't be ironic.'

'No, although I can't think why not. I'll ring later.'

Maggie wondered that Roland could have this whole conversation while she was still completely in the dark.

'What's happened?'

He was staring out of the windows, but it was black outside. He could see nothing. 'I'm sorry. The whole thing is very confusing, very upsetting.' He'd adopted what she called to the children 'Daddy's lawyer voice'. 'Did you say something about stew?'

'Roland! Has someone died?' Her voice had risen an octave.

'Sorry. Sorry.' He was moving back to the table. 'Someone has died. Not from our family, after all. No one we know. I'll explain in a moment.'

He looked shattered. Very pale and drawn.

'What's that red mark on your face?'

'A cut.' Roland slumped at the table, although she could sense his eyes on her as she dragged the heavy pot on to the hotplate.

'It won't take long. I'll just send the children to bed.' She could tell by his expression that he'd forgotten it was the Easter holidays. How odd it must feel to be so independent. She was aware of the people she cared about every single moment of the day. She couldn't imagine feeling as free as him. Maybe it was the difference between women and men.

'Jake! Tom!' she called, to give them time to stop any inappropriate activities. Trust was how she managed. Men lived in some other sphere.

Roland ate the stew slowly. Maggie was a casual but very good cook. Without surprise, he picked out a teabag from his plate. It might have been put there deliberately.

The police would talk to him. As the eldest son, he would represent the family. He shouldn't have let Leo go to the hospital but he had wanted to tell Imogen himself. He should stop Portia coming back from Mexico. There was no point in embroiling her. Now he would have to contact the nursing-home. He didn't envy them trying to convince Imogen that her beloved son was still alive. She was probably well set on her course to join him in Paradise.

What had Leo said? He mustn't be ironic. How odd of Leo not to understand that irony was an essential part of Roland's defence system. But, then, he'd never expected understanding from Leo. Their natures were too different: Leo was always direct, simple, clear about good and evil. He was good, of course. Even as a boy, he'd made Roland feel devious. Roland was the one who had told lies to get them out of trouble, never Leo.

Another call must be made to Father Bill. Perhaps he hadn't seen Charlie's weird bride yet. It was difficult getting in and out of prison, although Bill was part of the system. Presumably Mrs Potts would rather Charlie was alive, even if he was under suspicion of murder.

Roland pushed away his plate and tried to pour another glass of wine but the bottle was empty. In a moment he'd open another.

'I *love* having those boys around.' Maggie came back re-energised. When she saw Roland, she deflated abruptly. 'Now, you've got to tell me.'

'Actually, I find it very difficult to understand what it's all about.'

CHAPTER EIGHT

Answering Demands

Bill was asleep when the telephone rang. It had taken him hours to reach the point of letting go. It took him a couple of seconds to be fully awake. Priesthood, or his sort of priesthood, was about answering demands. 'Father Bill speaking.' His throat was so dry it hurt.

'Leo here. I hope I didn't wake you.'

Leo? But there could be no worse news. Charlie was dead. He must be asking about a funeral. The hands of his clock on the bedside table gleamed phosphorescently. One thirty.

'How can I help?' Or perhaps it was the misery of losing a brother. Perhaps he needed a companion in the darkest hours. Unlikely he would choose Bill.

'Have you told Lizzie about Charlie's suicide?'

'Yes. Yes. It was a terrible blow. Not just for her. I . . .'

'He's not dead. He's disappeared but, as far as we know now, he's not dead. Another man died.'

Bill found that, without conscious decision, he had rolled out of his bed and fallen on his knees. Thank God. Thank you, God. But for that sad other . . . He mustn't forget him.

'Bill. Bill!'

Bill picked up the receiver again. 'I can't help rejoicing, Leo, even though another man has died.'

'I thought you should know as quickly as possible. Lizzie must be suffering.'

'I'll go to her first thing. You say Charlie's disappeared?'

'Yes. The man who died was wearing his jacket. The police are treating his death as suspicious. Obviously, they want to talk to Charlie.'

'I see.' Bill, still on his knees, crossed himself. Years ago, he'd stopped finding himself ridiculous.

'They'll want to interview you. Maybe Lizzie. Try to be with her.'

'I will.'

'I'll keep in touch.'

'Thank you.'

Bill thought how difficult it was to believe they were brothers. Full brothers. Leo always talked down to him not unpleasantly but as if it was natural to behave that way. The way an older and more experienced man might talk to a young man at the start of his life. Yet Leo was only two years older than him, and his experience of this world was almost certainly narrower. Of course, it was a simple matter of class.

Smiling to himself, Bill got off his knees and went quietly to the kitchen. A sandwich was in order but he mustn't wake his sleeping housemate, who rose at five. Although he did the same, he didn't consider himself.

Over a honey sandwich and tea, he tried to put order into his confused mind. It was only three years ago that he'd discovered his birth parentage. Charlie, then unknown to him, had come to the church where he was saying Mass and afterwards the server, an old friend of his, had joked, 'Got any secret brothers, Bill? Did you see that big fellow in the front row? Spitting image, give or take a stone or three.'

It was astute of the server, an elderly man who'd always paid more attention to the congregation than to the Mass. Charlie, although fair and a good three stone heavier than Bill, had the long legs, broad shoulders, large head, curly hair, regular features shared by all four brothers.

He had laughed at the server but at other Masses, as he faced the congregation to give the homily, he'd become aware of the tall figure in the front row – his *doppelgänger*, or nearly.

The man's attendance was irregular, usually at an evening Mass. Then one morning there was a disturbance during the sung Latin Mass. He was not the celebrant and a woman reader came to find him. 'Father! Father!' she'd called. 'We need help in the church.'

He'd rushed along immediately, expecting the usual fainting old lady, ready with his mobile to call an ambulance. Instead there was Charlie, strutting in the sanctuary as if on a stage, bellowing (quite tunefully, actually) the responses to the Mass and trying to follow the priest up to the pulpit.

Bill had been summoned because he was big. But Charlie was bigger. Father Aloysius stopped pretending that nothing was happening and made for his chair, where he bent his head as if in prayer. The congregation, on the other hand, gave up prayer, and the antics on the altar were accompanied by animated if subdued chatter along the pews.

At first he'd chased Charlie round the altar, followed by the two female readers and two young boy servers. But this had quickly turned to farce as Charlie changed his booming Latin for cries of 'View halloo!' and imitations of a hunting horn.

So Bill had halted the chase and stood quietly at the side. Quite quickly, Charlie stopped too and came to him. '*Mea culpa, mea culpa, mea maxima culpa*!' He'd knelt theatrically, hands clasped. The congregation hushed.

'Come, my friend.' Bill had thought it was like dealing with a wild animal. Not a fox, something bigger, scarier and more scared. Even as he stood there he sweated and trembled.

'*Pax vobiscum*,' intoned Charlie.

'*Et cum spiritu tuo.*'

They went off together, bonded by Latin. Charlie would speak nothing else and Bill spent the next hour making coffee to his very exact specifications and trying to calm him. In the end he'd run off anyway, and Bill had heard no more for several months till he'd reappeared at an evening Mass. His manner was subdued and his hands shook visibly against the pew.

Bill had made a point of catching him before he left. 'I'm glad you're better.'

'From your point of view, that may be true.' Charlie spoke dully. His lids were swollen, his face pasty. 'I have been in the flames of hell.'

'I'm so sorry. Shall we have a coffee?' He had felt inadequate, of course, but determined to help. Why else would Charlie have returned?

So they became friends, more than priest to parishioner. Charlie told him he was a journalist, that his illness (not that he called it that) was unimportant to him, which was clearly a defensive and self-destructive lie. He said he was the only one of his family to be educated as a Catholic because his mother had got 'a bee in her bonnet'.

The 'bee' had prompted her to make a gift of her third son: Bill, at that time known as Orlando. Almost an anagram of Roland. One of Lady Shillingstone's famous witticisms, perhaps. So Charlie was Bill's younger brother.

CHAPTER NINE

Soyez Calme

Charlie flopped over the divan in the small dark room. He could have put the light on but he didn't. He'd rented the flat for Lizzie just before she went to court and prison in the same day. He'd paid in cash so no one knew about it. He told himself that. His head reached the floor.

Unless Lizzie had filled in the address on one of those fucking forms – the law liked forms – she'd never remember it.

Restlessly, Charlie swung his legs off the divan. Must stay calm. He'd been in prison – sorry, hospital – for six weeks. He'd co-operated. Madness, of course, but some would have called him mad. He'd stopped sleeping, stopped eating, mind chattering like a load of monkeys. It had amazed everyone, doctors, the family, himself. He'd never put himself in before. But he was getting older, more able to admit the black devils at his throat. He'd wanted to be well quickly, not captured, sectioned, imprisoned like poor Lizzie. He needed to be back on the job. Then they had sectioned him anyway. Insane, all of them.

He still believed in what he was doing. It was a job, *alleluia, alleluia*. Someone had had to do it. Griff, the old wanker, and he agreed about that. But things were worse now, more out of control. Most people had the good sense to stay out of dark cupboards. But most people weren't crazy, were they? *Alleluia* again. He felt in his trouser pocket for his carton of pills. In the circumstances, he'd break the habit of a lifetime, take one without being told to. If you're not actively unhappy, then you're very, very happy. There's a useful mantra. But not *too* happy.

He'd bought a bottle of vodka *en route* to the flat. Why should anybody understand about his drinking? It was his body. His fucking (not much of that lately) fucked-up mind. It was just a question of getting the balance right. He'd bought a box of panatelas in the same shop. Those Patels were on the ball. Not like a decent cigar, of course, but cheering, definitely cheering. Not *too* cheering, though.

Annoyed to find his legs trembling, Charlie stumbled to the cupboard that stood for a kitchen and put on a strip of neon light. What had made him buy such a puny bottle? He unscrewed the cap, took a long swig.

Better. Better. Soon he'd get himself on the road. Not literally. He'd stay where he was for twenty-four hours. No communication, that was the thing. Let the scent cool. Luckily he hadn't installed a telephone in the flat. Never believed in mobiles.

He took another pull at the vodka. Who would be looking for him hardest? He knew the answer. Not the hospital. They'd be glad to be rid of him. He'd have been out anyway in a day or two. Besides, they had the repercussions of pathetic old Horace's death to deal with. Death, rumour, wild speculation, just the thing to stir up the raving mad to further heights. It'd be lock up, shut down, away with the billiard cues and out with the pills – or the needles. Nothing like a good injection to restore calm and order.

The police might be more tenacious. For the wrong reasons, at the moment. At least some of them were on the side of right. What was wanking Griff up to? And Leo? Had he taken the bait? Leo was a believer. Not in God. But it took all sorts. Leo believed in him, Charlie. Poor sod. Leo was a good man, something Charlie never aspired to.

Charlie put out a hand for the box of panatelas and, once again, was annoyed to see it trembling badly. It was the filthy lithium, of course. Evil stuff. But without it, rocky shores and stormy seas. Not that he'd call the waters smooth. Crazy days and sleepless nights. Haywire. That was the word.

Stepping back into the room, he absentmindedly flicked the light switch. What a drear sight! Brown scuffed carpet, dark ragged curtains and a chair covered with black plastic, a dank, vegetable smell. Good enough for Lizzie, that's what he must have thought. Shameful. Not that his own flat was much better.

The point about this flat was that it was nondescript, in a

nondescript building in a nondescript area between Finsbury Park and Seven Sisters, just far enough from Lizzie's previous haunts.

Lizzie might have been safe here – except that now she was safe in prison, thanks to a magistrate with shit in his mouth. What good was it, putting away an innocent loser like her? Still, he'd be safe here now. With any luck. It wasn't that the third party wanted him more than the police but that they had far more to lose.

Trying not to be frantic about it, he searched poor old Horace's pockets for a matchbox. Tomorrow he'd go out for a paper, find out what the press had been given – or found out. *Soyez calme*, he told himself, rest easy.

CHAPTER TEN

Straightening Out

Portia flung herself into Leo's arms. 'You're such an angel to meet me! You must have so much . . . Oh . . .' She burst into tears.

Leo held her. He was always surprised by her size. They were so big, the brothers, and she was hardly more than five two or three. He must tell her the good news. That was why he'd come, and to warn her about the police. Not such good news. 'Let's get going.' He tried to extricate himself and lead her forward.

Still sobbing, she waved a hand behind her. A porter caught Leo's eye. He was wheeling a cart piled high with boxes.

'They're yours?' He tried not to sound horrified.

She nodded, speechless. Leo looked round. Hers had been one of the first flights in. The airport was still empty. The rows of shops, coffee bars, bureaux de change shone with unnecessary lighting. A few had grilles pulled up or half up. The floor space in front of them seemed wider, a startling silence rising.

'You'll be lucky to get them in one taxi, mate,' said the porter.

'Cheers. I've got a car.' He couldn't tell her here, now. She was just composing herself. He'd tell her as they drove into London. He took her arm again.

'Got your parking ticket, have you?'

He felt in his pocket and handed it over. Let the porter lead them. Yesterday had been a day from hell. At least he could bring comfort to Portia. They drove from the airport. Leo adjusted his wing mirror. The boxes had filled the boot and the back seat, blocking his view. Even now there was plenty of traffic around. He entered the tunnel.

'Do you want to tell me about it now? Or when we get back?'

Portia's voice was not quite steady, but controlled. She'd always been brave. Growing up among rowdy boys had taught her composure. Or perhaps she'd been born with it.

'There is extraordinary, wonderful news. Charlie is not dead.'

'What? *What?*' She grabbed his arm so that the car swerved.

Leo's hand was shaking on the wheel. He gripped harder. 'There was a mistake at the hospital. A case of mistaken identity. Another patient had died. I was called to identify the body and pointed out the error.'

'Oh, Leo. How terrible for you.' She laid a hand on his arm, gently this time.

It was the first sympathy he'd had all day and it nearly undid him. He felt his eyes bulging with tears. 'There's more,' he muttered.

'Don't tell me here, on this road. Let me get used to the idea that Charlie's alive.' She turned to him. 'Shall I come to your flat?'

'I'd like that.'

Leo's flat was in Pimlico, between Victoria station and the river, near enough to the Houses of Parliament. He'd bought it three years ago when life seemed to be opening: marriage and a ministerial job. But Suzanne had bunked off, insisting that although he might like her he certainly didn't *love* her, and the ministerial job had hit a snag when he'd voted against the government. It was supposed to be a free vote but nothing comes free in politics. Neither, to be honest, was it just that vote. The truth was he'd been out of sympathy with the government for many years. He'd given lunch in the House of Commons recently to a new acquaintance, the governor of HMP Wandsworth, which was in his constituency. This man had prepared for their meeting by Googling him. 'Do you realise you come up red for rebel more than anyone except the well-known dissidents?' he'd told him, as if it was a joke.

'The main backbench role is to question,' Leo had defended himself but, in fact, he'd been shocked. He didn't think of himself as a rebel, just as someone who stood up for what was right.

At least he didn't regret buying his flat. A man in his forties should have a proper home, wife or no wife, minister or humble Member of Parliament. Not so humble, in fact. Tomorrow he was set to ride the tiger with his claws in its back. Surprisingly, no one else seemed to have got hold of the story. Not a rumour. Or only the rumour he'd started himself, that his question was about the Met. The *Today* programme had put out feelers but he'd declined. That wasn't his job.

'You're all so unlike!' Portia stood in the parquet-floored hallway and looked around her.

Leo guessed she was referring to her brothers. They'd hardly spoken since he'd told her that Charlie was alive. 'You mean Charlie lives in a rat-hole and Roland has a grand country house plus a working flat in the City and Father Bill has – actually, what does he have? I've never been on his visiting list.'

'Nor me. Charlie once told me he shares a house with a gay priest and an unfrocked nun, in the sense that she wears trousers. He was probably making fun. I could do with a drink.'

Leo glanced at his watch. Not yet eight. 'Coffee? I don't expect there's any food.'

'Anything. Then you have to tell me. We have to sit down and you have to tell me. Everything.'

Leo had forgotten Portia's thoroughness. He didn't usually give her the time. The hall was filled with her boxes, which she'd refused to leave in the car. Now she was unwinding herself from a series of colourful capes and scarves. As she took off each one, she folded it carefully and laid it on a chair.

'Go on through. I'll get the coffee.'

Portia sat on one of Leo's long sofas. The room was comfortably male, just as Charlie's was uncomfortably male. (It was extraordinary to be able to think about Charlie without a dreadful wash of despair.) The furniture was modern, solid, sparse. On the white walls hung some of Leo's collection of sixties and seventies prints – a Warhol, a Hockney, a Kitaj. Briefly, she considered Leo's ex-girlfriend, Suzanne. Although they'd been an item for six or seven years, she didn't seem to have left any mark on this flat. Neither had Leo attempted to make her part of the family. Portia didn't even know who had left whom.

She leaned back wearily. After the hurly-burly of Mexico, it seemed very calm, very British. She laid her hands on her knees. They were trembling. They were also dirty.

44

Leo came back with the coffee plus two large brandies. He was in shirt-sleeves. Portia looked at him properly for the first time. 'You've got a black eye.'

'My fight with Roland.' Leo sat down.

'I'd forgotten. Over Charlie.' Portia sighed heavily and sipped her brandy.

CHAPTER ELEVEN

Starting the Avalanche

'A door ran into you, did it?'

Normally Leo enjoyed meeting the round, grinning face of this particular fellow MP – 'Hi, Jack' – Today nervousness made him irritable. 'Actually, my brother punched me.'

'Not the eminent QC?'

'The same.'

'You should get yourself a good lawyer.'

They were standing in the members' lobby of the House of Commons after picking up Hansard and other papers from the bookshop there. On one side a statue of Lloyd George stared disapprovingly. On the other a stone Mrs Thatcher, wearing a lumpy suit and what looked like lisle stockings, harangued them with pointed finger.

'I see you've got a question down.' Jack was leafing through the day's order paper.

'Number eight.'

'The speaker's had his skates on recently. You'll probably make it.'

It was a quarter to twelve, just before Prime Minister's Questions. Together they walked through to Central Lobby. The marbled floor and domed ceiling rang with the criss-cross of well-soled shoes, with the urgent, though lowered, voices of MPs and officials. Most of the visitors were already inside the chamber.

Leo looked at his watch. 'I'm going in. See you there?'

'Standing room only, I hear. Yes, I'll be there. Best of luck.'

Leo hurried across the lobby. He kept his head down to lessen the impact of his bruised eye. It was annoying that it had come up so violently purple, although he felt no pain – or no more than drinking brandy at breakfast time following a day that included the death of one brother, later resurrected, and a fight with another would induce. The important thing was to keep his mind on the job and not to think of Charlie.

'Number eight I see today, sir.'

Leo smiled. He was on good terms with all the parliamentary officials. The one who'd addressed him stood tall and imposing at the doorway to the debating chamber. For the last year or two, he'd worn a black toupee. It reminded Leo uncomfortably of the second police officer, who had led him to Charlie's alleged corpse. Where was Charlie now? That was the question. No! No. That was not the question. The question was the one he was about to put to the leader of his party. Unless the speaker decided not to call him. He wasn't as popular with the speaker as he was with the officials. His heart was beating rather too fast. Adrenalin was a useful tool, he reminded himself. Soldiers charging to certain death were jammed full of it.

Leo strode into the chamber, a handsome figure, with his long legs and broad shoulders well displayed in his sharply cut suit. After shaving his battered face, he had chosen, as an act of bravado, a scintillating pink tie, which now flowed backwards with the speed of his walking.

The benches were already two-thirds full and more MPs were hurrying in all the time, pausing for a second to nod to the speaker. The PM wasn't in yet but the opposition leader was in his place. He'd promised to grill the PM over a fresh scandal about payment for honours. Leo was glad the House was full. His question would get maximum attention. The press gallery was full too.

'Good morning, Polly.' Leo took his accustomed place beside the Member for Newcastle, who, as usual, was wearing a flowery scent, and took out his notes from his breast pocket. He'd finally got used to the number of women on his side of the House. He liked it, in fact. They were braver than the men, more ready to upset the applecart.

'Good luck with your question.' Polly smiled at him, not reacting to his eye. That was cheering.

High in the Visitors' Gallery Maggie, face cupped in her hands, peered down. It wasn't easy to see the MPs through the glass shield in front of her – a victory for terrorism, she supposed – but she'd spotted Leo's entrance, recognised his back view as he bowed slightly, tracked him to his seat, noting the bright tie and the livid eye – her husband's work. He sat next to a woman, young, well dressed in a pale suit. Idiotically, she felt jealous.

Her arrival there was unplanned, impulsive. She hadn't taken in that it was Prime Minister's Questions and had only managed to get a ticket because she was first in the queue. Only three more were let in after her.

The night before, Roland had told her the story: Charlie's supposed death, his own fight with Leo. They'd made love afterwards – the usual silent, businesslike affair. She'd lain awake for hours. Over the years the contradiction that stopped her sleeping had been repeated often. On the one side, her calm, rational self counted up the blessings of her life: health, wealth, a respectful marriage, wonderful children, responsibilities both inside and outside the home she took willingly and performed successfully. On the other hand, there was her love for Leo. It was extraordinary – pathetic, futile, perhaps – that it had survived for so many years, nearly twenty with so little encouragement. In all that time he'd said nothing, she'd said nothing. Yet he had never married, although there had been Suzanne. No longer, apparently. Maggie had seen her only once: very smart, slim.

Her sense that Leo and she loved each other, more than the brother and sister-in-law they were, was unreasonable, she knew that. But it had become part of her daily life, filling the vacuum left by Roland's coolness. In a way, it hardly mattered whether Leo loved her or not – of course he did in some way. She was like a schoolgirl hugging her passionate attachment to herself, warmed at its flame.

Mostly she behaved sensibly. No one must know. No one did know. Just now and again she felt the need to take a step out of the ordinary, to step closer to Leo.

That morning Roland had got up early. She'd heard his quiet movements in the darkness of their bedroom. She'd startled him by speaking, announcing she was going to London that day. She'd had no reason to tell him: he would catch an early train and not return that night. He showed little interest in how she planned her day. Nor would he link her decision (which he couldn't know was sudden) with his information, as a rather derisory aside the evening before, that Leo 'the idiot' would be on his feet the next day asking 'asking some damn-fool question about the police'. She told Roland her plans because it made her feel better, less of a liar. She did not, of course, tell him she was going to the House of Commons. After all, she might not have got a ticket. She might even have decided against going.

Yet she'd put on her prettiest pink and green tweed jacket, made arrangements for the children and driven herself, rather faster than usual, to the station.

Arriving at Waterloo, she'd decided to walk over Westminster Bridge. She took it slowly, lingering opposite Portcullis House where she knew Leo had an office, although she'd never been there. She didn't like the style of the building, too black with strange dark funnels, but the possibility of Leo's presence inside gave it a special attraction.

After she'd crossed the road towards the House of Commons, she'd had a panicky moment. Clandestine didn't suit her. And the place was so grand. She nearly cut and ran before a poster to her right, proclaiming the 186,000 murdered by the US and the UK in Iraq, shamed her: a cowardly country bumpkin who didn't dare walk through a few marble halls to see the man she loved.

So she'd continued, stood in Central Lobby with other visitors, heard the policeman bellow, 'Hats off, strangers!' before taking off his own, watched the speaker and other men in knee breeches, one carrying the great gold mace, march along the echoing corridors. At length she'd been politely herded into her seat and found herself, absurdly flushed and excited, in the third row of Visitors' Gallery, eyes fixed on Leo.

Around her, other eyes were on the front bench, anticipating the arrival of the prime minister. Maggie glanced in that direction and saw him, taller and more elegant than she'd expected. The noise from the floor, as MPs chatted to each other, almost drowned the question-and-answer session already in progress with the Northern Ireland secretary. At one point the speaker asked for 'less noise in chamber' but no one took much notice.

She didn't think she would have been able to concentrate on what they were saying anyway. Watching Leo and knowing he was going to stand up and speak – his name was down at number eight on the order paper she'd been given – made her as nervous as if he was one of her children about to perform in a school play. She reminded herself that Leo had been an MP for fifteen or more years, but her anticipatory nervousness grew.

At last the hands of the big wall clock moved to midday and the Northern Ireland secretary sat down. The chamber grew quiet.

Leo's hands were sweaty. The routine question about the PM's engagements had been dealt with. Now, as promised, the PM and the leader of the opposition were in a prolonged argy-bargy about cash for honours. It didn't get anyone anywhere but it entertained the faithful on both sides who hallooed and waved their papers when they thought their leader had scored a hit. The young MP opposite him was scarlet in the face with an orgasmic level of excitement.

Usually Leo enjoyed it as much as most – the leaders were both clever, witty men – but today he was on edge. Luckily this kind of sport never went on for longer than five or ten minutes. There, now they were done, and the speaker was indicating the first questioner.

Up in the gallery Maggie was finding the system, if there was a system, very confusing. Possibly this was due, at least in part, to her stupidity and her excitable state. At the end of each question, a dozen or more MPs stood up wanting to speak, and one who might or might not be on the order paper was chosen by the speaker. Only occasionally was she able to catch the name. It seemed being number eight was no guarantee to getting in your question.

She looked at the clock. Less than ten minutes to go. Why had she never paid more attention to the workings of Parliament? Because she hadn't been interested, although she declared (to herself) lasting attachment to an MP. She found herself willing, with prayerlike intensity, that the speaker's choice would fall on Leo.

When it did, with three minutes to go, she was so suffused with emotion that she hardly took in a word he said – something about the home secretary, illegal immigrants and the police. She couldn't avoid the reaction: a rising crescendo of 'Order! Order!', banging, baying, men and women on their feet, mostly from Leo's own side. Jeering from the other side. It looked almost as if he was in physical danger. Then the speaker said, quite loudly, 'The Honourable Gentleman knows he is out of order', and that calmed things enough for the prime minister to say a few words, which she was far too disturbed to hear, and suddenly the show was over.

The ministers were out of the door and the chamber emptied on a tide of noise. In a second there were only a few members left and no one on the front benches.

Around her she became aware of buzzing conversation. The entertainment had been far more exciting than the audience had expected. Then they, too, hurried from their seats. She knew she couldn't search for Leo but she wanted him to know that she'd been there and that she supported him. Still sitting in the gallery, with the chamber below, she tore a page from her diary and scribbled a message. She would give it to one of the polite officials.

Leo had thrown a bombshell, that much was clear. Downstairs in the lobbies, the atmosphere was highly charged, men huddled in groups. Visitors like herself were rushed through quickly as if, she thought sensitively, they had seen more than they had a right to see. But the MPs, she told herself firmly, were representatives of the people. Approaching an official, she handed over her note for Leo.

In another few moments, she found herself once again outside Parliament. The day had become very bright. Maggie shielded her eyes. On the other side of the busy road Westminster Abbey gleamed white. Alongside the House of Commons, men were unrolling carpets of fresh green turf. It was lunchtime. She was in London with nowhere to go, no wish, in fact, to go anywhere. She would tell Roland, if he showed any interest, that she had spent several hours recceing the small galleries in Cork Street. Actually, she would walk back over the bridge to the South Bank, grab something to eat by the river, then head for Waterloo station and home.

Slowly Maggie buttoned her jacket.

'Maggie!' She was passing the gates to the private, side entrance of Parliament when a loud voice stopped her. 'Wait! Maggie!'

She turned. Leo, dishevelled and flushed, had rushed out of a doorway and was crossing the courtyard. How could he be here? She felt confused and anxious. He ran towards her. She had time to register the surprise on the policeman's face before Leo grabbed her arm. 'Quick! Round the corner and over the bridge.'

They walked, almost ran, side by side. Leo didn't speak and

Maggie was out of breath. Vanity had encouraged her to wear high heels and a skirt, neither of which was her usual daytime mode and both of which she now regretted.

'I've got to slow down.' She stopped, panting. She gasped, 'I don't understand.'

'Oh, God.' He stopped and looked at her for the first time. 'You're smart. Are you off somewhere?'

'I've been somewhere.'

'You look pretty.' He glanced over his shoulder.

'Thanks. The press are after you, aren't they?' Across the road she caught a glimpse of the stone Boudicca beating along her horse and chariot.

'Think barracuda, Great White Shark, electric eel, giant octopus. How about lunch?'

'Lunch!' Maggie felt a ridiculous blush rising to her cheeks. 'I was going to pick up something along the river.'

'Better than my office and Denver, that's my PA, asking questions.' He was in a hurry again, taking her by the elbow and almost pushing her forward. 'Plenty of time for that.'

'I still can't walk so fast.'

'Sorry. It's been quite a strain. Charlie and then this. I expect I've got a bit of Charlie's mania.'

'You *are* his brother.' Maggie thought, I am walking across Waterloo Bridge with Leo in the sunshine. What had happened in there seemed hardly real. This moment was real.

Leo was silent now, walking a pace ahead and only turning to her when they needed to cross the road. He guided her dangerously between buses and taxis, and, against her will, she was reminded of Roland. The whole family shared that kind of high-handedness – except, perhaps, Portia who, although just as determined as the rest, didn't try to take others with her. Even Father Bill, whom she'd met twice and assumed to be a saintly character, must have certainty to be a priest. Imogen had it to such a degree that she hardly noticed anyone outside her own prism of life. And that wasn't because she was old and blind: she'd been like that ever since Maggie had first met her. 'You are a *nice* girl,' she'd said, as if such condemnation with faint praise was cancelled by the honour of being noticed at all. Of course she'd been young, pretty, and Imogen was nothing if not competitive.

But how annoying to be thinking of her now. They were walking by the river. A sharp breeze blew up it, fluttering the surface of the oily water. The trees were still leafless and cast a cat's cradle of black shade.

'It's too cold for outside,' said Leo. 'Let's try that pizza joint.'

'Good idea.' Why was he with her? How could he ask that question, whatever it was, and then do a bunk? Didn't he *want* to talk to the press?

The pizza house seemed very dark after the brightness outside. There was also music playing, quite loudly.

'Any port in a storm.' Leo got out a handkerchief and wiped his face. He was sweating. So was she. He winced as he reached the bruise round his eye.

They found a table. The waiter came quickly to Leo's peremptory signal. Maggie, always conscious of her weight, ordered a salad, Leo a pepperoni pizza.

'You know what that was all about back there?'

'How could I?' Maggie felt happy that she was not only a convenient escape route. He was actually prepared to talk to her. Roland almost never talked about his work. 'I must say, everybody seemed pretty surprised. Furious, actually. Are you allowed to do that sort of thing?'

'Allowed?' Leo smiled, then laughed.

'Aren't there whips? Or rules? Even conventions?'

'For the faint-hearted. We're supposed to be a democracy.' He waved at a waiter. 'I forgot to ask if you wanted wine?'

Maggie, who drank too much at night but never at lunch, found herself eagerly accepting a glass of Chianti.

'I do feel bad about my whip, a nice chap who's put up with what he sees as my foibles over the last few years. He'll be in trouble with our terrifying chief whip – no lady her – for not knowing what I was up to.' He grimaced wildly. 'But you can't make an omelette without breaking eggs and I like to remember . . .' Leo paused for a moment as the waiter came with their drinks '. . . that I'm elected by the good people of Wandsworth.'

'But would they want you to bring the government, your party, into – into – what's the word? Disrepute?'

'They love nothing better, however they voted. At least, I hope so.

All sensible people suspect politicians of being up to something. Don't you believe I was speaking the truth?'

Not wanting to admit that his actual words had become mazed in her emotions as he rose to his feet, she prevaricated. 'You didn't say very much.'

'Enough.' Leo waited while their food arrived, then asked, 'You're not much of a one for questions, are you?'

This was true. Roland had trained her out of the habit.

'It makes you very restful,' he added. He sighed. 'You know who got me into this business?'

'How could I?'

'That was a rhetorical question. The answer is Charlie. Charlie gave me some information.'

'But I thought . . .'

'He was in hospital, out of his mind. Quite right. He gave me the information via another. A journalist. And now I'm landed in it.' Leo smiled. 'Typical Charlie.'

'I'm surprised you could trust him,' said Maggie, feeling like a schoolmistress. 'Particularly with something as serious as this.' She pictured, with awe, the scene as Leo had stood up to speak. 'It will be on television.' A new acknowledgement. As her shock at being alone with Leo faded, she saw what a ludicrously inappropriate time it was to concentrate on her personal feelings for him. 'You must have more evidence than just Charlie?'

'You're asking a question.'

'Yes.' Maggie looked down at her salad. So, after all, he wouldn't answer her.

'What a coincidence you were in London today. Did you come for a good reason?'

But Maggie had seen him glance at his watch and knew he wasn't really interested. She could even be halfway honest. 'Just a jaunt.'

'Then you got more than you bargained for.'

She pushed away her plate. 'I should go for my train.' She tipped her glass for a final sip. 'I'll watch the news.'

'I'd like to think you were out there, watching. On my side. You are on my side, aren't you?'

'You know I am.' Did he understand what she meant by that? For a moment she thought he did – she'd smiled as she spoke, looked directly at him – but then he turned and waved at the waiter.

'We who are about to die salute you.' He decided to pay at the desk and they stood up. 'You go ahead, if you're in a hurry.'

She wasn't in a hurry but he was ordering her. Perhaps it was better to say goodbye in this dark space than face him outside in the windy brightness. Here she could kiss him without embarrassment. On the cheek, naturally, as she always did.

'Goodbye, Maggie. Thank you for being there.'

Maggie walked back along the river and turned left over the bridge. Leo's last words beat uncomfortably in her head. *Thank you for being there*. It had a vulgar, unreal ring to it. The sort of thing an unreal TV husband said to his unreal TV wife or buddy or secretary. It was not like him at all. Or not the him she thought she knew. Roland's brother, of course, but she had met him before Roland. Imogen had been giving one of her large dinner parties. She'd been invited, through a friend of a friend, for Charlie. But Charlie had failed to show and, at the last minute, to Imogen's obvious disappointment, Leo had taken his place. So, not Roland's brother but Charlie's brother. It sometimes seemed that Charlie was the key to the whole family. Typically, it was Charlie who had discovered Father Bill, although both insisted it was by chance. Chance seemed to play a not quite convincing role in Charlie's life.

She was skirting the roundabout before entering the tunnel that led to the station. It was a dirty, noisy area encouraging dark thought. Charlie frightened her: his unpredictability and the influence he had over Leo. Perhaps he was a force for good, as Leo obviously believed, but his excesses made her distrust him. Nor did she mean his drinking and womanising. Little things, like his habit of writing messages on his hands or arms made her nervous. She believed in abiding by the rules and Charlie, even when he was perfectly sane (and, truthfully, he was never perfectly sane), believed in breaking them.

Roland had a love of order. Maybe she had married him for it. As a barrister, he worked to uphold law and order. Why was nothing simple? She herself, a thoroughly sensible, unimaginative woman, refused to cut out her crush on Leo (was it no more that that?) and Roland, apparently so calmly controlled, was not quite what he seemed either. As the years of their marriage unrolled, she had gradually discovered another side to his personality that he hardly acknowledged and certainly kept secret from her. She couldn't define it but knew it was about anger. Perhaps it was to do with his jealousy of Charlie – that brotherly fight over his supposed dead body – but she felt instinctively that that was not the sum of it.

By now Maggie had reached the station side entrance. She'd walked fast enough to make herself sweat again. She was sure she had at least one blister and felt twinges of indigestion. The exhilaration of her weird and wonderful unexpected lunch with Leo, plus the large glass of thick red wine, had been overtaken by anxieties: Charlie had encouraged Leo to attack his own government. Even now the *Evening Standard*, ready piled in a stand by the bookseller, could be preparing a piece about the affair. It was too early for this edition but it would certainly be in the next and the next. Probably, it had been on the one o'clock news, the headline story. Leo had fired a shot to start an avalanche. And Charlie had loaded the gun. Charlie had always been dangerous.

Maggie stood blindly in front of the row of electronic timetables. Up till now, she had ignored the early-afternoon traffic of people, suddenly she felt pushed and threatened by the crowds.

She admitted, with a sense of disloyalty, that her love for Leo assumed his good sense and stability. She yearned for her yellow and blue kitchen, the daffodils outside the window, which she'd planted herself, every lovely bulb, her boys so innocently boisterous and self-centred, her properties in the town, which she managed so efficiently, the space for her new gallery where she would display beauty and talent.

'Sorry!' In her need to get on her train immediately, and remembering it always left from platform eight, she'd turned abruptly, knocking an old lady who reeled backwards uncomplainingly.

'I'm sorry,' repeated Maggie, steadying the woman with her arm. She was very small and leaned against a pull-along case.

'I'm partially sighted,' the woman murmured, waggling a white stick. 'Could you tell me the platform for Winchester?'

With relief, Maggie recognised the possibility of doing good. 'I'm going there, too. Can I help you?'

CHAPTER TWELVE

'Duck your tiny head, Pygmy!'

Portia was cross with herself. She crunched the gears of the rented van, then rammed on the brakes so the piles of boxes slid along the floor towards her. One toppled over. She should have transported them to Portobello much earlier so she'd have had the rest of the day and Thursday to unpack, sort and mark before Friday's big selling day. But when she'd reached her flat, she'd fallen asleep for an hour, dreaming of Charlie, unsurprisingly: Leo and she had talked of little else – at least, she could remember little else, although that might have been the effect of the brandy. Talking about Charlie left its own kind of hangover. Really, it was pointless trying to guess where he might be and why, and how he'd got involved in the death of a fellow patient. She suspected Leo had clues but, if so, he was not letting on to her.

Portia clambered out of the van and hurried round to the back. Any kind of manual labour made her feel like a pygmy. In a moment she'd find Brian, who sold antique cutlery in the stall next to hers and always volunteered to help. She had to pay for it with the odd stroke and appraising glance but she wasn't enough of a feminist to object. Conor didn't approve but, then, he was still up in Scotland. Brian knew her limits. He was married with two small daughters who visited with their mother on Saturday. He never helped Portia when they were around.

She'd grown up among men, of course, unless you counted her mother but, then, Imogen had seldom noticed her daughter's existence. The brothers had created her view of herself. At best they were patronising, at worst dismissive or even bullying in a casual, unknowing way. When she was ten, they were all teenagers, huge, sportive, loud, self-confident. She never spoke a word at meals and they wouldn't have heard if she'd tried. Naturally she hero-worshipped them all, taking turns for a particular allegiance, according to which had given her a glimmer of recognition. Sometimes Leo would take her to watch him play golf, or Roland to a tennis tournament or Charlie to act as ballast in his sailing boat. 'Duck, Pygmy!' he'd shout, as the boom came swinging over.

She'd never doubted that they loved her. Not really. It was just that they found her insignificant. You couldn't blame them but it wasn't good for her morale.

'I was watching you from inside. Too much of the Mexican mushroom, is it?'

Brian stood at her side. He'd bleached his hair since she'd last seen him, which made his reddish face redder and his blue eyes bluer. 'Wow!' she exclaimed.

'The days have been dull.'

'So you've turned yourself into a glowing beacon. And, yes, I would like help with my boxes.'

They worked amicably to unload the van. The boxes weren't heavy but Portia soon tired. She tried to work out what time it was in Mexico. Earlier, anyway. 'Want a coffee?'

'Sure.'

Soon Portobello Road would be one long chain of coffee shops. Then, on Fridays and Saturdays, a place for tourists to gawp. She bought two very expensive cartons of coffee and walked slowly back to the van. Brian and she leaned against it drinking.

'It looks like you had a good haul this trip,' said Brian. 'No boyfriend?'

'He's on a film.' Not Brian's business. 'The women are desperate for me to take their stuff.' Portia thought of her reason for coming back early. She could hardly believe it now: the death of a brother. She had lived through it even if the sentence had been reversed. It was no wonder she felt shattered. 'I'd better start unpacking.'

Portia sat on a stool doing nothing. She'd opened several boxes, pulled out a pile of blouses, then given up. Charlie's apparent death had jolted her, she decided, like the electric shocks that Charlie himself had been given on several occasions. The doctors had explained the treatment. It shook things up like a kaleidoscope, and when they settled down again they might be in a better order. Well, her bits were still whirling. She felt restless, muddled, her mind on her difficulties with the family which a sensible therapist had told her, years ago, she could never fix, probably not even understand, so her best bet was to accept. Since which she'd formed some kind of bond with Leo – on his terms, of course. Bonding didn't come naturally to any of them. Conor called them the *un*family. 'How's your *un*family?' He wouldn't be surprised by the latest news.

Out of the five siblings, which included the newly discovered Father Bill, only one, Roland, was married. Of course, Charlie had gone through the wedding service with Lizzie but, as far as Portia could see, it had been some kind of self-imposed penance, plus his special brand of rebellious up yours, and not a serious love affair with the intent of joining their lives. Even Roland, despite producing children with Maggie and owning a large family home, spent far more time in his London flat. By himself, she presumed. Certainly there had never been a whiff of another woman.

Leo was the oddest of all: handsome, clever, sympathetic and attractive to women, hence the glamorous Suzanne, yet still single.

Their parents' marriage had not been the best example. Imogen had treated their father as if he were a rather boorish schoolboy, unworthy of her attention for very long, although tolerated if he toed the line and didn't make trouble – in other words, accepted her lovers without complaint and paid the bills. The lovers, surprisingly to Portia, were never as distinguished as her father. They were usually younger, upper class and fair-haired. Although the upper-class bit had gone by the board as she'd got older. Maybe Esmond's undisputed intellectual superiority had allayed his jealousy. Maybe there was some sexual incompatibility. Thank heavens she didn't have to know about that.

Portia considered her own lover. Conor was an Irishman who'd come to England to make films. They'd known each other for a year and met when they found the time. No pressure on either side. He was tall and thin, with white skin that reddened when he became intense. Or when they made love. He always wanted to make love when they met. So did she. She sometimes wondered if it wasn't the sex that kept them together – as far as they were together. He'd accompanied her on the trip before this one to Mexico. He'd been sure he could get backing for a film about the women's co-operative. 'Beautiful visuals and heart-rending stories' that, he'd assured her, would cut purse-strings. Although he was now producing a TV documentary about teenage drug addicts, he was still trying, for which she gave him credit. This evening he'd be back and she'd call him. She wanted to tell him about Charlie. Where was Charlie? That was what Conor would ask.

She stood up. The boxes could wait till tomorrow.

The market stalls, selling guavas and strawberries from Israel, herbs from France and narcissi from the Isles of Scilly, were already beginning to shut down. It must be a slow day. Almost with a sense of duty – she'd never been much interested in day-to-day news – Portia went into the newsagent to buy a paper.

She picked up a *Guardian* and took it to the counter. A pile of *Evening Standard*s was slapped down in front of her. She couldn't avoid the heavy black headline: 'MP WHISTLEBLOWER'. Under it was a photograph of Leo, not with a black eye.

Her first reaction, before she even read the story, was to be annoyed that Leo had spent hours with her the night before and not even hinted that he had anything important on next day. It was typical and to be expected, but no less hurtful.

'And a *Standard*,' she said, taking a paper.

CHAPTER THIRTEEN

I'm Fine

Lizzie tried to understand what her resettlement officer was saying. He was the good sort, a big man, in his white shirt and epaulettes, filling the small room, encouraging but not patronising. She should listen. It was important. But how could she when she'd had the news, direct from the governor, that Charlie wasn't dead? Mr Potts wasn't dead. It had embarrassed her when Charlie took her name. Such an ugly name. She'd have been glad to be rid of it. That was Charlie, though. Do the opposite of what was expected. Charlie and Lizzie Potts. It sounded like a music-hall comedy turn. She'd tell him so when she saw him. Lizzie smiled to herself. She didn't know the details yet, of course, but the point was, he was alive. Alive. Now she felt like crying.

'So you have somewhere to go to? To live?'

She heard him this time. Charlie had found her a flat. But then they'd put her inside so she'd never been there. Fuckers.

'I've got a flat. I'm married, see.' She could hear the pride in her voice. Silly, really. They'd never even spent a night together. He wasn't dead, she reminded herself again. Anything could happen. You never knew with Charlie. He must love her a bit to have married her. Father Bill had done it in church, even if it was on a side altar, so it was good and binding.

'I don't seem to have the address.' He was looking through the papers in his folder.

'Well, I can't help you, can I. I've only been there once.' A small lie. 'It's OK, though. Finsbury Park area.' Suddenly she needed to convince him, herself too, that it existed. 'I came in here straight from the court. Fucking magistrates. You know. I didn't have nothing. Anything. The flat's there, all right.'

The prison officer, whose name, Derrick Whipple, was pinned to his shirt, continued to look doubtful.

'You can ask my husband. That's the best thing. You've got an address for him. If not, I have.'

'A different one, you mean?'

Lizzie found she was blushing. 'He hasn't sold his flat yet, has he. With me being in here . . .' Her voice trailed away.

'I'll get in touch with him, then.' He studied his paper again. 'Will you be resuming work?'

Would she be resuming work? Was he winding her up? He seemed straight enough. Maybe his notes didn't tell him about her line of work. Nights. 'I've got to keep away from people who do me no good, haven't I. You know.'

'I suppose your husband can support you. Is he employed?'

Lizzie thought about this. She chewed on an already well-bitten nail. Last time she knew about Charlie's whereabouts he'd been in hospital. Not long after she'd come in here. That letter just a few days ago. She supposed he was still there. Not working. She had no intention of telling this to Derrick Whipple, even if he was trying to help. 'He works for the papers.'

'Right. So you don't have money worries?'

They'd never talked about money. He didn't seem to have much, not like Mo or Arun with rolls of notes in their pockets. But he was educated, rich-feeling and, after all, he'd got her the flat. 'I'm fine.'

'Right, then.'

Taking more interest, she could see him ticking his sheet of paper. 'How long is it?'

'Till you come out? Don't you know?'

'The days aren't normal here.' Outside it was the nights that weren't normal. All those men willing to pay for what they could get from her. It didn't make sense. The way she'd been. Right out of it. Men and their needs. Make you laugh. But she'd always found it easy to pick up. Perhaps it was being so small. Made them feel big. She had nice eyes too. They often mentioned that.

'So you're clean. Right?'

'You know that. They slammed me in Detox straight away.' That wasn't fair. She'd gone willingly. Charlie had told her the drugs would be the death of her and she had to live now that she was a married woman.

'Anything I can do for you, Lizzie?' He smiled at her. A nice, comforting smile.

Did she want him to contact her mum? She'd thought of her lately. All those brothers and sisters. Six at the last count. Probably more now. It was just her bad luck to be the oldest. At least she'd managed to avoid kids. Something wrong with her insides, the doctor said. Hardly surprising, really. 'Thank God for small mercies' – that's what her mum used to say. Not that she'd said anything to her for two or three years. Couldn't blame her, really. With all those kids.

'I might want to contact my mum.'

'You want me to help with a letter?'

'I can write!' Her mum didn't even know about the wedding. It hadn't seemed the right moment to tell her, with court and, as it turned out, prison. 'Don't you worry. I'll think about it.'

'You'll do all right, Lizzie.'

It was his job to say things like that but she felt pleased all the same. She was off the drugs. She did have a husband, even if not quite in the regular way – but if it came to that, when had her life ever been regular? She saw he was preparing to go. 'I don't mind being in here,' she said impulsively.

'You don't?'

'I'm painting, you know. Walls, I mean.' She liked painting. Making something white and bright that had been a mucky yellow.

'Now you mention it I can see a few spots in your hair.'

She didn't want that. No personal comments from a screw. Anyway, that wasn't the real reason she liked being in prison. Course not. It was being safe. And what was she safe from? She was safe from fucking men. Maybe the lezzies had it right. She felt her mood blacken. This officer in here, with his well-ironed shirt (ironed by his wife, no doubt) and open, kindly face, he was a man too. Probably he fancied a bit of action like the rest of them. She stood up hurriedly. 'That's it, is it?'

He looked at his watch. 'Back to the wing, are you?'

It wasn't a question, though he tried to make it sound like one. She felt herself scurrying, like a scrawny little female mouse as he strode along ahead, unlocking the heavy doors, then slamming them after they'd gone through. Why had she told him she didn't mind it here? She hated every minute. When they got back and her new cellmate Yi Min was cleaning her nails, she didn't even say goodbye to him. Who did he think he was, clumping about with his clipboard and thinking he could solve her problems? Ignoring Yi Min, who only spoke a few English words anyway, she crawled into her bed and shut her eyes.

Perhaps if she lay still enough for long enough she'd recapture that joyous feeling when she was told Charlie was alive. He lived. Desperately, she tried to place him between other images of humiliation and disgust. Tall and solid, blue eyes, flushed skin, a brick wall. 'Don't kill yourself, Lizzie Potts,' he'd said to her. But what had they done to him in hospital? Why had she been told he was dead by Father Bill, his own brother, when he wasn't? If he wasn't. What might she be told tomorrow? Or later today? Nobody to trust. Nobody to lean on. She'd never cut herself, like so many in here did. That's why Yi Min was here, not Leona any more. Too much blood. It had disgusted Lizzie. So much disgusted her. Bleeding was horrible. She was glad her period didn't come any more. She wouldn't cut herself. But the pain was coming in her head. How could she bear it? Charlie! Charlie! Where are you? Where are you when I need you?

CHAPTER FOURTEEN

Naked on the Naked Earth

It was Bill's turn for taking confession in church. Father Aloysius, the parish priest and therefore his superior, insisted on the black boxes with their absurd grilles being used at least once a week. He said old people felt more secure in darkness with the priest an anonymous shadow. To Bill, it was a step backwards into medievalism where the power of the priest was a source of fear, not comfort. He much preferred the modern style, a chat in something called, rather charmingly, the parlour, with both sinner and Christ's representative on earth praying together in their chairs, followed quite often by a reviving cup of tea.

But Wednesday was his turn for midday confession in church so that was what he was doing. Obedience remained an important part of church order. Father Bill sat in the little dark box from midday to one o'clock and in the first half-hour no one came, and in the second, Loretta, an old and pious lady of vaguely Portuguese origins, who confessed her sins (mostly of greed and covetousness) at every opportunity, came to spend a long ten minutes of shame, which Bill tried hard not to believe she found pleasurable. After her departure – he knew she hoped for a heavy penance so he obliged with a whole rosary – he decided to do some serious praying. The subject of his prayer would be Charlie, his brother, for whom he felt great affection and about whom he knew so little. He was in deep trouble, that was clear, and not just because of his mental instability.

Bill, head in hands, found himself recalling the great saints of the Church, and estimating how many, in modern terms, would be declared insane and removed to a secure unit. St John the Baptist roamed naked through the wilderness, a wild man living off insects and honey. St Francis, from a solid merchant background, started his progression towards sainthood by stripping himself naked in Assisi's main piazza, much to the amusement of a large crowd. The compulsion to be naked was, of course, classic manic behaviour. The acknowledged lunatic in the New Testament, hiding out in the tombs at Gadara, was also naked, and strong enough to break free of his chains. Jesus identified him as being filled with devils, which it was his job to drive out – extremely dramatically as the devils entered a herd of swine that flung themselves over a cliff to their death.

Bill found he was going off the point. It was the drama of the Church that had first drawn him to it. Perhaps that, too, was Charlie's attraction. Before he began his training for the priesthood Bill's own life had been unbearably confined and drab. Brought up as an only child (adopted, of course) by elderly parents in Birkenhead, his only escape had been books and school: St Anselm's College, a Christian Brothers grammar school in Birkenhead. It was a famously strict place but his parents had already passed on to him the gift of faith so he was happy there. He'd thanked them for that as they died, his mother six weeks after his father. To have their own son (nearly their own) giving them the last rites had sent them off feeling as if heaven had already reached down to them. Bill smiled in the darkness, then reproved himself for allowing his planned praying time to be taken over entirely by thoughts of self.

St Francis had said he wanted to die 'naked on the naked earth', although in the event he passed away surrounded by his loving brothers, and when his soul flew to heaven it had been accompanied by a thousand swallows whirling upwards in the evening light. What was nakedness but a seeking after purity, a seeking after God? Is that what linked the madman and the saint?

His superior in the English College at Rome had told him that the worst trial facing a young priest was how to purify the self without becoming self-centred. The textbook answer was to hand yourself over to God and let him do the purifying. 'But if I'm examining my conscience on a regular basis,' Bill had asked, 'how can I avoid being self-centred?'

The priest had smiled kindly, 'That's why I called it the worst trial.'

Yet his own start in life had been strange enough to encourage him into self-analysis. His parents, perhaps embarrassed, had only hinted at the circumstances in which they'd adopted him, mention of 'a good Catholic woman', 'a large family' and 'health problems' so that he'd imagined a working-class Irish mother burdened by poverty and constant conceptions; perhaps she'd even died. Lady Shillingstone had been quite a shock. A year or so ago Charlie had passed on a story that he said came from his mother.

During Bill's baptism (as Orlando) Imogen, at the height of her short-lived Catholic fervour, had noticed a middle-aged couple pretending to pray in the pews, 'pretending' because their real attention was on the service taking place over the font, the two little boys playing and the baby being received into the Church.

Imogen found them, talked to them, discovered they were child-less and decided it was God's will that she should give away one of her sons. Charlie had retailed this mockingly and it was quite possible he'd made the whole thing up. But, if so, there was no other story to replace it. Whether Imogen regretted such an extra-ordinary action no one, not even Charlie, hinted. Certainly she'd never made contact and showed no particular interest when Or-lando, now Bill Wright, reappeared. But, of course, she had Charlie, another, beloved, third son.

At one o'clock, Bill left the confessional and, genuflecting jauntily, headed for Wednesday's lunch of spaghetti Bolognese. Not his favourite but he was hungry enough to enjoy it.

Aloysius had already eaten so the food was left by the microwave. Beside it was a note from the housekeeper: 'Your brother called.' How annoying was that! Mary O'Brien knew perfectly well he had three. Now she wouldn't be back till tomorrow so he couldn't ask. Moreover, 'called' in her language could mean either 'paid a visit' or 'rang', although if the former it would certainly be Charlie as neither Roland nor Leo had ever come near the church or presbytery. They were not Catholics, so there was no reason why they should.

Eating the Bolognese in his usual hurried way, Bill decided he would visit Lady Shillingstone – he could never manage to think of her as Imogen or even as 'mother'. He would just make a ten-minute call, which was her preferred length of time, before the finance meeting. It was six months since he'd seen her. Under the present circumstances, she might be more welcoming than usual.

CHAPTER FIFTEEN

Separate Realms

The small room was dim, curtains drawn, the only sound the restless movement of Imogen's legs under the covers. She'd been unwell all day, the shock of Charlie's supposed death producing what the doctors termed, not very certainly, 'another minor stroke'.

It was two thirty. Wednesday. Roland, who had cut short lunch with the president of the Law Society to see the doctor, and his mother, of course, hesitated by the door. He had always thought Imogen would arrange her death in a grand manner, as she had her life, but perhaps it was beyond even her controlling powers. Her face on the pillow, shining white out of the darkness, was like that of any other very old lady – in fact, any very old person since she seemed, with her prominent bone structure, as much man as woman.

'Oh, Roland! No one told me you were here.'

Roland looked at his sister with surprise. Portia had surprised him ever since her arrival in his life. He'd been twelve, firmly convinced that their family consisted of males – apart from Imogen who belonged to some other distant and more perfect species. Portia, noticeably small while they were all big, quiet where they were noisy, unselfish when even as boy he had known he had to fight for his place at the centre of the world, was out of place and a puzzle – if he'd ever stopped to think about her.

Now here she was at his elbow, dressed in her usual assortment of bright colours, red predominating.

'You've come to see Imogen.'

'Yes. She's not well. More not well than usual, I mean.'

'Look at her.'

They stared at their mother before Portia pulled away. 'Have you seen the *Standard*?'

'I've been busy.'

'Actually, it's just as well Mother's not too *compos*.' Portia was the only one of them who ever called Imogen 'Mother' with any conviction. He wondered whether it showed a lack of awe and whether she was making a claim on Imogen that none of the rest of them dared. He turned to look at her as if for the first time. Was she stronger than she seemed?

'You're not taking me seriously.' Portia was blushing. She took Roland's arm. 'Come into the sitting room and I'll show you.'

Roland studied his watch. 'I've only got five minutes.' He had wanted to be alone with Imogen. He sighed. 'What a dreadful twenty-four hours this has been. We still don't know where Charlie is and the police want all sorts of information. I've never expected Charlie to behave reasonably but Leo seems to have gone off at the deep end too.' Unconsciously, he fingered the cut on his cheek.

'It's Leo who's in the news. Actually, he's making the news.'

The moment they were in the softly carpeted room, Portia thrust the newspaper at Roland. 'If it was Mexico, I'd understand it.'

'What do you mean?'

She watched as he arranged his long limbs in an armchair and finally took up the paper. She thought, he's already angry with Leo and now he'll go mad. He was handsome, but there was something tight and fractious about him. No wonder he couldn't stand Charlie.

Roland set aside the paper. He seemed more weary than angry.

'Do you think it's true?' asked Portia. 'The head of the Met blackmailing our home secretary? I mean, it's hard to believe, isn't it? In England. We don't have that sort of corruption, do we? Serious corruption. I know politicians get dumped regularly for various kinds of bad behaviour. Sexual "indiscretions", isn't that the word? Sex stuff seems almost normal. This is different, isn't it? If it's true. What do you think, Roland?'

Her brothers were so clever, that was the point: at Eton with exotic flower-embroidered waistcoats, at Oxford, all three of them, knowing everything long before she knew anything, in high-profile jobs, even if Charlie's career was hampered by his illness. Probably he was so clever that his brain couldn't cope, or that was how Imogen had explained it when Charlie had had his first breakdown. Portia had been just ten, terrified by a rumbustiousness that had tipped over the edge into madness. Charlie had insisted she was Cinderella and he was her Prince Charming; he'd danced with her, swinging her feet off the ground. Then he'd begun to sing and stripped off his clothes and soon after 'the men in white coats', as he called them later, had come to take him away.

Even when Charlie was in hospital, he was cleverer than her. Once he'd recited the whole of *Macbeth*, although he left out what he described as 'Shakespeare's low moments'. Then he'd bet her a hundred pounds he could do it backwards. He failed, of course, but she kept the IOU he'd written her for years. 'Gentlemen always pay their debts,' he told her, 'but I'm not a gentleman. I'm a hobbit!' He'd screwed up his face and leered.

'So, what do you think?' asked Portia again.

'I don't know.' Roland frowned. 'What do I know? I deal in evidence.'

'I saw him last night and he never said a thing. Did he warn *you*?'

Roland didn't bother to answer this. He stood up and handed the newspaper back to her. 'It's not my business.'

'But you must have a view! And he is your brother.' Portia was conscious that she had never pressed him like this before. As if she had a right to access his thoughts. But she did, didn't she?

Perhaps Roland would have answered her appeal except that they were joined at that moment by a third person.

'Bill!' Portia was pleased. Although not a believer herself, she liked having a priest as a brother. On his arrival in the family, she'd automatically ascribed to him the same power of intelligence and success as she gave to her three other brothers so it was a pleasant surprise when he treated her as an equal, even deferring to her on the few occasions they'd met as someone who devoted her life to helping others without the support of faith.

'Quite a family gathering!' Portia smiled. It was her attempts at optimism, she noted, that caused her to be ignored.

'I'm just going.' Roland made as if to pass by Bill. Portia was not even certain they'd met before.

'I'm sorry if I'm out of place.' Bill was calmly humble. 'I'm anxious about Charlie and it reminded me I hadn't seen Lady

Shillingstone for months.' His formality sounded vaguely absurd. Imogen was his mother too.

'What a mess!' Roland seemed to change his mind and went back to the chair. He sat down heavily. 'Imogen's like a death's head, Charlie's not only mad but wanted by the police and now Leo's gone berserk. You'll have to do an awful lot of praying to sort this lot out.' He smiled slightly at Bill.

'He means this,' said Portia, holding out the paper to Bill. It was strange how physically alike the brothers were when their characters were so different. Their voices were unlike, of course, Roland's exceedingly upper class and Bill's still accented by his northern roots. Even so, the deep timbre was the same.

Bill took the paper and sat in the armchair opposite Roland, who closed his eyes. The room was not large but heavily furnished as if for a group who needed comfort or perhaps for the rich. This was, after all, an expensive nursing-home.

Portia continued to stand, now watching Bill. He was wearing a dark jacket and trousers but no priestly collar. His clothes were cheap and well-worn and his face, although so like Roland's in features, had a less cared-for look, as if he had used a blunt razor and coarser soap, while his hair, thinning like Roland's, had not been sleekly cut but straggled in uneven lengths. In brief, he looked poor.

Portia immediately doubted her judgement because it shouldn't be possible to make such a distinction in the twenty-first century in a western country. She could tell the poor in Mexico easily enough because they carried their babies on their backs and lived in mud-baked houses with no running water and ate meat only on a feast day. But surely in Britain 'the poor', like 'the working class', was a thing of the past. Everybody had a TV, used hair conditioner, bought expensive, unnecessary and unnutritious food. The difference now, so she'd believed, was in education and culture. The poor were trapped in unattractive ghettos but this didn't mean they were without money to spend – compared to her Mexican women.

So what did she mean when she relegated Bill to the poor? The answer came as Roland opened his eyes and said bitterly, 'I don't expect he mentioned anything about this to you either.'

Of course! It was not that Bill looked so poor but that Roland looked so very rich! It was the contrast that had confused her. The poor might have changed their nature but the rich had only become more what they had always been: expensively dressed, expensively serviced and thoroughly convinced of their own superiority.

'No. I knew nothing,' said Bill. 'Nor would I expect to.' He hesitated. 'You don't think it has anything to do with Charlie's disappearance? That poor man hanging from a tree.'

'I understood you were close to Charlie.'

'We respect each other.'

'Respect!'

'But I don't ask him questions,' continued Bill, serenely. 'Perhaps priests get out of the habit.'

Portia thought that she might as well not have been present. 'Is there a radio here? We could listen to the news and see how seriously the press are taking it.'

'It has to be taken seriously.' Roland didn't even bother to look at her. ' "Leo Barr MP, younger brother of prominent QC Roland Norrington Barr who successfully prosecuted the so-called chloroform murderer." '

Bill had returned to the paper. He read aloud: ' "Is the prime minister aware that the home secretary made a private arrangement with the chief of the Metropolitan Police to ensure that the latter was appointed to his position?" '

'Doubtless we'll know all too much about it in the weeks ahead.' Roland stood, took his BlackBerry from his pocket and turned it on. Portia saw him bring up his emails. 'A message from Leo. That's very gracious of him.'

'What does he say?' Portia moved closer to him.

Before he could answer, an urgent figure appeared in the doorway.

'What is it, Matron?' Roland held up an arm, as if appealing for order.

The matron, who was portly, checked the buttons of her blue uniform, then replied gravely, 'I've called back the doctor. I'm afraid your mother has had another episode. A turn for the worse.'

'Oh God!' Roland was clearly not invoking the name of the Lord with any religious fervour.

Bill had stood up at Matron's entry. Portia looked from one brother to the other, one shocked, the other businesslike. 'Can I go to her?' She wanted to sit by her, hold her hand. Why did no one ask, 'What do you mean, *worse*?'

'A nurse is with her.' Matron turned to Roland. 'We have it in writing that under no circumstances should she be removed to hospital.'

'Yes. No.' He was muttering, distressed.

'We must tell Leo,' Portia said, forgetting for a moment the unfolding of a more public drama. 'And what about Charlie?' A feeling of terrible anxiety took hold of her. Up till now her worries about Charlie had been mitigated by the glorious news that he'd escaped death. But what if he hadn't or something bad was happening to him? He was a risk-taker and had probably not entirely recovered from his manic episode. Mother and son, both undergoing *episodes*. It was too much, near farce: her mother dying (because surely that must be the case), her father out of his mind, one brother on the run and another brother intent on bringing down the government. This was her family.

'I'm going to her.' She felt near to tears.

Bill and Portia sat on either side of Imogen's bed. They'd spoken only once when Bill had recalled his finance meeting. 'I should be elsewhere,' he'd said, 'but my mobile's packed it in. Can I borrow yours?'

'Mine's out of juice. Sorry.'

They stared at each other, divided by the prone figure of their mother. They were brother and sister but, to Bill, it didn't feel like that.

A nurse sat further away. She had put an oxygen mask on Imogen, which seemed to exaggerate the irregularity of her breathing. The only other sound was that of a blackbird cheeping insistently outside the window. It would remain silent for several minutes, then start again, the sound scarcely muffled by the curtains drawn against the light.

Portia stood up abruptly. 'I can't bear it!'

Bill tried to imagine how many deathbeds he'd attended. Including those of his parents. Not many people were called to watch over the deaths of two mothers. 'Don't worry, I'll stay. I hate the finance committee anyway and they hate me. I can't bring myself to take money seriously.'

'It's lucky you're a priest, then.'

'Priests have to manage budgets like everyone else. More so, really, with the church to look after, the church house and the parishioners.' He was using his normal tone and he could see it was grating on Portia. She left the room, mumbling something he couldn't hear.

The nurse, sitting heavily in the chair, shifted her position and sighed. 'It's hard to let a loved one go, however old and infirm.'

Bill said nothing. He thought that, by all accounts, Imogen had taken more interest in power than love. Apart from Charlie. He began to worry about Charlie again and to channel his thoughts took out the small book of prayers and spiritual ideals he always carried. He read:

> 'Modernity partitions each human life into a variety of segments, each with its own norms and modes of behaviour. So work is divided from leisure, private life from public, the corporate from the personal. Both childhood and old age have been wrenched away from the rest of human life and made into distinct realms. And all these separations have been achieved so that it is the distinctiveness of each and not the unity of the life of the individual who passes through those parts in terms of, which we are taught to think and to feel.'

Then he thought it was surprising that Roland, whom he'd judged a cold fish, had appeared so upset by his mother's deterioration. Maybe he was a weak man who'd built a tough, protective wall. In Bill's experience, people were seldom as they seemed. Or that was what he liked to believe.

When Portia returned to the sitting room, Roland was standing in the middle of the room apparently concentrating on his BlackBerry. Against her wishes, she burst into tears. Roland looked up and, even through her sobs, Portia could see his startled embarrassment. Had the act of managing his affairs wiped out the present situation? 'I'm sorry,' she gasped, adding, ridiculously, as if there weren't enough reasons to sob, 'it must be jet lag. I mean the reason I'm not coping very well. Although there's certainly plenty to cope with.'

Like a character from an old-fashioned play, Roland handed her a very large folded handkerchief. How could the warm-hearted, even saintly Maggie be married to such a man? Then, to her surprise, she felt a tentative pat on her shoulder. Portia's mind was swinging wildly from one thing to another. Now that she'd mopped her tears she felt a strong urge to put on the television, which she'd just noticed in the corner.

Would Leo appear, explaining to the nation his accusations? It struck her that everyone except her seemed to do exactly what they wanted. It was only she who was constantly second-guessing, trying to do what she, or rather some unknown arbiter, wanted her to do. Even in Mexico, where she was trying so hard to improve women's lives in a practical way, she felt as if she was acting at one remove, a mystery both to herself and to them. She went over and turned on the television.

Roland slid the BlackBerry into his pocket. Not yet having the courage to go to his mother, he'd been watching BBC World News on its tiny screen. They had used a clip from Prime Minister's Questions. It seemed Leo had avoided on-screen interviews so far and the reporter had nothing more to go on than his question at midday. Usually any major scandal was heralded by gossip and rumour but Leo's accusation seemed to have come from nowhere.

Behind him, he heard Portia switching through the channels. She'd stopped crying as quickly as she'd started. Obviously she, too, was searching for explanations. But how despicable! Their mother was dying and they were trying to catch Leo on television. It was another black mark against his brother. Roland could never forgive him for having been born hardly a year after him. Roland had never had Imogen to himself. Charlie had not been a rival in the same way: Imogen had loved him as you do a force of nature, a mighty sunset, a turbulent sea. Besides, he had been set in his rivalry with Leo before Charlie was born.

'I'm going in to see Imogen.'

Portia, who had reached a wildlife programme overflowing with monkeys, peered up at him. Her eyes were large and appealing. Not a monkey's but some other animal's. 'Bill's going to stay with her. Have you called Leo?'

75

'I've left a message.' At least he knew how to behave. 'And one for Maggie, who probably won't tell Father. Apparently, he spends most of his time on the high seas.'

'It's strange, that.' Portia seemed to be contemplating the idea seriously. 'Do you remember when he had a passion for those O'Brian books? Perhaps that's where it came from.'

'Possibly.' Esmond's failure of control over his mind frightened Roland. From an early age, he'd been told – erroneously, in his view – that he was like his father. True, they were both lawyers but Esmond had specialised in libel, never afraid to take on the most powerful opponents in the world of business or of media and most often winning, while Roland prosecuted or defended criminals. His was a murky world in which the concepts of good and evil were swapped for not guilty and guilty. He was paid to win the case, not to seek justice.

During his twenty years at the bar he'd seen the worst of human nature, and he was good at his job because he understood it. It struck him that Leo would have considered none of this when he asked his question in the House. He still believed in black and white. What a crass luxury!

'I suppose Mother really is dying?' Portia looked aghast at her own words.

Roland stared at her. He felt a wild urge to cry out, 'What do you care? Any of you! I'm the eldest! I *love* her!' He suppressed it with rigid control.

Esmond, in his neat bedroom at the top of the house, twisted and turned. Damn this wind, he swore, as one great toss nearly had him out of bed. I'll not wait for eight bells tonight.

Those young fools need their sleep, although they pretend I do. Bollocks! What I need is my hat and coat, the deck under my boots, the water thrashing port and starboard. She's a good, strong ship, that's the truth. Nothing will break her. But she still needs her captain. Captain and commander.

That's it. That's better. With one splendid roll, Esmond ejected himself from the bed and landed on the floor with a thump loud enough for Tom to hear and call to his mother in the kitchen, 'Mum! Grandpa's fallen out of his bed again!'

On the floor, Esmond felt his old bones rattled and bruised. For a moment, his mind cleared and he felt the thick carpet with gratitude. On board ship, he'd have landed on wooden planks.

CHAPTER SIXTEEN

Extasie

Charlie planned to pick up a book from his flat: *The Collected Works of John Donne*. The first line of 'The Extasie' had been driving him mad – more mad (ha!) – all day. Could it really start 'Where'? *Where, like a pillow on a bed* . . . He'd written the alternatives on either forearm: *When, like a pillow on a bed* . . . and EXTASIE on his inner arm.

He needed the line to complete *The Times* crossword puzzle but he also needed an excuse to move out of the disgusting room. In the night the brownish walls had run with slime, closing in on where he lay, trapped in pill-induced somnolence. A loathsome odour filled his nostrils and he'd nearly puked. The stained felt carpet had turned to a marshy moss sucking him downwards.

He couldn't move that night but in the morning he'd put one heavy foot in front of the other and forced his trembling fingers to unlock the door. He'd staggered to the corner shop, as he had the evening before, bought a newspaper and a pork pie, then returned to his room. He knew he seemed drunk – not just his gait but his slurred speech – and was afraid of attracting attention.

In the light of day, dim and greenish from a small window, the room seemed less threatening. For the first time in weeks, he was able to concentrate on the newspaper, reading every page, from news, through business and features to sport. The papers were his work, another kind of drug. Soon they'd be blown apart by his story. Good old Leo wouldn't let him down. Or Griff. Like a terrier with a rat. Feeling his mind beginning to race, he'd turned hastily to the crossword.

At first it had been fine, memory as sharp as ever, brain drawing the right conclusions. Then came Donne. Unlike his brothers who'd read classics at university, Charlie had scandalised his parents by opting for English. He'd informed them that the language of the Anglo-Saxons, the Chaucerian writers and the Metaphysical poets had far more to teach him than the predictability of Greek and Latin. (He'd read the classics in his spare time anyway.) They'd told him he was MAD – ha! again. With the same dazzling memory as his father and brothers (his mother too), he'd made a start by learning the whole of *Beowulf*, followed it up with Spenser's *Faerie Queene* and crowned it with Shakespeare's history plays because the tragedies and comedies were too easy to remember. (Later, he'd regretted this and added the tragedies to his portfolio.)

Memory was his stock-in-trade, making it easy to dabble in journalism. Thanks to the intercession of the Blessed Virgin, neither a heavy load of drugs nor half a dozen bouts of ECT (known in medical circles as 'a kick in the head' but effective all the same) had fucked up his memory. So what was that Donne line? 'Here' would seem more likely than 'where', but when had genius chosen the more likely?

He'd waited too long. Three-quarters of the day was gone. *Fast falls the eventide.* It needed resolving instantly. To his flat, then. Abandon his place of sanctuary for the area most dangerous to him. 'Where' or 'when'? Charlie dashed out of the flat and down the echoing stairs. Just two tube journeys. He would emerge in Knightsbridge with the rush-hour crowds, mingle and become invisible. Invisible? He was too big, too dishevelled. He walked with too much staggering energy. Taking a bottle from his pocket, Charlie popped a single pill into his mouth. *Soyez calme*, Charlie, old dear.

The first tube was nearly empty. He tried hard not to catch the eye of the two women and one man in the carriage. Yet he could feel himself a magnet, drawing their eyes to him. The man who was sitting opposite and who wore a nose ring and black T-shirt, although the weather was cool, suddenly leaned forward, smiled and said, quite loudly, 'Yeah, man.'

This was intolerable! Did such a jerk think he was a pick-up? Charlie was on the point of starting an angry diatribe on the right to privacy in public places when he recalled that he was on the run, keeping a low profile and doing nothing to draw attention to himself. Even so, he couldn't resist crossing himself against the devil's lures, then moving to another seat at the end of the carriage.

It was true that the woman sitting there looked at him too, and even smiled, but he judged her the motherly sort.

Charlie rarely thought about his appearance. For his marriage, he'd found a pair of purple velvet braces decorated with naked women who danced when he stretched the elastic. Looking back, it hadn't been too tactful a choice, given Lizzie's (hopefully abandoned) profession. If asked what he was wearing on a particular day he'd only have been certain that he was *not* wearing a suit.

However, something in the woman's sympathetic smile told him that all was not entirely well. Automatically, he checked his flies but the zip was firm. Mustn't get done for indecent exposure just at the moment. Nothing else occurred to him, and his attention was diverted by the station they'd just entered: *Holloway*.

The name of Lizzie's present residence galvanised him into action and he lurched out of the train just before the doors closed. Donne must wait an hour or two. Like the knight in shining armour, as he'd first presented himself to her, he must charge to her defence, wave his silvery blade like a wand, turn her situation from dark to light.

Charlie felt his spirits rising wonderfully, overwhelming a cautionary inner voice. He pictured Lizzie's pinched face flushing at the joy of seeing him, her pale little fingers fluttering in celebration. To him, she was an abused child, infinitely pathetic, and lovable only as she found some strength and courage.

Bounding along the wide streets – he'd remembered too late that Holloway the prison was not very near to Holloway the underground station – Charlie felt the last two days recede into a nightmare of horror and despair. Poor old Horace Silver (real name Brendan Hennessy) as he hung on that tree, far too great a punishment for borrowing another man's jacket. As the slimy walls had closed on him the night before, one of the nastiest images was of Horace's bulbous face, still expressing the surprise he'd felt as they'd snuffed out his sad life. It was insulting, of course, that Horace, a down-and-out with shamrocks for ears, could be mistaken for him, a virile man in the prime of life but, under the circumstances, he wasn't complaining. They were both big men, that was true, with curly hair, and they'd been mates. Poor old Horace, he thought again.

At last the massing red brick of the prison appeared across two roads. Not waiting for the lights and congratulating himself on his nifty dodging of a bus, a taxi and a lorry bearing scaffolding, Charlie arrived, sweating, panting and trembling (although he didn't notice it) at the entrance. To his right was the visitors' centre where a busy crowd of women, children and some young men came and went.

After his dash across the road, a belief in his godlike invincibility was adding to his good spirits. He strode up to the small open door, which was the main entrance, passed through it, and confronted the female officer behind the glass panel.

'Yes?' Merely a grunt. Behind her a group of officers, men and women, all unnaturally large, were laughing at some shared joke. No respect.

'I'm visiting my wife, Lizzie Potts.' Charlie was glad at the clarity of his voice. In his view, prison for women was an abomination, these monstrous keepers of the gate tarred by the brush of brutality.

'Visitor's order. Proof of identity,' grunted the woman behind the window. She might as well have been a warthog. If warthogs grunt. Charlie experimented with a few grunts himself. Gales of laughter penetrated the thick glass.

'Enough is enough!' bellowed Charlie, thumping the window. 'Can a man not visit his own wife?'

Four faces wearing the same expression of warthog hostility turned towards him. One leaned forward to press an alarm bell.

Almost too late, Charlie remembered his vulnerable situation. Stumbling, pushing himself off the doorpost, he beat an undignified retreat. Gone Lizzie's knight in shining armour, in its place a semi-deranged man on the run.

This was a downer, but as soon as he'd escaped his spirits rose miraculously. He even dared a further thump on the window of the visitors' centre, accompanied by a rousing cry of 'VO to you too!' A group of astonished faces turned his way as, giving them two fingers, he skipped off.

Passing a newspaper kiosk, he bought a paper, which he attempted, in the usual way, to put into his pocket. It was only then he realised that he was wearing a pyjama jacket over his sweater. It didn't worry him unduly. There were no rules yet about confining pyjamas to the bedroom.

He was back on track now for his flat and *The Collected Works of John Donne* except that, as he stepped on to the underground train, the entirety of 'The Extasie' flooded into his brain.

The train was very crowded now and although, a head above most people in the carriage, he was jostled and constrained, the exquisite words of the poem freed him into another world:

> *Where, like a pillow on a bed,*
> *A Pregnant banke swel'd up, to rest*
> *The violets reclining head,*
> *Sat we two, one anothers best.*

It was impossible to refrain from filling the grimy, over-inhabited underworld with such beauty. His voice, reciting sonorously, cleared a space like a police car through traffic. As the doors opened for the next station, he stood alone, celebrating all the wonder of English Metaphysical poetry. Carried on its wings, he left the train and soared upwards to light and air.

In his absence darkness had closed on the city. Immediately his mood changed, the exhilaration grounded to exhaustion and anxiety. He took his remaining money from his trouser pocket, enough for a visit to a pub, a double vod and a packet of crisps. It was human contact he needed, a warm face, an arm on his shoulder. He looked round, trying to take his bearings. Father Bill would do if he could only remember the way to his church. Bill's telephone number sprang into his head. Now all he needed were some coins and a telephone kiosk. Extraordinary how difficult such basic perform-ances became if you gave them a chance.

Crammed against the balloon-shaped breasts of 'Jonni, the perfect plaything', Charlie juggled with ten-pence coins, two slipping through his shaking fingers to the floor. *'Domine non sum dignis!'* He sent the cry of his own unworthiness up to the heavens – or maybe to the 'perfect plaything'. He felt God should give one of his own a bit more help; he would tell his brotherly priest so when he got through to him.

'St Mary's.' It was a man's voice but not his saintly brother's.

'Is Father Bill available?' He had assumed a strong Irish accent.

'He's out at this moment. It's Father Aloysius here. Can I be of any help?'

'I n-need B-Bill.' Now he had become a stuttering man. 'It's Ch-Charlie. His own brother Charlie!' he cried, losing both the bogs of Old Ireland and the stutter.

'Is it so?' The voice at the other end seemed full of doubt.

'What is it, my man?' He had become a commanding officer. 'Speak up. Is there a problem?'

'Perhaps I should not be the one to tell you or perhaps it is good fortune you phoned.'

'Yes? Yes?' The fellow was mumbling and bumbling.

'Bill is away because your mother is seriously unwell. He has postponed the finance meeting to be with her.'

'Postponed the finance meeting? Then it must be serious.' Charlie felt the beginnings of inappropriate hilarity. 'Do you mean my frightful old mother is dying?' He tried to avoid laughing aloud. It was not that he didn't feel sorry for Imogen brought so low, but in competition with a finance committee and Bill, whom she barely tolerated, sitting assiduously by her bed . . .

'I am afraid so,' confirmed Aloysius.

'Then I must take wing to her side.' Now he had become a minor figure in a recently discovered Shakespeare play. The route to Imogen's nursing-home was better known to him than that to Father Bill's domain. Luckily, one destination would find both.

Momentarily, as he headed back to the underground station, Charlie considered the risk in surfacing at a family scene, before deciding that personal safety must give way to a mother's death, just as the finance committee had. This time he couldn't control gales of hysterical laughter.

CHAPTER SEVENTEEN

Great Things

Leo had decided to give his first interview to a seven o'clock TV news programme. He sat in a small, hermetically sealed room, waiting for the interviewer to spare him a few moments before going on air. A researcher had already been in. She'd appeared so young that he'd made the mistake of patronising her. 'It is only the chief of the *Metropolitan* Police who needs the home secretary's approval,' he had told her, perhaps irritably. He had not wanted to talk to her. He'd always hated this kind of pre-interviewing, as if to check whether he had something worth saying. Well, in this case there could be no doubt about that. Leo realised he must have smiled a little, cut quickly short as the girl snapped at him, 'And do you expect to protect your sources, Mr Barr?'

It was the serious question. Of course he had given an emphatic 'yes'. But he wasn't a journalist. He was an MP with a duty of openness to his constituents and to the House. An 'unnamed source within the Police Service' would satisfy no one. Would anyone believe that he really had nothing else to say? Perhaps when Charlie disappeared he should have dropped the whole thing. It was difficult to believe after what had happened at the hospital that his brother wasn't in danger. But the reporter, Griff, had been so insistent. 'Charlie says you're to go ahead *whatever the situation*. Appear on the television programme,' he'd told him, 'just to keep up the pressure. Trust me to do the work. Say nothing.' At least that wouldn't be difficult.

He stood up restlessly. It was already nearly a quarter to seven. A silent television on the wall showed two heavily made-up women drinking beer in a pub. A beastlike man appeared and slapped the face of the bigger woman. Leo turned his back on the set.

Why was he taking such risks with his life, let alone Charlie's? He reminded himself that he was upholding a moral force. Girls like Lizzie were still out there being used and abused. It was indisputably deplorable that first, even if currently single, the home secretary could get involved in such a squalid sexual scene and that, second, the commissioner would feel able to blackmail him successfully.

Doubtless, they had both worked hard to avoid seeing it in such a damning light. They were past colleagues of numerous committees. They'd met openly for lunch at the home secretary's club. Griff admitted no one had overheard their conversation but he insisted they both knew why they were there. Ten days later the new head of the Met was announced. It had not been a very surprising appointment. He was second in the running; no one questioned why he had overtaken the front runner.

During the two years he'd been in charge, he'd done his job well: fewer press conferences than his predecessor and more quiet, behind-the-scenes reorganisation. The press liked his modest bearing. He was not very tall, not very handsome, but possessed a kind, open face, an old-fashioned bobby-on-the-beat look, which reassured the public. He was liked. He was a success. Perhaps it was a pity his career would soon be over.

Leo had been trained by his parents to believe that success was by far the most important virtue. When he'd first been adopted as a Labour candidate, Imogen had commented without missing a beat – they were in the London drawing room, dappled sunlight through the trees in the road outside, both with a glass in hand – 'There's no point in being elected Member of Parliament unless you become prime minister.'

At that moment Esmond had come in, tall and dark in his court clothes. 'And no point in joining a committee unless you're chairman.'

Suspecting that he had no stomach for high office, Leo immediately knew the possibility of failure. Without his parents, he might have chosen a quiet, low-profile job. Yet he had become an MP, then a minister. He'd chosen a job in the public eye and found he was good at it. In the beginning he'd believed in his power to change things for the better, even beyond his constituency. He could still remember the excitement of his first appearance in Hansard. He'd asked a question about the use of police batons and horses to break up a demonstration over discrimination against black workers. He'd never been a favourite with the Met.

'Mr Barr.'

Leo turned to acknowledge the presence of his interviewer. Unlike many screen personalities, he was much bigger than Leo had expected, as tall as himself, wearing a turquoise tie and a silver-grey suit, just a shade darker than his hair. They shook hands. They'd met before in clubs, at conferences. He was a likeable man.

'You've certainly got them scared.' The interviewer began at once. 'I can't get anyone to speak on air either from the government or the police. I assume you're willing to give us more detail than you did to the House?'

'It was Prime Minister's Questions.' Leo saw that credits were rolling on the television screen. 'Aren't we on?'

'Commercials first.'

Leo understood that, despite or because of his well-known criticism of the government, this presenter didn't want to back some MP's random fantasy. He could at least tell him the name of his journalistic contact, famous enough (or infamous in some circles) to be taken seriously. Off the record, of course. 'Trust me,' he said, as Griff had said to him, 'This story will run.'

In another second they were striding side by side to the studio. Leo found that, to his surprise, a surge of adrenalin was giving a spring to his step and sharpening his mind. Maybe, after all, he was meant for great things.

CHAPTER EIGHTEEN

A Miracle

'He's dreadfully pale.' Portia and Roland were watching Leo interviewed on the television in the sitting room at Imogen's nursing-
home. It was now nearly five hours since Roland had arrived. He
was suffering from a mixture of despair and irritation.

'His black eye isn't very pale. Silly bugger.' It was true, however,
that Leo was pale, almost ashen – particularly in contrast to his
interviewer, whose bronzed face was set off by a luminous turquoise
tie. He was engaged in asking Leo how long he had had this
information and why he had chosen to reveal it on this particular
Wednesday.

'As you know, not everyone gets a chance at Prime Minister's
Questions. You have to wait your turn.'

'But why deliver it as a bombshell? Surely that's hardly playing fair
with what, after all, is your own government. Your own leader.'

'My constituents are my leaders.'

'So you talked to them about it first?'

'Let's get this straight. I wanted to put the information I'd
received into the public arena, with no chance for anyone to twist
and turn. I believe in my story. I believe in my source. I wouldn't put
my career on the line if I wasn't convinced of its rightness. As far as
I'm concerned, the home secretary can have any sexual liaison he
chooses but when he allows it to lead to corruption the country
should know about it. If he can disprove it or produce any kind of
defence, ditto the Metropolitan Police commissioner, let him do so.
I will resign on the day they convince me and everyone else. So far
there have been no denials.'

'Phew.' Portia squeezed one hand in the other.

'He's mad. You're all mad.' Roland turned his back on the set. When he'd rung Maggie to tell her about Imogen, she'd asked if she should tell Esmond and he'd stumbled over the proper answer: wait till she dies. All his life he'd tried to please his mother and soon it would be too late. She'd leave him in the midst of turmoil and discord, his own superiority in the family unacknowledged. To his shame, Roland felt tears in his eyes, an accompaniment to a painful cocktail of misery, fear and anger.

'Surely, Mr Barr,' said the interviewer, who suddenly seemed nervous as if he'd only just taken in he might be tarred by Leo's audacity, 'the accused are innocent until proved guilty.'

'In a court of law, that's true. Politics is a different game altogether.'

'You're making an accusation without giving any facts to back it up?'

'I had a meeting with the chief whip today. I shall have another later. I shall give her any facts. If the government chooses, they can convene a committee and I'll give the members any facts too.' A bitter note had entered Leo's voice.

Portia sat down close to the screen.

The interviewer consulted his clipboard. 'Two years ago you resigned from the culture, media and sport committee in acrimonious circumstances. You accused the government of cronyism, among other things. Since then, you have voted against it on seven separate occasions. Could this have anything to do with your present accusations?'

'No!' Leo's ghostly pallor had changed suddenly to a mottled red, tonally in the same range as the bruising round his eye.

Far from intimidating his interviewer, this show of emotion seemed to give him new heart, and he leaned across the table almost eagerly. 'There's also the recent problem with your brother.'

At this Roland swung round. 'The bastard!' It seemed inconceivable that Leo could have mentioned their brawl, but nothing would surprise him.

'I have three brothers. I have not come here to talk about any of them.' For a moment Leo half rose from his seat, as if he was about to depart, then sank back again, glaring.

'He probably meant Charlie,' whispered Portia. 'That's really not fair.'

'My dear girl, when have our media appreciated the value of fairness?'

Meanwhile, on screen, the interviewer had embarked on a garbled account of a murder in a mental hospital and Charlie's disappearance.

'The Met fights back,' commented Roland, almost with satisfaction.

'What possible link—' began Portia, but at that moment both she and Roland were diverted by a loud noise outside the room.

A man's voice, at first belligerent, burst into song: 'For she's a jolly good fellow, for she's a jolly good fellow, for she's a jolly good fellow and so say all of us!' The voice rose to a crescendo.

'So now we know where Charlie is,' said Portia, attempting a smile.

Not bothering to respond, Roland headed for the door. Unfortunately, he flung it open just as Matron tried to pass through it. The short, stocky figure and the tall, bony one collided. She came off worst, but before she collapsed into a chair, she panted, 'Your brother. Mr Potts. I'm afraid he's not very well.'

'Typical!' Without apologising but with a recriminatory glance at the television screen, as if Leo could be blamed for this latest débâcle, Roland left the room.

Father Bill, meditating on madness while trying to say his prayers, wasn't particularly surprised when he heard Charlie's unmistakable tones outside Lady Shillingstone's door. Up till then the only sound had been her irregular breathing into the oxygen mask and, occasionally, her legs moving under the sheet.

The nurse rose to her feet with alarm.

'It's another son,' explained Bill, soothingly. He was extremely relieved that Charlie had surfaced, not only because he'd be able to say farewell to his mother but also because he was obviously in good health, if some way over the top.

The door burst open and Charlie, striding over the small matron, entered. He stood at the end of the bed and again sang lustily the whole of 'For She's a Jolly Good Fellow!' followed by some rousing alleluias.

Even Bill had to admit his appearance was enough to cause

disquiet to any respectable nurse. His lower half was fairly ordinary –
by Charlie's standards: sandals with one red and one blue sock,
amber-coloured corduroys, with a rip big enough to reveal his thigh
– but above he had excelled with a striped pyjama jacket over a
purple sweater, a red silk handkerchief tumbling out of the top
pocket and what looked like a once white hand towel tied as a cravat.
Presumably disappointed with his mother's lack of reaction to his
entrance, he picked up the (luckily empty) wastepaper basket and put
it on his head where it sat jauntily. This action was explained when
he began to march up and down, swinging his arms like a soldier and
singing, 'The Grand Old Duke of York, he had ten thousand men.
He marched them up to the top of the hill and marched them
down—'

He was interrupted by Roland, entering in what looked like a
passion of fury. For a second, Bill thought of intervening between
the brothers, then decided that Charlie, crazy or not, was much the
biggest and strongest person in the room.

'What do you think you're doing?' shouted Roland, then glanced
towards their mother and lowered his voice to a hiss. 'Bringing your
self-centred antics into the room where your own mother's dying!
Have you no respect?' He interrupted himself to look at Charlie,
who had stopped ramrod straight before raising his hand in a salute
to his brother. 'No, of course you haven't,' continued Roland, the
fury fighting a battle with what might have been despair.

'Dying!' pronounced Charlie, in a voice of thunder. He peered
theatrically towards the bed where his mother, silver hair spread on
the pillow, breathed into her oxygen mask. Bill, backed against the
wall, also peered and heard, or thought he heard, as Charlie's 'Dying'
rang out, an answering mumble from within the mask.

Portia, by the door but with the sharpest ears and the most
sympathetic nature, murmured, as if to herself, 'Never. She said
"never".'

Neither Roland nor Charlie took any notice. Removing the basket
and striking a classical pose, Charlie declaimed, with no obvious
sense of sorrow, ' "O! what a noble mind is here o'erthrown . . ." '

Meanwhile the matron was whispering to Portia, 'Shall we try to
get a doctor? I'm afraid he's not quite himself.'

'Not quite,' agreed Portia. 'He must be disturbing other patients.'
Despite this understanding approach, her expression was surprisingly

cheerful, as if Charlie's presence, however out of control, was cause for celebration rather than anxiety. In that, she resembled Bill, who wore a look near admiration as Charlie began to recite *The Lays of Ancient Rome*. 'Lars Porsena of Clusium/By the nine gods he swore that the great house of Tarquin should suffer wrong no more . . .'

'He has an astonishing memory,' whispered Portia.

'What about a doctor?' asked the matron. 'Of course we're still waiting for the doctor to come to your mother.'

All such considerations were put on hold by a sound from the bed that could be missed by nobody. 'I am not dying.'

The nurse was first at Imogen's side. She removed the mask and stared in wonder.

Imogen woke to shadows and noise. Together, particularly as the shadows were huge and the noise booming, they reminded her of Kabuki theatre for which she had once had a passion. The incomprehensibility had appealed when so much in life was boringly predictable. It seemed as if she was on stage herself, surrounded by action. That had been true once, too. Dressed like a princess with clipped waist and swirling skirt, stepping along the stage – no, not stage. Catwalk. How the audience had gasped in admiration! She had been the centre of attention. Paris. A lover and a career. No! No! Not to be remembered. Too painful. Better send that young life back to the shadows.

What had been said about death? Had she cried out? Her throat felt sore and cracked. She was scarcely able to force out a word, let alone a cry. Perhaps it had been inside her head. After all, she could do with more clarity – failing that, a glass of champagne.

A soft, dark face came close to hers. 'Madam, you feel better?'

The present was a place where women, always women, asked her that unanswerable question. 'Better than what?' she wanted to respond. But they were kind. Good servants who looked after her to the best of their ability. They wouldn't have understood her question.

'A drink,' she mouthed.

Her mind was sharpening, not, these days, always a good thing, and now she heard Charlie's voice. Such a beautiful voice now reciting Macaulay's great poem. How glorious, how elevating! She lifted her skeletal arms from the bed and spread them wide: 'Charlie, my darling Charlie!'

'My God, now he's raised his mother from the dead.'

Another shadow spoke. Roland. So satirical, so jealous of his brother. But what did he mean?

'I'm not Lazarus,' she tried to say.

The soft brown hand was putting a glass to her lips. 'Ugh.' She spat it out.

'She wants champagne,' said a gentle voice, Portia. Portia understood what she wanted. Dear Portia. So good. No beauty, of course.

The voices continued. So many she couldn't understand them. Even in her triumph women had got at her, scissors threatening her beauty. Only jealousy. She *was* the New Look. Charlie didn't come to her welcoming arms but the cold bubbles of the champagne broke against her lips.

'Ah, Mother dearest.' There he was now, crouching or kneeling beside her. But why was he calling her 'Mother'? She tried to put out a hand to touch him, but he was out of reach.

'O Fount of Wisdom, Hope of the Hopeless, Queen of the Starry Night!'

Charlie always knew how to please her. Flattery and fun. Like the one in Paris she mustn't remember. He used to make her laugh but now she felt too removed for laughter.

'I've been in hell,' said Charlie, 'but since entering into your presence, Light of my Life, I've entered heaven.'

She would have liked to contradict him there: only a fool would believe in heaven and hell. No longer remembering that she herself had had him baptised into the Catholic Church, she thought he had become a Catholic to scandalise, like everything else unknowable in his life. He wanted a reaction. It was a game with him. But she always won. She always forgave him. It was that brother she'd given away, coming back where he wasn't wanted. Far too humble for her taste. Humility had always irritated her more than anything. That was why she liked Charlie. So confident.

'*Confiteor Deo omnipotenti et vobis, fratres, quia peccavi . . .*'

Latin was it now? She wanted to say, 'You don't need Latin to impress me, Charlie.' But her voice was too small, even with the trickles of lovely champagne as encouragement.

'Have you given her the last rites?' a voice cried. Charlie again. Why did he joke so much? One so brilliant. *Un homme sérieux*, although also wild. Always wild.

'I didn't want to presume.' Another voice. Lying, probably. The priest. That cast-off boy who, losing a mother, had turned to Mother Church. Her mind was so clear. She could understand anything, everybody. Except those voices, those black shadows. They were beyond her. The words came to her ears but without meaning.

'She's been a wicked woman. She must be shriven! Take out the tools of your trade!'

Charlie. Why wouldn't his name come out of her mouth? What curls he'd had! What plump red cheeks. How straight and strong his body. It was no wonder the girls had always gone for him. He was hardly more than a boy when the first one had come sobbing to her. Of course his head was turned. Oh, Charlie!

Imogen's apparent revival hardly surprised Bill. He'd seen it before in the dying. Perhaps it was the blessing he'd given her as she lay unconscious. The confusion in the room was so great that he would have left, had Charlie not clung to his arm. He rocked now and again, like a ship hit by a blast of wind.

Bill was struck by the suffering that lay behind the bull-like charging.

He was also struck by Roland's obvious aversion to the whole business, his face so pale and tight as if he, too, was undergoing physical pain. Only Portia appeared to accept the situation, even smiling and once laughing at Charlie's lunatic remarks.

Bill felt able to do nothing about the suffering or the mania, apart from lending his arm. The nurse and matron seemed equally helpless. Perhaps they felt their responsibility stopped with Imogen, who was still prone but accepting dribbles of champagne off a spoon. Her blind eyes were open but she didn't seem to react to anything Charlie shouted at her.

He thought she would leave them again soon, and this time for good.

Charlie spotted the doctor first. He felt he was conducting the room and had a duty to welcome a new entrant on to the stage. Letting go of Bill, he pulled the doctor in with a bear embrace, not noticing the man's confused resistance and his pursed mouth of disapproval.

'This is an unexpected family party but you are a welcome guest, an honoured guest. Your name, please, so I can introduce you to my distinguished mother – not a good woman, we must admit, we just have admitted to the son she gave away, but a woman of distinction. During her reign as queen empress of the London section of the Nobel Order of Royal Embroiderers, she was feared and admired in equal parts. Their meetings at Hampton Court Palace gained a world-wide reputation. Their skills were in demand from Colorado to Kosovo.'

'Charlie. Charlie.'

'Yes, Portia.' He looked down kindly as his pygmy sister. She was a sweet girl. Never ticked him off.

'You must let the doctor go. You're holding him too tightly.'

So now she was ticking him off. How sad! How truly sad! Yet she was right. Why was he hugging this unattractive man in a dark suit? Who was he anyway? Suddenly, he was hit by the word 'doctor'.

'What? The men in white coats come to get me?' Escape! He must escape at once.

'No, Charlie. He's come to see Mother.' Mother again. Portia again. But he didn't trust her for a second.

Horrible images of the hospital entered the stuffy little room. A man's face, red and bulbous. The chase. Being chased. No. Not chased. But he'd run. Now he must run again.

When Charlie blundered from the room no one tried to stop him. He was too big. Too strong. Too mad. Besides, the doctor hardly knew the set-up, quite apart from his need to recover from his unexpected close encounter with what seemed a cross between a grizzly bear and a stand-up comic.

Portia followed him down the hallway. She heard her bleating voice, 'Stop, Charlie, darling Charlie, do stop', and knew it had got nowhere near his consciousness. Pushing past an unwary nurse carrying a tray of medicines, which scattered to the floor, he was out of the front door in a flash, battling his way, in unsteady tacks, down the pavement. And now, she thought, as she trailed back to Imogen's door, they were as ignorant as ever about what had happened to him. The death that had occurred at the hospital. The man Leo had described to her lying in the morgue. They had questioned him about none of it.

Roland hadn't even tried to ring the police, which could be seen as a blessing. All they did know was that Charlie was as high as a kite again.

Drearily but not without hope, because seeing Charlie, in whatever state, always made her happy, Portia re-entered the room.

CHAPTER NINETEEN

Doing the Appropriate Thing

'Isn't that Uncle Leo?'

Maggie swivelled from the television and stared at her son as if she'd never seen him before. Tom took a step backward. His baggy trousers fell another inch as his shoulders slouched.

Maggie regrouped. 'What do you want?' There was no point in answering his question. It was obviously Uncle Leo, coming to the end of a bad-tempered interview during which she'd felt no closer to understanding what he was getting at. 'Darling,' she added, giving Tom a smile. 'I'll be with you in a moment.'

Tom withdrew with the furtive expression of a boy who'd been turned down by his mother. Unexpectedly. Maggie was always loving.

'I'm going straight to my constituency now. If they think I've behaved wrongly, they'll tell me so. I have a very strong and open relationship with them.' Leo seemed more certain now than he had earlier.

'You may like to know that we have emails and calls flooding in. Are you planning to speak to a newspaper? You could make hundreds of thousands of pounds.' Perhaps insults would work.

'I have no such plans.'

'You expect the information to come from other sources?'

'I expect men who are leaders of this country and paid by the people to do their duty honestly and truly. I have nothing more to add.'

The interviewer gave up. Clearly, like Maggie, he found this sword of righteousness that had popped off the back benches quite extra-ordinary. 'Thank you, Mr Barr.'

Leo rose to his feet before the cameras cut away.

Maggie turned off the television and returned to her chair. She wondered if Roland would ring Leo and tell him his mother was dying. Or perhaps she should. This reminded her of Esmond. She was late with his supper. Although his wits were so tangled, he had an animal's instinct for mealtimes. It was surprising he hadn't banged on the floor with his stick. Or perhaps he had and she'd been too engrossed to hear him. Tom would have to wait. She thought of the two boys, of their certainty. Tom would take what he wanted. That hangdog look of his was only the twelve-year-old style of the moment. She had taught them to be independent.

In a flash the wish came that they'd been Leo's children.

The telephone ringing on the other side of the room finally got her up from the chair.

'Oh, Maggie. It's all such a mess!'

'Portia, darling.' They were not close but, still, Maggie liked her sister-in-law. She admired what she saw as her free spirit, particularly when she might so easily have caved in under the weight of all those brothers. 'I'm proud of him. He's so brave.'

'Brave? Oh, you're talking about Leo. I wasn't thinking about him. I don't understand that one bit. I mean Charlie. Charlie's been here. Absolutely flying. Then he ran off. Roland's determined to ring the police.' Portia sounded near tears.

Maggie didn't want to think about Charlie. 'Where did this happen?' She tried to sound caring.

'At the nursing-home. I'm there now.'

Now Maggie had to take notice. 'Isn't Imogen supposed to be dying?'

'Charlie raised her from the dead.'

'He's there too!'

'I told you. Oh, Maggie. Please tell Roland not to get the police. It's so cruel, and Leo told me that only a few days ago Charlie was virtually OK.'

'Is that why you're ringing?' Maggie felt too tired to make sense of this. Her visit to London, her lunch with Leo, his performance on TV was enough for one day. 'I haven't even given Esmond his supper,' she said, in unusually self-pitying tones.

'But, Maggie, you're the only one Roland will listen to.'

Could Portia really believe that? 'We've got to remember there's someone's death involved, not just poor Charlie's state of mind.'

At this Portia seemed to give up. 'I'd better get off the phone. My mobile's run out of juice, as usual, so I'm using the nursing-home's landline.'

'Keep me in touch,' said Maggie, which was the last thing she wanted.

Walking wearily to Esmond's room, she thought how much of her life she spent trying to do the appropriate thing and never more than partially succeeding. Portia, on the other hand, took the passionate approach.

It was a small but welcome blessing when she found Esmond sitting up in bed with a contented smile. 'You are a wonderful woman,' he said, his smile becoming almost seraphic, and he began to recite, in the sing-song voice of the past, 'Quinquireme of Nineveh from distant Ophir . . .' With a flood of well-being, Maggie's pleasure in caring for people returned. She had been sour with Portia but she could ring her back. When Esmond had finished his poem, she straightened his pillows and, patting his hand, promised him his favourite snack of soft cheese on white bread. 'Just as long as you don't fall out of bed again.' Afterwards she would make mountains of spaghetti for the boys.

By midnight Maggie was asleep in bed. Unusually Roland hadn't telephoned but although that was a slight worry it was also a relief. She was ruling her own domain efficiently.

At one o'clock, at the time of her deepest sleeping, she was woken by a loud noise. First there was thudding and then, soon after, the breaking of glass. The house alarm did not go off. But now she remembered she had not set it. With heart thudding and guilt added to fear and sleepiness, she sat on the edge of her bed.

The boys wouldn't hear anything. They were at the back of the house. Esmond wouldn't hear if a burglar broke into his bedroom. He might offer a welcome.

Maggie tried to shake her head free of sleep, her thick blonde hair whipping across her cheeks. Her only reward was a voice echoing from the targeted room below and a suspicion nearly as threatening as the presence of an intruder.

At last she was fully awake and, without putting on a light, creeping towards the stairs. There, she hesitated. The noise seemed to have settled into occasional furniture movements. Possibly a burglar pulling choice pieces towards the window prior to removing them, or possibly not.

Tiptoeing downstairs, she could see light coming from the open door of the drawing room.

Charlie had come here ten years ago, during one of his 'episodes', stayed for an hour – it was the children's teatime and he had attempted to eat a spoon – before leaving precipitately. Two days later he had been found at Nice airport on the verge of convincing a pretty Air France stewardess that he was an off-duty pilot. To prove his point he'd run round, like a child, arms outstretched, imitating an aeroplane landing on a dangerously short runway.

'Charlie!' Maggie entered the drawing room. She tried to inject normality into her voice. 'Did you have to break the window? Roland will be incandescent.'

'Bugger Roland. I expect he hides his drink too.'

Maggie was surprised that Charlie accepted her appearance so easily. She supposed that, in his present state of mind, the Angel Gabriel would hardly have caused amazement. 'I'll get you a drink. What do you want?'

This acquiescence seemed to deflate Charlie. He had been standing in the middle of the room rather like a boxing champion at the end of the final bout before the result was announced, but now he collapsed suddenly into a chair. 'Oh, Maggie, Maggie. What a wicked world we live in!'

Despite her lack of sympathy for her brother-in-law and her wish to avoid him if possible, Maggie couldn't resist the appeal. 'Don't have a drink, Charlie. I'll bring you a cup of tea.'

'I've come to see my father.' There was a new solemnity in his tone. Maggie's heart hardened. His visits to Esmond were rare, mistimed and upsetting to everybody. 'He's asleep,' she said briefly, then added, in case he hadn't noticed, 'It's the middle of the night.' She hardened her heart further. 'Shouldn't you go back to hospital? Portia rang earlier. She said Roland's got the police looking for you.'

Charlie lifted his head and stared at her. 'Would you say you were a woman of discrimination?' For a moment, although his speech was thick, he seemed much less mad. 'Would you understand if I said I was in hiding, in fear of my life?'

'I don't know. Look, you can have the spare room.'

'Spare room. Spare bed. Spare man. Have you ever looked on the face of the dead?' Now his face expressed deep grieving.

Maggie didn't answer. The room was cold but she didn't dare go for a dressing-gown for fear of what Charlie might do. Instead she sat in a chair, curling her bare feet under her. Although she was large, she had always been supple.

Charlie seemed grateful for her company. He didn't smile or speak, but there was a lessening in the air of tension around him. He even shut his eyes momentarily.

'You're exhausted, Charlie.' She was using the tone appropriate for a toddler who couldn't get to sleep.

It didn't work because Charlie sprang instantly to his feet and began to march up and down singing 'Rule Britannia' in an Irish accent. Just as Maggie was considering sneaking off to ring Roland, he stopped equally abruptly and collapsed once more into the chair.

'You see, they'd like to find me. I slunk into my flat like a burglar, found my car key, drove here. At the heart of darkness. They'd like to find me very much. But I won't let them. They're like a plague, bringing sickness, death and lies.'

Maggie knew about the paranoia visited on the mentally ill, the threats and commands of alien voices, but she hadn't known it was one of Charlie's symptoms. 'I'm sorry,' she said.

Again he assumed the less wild expression, which, oddly, she found more upsetting. It carried with it a look of tearfulness she'd never seen on his face before. What had happened to him? Vaguely, she recalled Leo telling her that Charlie had been behind his question to the prime minister.

'Dearest Charlie, please let me get help for you.'

Suddenly he was crouched at her knees, head in her lap, arms round her waist. The physical contact shocked her, wiping out her maternal feelings. He was too crudely masculine, a huge fraternal parody of Leo. She was only wearing a nightdress, and could feel her nipples hardening against his head. Even if he was only looking for comfort, she couldn't give it.

'No, Charlie! You can't.' She pushed at him almost angrily but he was like a boulder across her body.

She had a horrible feeling that he might grab at her heavy breasts. Now she was truly frightened. He had become repulsive, a dangerous, repulsive maniac. 'Get off! Go away!' She began to scream. She scrabbled at his torso, pulled his hair, her head bent over his. Then, as she glanced up, she saw two naked legs.

'Mum. Mum.'

She raised her eyes further. Tom still looked half asleep in his bed uniform of T-shirt and underpants. She noticed with a pang, as if the situation had made her perception more acute, that the shadowy down on his legs had become darker. Soon he would reach puberty and cross the mysterious gateway into manhood.

'It's only Charlie, Mum.'

He was reassuring her. Annoyingly, the children had always loved their crazy uncle, welcoming him at whatever time, day or night, he appeared, in whatever condition.

'I know it's Charlie.'

Tom approached closer. He was shivering with cold. 'Charlie. Charlie.' There was no reaction. 'You know what, Mum? I think he's asleep.'

Maggie knew immediately that he was right. Her panic subsided. That was why he was slumped so heavily.

'Maybe we can roll him on to the sofa.'

Maggie looked at her son with new respect. He was so practical, so unafraid. 'I don't think we can manage that but, if you help me, I expect I can get out and he can sleep where he is.'

Fifteen minutes later, Maggie and Tom, with the new addition of Jake, sat by the Aga, drinking, respectively, tea and Coke. Surprisingly, the boys asked no questions, as if anything to do with their eccentric uncle was beyond explanation.

'I suppose I should ring Dad.' Maggie yawned.

'It's the middle of the night,' objected Tom, in a sensible voice. But Maggie knew that to him Roland represented the law and he didn't want to hand over Charlie.

'Well, I expect it can wait till morning.' Either she wanted to reward her son or she wanted to punish her husband.

Together, mother and sons went up to bed.

CHAPTER TWENTY

Not a Whimper

Too pumped up for bed, Leo sprawled across his white sofa. His television appearance, a long meeting with the staff and key workers at his constituency and an even longer one with the chief whip had to be digested before he could even think of sleeping. Now and again he sipped at a glass of whisky. But alcohol wasn't the answer.

Catherine, the chief whip, had not behaved like a 'human-resources manager', as she sometimes liked to portray herself. 'Breaking the tradition and probably the rules of the House . . .'; 'showing no ordinary human sense of decency or respect'. After a while her outrage had turned to disgust with an edge of self-pity: 'Have you any idea of the amount of damage you've caused? Even if your allegations are completely unfounded, about which I've no doubt at all, the papers will have a field day, the opposition will make you a hero . . .' She'd paused for a moment and looked at Leo for the first time. She was a stout woman with slightly bulging blue eyes underlined by pouches from lack of sleep. 'You're not having a breakdown, are you?' It was the nearest to sympathy he would receive and quickly commuted to derision: 'Men like you are contemptible. Trying to pretend they have a personal hold on the nation's morals.' Then she'd reverted to the breakdown line but with a new slant. 'If you were having a breakdown, seeing a shrink, weekly visits to hospital . . .' She'd seemed to be musing to herself.

Leo, who hadn't spoken for half an hour – there seemed little to say, apart from repeating his accusations, which was clearly unnecessary – couldn't resist putting in a few words: 'The KGB committed awkward customers to mental institutions.'

Catherine had repaid this sally with total venom. 'They say mental illness runs in the family. It's your brother, isn't it, who goes in and out of hospital? And now in trouble with the police?'

Leo felt a spume of bile rising in his throat. 'My brother has nothing to do with this.' It had the virtue of sounding true.

Catherine had picked up a sheet of paper from her desk. 'You're not on any committees, I know.' She'd made it sound like a sin as well as a failure. 'But what about your constituents? I gather you didn't even see fit to inform them.'

Leo wondered if he should feel sorry for causing this woman so much aggravation. If she hadn't mentioned Charlie, he might have tried to build a bridge to the future. Her job was to be a fixer and she'd failed to fix him. She would be in huge trouble with Downing Street. Maybe her career was on the line too. But her assumption that he'd made up the story was galling. Probably, truth had no meaning for her any more. It was 'my party', good or bad, 'my prime minister', 'my home secretary'. Like a soldier she was doing her job and letting others look after the morals.

'My office manager believes in me. Bob' – he needed to produce a friendly name in the bitter atmosphere – 'has supported me for fifteen years. He respects me. I've got a great team of case workers. Tomorrow we're calling an open meeting.'

'Open meeting. Fuck your open meeting!' the whip spat, with disgust. The words and expression sat oddly with her neat make-up and well-coiffured hair. Then she'd reconsidered. 'What time is it?'

'Midday. Catch people at lunchtime.' He guessed that she was considering her options. 'You could organise a press conference.' He spoke ironically. 'Have it at midday too. At some point someone's got to confess or deny.'

From here on the interview had taken a slightly different tone. In fact, the whips' office couldn't do much to improve the situation. It would be for Downing Street, the Home Office and the Metropolitan Police to handle things outside the House of Commons.

They were both aware of this. Even so, Catherine could not bring herself to shake hands with Leo as he left. He imagined she'd take it out on poor old Alan, his regional whip, who really did behave like a human-resources manager. And a lot of good it had done him.

Leo drank his whisky a little more energetically. If he'd been the whip, he'd have asked, 'why?' Bob hadn't asked either, but he was a mate, an admirer. 'Why' would have implied doubt. Or maybe he was waiting to see how tomorrow's meeting went. He had asked one important question: 'Will others come forward to corroborate your allegation?'

Leo had answered briefly, 'That's for others.' He could have added, 'I'm the stalking horse.' Instead he'd burst out impulsively, 'How would you feel about having an independent MP?'

'Independent?' Bob's shocked face had been enough.

Leo got up restlessly and went to the kitchen, although he knew there was nothing to eat beyond a packet of dry biscuits. He was reminded of his lunch with Maggie. Much had happened since and at the time he had been so hyped by the drama of his question and his flight from the press that now it had the unreality of a dream.

She'd looked particularly pretty, he remembered, her girlish complexion and fair hair glowingly out of place in the dark pizza house. He always thought of her in that big house in the country, which seemed to have everything to do with her and absolutely nothing to do with Roland. Roland's London flat, where he seemed to spend much of the week, could have been a set of rooms in a college *circa* 1950: heavy furniture, dark flooring, little light. Maggie seemed to create light and colour around her. Even Esmond's sarcastic old age had converted into a crazed good humour once he was in her care. Or so she presented him.

What did she see in Roland? He could only vaguely recall her first appearance in the family circle. She'd been a *protégée* of Imogen so she couldn't have been as pretty then. Imogen didn't like competition. But Maggie was a little plump. Perhaps that was it. Imogen, who would have been called anorexic in another generation, counted slimness the prerequisite of beauty.

Charlie had first choice, of course. Usually the girls fell easily to his charming full-frontal approach. Maggie had not, Leo thought, or perhaps Charlie found her too real.

He himself had hardly been at home during that period. He'd been nursing one of the Manchester constituencies. By the time he had focused on Maggie, she was already married to Roland and pregnant probably. She always seemed pregnant in those early years.

But he'd fancied her all right.

One night two or three years into Maggie's marriage, they'd stayed up late drinking. They'd been in the country together. A Sunday night, Roland already gone back to London. They were in the garden but every now and again there'd been a squawk from a microphone she had tuned into the baby's bedroom.

They'd talked about growing up and he'd tried to explain what it was being positioned above 'the charming, volatile Charlie' and below 'the cold fish Roland'. Then he'd remembered he was talking about her husband.

She'd laughed, almost giggled. 'I felt sorry for him,' she'd said.

He'd exclaimed, 'Sorry for Roland?' with such amazement and depth of emotion that they'd both laughed.

Somehow that had led to a kiss. Nothing more. But enough. He didn't want to have an affair with his brother's wife. Presumably, she felt the same.

They'd never referred to it afterwards. The danger was too great to risk a repeat. Over the years he'd taught himself to see her as a good wife, a good mother. At first he'd been wary about seeing her on her own.

Strange, therefore, that they'd had lunch together on this extra-ordinary day. Now yesterday. He looked at his watch. Two a.m. The night before he'd stayed up late, then got up early to collect Portia. At the time Charlie had been the only issue on the agenda. At least, the only issue he'd cared to discuss with her. Of course he'd told no one about the news he was about to launch in deadly rocket fashion. But it seemed odd he hadn't been tempted to make a discreet, loving sister his confidante?

Again, he found himself thinking about Maggie. How would it be if she were with him now? They would go to bed, of course. Her body would be soft, unlike his ex-fiancée's. Suzanne was beautiful. People stared at her in the street. She was nearly as tall as him; they'd made a striking couple. His constituents always asked if she was a model and tried not to be disappointed when he said she was a radiologist.

Looking back, it was amazing she'd stayed with him so long. She'd rung him a few weeks ago to tell him she was getting married. 'That's terrific!' he'd said, and thought he meant it. He told himself his constituents missed her more than he did. 'You haven't let that model get away, have you?' He'd definitely gone down in their estimation.

Yet Suzanne's announcement of her marriage had disturbed him. She was right to think he didn't love her, but it felt nonetheless as if some door had closed on him, as if no one could be more suitable than Suzanne. It was depressing. No wife. No children. Single all his life. Why not admit to himself that her news had made him feel obscurely outlawed, unstable? Wasn't there some psychobabble cliché called a mid-life crisis? The chief whip might not have been so far off the target. Maybe the prospect of Suzanne's happy future without him had precipitated him into crisis. After all, they'd been a team for over six years. He'd proposed to her, for Christ's sake! One problem: he still didn't want her. Forget Suzanne.

Now he really began to worry about his constituency meeting the next day. It was true that Bob had been sympathetic, even ebullient about his behaviour. He was as fed up as Leo with the present government and quite ready for a fight. But tomorrow would be a different story. There was a group of self-made or up-and-coming businessmen who were already disappointed with their MP. They'd liked him best when he was a minister, close to the government, close to the centre of power. They didn't want a rebel. They wanted someone who could help them with special deals, grants and, at the very least, give them a posh lunch in the House of Commons. When they hired the corporate dining room for a lunch to impress their investors, they wanted their MP to invite along politicians with clout, men or women who were otherwise out of their range. The last thing they needed was to be represented by a pariah. These men and a couple of women he'd flirted with, and one a bit more, would certainly call for his resignation.

He was a good MP. He liked the role. And what else would he do? He was one of the lucky ones, too, having a London constituency. He could think of at least four Labour Party hopefuls who would kill to get their hands on his seat. Including Eloise in his own office.

The idea of killing was unfortunate because it conjured up the image of the dead man in the psychiatric hospital who, for a few seconds, Leo had looked on as if he were his dead brother.

All the same, he didn't regret his action, even if it did turn him into modern Guy Fawkes. In fact, he was proud of himself.

Giving up any idea of sleep, Leo decided to take the opposite approach. He picked up his coat from the chair where he'd thrown it and was heading for his computer when the phone rang.

'Hello.'

'Leo. I know it's the middle of the night and you've got other important things—'

'Maggie?'

'Yes. It's Charlie.' Her voice sounded muffled. 'I thought you should know. He was here in quite a state. Then he went to sleep on a chair. A moment ago I checked on him and he was gone. He said he was fleeing for his life but I suppose that was just his illness speaking.'

'Oh, God.' Leo sat down abruptly. 'Roland's not with you?'

'No. I couldn't get hold of him. That's why I'm ringing you.'

Leo remembered he couldn't leave the flat because reporters and cameramen were camped outside. He needed to reassure Maggie. 'There's nothing we can do about Charlie till he surfaces again.' Of course she knew that, so why was she ringing in the middle of the night? 'He must have got hold of a car.'

'He said he went to his flat. He would have got his own car then.'

'Yes.' Leo thought about Charlie driving through the night with his head full of fear and craziness. 'Thanks for telling me, Maggie, but go to bed now.'

'Are you all right?' Her voice was filled with tenderness.

'I suppose so. I sneaked back into the flat just before a football crowd gathered.'

'I watched you on the TV.'

'Did you? Did my black eye come out well?'

'More technicolour, I'd say.'

'Good night, Maggie.'

Roland was tiring. His brain was reasserting control, always a painful moment. Didi was as beautiful as ever: his smooth, almond-coloured buttocks, his narrow waist with surprisingly broad shoulders, his heart-shaped face with the black eyes veiled by long lashes, his cock so obligingly ready to rise out of its bed of curly hair.

Roland feared he was becoming obsessed with Didi. Not love, of course, but just as dangerous. At first he'd only been one of the boys he called on when the strain of resisting became too great. He took them, paid them, and never thought about them again till the next time of need. But Didi's image stayed with him when he was in his chambers or at home.

Didi was a flirt, that was the trouble. His cock might be obliging, but he liked to play games, withholding, forcing Roland to take note of him as more than just a body. He'd pretended, for instance, that the cut on Roland's face had been given him by a rival lover, 'a rough man'. Did Roland think he couldn't be rough if that was what he enjoyed? He'd flounced and sulked.

Sometimes he sang songs in his brand of Moroccan French as Roland fucked him. It was impossible to tell whether it was in the spirit of celebration or mockery. He told Roland stories, in his delightful, husky, accented voice, about the other bad boys in the restaurant where he worked as a waiter, about his brother who was straight and 'escorted' older women, even, proclaimed Didi, widening his eyes, Jews. He only had about fifty English words but they seemed enough.

The brothers were in England illegally, of course. When Roland's brain fully asserted itself, he felt a terrifying sense of impending doom. On this night it was coupled with an immense lassitude. Yet he daren't sleep.

He stared at Didi, naked at his side. He knew he was looking at him like a lover, desperate for many reasons, but also at their parting.

'You go? *Tout d'un coup.*'

Roland tried to stroke his shoulder but he pulled away.

'I not see you. Come to the restaurant?'

Desire and danger. Without answering, Roland got up and went towards the shower. The hotel room was plain, almost unfurnished, a room used for clandestine meetings.

The water fell on him hard, clearing his head further. Soon his desire for Didi would be mixed with hatred and disgust – of himself. He'd known he was homosexual from schooldays but it hadn't suited him to acknowledge it publicly. Imogen had expected so much of him. How often she'd reminded him he was the eldest son! And now they said she was dying.

He turned off the shower and watched as the wavery shadow of

Didi approached the glass door. His body responded even to this insubstantial and doubtless reproachful ghost.

He opened the door and reached for a towel, trying hard not to raise his eyes. Didi said nothing. Then, after a moment or two, he brushed past him into the shower.

Roland thought he would give him more money than usual, then felt ashamed and, with another turnaround, defiant. Didi was a male prostitute, a rent-boy. Why pretend otherwise? Money would make him happy, however he postured.

Money made everyone happy. Money, or what it could buy, made Maggie happy: a lovely house and garden with appropriate gardening and cleaning help, three children, all educated at the most expensive schools, the opportunity to play games with property and even, apparently, to have the satisfaction of making money for herself, although it could only happen through his investment. Money gave her freedom to toy with running an art gallery, to pop up to London when she felt like an outing. He didn't have to feel guilty about Maggie. He even found he could service her sexually, which came as a surprise and a relief each time. He was a good husband in every way.

By now he was fully dressed and tidying the room. He always made sure to take away the used condoms and any other evidence. He was a lawyer, after all.

Didi was dressed too. He wore a tightly belted gabardine coat, Humphrey Bogart style, teamed with a rather strange woollen cap pulled low over his eyes, which emphasised his red, pouting mouth. He had his hands deep in his pockets. It was a studied pose but appealing.

Roland had a roll of notes in his palm so it made sense to join his hand to Didi's. Didi started to pull away but as his fingers felt the notes forcing them open, he stood completely still and turned his wonderful eyes on Roland. Their extreme darkness made them hard to read but Roland thought he saw gratitude and excitement. There would be another time.

'Thank you.' Roland liked to say 'thank you' as he pressed money upon his lover. Yet he was disappointed too. 'I'll call you.'

'Yes.' Didi modestly lowered his extravagant eyelashes as Roland felt across the pocket to touch his cock.

'We'll meet soon.'

Didi smiled wistfully but said nothing. Roland withdrew his hand. He looked at his watch. It was nearly five a.m. They never kissed goodbye or left together. He would scarcely get two hours' sleep. But he was happy, happy. Surely.

CHAPTER TWENTY-ONE

The Devil and the Deep Blue Sea

Father Bill woke up suddenly, sweating. What dreams of unholy rage and perversion! Such nightmares made the devil substantial, torturing him with the temptations of the flesh. They came so seldom now that it was always more shocking that such evil could still find a way into his imagination.

Doubtless it was the disturbance of yesterday's visit to the nursing-home: Imogen's approaching death, repelled whether by the forces of good (he'd recited the last rites, although without white cloth, oil or water) or by the forces of madness, as Roland had suggested. But was Charlie possessed of the devil?

Bill woke up further and his dreams squashed back into the horrid place they'd been called from. The reality, although not personally threatening, gave quite enough exercise for his moral judgement. When Charlie turned up at the church, which he very well might, was it his duty to hand him over to the police?

The police had arrived shortly after Charlie's abrupt exit. There'd been six originally, all big, two armed. The sight of the guns had been shocking. When they discovered their prey had fled they reduced their numbers to three, but their stance of rough accusation didn't change.

The matron had tipped them off about Charlie's presence but finding two of his brothers, one sister and a mother (comatose – although taking an occasional sip of champagne) was clearly a setback. One spoke to his boss for further instructions while the siblings were herded into the sitting room.

Already bad-tempered, Roland had soared into a fearful rage before, quite suddenly, as if a switch had clicked, he became utterly calm and courteous. Bill found this level of self-control alarming and reminded himself that lawyers were unlike normal people.

He himself, free of any wrong-doing, nevertheless felt both nervously excited and guilty. The policemen, however unprepossessing, had assumed the majestic mantle of authority. Of course, as a priest, he had learned obedience.

'We need to interview you about your brother,' the leader policeman had pronounced.

'In what reference, Officer?' Roland had asked suavely.

'He is wanted in connection with a murder inquiry. We would like you to come down to the station. At your convenience, of course, sir. Just to answer a few questions. Sir,' he had added again, although Bill couldn't tell if it was in true deference or mockery.

They had all gone in the end, taken in two police cars with sirens, quite unnecessarily. Bill assumed it was to intimidate them. Things were surprisingly chaotic in the police station. By the time they arrived it was after seven and they were told that the officer in charge of the case, a Chief Inspector Roger Burrows, wanted to interview them in person but he had to drive from South London. They must wait. But where? The station was undergoing renovation, some rooms were uninhabited, some locked, a mobile cabin parked in the road already, apparently overflowing with people. Neither, owing to a lack of facilities, was the proverbial cup of tea available, let alone a sandwich.

Eventually, after more than an hour, Bill had been allowed to nip out for coffee and snacks. When he arrived back, Roland had disappeared into an upper room.

'Two grisly characters took him away,' Portia had informed him, 'One wearing a wig. Do you think he was in disguise?'

Bill admired her approach to the situation. She appeared to share none of his trepidation. 'I'm in favour of solving murders,' she told Bill, as they munched on chicken samosas (dry and smelly), 'but I can't say I'm too impressed by the police's approach. I mean, is it right to keep us hanging round here when our mother might be dying?'

This was the longest time Bill had ever spent with his sister and, if the circumstances weren't perfect, it still seemed a good opportunity to inform himself of more about his birth family. It was soon clear that she, born a decade after his adoption, had scarcely been aware of his existence. 'Mother believed in the world as she saw it and the world didn't include you.'

Doubtless this was an accurate description of Imogen's approach to life but Bill couldn't help feeling disappointed. The trouble was that, with years of experience to the contrary, he still believed in the essential goodness of man. He had begun to say, 'I suppose she was a very encouraging mother,' then admitted to himself it was unlikely and changed it to 'demanding'.

'No demands on me,' Portia had replied matter-of-factly. 'First, I was a girl, second, I was plain and, third, I was a mistake.'

'You're not plain,' Bill had replied quickly. Although he tried to notice the spiritual side of people rather than the physical, it was difficult to avoid Portia's striking good looks: the mass of dark curly hair, the large blue eyes and the rosy complexion. Admittedly, she was so tied about with bits of material, including a spotted scarf in her hair, that her appearance, good or bad, wasn't easy to discern.

But she had discounted his view, content, it seemed, to remain 'plain'. 'The brothers had a terrible time. They were my heroes, of course, but Mother treated them like lovers. Well, Charlie was the principal lover with Roland and Leo more like courtiers vying for her favours. Worse for Roland, thinking it was his right as the eldest. Think Queen Elizabeth the First. Poor Mother. There was no Tower for her enemies. There could be an argument for saying you were well out of it.'

Through this chilling condemnation, Portia remained perfectly cheerful, as if it were no more than historical fact, just set a little closer than the sixteenth century.

'But you love her?' Bill had murmured, feeling, obscurely, he must mount a defence.

'She's my mother, isn't she?' Portia had seemed surprised and Bill thought it best not to point out how many daughters hated their mothers with far less cause.

'It's in my nature to serve,' Portia added, as if that explained everything. Perhaps she was making a link between them.

Bill had wanted to ask about Esmond, who had been more or less beyond the reach of rational conversation by the time Bill had entered the family fold. He would have liked to hear about the greatness of the lawyer. He had been made knight and peer, after all.

Unfortunately Roland had returned before he'd been able to

question Portia further. Roland's cloak of suavity was still in place but barely disguising a frightening tension. Was it possible that both qualities were inherited from his father and that Esmond's mind had cracked when he could no longer control the passion inside the suavity?

Roland had left almost at once with scarcely a word, but before being led off like a beast to the slaughter, as Bill couldn't help thinking, Portia whispered, 'Roland's no use to them. Personally, I think Leo knows something but I shan't tell. They must hate him enough already.'

Brought up to be law-abiding and God-fearing, Bill was shocked by the idea of withholding information from the police. However, when his turn came, the two detectives held him for less than ten minutes, as if they sensed somehow that he was not really part of the family. Perhaps Roland had told them. Fighting to place his humiliation to the honour and glory of God, he had nevertheless decided not to inform them that it was to him and his church that, *in extremis*, Charlie tended to direct his steps. They had already searched his flat and taken his passport. Let them be content with that.

As if in time with the final act of last night's events, Bill's alarm went off. Its ringing always calmed him, an echo of his seminary days when bells marked every important hour. Order was what he'd appreciated, and still did appreciate, about the Catholic Church, order out of chaos. He supposed his nature was fearful. It was like a man teetering on the edge of a cliff, drawn to jump yet looking for a strong arm to hold him back. Bill was the product of elderly parents who found contentment in hard work and regularity. Yet he was drawn to his birth family, so disunited that they couldn't even decide on the same surname. When he was with them, the cliff's edge was higher, more dangerous and more alluring.

Shakily, Bill rolled out of his bed on to his knees, and began the first prayers of the day.

CHAPTER TWENTY-TWO

Arrivals and Departures

Leo arrived at Maggie's very early in the morning. He pretended to be looking for Roland. 'I need a family consultation,' he said.

It was still fairly dark. When the doorbell had rung, Maggie had thought it must be Charlie back or the police or even Roland, although he was least likely, being methodical in his habits.

She stood shivering in the hallway, a shawl wrapped round her nightdress. 'What is it? Roland's not here. Didn't I tell you?'

'Can I come in all the same?'

Maggie took in Leo's exhausted face with the livid bruising round the eye. 'Of course you can.' She hugged him, put heavy emotion on hold, and drew him to the kitchen. 'I'm glad you came. It must be dreadful to be alone at such a difficult time. Roland will be glad.' This was untrue, of course, but sounded sensible, or so she hoped. Anyway, she could see that Leo wasn't listening. He had the seeking-comfort look she recognised from the boys.

The kitchen was warm and cosy. 'I don't expect you've eaten,' said Maggie, and Leo didn't deny it. He sat, still in his coat, hunched in her big armchair. When she handed him a cup of tea and a large slice of cake, he took them gratefully.

Maggie leaned against the Aga and watched him. She thought how pleased she was not to be a man. They seemed programmed to fight all these terrifying dragons but, really, it was too much for them. Even Roland, in all his knowingness, gave evidence, in a night-time muttering or a first drawn look on waking, that a shaky person was hiding inside him. Men tried to be bold and brave, yet often they acted in blindness. Women were much better at seeing things in all their complicated aspects.

'How did it go after your TV interview?'

'I had a tolerable meeting with my constituency staff and an intolerable one with the government chief whip. After we spoke, I couldn't sleep.'

'Oh dear. I suppose I woke you.' Had she really dared ring him in the middle of the night? Even with the excuse of Charlie's arrival and departure.

'Absolutely not. I thought I couldn't escape from my flat because of the press camped there. But around four they bunked off. I expect they assumed I was asleep and they needed food or warmth. So I came here.' Maggie wondered if he knew about Imogen's crisis and, if not, whether she should tell him. There seemed no point. After all, it had passed. She took his empty plate and mug. 'Do you want a bed?'

'No. No.' He looked at her for the first time, then away. 'The second brother to keep you out of yours.'

Maggie tried to make a joke of it. 'I'm not expecting Father Bill.'

'Was Charlie very bad?'

'He did a bit of singing. Then he went to sleep.' Maggie remembered how she'd panicked as Charlie's heavy body slumped across hers. She felt ashamed now. 'The boys came down. We thought he'd be out of it till morning.'

'When he's mad, he can't sleep. Or, rather, stay asleep. He gave no clues where he might go?'

'None. He left a broken window, that's all.'

Leo stood up and came over to Maggie. She knew he wanted to kiss her but she didn't want to give or receive a comfort kiss. She stood with her back to the Aga.

Leo put his arms round her.

'You've got so much to deal with,' she said, and let him kiss her, after all. It was very sweet after so long to feel their mouths joined. Although exciting, mostly it was a relief, an acceptance of the feeling they had for each other.

When he put his hand on her breast she didn't object either, but she knew there must be nothing more. Not now. She thought of her sons sprawled in their beds. Of Esmond stiff and straight, as if he was already a skeleton. Probably not ever.

She didn't have to push very hard for Leo to move away a little.

His arms went back round her and for a moment he laid his head on her shoulder.

Neither of them said anything, but they were both smiling. Leo went back to the chair and shut his eyes. Maggie saw that he would sleep for a bit and looked at the round clock on the wall. She would leave him for a couple of hours.

For a moment she felt uneasy about his similarity to Charlie and the repetition of the act played out a few hours earlier. Then she smiled again and, after switching off the lights, left the room.

The garden shed had seemed a haven of peace and security. He'd tried the car first but the door wouldn't open, although it couldn't have been locked because he could see the keys inside. He saw the glint of moonlight on steel. Unless it was an eyeball. Glaring. A glaring eyeball on the dashboard had sent Charlie tottering back among the trees, which poked out bony fingers to scratch his face or entangled his feet with tripwire roots.

Until *she*'d appeared, the shed had been a refuge. He'd fallen on a pile of plastic sacks and thanked God as his saviour. Invoking God had been a mistake. *She*, the Madonna, had popped up at the window. Her face, backlit by the moonlight, was heavy with mourning, huge, tear-filled eyes. He guessed she was the Black Madonna of Częstochowa come to reproach him. But why reproaches? OK. He'd slept with a multitude of girls in his time but they'd always been more than willing and had mostly dumped him. The tarts were another matter. In the early years it had been a jolly night out with the boys – pay your dues and no questions asked. Gradually things had changed.

'O Mother of Goodness, O Innocent Bride of Christ, O Virgin of Virgins, I humbly pray you, stop looking at me in that tragic way. Have I not tried to save rather than corrupt? Is not my own bride, if not virginal, untouched by me?'

Now the face of the Madonna began to change. The skin and eyes paled. She had become Lizzie Potts. But a Lizzie Potts whose mouth was cruel and lascivious. Although she didn't speak, Charlie could hear her accusations: he'd only not fucked her because he didn't fancy her – no virtue there. He'd locked her away, taken her to court and shut her in prison.

'No, Lizzie!' He tried to tell her that he was on her side, that he knew all about being locked up with men who threw billiard balls at you and spat as you passed. How had he kept up his spirits in such circumstances? 'You have to pray, Lizzie, you have to hang on to what's good. You need the Madonna of Sorrows, Lizzie, who saw her own son crucified, to come to your aid.'

If he'd been able to speak, he'd have said all this, an appeal for both of them, but his mouth was clamped shut and his body was clamped to the floor.

When he next looked up there were no faces at the window, but he was icy cold and his limbs shook. He staggered to his feet, unsure of where he was or why.

He jerked open the shed door and found himself confronted by a stage, garishly lit in every detail. Front centre, there was a covered swimming-pool, to the left a long wall, to the right an avenue of trees, further away more trees, shrubs, terracing, flower borders and swathes of daffodils, like yellow sashes on the grass. A brisk wind made the growing things move while birds flittered about, some carolling, some cheeping, all filled with startling energy. At a distance the backcloth, an elegant red-brick building, stayed reassuringly still, although the number of windows and doors, black holes into the fabric, was threatening.

Charlie gazed out for quite a while, wondering what to make of the scene in front of him and his role in it. What he needed was a vod to steady his mind. It seemed like he'd been low on the vod stakes for far too long.

Without warning, a low-down black hole disgorged two figures, a man and a woman. Almost immediately, they were hidden by a row of shrubs.

Charlie felt drawn to them, fellow human beings in this alien land. He started urgently in their direction, managing only at the last minute to avoid falling on to the swimming-pool cover.

The noise of an engine starting was accompanied by a woman's cry. The vehicle went a short way, then stopped again.

'There's Charlie's car!'

Maggie's cry only just reached Leo through the car window. He was feeling remarkably optimistic and alert. How right he'd been to come to Maggie! He wasn't going to look too closely at their kiss but her presence, plus two hours of dreamless sleep, had radically altered his mood.

He had considered his actions carefully and done what he thought was right. Whatever abuse came his way, he was a man of principle. A line popped into his head: 'Charlie would be proud of me.' Possibly, a delayed echo of Maggie's shout.

He stopped the car. Indeed. There, behind a large oak tree, was Charlie's battered silver car. Leo's heart sank. It was all very well acknowledging Charlie in his absence as some kind of moral yardstick but in the flesh things were never so easy.

Maggie panted up to him. 'He must be here somewhere.'

'Shit!' Leo knew he had just time to drive to London, negotiate entry to his flat with the media, shower, change into appropriate clothes, and arrive, once again media-permitting, at his office for a smaller meeting before the general one at midday. 'Shit,' he said again.

'I know.' Maggie's face screwed up with anxiety. 'I could call the police, the hospital or Roland.'

The shrubbery on their left rustled as if a beast was coming out of the jungle. They turned.

Charlie, hair in a curly halo, pyjama-top tied at his midriff like a fifties pin-up, with leaves, twigs and earthy deposits adhering to various parts of him, advanced at an uncoordinated run. 'Good! Good! Need a lift. Not in a fit state. Your car. Leo?'

Before Leo could object, the large and extremely smelly – sweat, dirt and worse – Charlie had deposited himself on the seat beside him. From outside the window, he heard Maggie calling, in girlish, cheerful tones, 'Just like the Green Man!'

'I can't take you anywhere,' said Leo, brusquely. Faced with his crazed brother, his careless optimism had given way to panic and despair. Even pangs of ambition and obedience came to unsteady him. It was all very well to call the shots, a whistleblower extraordinary, to face his constituency party with panache, but how could he think straight with Charlie as baggage?

'Don't worry about a thing.' Charlie waved his hand magnanimously. 'I won't say a word. Quiet as a mouse.' Here he couldn't resist a squeak or two to prove his point. 'Carry on as before.'

'Oh, Leo.' Maggie was peering in at the window but Leo noticed she hadn't ventured to Charlie's side of the car. 'Perhaps I could persuade him out.' Understandably, she sounded doubtful.

'A bottle of vodka might do it.' They looked at Charlie, who was hunched in his seat as if trying to prove he was invisible – or perhaps a mouse. Leo didn't find the idea funny. This was one of the most important days of his life. 'I can't afford to be late.' He felt Maggie could see the naked ambition in his eyes. He sighed and even groaned. 'I'll just have to take him.'

'Squeak.' Charlie squeaked.

'Well done,' Maggie called after them.

For the next twenty-five miles nothing more was said by either brother because Charlie fell asleep. Leo became calmer. He managed to think of his brother, tenderly, as the holy idiot, the Prince Myshkin of the Home Counties. He also reminded himself that Charlie was in danger and needed care. He should be pleased he'd surfaced. The problem was how to dispose of him safely before they reached Leo's flat with its media accompaniment.

They were soon in the London suburbs, bright with tiny spring leaves. Another half an hour and they would arrive.

Charlie woke with a snort and a shifting that set off new odorous waves. He peered forward with what Leo assumed were blind-lunatic eyes. 'Right here,' he commanded.

Leo grasped, with an extraordinary sense of virtue rewarded, that Charlie was indicating the route to the hospital he'd only recently fled. Did he really plan to return? Not that his doctor was unsympathetic. On visiting Charlie or, indeed, committing him, Leo had often felt sorry for the various medical men who had to deal with him and his fellow inmates.

'We're going to the hospital,' said Charlie, lest there should be doubt. 'Lock me up, that's the thing. Safety in numbers. Secure unit *numero uno*.'

Despite the slur in his brother's voice and the tremble in his hands, Leo believed what he wanted to believe, that for once in his life his brother was doing the sensible thing voluntarily.

'I'll have to drop you and run.' Charlie made no comment as Leo looked at his watch anxiously. In another ten minutes they were going through the gates to the hospital and Leo thought, with a rush of unselfish emotion, that the present scenario, although far from ideal, was immeasurably better than his last visit – was it really only two days ago? – when he'd been summoned to identify his brother's corpse.

He noted that the orange police tapes and blue sheeting were still visible further down the garden. Was Charlie sane enough to ask if there was any way to contact Griff? In normal circumstances he would certainly know his telephone number by heart. On the other hand, the most important thing was to turn him in before he changed his mind or a cohort of zealous police popped out from behind a tree.

He parked the car and got out. Luckily, Charlie seemed equally keen on a quick and anonymous entry. Raising a shaky hand in salute, he loped off round a corner.

Maybe Griff would give him a progress report without prompting.

Doubtless he was keeping a low profile himself. He, Leo, had been the one to stick his neck out.

CHAPTER TWENTY-THREE

Doing Good

Portia woke to find herself face to face with Conor. His long eyes were still closed. After last night's disturbances at the nursing-home and the police station, she had felt the need of companionship.

He liked coming to her flat, saying it gave him psychedelic insights. She'd decorated it during her pre-Mexican Indian phase, and following her recent discovery of the staple gun. Every surface, walls, ceilings and a good deal of the furniture, was stapled with Indian fabrics, ranging in colour from deepest purple through magenta and orange to gold and silver. Charlie had paid her a visit a few years ago and beaten a retreat almost at once, explaining with a wink that he feared for his sanity. Even her sheets were a rich crimson, highlighting Conor's ivory skin.

His eyes opened slowly. 'Hi, Princess.' It was one of his conceits that he was the poor lad plucked from his hovel to his rich lover's castle. In fact, his flat was neat and clean and larger than hers, and he came from a family of Dublin lawyers rich enough to send him to film school in New York.

In many ways he'd had a far more privileged background than Portia, who at sixteen had been more or less cast out from home.

'So, now, have you got over the incursions of the Gardai?'

'Police,' corrected Portia, automatically. She liked Conor's cod-Irishness and, of course, his attention to her. Yet she still found it hard to believe that he thought her special. Equally, she couldn't quite believe in his job or his apparent success in it. Even if he hadn't got the Mexican documentary off the ground, he was always employed. When she saw his name on the screen, she wanted to boast, 'That's my boyfriend,' but it seemed too unlikely. His habit of self-aggrandisement cheered and comforted her. Perhaps some of his confidence would rub off on her. Perhaps her boxes of embroidered blouses in Unit D, 17A Portobello Road would come to feel like a real achievement, not a pathetic and inefficient glimmer of charity.

'Oh, Conor.' He was stroking her breasts now. That was another thing. He often admired her body, particularly that her breasts were large in proportion with her small frame – she'd always been vaguely embarrassed by them, which was the original reason for her disguising layers of shawls and jackets. (Imogen, of course, had perfectly proportioned breasts.)

She was not only Conor's 'Princess' but his 'Venus' and sometimes 'Queen of the Persian Miniatures'. He was tall, of course, but in his slenderness unlike her brothers who, even when spare of flesh like Roland, had a formidable solidity.

'You were sweet last night. On and on about your monstrous family and then the police. I do believe you bear the weight of each and every one on your own lovely shoulders.'

Now he was kissing her breasts, his mouth circled and light on her nipples. She had planned to set off early but she could never resist Conor's touch. Sometimes when her body throbbed for him, as it did now, she wondered if this could be love.

'Put your hand here,' said Conor, 'and here.' For someone so playful, he was a surprisingly direct lover. She liked that too. Direct, but not bullying, she thought, as obediently she slid her fingers down his body.

It was still early. Plenty of time to make love and then do good.

Leo stared through the windscreen of his car. He hoped it was protection enough against the eyes of the hordes of journalists collected outside his flat. At least he had had the good sense to stop at the top of the street. There was no way he was going through that lot.

He backed away carefully. Once round the corner, he pulled towards him the newspapers he'd bought and thrown on to the passenger seat. Something fell to the floor. He drew in to the side of the road, felt around and picked up a bunch of keys. Not his, attached to a medallion of the Virgin. They could only belong to Charlie.

Portia had a key to Charlie's flat. She treasured it, in ridiculous sibling wishful thinking, as a sign of trust. Probably Charlie had forgotten.

Once Conor and she had finished making love, she'd identified that her main source of anxiety, well above laying out her stall, was Charlie's whereabouts and state of mind.

'Why wouldn't I come with you?' He'd seemed surprised by her pleading note. 'Sure, the film [or 'fillum', as he pronounced it] won't stop if I don't turn up.'

So here they were, cautiously opening the door to Charlie's flat, after vainly knocking and ringing.

'Mucky, I'd call it. Mucky,' commented Conor, as Portia gave a comprehensive gasp.

Even in the dimness of the basement, they could see the place had been trashed. Conor found a light switch. 'Is it burglars now?'

'Or the police.' Portia pushed away some books with her foot as she tried to get further in. 'I told you how they questioned us.'

'Poor old Charlie,' said Conor, wading after her through more books and papers. Ahead of them, in the large open-plan room, bookcases, tables and chairs had been turned over.

Portia picked up a chair and sat on it. She felt stronger. 'Charlie won't mind. It doesn't take burglars or the police to make his flat a tip.'

Conor patted her shoulder. 'So now we're here and Charlie's definitely not, what do we do next?'

'I wonder what they were looking for.'

'Evidence. A murder weapon. Bloodstains.'

'The poor madman was strangled.'

'Gloves?' Conor righted a second chair and sat on it, then said, in a dramatic whisper, 'Pssst. Something wicked this way comes.'

They both stared at the door, which was still open.

'Leo!' exclaimed Portia. She felt herself blushing as if at the entrance of a lover.

Leo's gaze took in the scene. 'I haven't time for this!' He headed for the bathroom.

'Sure, families can be fun,' murmured Conor, under his breath. They both listened to the sound of water running, followed by objects falling and a certain amount of high-powered swearing. 'That's the TV star, isn't it?'

Portia wrung her hands. 'Why is he here? I really don't understand it.' She added with untypical bitterness, 'Which is nothing new.'

Conor leaned forward in his chair. 'Just remember, you're beautiful, good and extraordinarily sexy.'

Portia found her eyes filling with tears. She was convinced he meant it.

Since the contents of the bathroom cupboard were in the basin, it took Leo a moment to find a razor. When he did, it was so revolting that he almost abandoned the project. That was when he began to swear. But his constituents wouldn't go for the designer-stubble line. In fact now, too late, he remembered Bob's first advice when he'd won the seat: 'Remember, no successful Member of Parliament is ever without a razor in his pocket.'

The shower and bath were beyond use so he dabbed himself with water and re-emerged.

'Be an angel, Porsh, and find me a clean shirt and tie.' He always called her 'Porsh' when he wanted help.

'I should be in a suit. Oh, fuck.'

Portia stared at him. 'Charlie never wears ties – or clean shirts, if it comes to that. And he's much fatter than you.'

'How about mine?' Conor stood up.

Leo, who'd hardly acknowledged his existence up to now, took in the neat grey suit, the pale blue shirt and red tie. 'Do you think I'd fit?'

'Appearances can be deceptive. Thirty-four waist. Fifteen-and-a-half collar.'

Already Leo was stripping. He took out his mobile and laid it on the chair, turning it on in the process. It rang immediately. Leo hesitated.

'Shall I get it?' Portia reached out.

'Thanks.' One arm still in his shirt, the other out, Leo took it from her firmly.

'Leo. Have you heard the news?'

Leo had never known Bob sound stressed and tried to lighten the tone. 'I thought I was the news.'

'The commissioner has resigned.'

'What?' Leo tried to clear his mind. 'You mean he's admitting . . . ?'

'He's admitting his wife's got terminal cancer. He needs to be with her and their children. A boy and a girl. Twelve and fourteen. Boy autistic.'

Leo felt he was being given too much information. 'Hold on.' He finished taking off his shirt and put on Conor's.

'He gave him the shirt off his back,' intoned Conor. 'Greater love . . .'

Leo grabbed the phone again. 'Who's that with you?' asked Bob, sounding nervous. 'Where are you?'

'Charlie's flat. Preparing for the meeting.'

'Isn't that the insane brother suspected of murder?'

'He's in hospital, Bob. I just took him there.' Leo wanted to be calm, particularly with Bob, but he could feel impatience gaining ground. 'I had to come here because my flat's surrounded by the man-eating hounds of the press. I'm just putting on a suit belonging to my sister's boyfriend.'

Leo listened to Bob's heavy sigh down the line and feared it didn't bode well for the morning ahead. 'The resignation must be good news,' he said, in what he hoped were decisive yet calm tones. 'Thanks for letting me know. See you in half an hour.'

'Hospital?' wondered Portia. 'Charlie's back in hospital?'

Leo didn't look up from knotting Conor's tie. 'He made me take him there. Wish you'd call them, Porsh. Check out the scene. As you see, I've got to dash.' He was already half through the door before he remembered Conor. 'OK if I keep your stuff for the day?'

'Be my guest.'

After Leo had gone, Conor completed the clothes changeover under Portia's anxious gaze. There was something sexually disturbing about seeing your lover kitted out as your brother.

'I thought you were much slimmer than him.'

'Maybe you underestimate men unrelated to you.'

'And why were you in a suit? You never wear a suit.'

'Last night I was summoned by you from a fund-raiser. In total we made love three times, which is not bad for starters. Remember, my darling?'

He was interrupted by a mobile, on the table but hardly visible among the mess. 'Oh dear.' Portia picked it up. 'It's Leo's.'

'Come to think of it, he's got mine in my jacket pocket. Go on, answer it. You never know what you might learn.'

'Hello.'

'Mr Barr, please.'

'Who is it?'

It turned out to be Dr Cass Heilbrand, the loquacious psychiatrist whom Portia knew from her visits to Charlie in hospital. She'd sometimes wondered if his duty of listening to patients built up a need in him to speak at length to non-patients. She liked him, however, because he'd always treated Charlie as someone out of the run of the normally insane. Possibly a contradictory description but she knew what she meant.

'I have to admit to surprise when a nurse informed me, with some trepidation, "Mr Potts has reappeared on the ward." He was securely here when I left for Paris to give a lecture on the benefits of the male menopause – benefits to the mentally ill, that is. Bad timing as it turned out, with this dreadful Horace Silver disaster, as he likes or, I should say, *liked* to style himself. A most unfortunate man. Spent more time here than anywhere. Male menopause didn't help him. Tried and failed to do away with himself more times than I can count. Serious attempts, too, with enough pills to fell an ox – quite an expert at the false-swallow technique – and now the police assure me that, far from topping himself, he's been topped by another. Murdered, in other words. Frankly, I find it almost impossible to believe. These police doctors are a law unto themselves. Always touting for work. Ditto Forensics.'

As he drew breath, Portia intervened: 'Leo brought Charlie in?'

'Charlie brought himself in. Astonishing . . .'

Portia listened patiently as the doctor enjoyed recapping the various ways that Charlie had entered the hospital, including an occasion when he'd been strapped to the table inside a mobile home. At length she got another chance to speak. 'Apparently the police suspect Charlie.'

'Ridiculous. In fact, my real purpose in ringing Leo was to say that I've prescribed heavy sedation for your brother and he'll be in no state for police interviews. Not for days, even weeks. It's up to me. I have to give permission.'

'Oh. I didn't know.' Portia began to see why Charlie might decide hospital was, for once, the safest place.

'Yes. Yes. A little bit of power we doctors cling to. I'd recommend giving visits a miss for two or three days. Ring me on Monday. Thank you.'

Portia was surprised at how relieved she felt by the doctor's news. It made her unwilling to dwell on Leo's political shenanigans or rush to her (possibly dying) mother's side.

Conor seemed to catch her mood. 'So, is it Portobello now and that lecherous, treacherous neighbouring stall-holder?'

'Yes,' agreed Portia. She looked round and sighed. 'I can't face serious clearing up. I'll just tidy a little.'

She thought, Lizzie can do it. She might enjoy doing something useful when she comes out of prison.

CHAPTER TWENTY-FOUR

Resettlement

At ten o'clock Roland rang Maggie. Since Leo's departure with Charlie, she'd thrown herself into household matters, as if to salve her slightly rocky conscience (they had kissed after twenty years of abstinence – they had *kissed*), changing sheets, cleaning out the cupboards in the kitchen and making lasagne for the boys' lunch – their favourite dish. Tom and Jake repaid her virtuous activity by playing football too near the house and breaking a window pane. The second pane broken in less than twenty-four hours. Admittedly it was a small, unimportant one in a downstairs lavatory but enough to consider withholding the lasagne – except that would be to punish herself.

None of this would interest Roland. 'You didn't ring last night.' She hadn't intended to accuse and even regretted the impulse to question. She wanted him to feel free. She wanted to be free.

'No. I'm sorry.' He began a description of the infuriating evening at the police station, the casual inefficiency of the officers and his relief to arrive back finally in his flat. 'It was a tin of soup and bed for me.'

Maggie was surprised by this long explanation delivered in conciliatory tones. She almost asked if he was all right, then recalled how much he disliked giving that sort of information. Perhaps she should take the plunge instead. 'Leo and Charlie were here earlier,' she said.

'What? Whatever were they doing with you?'

She decided not to answer this too exactly. 'They left together. Charlie was pretty high, I'm afraid.'

'Of course he was!'

The conciliatory tone had now departed and Maggie felt more relaxed. 'Leo hasn't been in touch with you?'

'Don't you read the papers? I can't think what he was doing out there with you.'

'I suppose he was looking for Charlie.' Maggie tried not to sound smug. Or secretive. Or happy. Then she felt guilty. 'I've got a problem with the decorators in the gallery. I've got to go to town.' This was true. 'I'll take the boys with me.' She would. 'We can have a pizza.' But what would happen to the lasagne? And what about the broken panes?

Roland was saying goodbye. She had bored him into getting off the line. The smug happiness welled back.

Roland wished he was in court. Only there could he rid his mind of Didi, and his own disastrous emotions. He had a big case starting on Monday for which he needed to study the papers. The defence counsel who'd once been in his chambers was a bit of a friend and more than a bit of a rival. The clerks liked that sort of thing. It made them feel as if they were promoting a pit-bull fight.

Perhaps he would report Didi to the authorities who, with any luck, would deport him and his brother as illegal immigrants. He tried to imagine the relief of putting Didi beyond temptation but only succeeded in picturing him naked in certain postures.

There was a chirpy knock at the door. It would be one of the junior clerks, bringing him more papers.

'Yes.'

The boy – still boyish despite his pinstriped suit – juggled a load of files across the room and unloaded them noisily on to Roland's desk. Then he stood, apparently waiting, with an expectant air.

'What is it?' Roland asked reluctantly.

'Just thought you'd want to hear the news, sir. The Met chief's resigned. He says it's because his wife is dying of cancer. But, of course, your brother . . .'

He had asked him a question so now he had the answer. In the boy's sharp, curious eyes he saw reflected the idiotic scuffle between himself and Leo. Doubtless he was trying to conflate disparate scenarios. Before he showed his irritation too obviously, though, he should remind himself that the clerks were on his side.

'It's been a difficult couple of days.' He was amazed that he should even admit this much to a *junior* clerk.

'Understood, sir.'

'However, I am nowhere near the loop in this business of charges of corruption against the home secretary. To be honest, I'm pissed off about the whole thing.' He hadn't had any intention of saying so much. Worse, he could hear the whine of emotion – Didi's fault, not Leo's.

'Yes, sir.' The boy, brash as he'd first appeared, good-looking too, was clearly embarrassed by this unprecedented confidence.

Forcing down a horrifying impulse to burst into tears, Roland bent his head and pulled towards him the piles of folders. He tried not to imagine the gossip in the clerks' room. He heard the door being shut quietly, as on a sick room.

'You're being released tomorrow.' The officer who delivered this news to Lizzie seemed fairly surprised.

She was even more so. 'But I haven't finished my resettlement course.' It was not her nice resettlement officer who stood filling the doorway of her cell but one of the lezzie sports teachers who'd always rather fancied her.

'It says so here, on my list. You've heard about overcrowding, haven't you? Have it your own way, don't believe me. If you've grown to enjoy the banged-up life, we'll always find you a corner.' She leered mockingly.

'Fuck off, can't you!'

'Suit yourself.'

Left alone Lizzie tried to control a wave of panic. You couldn't expect prison to make any sense but Holloway hadn't been so bad. No attacks and one or two screws who seemed to care. She'd even seen the governor once, a tubby chap who'd asked her if she got enough outside exercise. She'd said, 'Yes,' without explaining that the twenty minutes a day in a yard had no interest for her. She was keeping her head down, wasn't she?

What was her next step? In her agitation, Lizzie began to tear at her fingernails. Charlie. Charlie. Now she couldn't even remember where he was. Not dead, that was all she'd taken in. So, back in hospital? Her mind skittered all over the place. Tomorrow. Was she really going out tomorrow? But what about that wall she was painting? She'd have liked to finish it. 'Satisfaction of a job well done.' That's what the screw said. Well, she wouldn't get that now. Although there was today. They'd be coming to take her down soon, if they remembered.

It was harder to think of the future, that was the point. So suddenly. Where was that flat Charlie had got her? He'd been so pleased about it. How did she get in touch with him? The hospital? Perhaps that nice resettlement officer would help. But hadn't he told her he was off this week? She'd have to ring the hospital herself. At least she had phone credit because she hadn't had anyone to ring.

Why was she being let out early? She'd never get an answer to that one and it wasn't important anyway. Like the whole of her life, it had just happened to her.

Lizzie got up – her legs a bit wobbly after the surprise – and went to a plastic bag under her bed. Other girls complained about 'volume control', which meant not being allowed enough things in their cell, but she never had a problem.

Inside the bag, she found an envelope with Charlie's letter from the hospital. There was the telephone number. Now she had to get up enough nerve to ring, wait for 'association' and brave the queue. No way was she going to *beg* to stay in prison.

Bill was enduring a bad day. Sometimes recently he'd wondered whether he would have made a better monk than priest. Perhaps a Benedictine with their founder's vow of stability, obedience and *conversatio morum*. The lack of a rule, or order, might be what made his life so difficult – although probably it was a weakness in his nature. A stronger man, more centred and less prone to emotion, might deal with the challenges presented daily to an inner-city parish priest. He didn't fool himself that the monkish life was easy, of course. He'd chosen to be a priest because he enjoyed (not the right word) the variety and drama, and he knew obedience either to God or a superior was not his strong point. But he felt in need of guidance, a steadying hand, a daily routine. Stability instead of the random.

These thoughts reminded him that at that very moment, midday, he should be reciting his chosen prayer for the week: the Angelus. Yet here he was, once again, thinking about his own problems.

On the other hand, Christ was/is mercifully understanding about human weakness and last night's goings-on in the nursing-home and the police station were enough to rock the concentration of a saint. The worst thing about it, and he had been taught to confess the worst to another, or to himself if another was unavailable, was how excited he'd been by the incident. He might have appeared outwardly calm, as a priest should, but he had been far more aware of his own feelings than anyone else's. He would confess that to Father Aloysius when the time came

Now, thankfully, he felt himself about to pray. Then, just as he started, there came a brief and agitated realisation that all his most selfish behaviour arose in conjunction with his birth family. 'O God, come to my assistance, O Lord, make haste to help me.'

Lizzie crept back to her cell, head down, hands sweating and trembling. The hospital had made her feel a fool, even after she'd told them she was Charlie's wife. He wasn't taking calls, they'd said, as if a wife should know that, wouldn't be for days yet. What was her number, they'd asked, as if they didn't really care, because Dr Someone-or-other, she didn't catch the name, just might find time to give her a buzz. Of course, a buzz was a joke. She could hardly tell them she was in Her Majesty's Prison Holloway and, anyway, she wouldn't be tomorrow.

Lizzie lay on her bunk, desperate for a fix or a snort or a spliff, or even a drag. But she had promised Charlie.

In penitential mood, Bill had skipped lunch to visit a bad-tempered old man who believed the devil lived in his dustbin. Actually, it was his wife who needed the visit.

He was walking away when his mobile rang. Whenever he doubted the appropriateness of this form of interruptive communication for a man of God, he remembered that Jesus, in his ministry, was always available, even for the most intransigent of his flock: women who bled too much, fathers who feared for their daughters, lepers, laggards and sinners.

'Father Bill here.'

'Oh, Father.'

The caller was young, female, hesitant.

'How can I help?'

'It's me. Lizzie.'

He heard the snuffling wordlessness of tears, the tragedy of being human. 'Dear Lizzie. God bless you, my dear.' Still, she couldn't speak. 'Shall I come to you?'

No answer. Then a few barely discernible words, among them, 'Charlie'. He thought of Charlie as he'd seen him yesterday – not a very stable husband.

'I'm getting out tomorrow.'

Ah, so she had had to submit to the sudden-release technique. Prolonged contact with prison encouraged cynicism and sometimes he wondered whether making it particularly difficult for released offenders to settle into a non-criminal life outside suited a Prison Service subtext. After all, recidivism enlarged their empire. He understood her nervousness now. 'I'm afraid Charlie's not quite better.'

'Where . . . ?'

Well, that was a question. 'I'll be sure to meet you. Don't worry too much.' So easy for him to say. 'Didn't Charlie rent you a flat?'

The snuffling, which had lessened, increased. Oh, God, guessed Bill, inspired by the dreadful sounds of her loneliness, she doesn't even know where the flat is. 'I'll find you somewhere, Lizzie. I'll be there.'

The snuffling lessened. He should be used by now to the hopelessness, in every sense, of those who dropped through the net. He could say, 'Don't Probation have a plan for you?' but there seemed little point. If her release plan didn't insist on a stay in a hostel, she was well out of it. 'I'll ring Probation – Shirley, isn't it? – and be at the gates.' He pictured the desolate figure carrying a plastic bag. 'Don't worry,' he found himself saying again.

Portia was being busy. Her busyness pleased her. During her Indian phase she had tried silence and meditation but it had felt like doing nothing, a self-centred denial of life. In busyness she found a greater peace. As she sliced open each cardboard box and carefully took out the piles of white, red and yellow blouses the action formed a kind of satisfying shape in her head. She recalled the brown hands of the women who had made and embroidered the clothes and had laid them in the box as carefully as she was taking them out. They were closely linked, those poor, uneducated peasants and her. It was a ritual they were embarked on. Even if it seemed to be about money, it was more than that. Reverently, she spread the first ten blouses in a line on the table.

'Portia. Portia. Will you marry me?'

Conor was still hovering about, Conor who touched her body and who had turned out to be taller and wider than she'd thought. The last few days had been so peculiar that she could almost believe he was being serious.

'I've been watching you. You're like a high priestess.'

'I was feeling that too.' Of course he hadn't meant it. 'Shouldn't you go to work?'

'You've mesmerised me.'

'What about Leo's clothes? You can't wear that all day.' Although she loved him, she wanted to be on her own now, undisturbed.

'He's wearing mine. Will I be seeing my lady tonight?'

'Yes. Yes.' Against her will, she watched him walk away: the expensive jacket hanging a little loosely, the trousers bunching over his shoes, his hair just too long over his collar. The sight made her consider Leo. It wasn't only a suit that made him a Member of Parliament. What, then? It had never been her role to question her brothers, in their presence or in their absence.

Portia returned to her blouses and marvelled at the energy in the embroidery, at the birds and flowers, the brilliant colours, the trimming and tassels. She laid out the bottle-top earrings in rows, as brilliant as emeralds and rubies. Surely she would sell them all and send the money to the mountains.

It was well into the afternoon when her mobile rang, a number she didn't know.

'Yes?'

'I hope I'm not disturbing you. It's Bill here.'

Bill? 'Oh, Bill.' Silly he didn't come instantly to mind when she'd spent most of yesterday evening with him.

'I have a problem. You might be able to help.' His northern accent seemed more pronounced over the phone. 'It's Lizzie. She's coming out of prison tomorrow. Without warning so no place to go. Charlie rented a flat for her but she doesn't know where and, of course, he's not exactly available . . .'

'Charlie's in hospital, under heavy sedation.' She could clear that up.

'Thank God.'

When he said 'thank God', he meant it. How strange it must be to feel another presence directing your life.

A few pleas later and Portia had agreed to find a bed for Lizzie – or, rather, a sofa. What would Lizzie make of Conor? Even allowing for Charlie's theatricals, it seemed prostitution had been her line of business. And didn't that mean she hated men? 'So Charlie really did marry her?'

'Oh, yes. I performed the ceremony myself.'

'I wasn't invited.'

'Perhaps I was wrong to do so but, as you know well, your brother is a persuasive fellow. The Christian marriage service demands all kinds of vows but I fear his motives were unusual. Non-consummation, you know, provides grounds for annulment. I think it unlikely such information would have come Lizzie's way, poor girl, although she is a cradle Catholic. It would undermine her confidence.'

'Heavens!' Portia noted that since her brother's call she had been drawn to Christian exclamations. It seemed to her that non-consummation was undermining in itself, quite apart from the question of annulment. An image of herself and Conor so happily in bed that morning came into her head. How long would Lizzie stay?

'I'm meeting her outside the prison some time between eight and ten so when shall I deliver her to you?'

'I'll be here all day.'

'Where is that?'

He was being humble again, aware of how much he was asking of her when she was not even one of his flock. But presumably he thought of Lizzie as part of the family, although after yesterday evening's example of their family life, you might have thought he would keep poor, fragile Lizzie out of their orbit. 'She can come and help me on the stall or at my flat after eight p.m.'

It was only after Bill had rung off that Portia saw it was perfectly obvious where Lizzie should stay: in Charlie's flat. Admittedly it was pretty revolting but after prison it wouldn't be so bad. Wasn't Holloway famous for its cockroaches?

Immediately admonishing herself for such meanness – could she only help women who lived on the other side of the world? – she decided to welcome Lizzie for a few days and make Charlie's flat habitable.

She even tried to call Bill with this idea but his number didn't come up. She found herself surprised that a priest should block access.

CHAPTER TWENTY-FIVE

Being Realistic

Bob took Leo's arm and hustled him into the offices. A single photographer, wearing shades although it was a cold, dull day, took a flashlight snap. Leo flinched.

'It's all right. He's one of ours. I've diverted the main group of wankers to the hall – where we're due, incidentally, in less than an hour. TV, too.' He took a look at Leo. 'What's happened to you?'

'I told you. I couldn't get into my flat.' Leo had always enjoyed Bob's uncompromising manner but, then, Bob had been on his side.

'That suit doesn't fit you.'

'Aren't you going to ask about my designer stubble?'

Bob didn't answer. Eloise who had followed them gave an encouraging wink.

They went inside and the two men sat on either side of a table.

'I need coffee,' said Leo, 'and something to eat.'

'Did I start all this or did you?'

'I still need a coffee.'

Eloise slid away to the kitchen.

'I've been getting constant calls from that rapper of yours.' Bob drummed the table.

'Denver's a natural communicator.' He was Leo's PA in the House of Commons – or, rather, in his office at Portcullis House. His ambition was to be the first black rapper MP.

'He says he can't communicate with you. Your mobile's on constant message service.'

Leo felt his pocket. 'Shit.' He'd left it in Charlie's flat. Or in his jacket, which was now on Portia's nameless boyfriend's back. 'Denver's good at repelling boarders.' Two years ago Denver had

walked into this very office. He and his mother, whom he accompanied, came from one of the worst estates in Leo's constituency.

'He'll need to be,' grumbled Bob.

It was time to get serious. 'Any reaction from Downing Street?'

'A waiting game. That's what they're playing.' Bob leaned across
the table and stared into Leo's eyes. His own were rather small and
close together. Leo had never noticed this before. 'Is it true, this
story you've set loose? Do you believe it to be true?'

Leo felt like a suspected murderer under interrogation. He was
about to respond, 'No, I made it up on a dull afternoon in the
House,' when Bob put his head in his hands and said, in muffled
tones, 'I've given my life to this constituency.'

'I'm sorry.' It was true. But it was Leo's life too. He frowned at
Bob's thinning hair and heavy slumped shoulders. 'Perhaps I should
have passed it up.'

'Perhaps you should have spoken to me first.' Bob took his head
out of his hands and glared, if feebly. They were in it together.

'Yesterday you didn't seem so depressed.'

They paused as Eloise brought Leo his coffee and biscuits with a
nurse-to-patient smile.

'Yesterday I hadn't spoken to the party – laughingly called
"faithfuls".'

'Ah.' Leo drank and ate hastily.

Bob watched him gloomily. 'You haven't enough evidence,' he
said eventually. 'Any evidence.'

'What about this police chief going? Isn't that just a little bit
incriminating?'

'His wife's dying.'

'We're all dying.'

Bob gave another glare, more convincing this time. 'The police
will close ranks – they have already.'

There was a longer pause, during which Leo thought hard and
also longed but didn't dare ask for another cup of coffee.

'You think the home secretary will just ride it?'

'The red-tops haven't found anything yet.'

Leo looked down at his fingers. He noticed the nails were dirty –
contact with Charlie or Charlie's flat, he decided. 'What if I produced
the girl? Or someone else produced the girl? Or, better still, an
appropriate photograph. You get my point.' He raised his head and

felt a flush in his cheeks. 'One of the young illegal-immigrant girls who our dear minister had sex with before sorting out her stay in Great Britain. Not that her stay was ever going to be much fun, given the circumstances. You know the sort of circumstances I'm talking about?' His voice was loud and passionate and he found himself staring hard into Eloise's bright eyes. Why was she in the room anyway? She moved her mouth a little, as if murmuring. At least he'd lost his patient status.

'So that's what it's all about,' said Bob, sombrely, but his face had lost its grey cast. 'How long?'

'These things take time.' Leo thought of Griff. He was an unassuming little man but he had a reputation for never letting a story go. All the same, maybe he could do with a little help.

Maggie looked aghast at the walls of her gallery. Could she really have chosen this mucky brown, a kind of farmyard sludge? The decorator stood beside her with the cheerful expression of a man expecting plaudits.

'We're pretty hungry, Mum.' To be fair, Tom was trying not to sound whiny.

'It's half past one.' Jake showed his watch as objective evidence.

Maggie thought about all the hours, days, weeks she'd studied colours, different brands, different mixes, which all looked different when she'd painted them on these walls at different times of day in different lights. She could have taken a PhD in paint colours.

'It's quite strong, isn't it?' said the decorator, complacently.

'Oh dear.' Maggie found a chair and sat down heavily.

'We're starving,' chorused the boys, clearly alarmed at her fixed posture.

Maggie remembered that she had been up in the night with Charlie (and where was *he* now?), then at dawn with Leo. Somehow the thought of Leo and their kiss was no longer uplifting but made her want to burst into tears. 'I'm hungry too!' she snarled at the boys who retreated to the door where they stood sulkily sentinel.

'Are you not too sure?' The decorator had painted hundreds of experiments on these very walls, had witnessed the moment of choice.

'It's darker than I imagined,' said Maggie. 'Muddier. Even op-pressive.'

'Oppressive,' repeated the decorator, seriously.

He'd been very kind during the process of decision-making. Of course, she was paying him by the hour. He'd probably be happy to do it all over again.

'It's not easy to lighten a colour. How about you try hanging a few pictures?'

Maggie thought of the first three exhibitions she had lined up. By chance the painters all used a pale palette: still lives of flowers, usually lilies in white china pots, seascapes with bleached skies, and an abstract painter who favoured shades of white varied with ice blue. Her spirits lifted. She possessed a placid nature but recently she had noticed alarming mood swings.

'You're right! The pictures will make all the difference. Come on, boys. We're off.'

'It just takes time getting used to it,' commented the decorator, to Maggie's retreating back.

Outside, the grey skies were delivering dribbles of rain. By now, thought Maggie, Leo's fate will be decided. If his constituents kicked him out, although she was not certain if that was possible, he might become another person. He might want to lead a new life.

'It's really pouring.' Now Tom *was* whining.

Imogen had a dreadful sense that someone was weeping close by her. The looming size made him a man. She hated men who cried. The tears were wetting her – she could feel the dampness on her cheeks, hear the gushing.

'No! No!' She plucked and pulled at her body, at the swathings round her.

The presence bent and whispered something in her ear, but she couldn't make out the words. They merged into the hissing of the tide on a beach. Water, more water. Where was the sunlight? The boy by the lake, the swimming and laughter? So many boys and men who'd taken her in their arms. Where were they now? Why was she all alone on this beach, the tide ebbing away?

'Esmond.' A hissing sort of name. Not heroic. Where was he now? Always the last resort. But she'd known he was at the helm.

Alone. Alone. She tried to struggle upwards but the dark presence held her back. Men never held her back. Don't remember that one. How she'd loved him. Long ago. When she was young. Swirling skirts. Only one. Men always let her do what she liked. Men loved her. And she loved them. Why was this man forcing her down? Ah, but perhaps he was a woman. Women did not like her. No sisters for her, no girlfriends to play with on the beach.

It was a woman who held her down! Who spouted water over her. Now she understood. Now she understood her fate. Dropping her clawing hands to her side, quietening her tossing head and arching back, she lay still. She was truly on her own. Finally the men had deserted her – even Esmond. Esmond, who had saved her once. He was old, too. Feeble. Esmond couldn't save her now. She must allow the black waves to envelop her with dignity and without protest.

Beside the bed, the nurse noticed her patient's restlessness suddenly abate. She felt the pulse with her fingers and listened to the breathing. Death had moved another stage closer. Perhaps the old lady was now in her final hours and she should inform the matron who, once again, would summon the relatives.

Yet, after last night's hullabaloo, she felt reluctant. She liked her patients to die peacefully – it was a last human right, she considered, and she tried to help them towards this. Relatives had rights, too, of course, she admitted this, but perhaps not so many when they behaved as badly as Lady Shillingstone's children. Shameless! As if they were hardly aware of their poor mother so near her departure from this world and entry into another.

The nurse, who was religious and believed fervently in a further happier kingdom, felt a tear in her eye. She'd looked after many men and women at the last stages of life but had never lost her sense of the great drama.

Maybe she would hold off informing Matron a little while longer.

Leo entered Charlie's flat. He had just about survived his meeting, backed by a newly stalwart Bob. 'We've bought time,' Bob had told him, 'while we await further developments.'

Downing Street was holding a press briefing at two p.m. so the senior hounds of horror had gone there. According to Bob, the junior, after grabbing photographs outside the hall, had gone to cover a speech being given by the home secretary at a Guildhall lunch in the City.

A few cub hounds had tailed Leo's car but they seemed to give up or were called away. Nevertheless, he had felt more likely to be left alone in Charlie's flat, however unwelcoming, than in his own.

With relief, he took off the rather too tight jacket and trousers. He opened the shirt collar and pulled off the tie. The flat was cold, he noticed, but someone, probably Portia, had tidied it up a bit. In the corner, a bed had been uncovered, the bedclothes draped roughly across it. If he was to think straight ever again, he had to snatch an hour's sleep.

When he flung himself down, a scattering of moths flew up, then settled again.

Charlie, in his hospital bed, lay still as a martyr, pressed under the black weight of drugs. He might as well have been at the bottom of the ocean.

Esmond, more fortunate, was watching the wake of his ship recede from his position on the poop. A small flock of birds had settled at the centre attracted by the calmer water and food scraps from the galley. They were sharply black and white, northern birds, he thought. He had no name to give them but still felt proprietorial, pleased they were under his command. That was the job of a ship's captain: to take responsibility for those on board – or near enough on board, as in the case of the birds.

How happily they bobbed up and down. How confidently. Some-where, far from the sea, he'd watched over boys just as happy, just as confident.

CHAPTER TWENTY-SIX

Present Comfort

It was raining, of course. Whenever Bill went to meet a prisoner being released, it always rained. Also as usual, the prison had only told him that Lizzie would come out somewhere between eight and ten. It was already nine so he was thoroughly wet and cold.

Bill looked longingly at the visitors' centre, a modern building standing fifty yards from the gate, but of course it was not yet open. He could sit in the waiting area for those who had appointments in the prison but then he risked missing Lizzie.

Behind him the rush-hour traffic on Camden Road reminded him of how right he was to be standing there for Lizzie, like a post she could cling to before she was swept away by the flood. He felt for a moment the warmth of virtue, and when the big gates began to open, he was sure he'd be rewarded by the sight of her.

Instead, a man he recognised as one of the prison doctors emerged with an officer at his side. He came over. 'Tell me, Father, you're a doctor of the soul. Why do these girls do such dreadful things to their bodies? Don't they know they've only got one?'

'Not a suicide?' asked Bill, gloomily.

'Averted just in time. The prison's getting better at that. So, you've no answer for me?' The doctor was an oldish man with a scratchy grey beard but his physique was strong and exercised.

'Nothing to live for?' suggested Bill.

'Many of them have children.' The doctor sounded suddenly exasperated instead of depressed. 'I'm off to see if I can find some sick people who actually want to get well.' He walked away briskly, swinging his arms.

After he'd gone Bill also began to walk swinging his arms. He thought about 'community', a word government and media used freely, as if it was the answer to everyone's prayers, certain antidote to poverty, sickness or violence. In his experience, the only communities that worked were healthy families – and there were few enough of those on his beat. To be part of a true community you had to accept and take responsibility for all the failings of all the members and, as far as he could see, very few people were willing to do that. It was perfectly acceptable, in fact widely encouraged, to look out for yourself and blame anyone who stood in your way or just made life more difficult.

You could find the roots in Mrs Thatcher's attitudes or in capitalism or the pressures of too much immigration, but that didn't help. Nor did it help to pretend that 'community' was the proper word for what were merely postal districts. Or worse. He'd once heard an official refer to the 'paedophile community'. During his training he'd been taught the true meaning of 'communion' on which 'community' was based. Now he only truly believed in the communion of souls. But a priest might do a little to bring those souls together.

Bill was enjoying a quick prayer for Portia, giving thanks that she was taking in Lizzie and asking that she would receive the grace to make it less of a pain and more of a pleasure, when Lizzie finally sidled out of the door. Adding a prayer for himself – did she have to appear so miserable when he'd promised to care for her? Well, of course she did – he went forward, arms outstretched in welcome.

'Hi, Father.' She looked upwards with a bewildered expression on her pale face. 'It's raining.'

'It is. I'm sorry.' She might have enjoyed the rain, he supposed, after being cooped up for weeks. But he was on her side. 'Let's go and warm ourselves up with a hot drink. Here, let me carry your bag.'

It was the plastic bag that touched him most, so light it could hardly hold more than a toothbrush and one or two items of clothing. Even he, as a priest who'd vowed to leave everything and follow Christ, would be hard-pressed to fit all his possessions into two substantial suitcases and that would entail leaving behind the china he'd inherited from his parents (adoptive) and a particularly cosy blanket from the same source.

Lizzie was silent until they entered the small coffee bar, dimly lit with orange lights. Then she gave a sigh, sat down at the nearest empty table and said, quite firmly, 'That's better, isn't it.'

Bill felt a sense of achievement: first step successful. What more did she expect but present comfort? He ordered coffee and a heavily sugared pastry for her. He knew the recovered drug user's need for sweetness.

When she'd eaten and drunk and her skin had gained a slight pinkness, he leaned forward, just enough to provide reassurance without what the psychiatric types called 'crowding her space'. 'I'm taking you to Portia, Charlie's sister. She's giving you a place to stay.'

Lizzie stared at her plate as if she hadn't heard.

It struck Bill belatedly that she might not even know of the existence of a sister, her sister-in-law. 'She's very nice. Quiet. Unmarried. In her middle thirties, I'd say. I've fixed it with your probation officer. It'll give you time to breathe.'

As she failed to react, Bill felt the rest of his day pressing on him: the christening at midday (a joy, of course), the meeting for Catholic Nigerian Women, the postponed finance meeting, the evening mass at six p.m. He thought that loving poor Lizzie was easy enough but finding the patience to stay alongside her gaping lack of energy was very difficult indeed. In this case patience was the greater virtue, whatever St Paul might teach.

'Shall we go now?' he suggested gently. It seemed wisest not to inform her that delivery to Portia would take place at a stall in Portobello Road. Sufficient unto the moment.

Portia was dazed. Conor had come back to her again the night before, still incidentally, wearing Leo's jacket and trousers. Perhaps it wasn't altogether incidental for something had changed him in her eyes. Over a Marks & Spencer dinner he'd brought with him, he'd talked about his film and she'd suddenly understood that it was real, a serious project in which he was employed with a serious role. She couldn't understand why she'd so underrated him. As he talked in his quirky and amusing way about the influx of new money that would allow them to travel to the west coast of Scotland – to investigate drug use in small fishing villages – she realised that the problem had been on her side, not his. Only now was she seeing him as he was, undisguised by her own layers of failing self-esteem.

She didn't even try to understand the change – something to do with the scarifying events of the last few days, perhaps – but now she declared herself, with certainty, in love. The big or even biggest L. Moreover, in love with a man she respected and who, she dared to hope, respected her. For too many years she'd been drawn to men who took her at her own evaluation and left her for someone less adoring and more demanding. Of course she hadn't told Conor about her new feelings. That would be too dangerous. She felt it in the glorious levity of her spirits as she kissed him goodbye, took the crushed early-morning tube to Ladroke Grove, walked to Portobello and opened her stall. She was in love and, judging by last night, Conor might just conceivably be pretty keen on her too.

In this ebullient mood, she had quite forgotten her promise to Bill. She smiled, she sang, and found customers massed before her as if drawn by the magnet of her happiness. She was conscious enough of others in her sphere to consider it slightly shameful that she was no longer worrying about Leo (she hadn't even listened to the news and purposely not bought a paper) or Charlie (safe in hospital) or her mother (but death must come to us all at a certain age). Love had made her selfish for the first time in her life and the world must take care of itself.

Lizzie had shown signs of flight when she and Bill reached the noisy market so he had a good grip on her arm as they entered the building where Portia had her stall.

'There she is. Straight ahead.' There was no time for misgivings that these two women were not made for each other. 'Portia!' He waved to get her attention. Then, since she seemed not to see him, he elbowed his way to the front of her stall, dragging Lizzie.

Portia looked at him vaguely, smiled. 'Hi, Bill. I didn't know you liked embroidered blouses. Or is Portobello on your beat?'

Bill was used to the short-term memory loss of those doing favours, even when they were as kind as Portia, so he continued as planned. 'Here's Lizzie. I'm sure she'll help out till you're ready for home. I've got to be on my way. She hasn't got her forty-six pounds from the prison yet, some mix-up, but I've given her twenty so she's all right for cash. Remind her to report to her probation officer later. Thanks.'

During this transaction, Lizzie seemed struck dumb and unmoving so Bill, much to his relief, was able to make a quick exit. He thought it best not to look round. It occurred to him that he seldom felt the satisfaction of doing good because he had never done quite enough before it became necessary to move on to the next needy soul. He sighed, then flinched as an elbow jabbed his arm, followed quickly by a *'Scusi, Padre.'* An Italian. Oh, yes. He was wearing his priestly collar in honour of the baptism. How lucky he was to be in the service of the Lord!

The two women looked at each other warily. Lizzie recovered first. Considering her slight figure, she fought her way round to the back of the stall with remarkable ease. 'Nice stuff you've got. I can show them off for you a bit.' She seemed filled with energy and enthusiasm. 'And watch for those thieving fingers.' Clearly she had been on a market stall before. 'My nan says you should always work in pairs.'

'She had a stall, did she?' Valiantly, Portia swept aside the gauzy veils of love and peered at the pale, pin-thin apparition that Bill had swept upon her.

'Forty years. They gave a party when she stopped. My mum never had the flair. I could have done it, but she sold it on.' As Lizzie spoke, she shook out a shawl and displayed it on hooks behind the stall that Portia had never noticed before.

'I'm afraid it'll be a long day for you,' said Portia, weakly.

'If you like one,' said Lizzie, to a customer with a blouse in her hands, 'you should take three. At this price they're a giveaway.'

In the glowing morning Portia had already been selling more than usual, but with Lizzie at her side, the stock disappeared at a remarkable speed.

In a slight break, Lizzie turned to Portia with her face wrinkled in serious-advice mode. 'You're selling way too cheap. You know that.'

'They're not at all well made.' Portia was surprised to find herself defensive.

'That's not the point, is it? They attract, don't they. People don't expect good finishing at a market. Besides, they'll be home before they notice, won't they?'

'Yes,' agreed Portia, while noting Lizzie's habit of ending every definitive statement with an automatic and meaningless question.

She was amazed by this invasion of her love fest and by the confidence of one who, in family lore, was beyond hopeless.

'I'll tell you what, you get a coffee. You've been here from crack of dawn, haven't you? I can manage for half an hour, can't I?'

For a wild moment Portia considered whether this strange new sister-in-law would pinch the stock and run the moment her back was turned. After all, she was only just out of prison. Perhaps she had an accomplice round the corner.

Lizzie seemed to catch something in her face. 'You see, where I've been, and before if it comes to that, I never was useful. Well, not in ways I'd want to shout about, so if you'd let me . . .' Her voice trailed away.

Now Portia saw the face of the woman she'd been told about: abjectly humble, desolate, huge eyes on the edge of tears. 'It's so nice of you,' she said quickly. 'I'm dying for a coffee, actually. I'll bring you one too.'

As she made her way through the crowds Portia turned back and was struck by Lizzie's waif-like presence. Yet there she was, gamely managing the stall. It was a piece of luck, thought Portia, generously, that the market drew on her area of expertise.

There was a queue at the coffee stall and while she waited the world did a swing, the way it sometimes does, and she saw how narrow her own experience of life was. Her links with poor Mexican women and her Portobello venture were merely games. She was a product of her family, tethered to their success. Even her love object, darling Conor, had been born with invincible security. Charlie, it was true, escaped periodically into the void of madness where he resided now. But he returned. He would return.

How different was Lizzie's experience of life! A line from *Antony and Cleopatra* came into Portia's head, about Octavia, the pawn in the Roman game of marriage, 'a swansdown feather on the swell of tide' or something like.

A feather was fragile, right, but it didn't sink and it could even make its own way down the therms, travelling the sky with the panache of an astronaut. She began to see why Charlie had thrown his grapple at Lizzie. Maybe it was not only in order to save her.

'You want something?' It was the bored but aggressive face of the girl behind the counter.

'Two *latte*s, please.' Lizzie had sunk near the bottom. Charlie had found her there. He was attracted by the world she inhabited. He'd once told Portia that prostitutes 'didn't mess about'. They hadn't the time or the energy: they just wanted the sex bit over so they could have a line and chill out somewhere nicer. They weren't a burden.

She hadn't really believed him. He'd been on his way to a manic episode when he'd told her. Then he'd married Lizzie and she hadn't believed that either. Now here she was, carrying a carton of coffee, and there Lizzie was, chatting up Brian, his wife and daughter. Even at this distance Portia could see that her thin cheeks were flushed with success.

'Hi, Lizzie!'

As the day progressed Portia watched Lizzie gradually wilt. She refused a sandwich and sat hunched on a chair, reducing her size to that of a ten-year-old. When Portia commented and even suggested shutting up shop early, she told her to go away and leave her alone. Then she put her head in her hands.

Brian, whose wife and child had now left, raised his eyes to Portia. A little later he whispered, 'Where did you find her, then?'

'My brother brought her, didn't he?' replied Portia, rather tartly – and noticed that she had caught the habit of Lizzie's rhetorical questions.

'You and your brothers.' Brian nodded wisely while staring into her face.

She decided that his very blue eyes were created by contact lenses. She recalled Conor's heavy-lidded brown eyes. Like a Giotto saint. 'She just lacks stamina. I've done so well, I can afford to head off soon.'

'With her?' His voice was disparaging, contradicting his previous chumminess.

'Why not with her?' Had Lizzie told him of her most recent domicile? Unlikely. It was probably something in the air around her.

'I'm getting us two more coffees,' she said to Lizzie, speaking loudly as if to a dimwit or a child.

Lizzie shifted her narrow shoulders a little but didn't look up.

'Don't worry.' Brian smiled knowingly. 'I'll tend the stall.'

Surprisingly, the crowds of the morning hadn't built up in the afternoon. Portia came out of her building and looked up at a drizzly grey sky. In the beginning she'd rented a stall on the road so this was her first year under cover. On the whole she liked the greater security and the warmth, yet she missed the special atmosphere of the street, the shouts of the stall-holders, the continual flow of people from all over the globe, many with children, some with dogs, one with a monkey, some dressed, even on this grim March day, in glittering tops, feathered scarves, embroidered hats or patchwork coats.

'Isn't that your phone, lovey?'

It was. Of course it would be Conor.

'Hi, darling.'

'Porsh? God, you're hard to track down.'

She'd never been disappointed before when Leo had rung. 'I guess you want your suit. And we've got your phone too.'

'I'm calling from Charlie's disgusting flat. Bill says you've got Lizzie with you. I need to speak to her. Remind me of your address?'

Portia pictured the collapsed figure behind the stall. 'I don't think that's a very good—'

'It's important.'

'We won't be back for a bit.'

'Back?' Apparently, he'd expected her to be in her flat all day.

'Didn't Bill tell you we're in Portobello?'

'So he did.' There was the sound of a heaving sigh.

'Are you all right?'

'Just tell me where your stall is.'

Portia obliged.

CHAPTER TWENTY-SEVEN

The Tower of Babel

Roland had woken with a hangover and the realisation he'd called Maggie after drinking a bottle of wine and talked garbled nonsense. The bottle and the conversation had followed a call from Didi, who was not even supposed to know his telephone number, and a news item on 'The Barr Allegations'. It was a small consolation that Leo had dropped the 'Norrington' out of their originally compound surname while Roland had retained it. The BBC political correspondent had said that either Leo Barr or the home secretary would lose his job and there were no bets on the former.

Serve him right, thought Roland, viciously, as he shook out two paracetamols. Then he relented. Although a pain in the neck, Leo had always been a reliable constituency MP who could have risen higher if he'd played his cards right. He'd never shown signs of an insane death-wish.

The telephone rang as Roland was reluctantly raising the blinds on a murky day. It was the nursing-home with their daily report on Imogen, as agreed. He was aware of his heart beating irregularly. While he had been making a fool of himself, she might have been dying. He sometimes questioned why he loved his mother so much when he was well aware that what little love she allowed to escape from herself went in Charlie's direction. Yet there it was. He loved her more than anyone, more than Maggie, who represented the good side of himself and, of course, on a quite different scale from his feelings for Didi, who represented – well, whatever he represented.

'Her ladyship is struggling, Mr Norrington Barr,' the matron said. 'The night nurse was on the point of calling the family.'

'And why didn't she?'

'Lady Shillingstone rallied, sir.'

The woman sounded miffed, as if he were doubting the competence of her staff. He would have liked to be summoned. He would have sat holding Imogen's fragile hand in the darkness. Just the two of them. Instead, he'd been with Didi.

'Call me any time. *Any* time,' he emphasised. He must be there when she died. Perhaps she would give him a final benediction, which he had to admit was unlikely, or perhaps they would be in unspoken communion. The eldest should sit at the deathbed of his mother. The idea soothed him as he dressed, ate breakfast and set off for work.

Proportionality was a good system for self-governance, and a mother's imminent passing put everything else in its proper place. Who knows. Perhaps Didi would sink quietly from his life.

Things were not so calmly proportionate at his chambers. Mike, his clerk, unusually for him, was throwing a minor wobbly. 'He keeps ringing,' he said, without preamble. 'We expected the newspapers to be a nuisance, sir, what with this Barr versus home secretary business. We just give them the silly buggers treatment. If you know what I mean, sir. No holds barred. But this man.' Mike rolled his eyes theatrically.

'What man?' Roland set his face in stern lines. Flaky he was not. At least, not in his chambers. Mike's pugnacious expression now was similar to the one he assumed when bartering over the telephone for a better deal for one of his barristers.

'He said he was an old friend of yours. First name Smith, second name Dunbar.'

'Shit,' said Roland.

'Exactly my impression, sir.'

'Thanks anyway.' Roland went into the office and closed the door. Smith Dunbar was a South African who'd attended his public school before being thrown out in his final year and returning home. Roland might have been sacked, too, but his father, then at the height of his fame as a judge, had intervened. A few years ago, someone had mentioned his name in connection with the *Cape Times*. Roland had been glad he was still in South Africa.

The pile of folders still sat on the desk where he'd left them. Most evenings he would have taken them home, got ahead a bit before the weekend. On Monday he was the prosecuting counsel in the case against a woman who had killed her husband. She was pleading self-defence, following physical abuse over many years. This would have been more convincing if she hadn't weighed twice as much as her extremely puny husband. The only problem was that, since the attack, she had been held on bail, now for over nine months, and had lost eight stone, making her a normal sort of woman shape. They would have to rely on photographs, of which there were suspiciously few. The other problem was that she was a police officer.

It would be a high-emotion case – Roland had built up a reputation for dealing coolly with such difficult situations. And now Smith Dunbar. What did he want?

Deciding on action rather than passivity, Roland walked out to the clerks' room to find Mike, and Dunbar's telephone number.

Leo felt like a wanted man. His face had been in too many papers, often on the front page. Only dramatic news elsewhere would wipe it off. The story he'd chosen to uncover had probably already claimed one innocent victim: the-wrong-place-at-the-wrong-time Horace Silver. For once Charlie had it best, lying peacefully in his drug-induced coma. Griff should never have told him the name if he hadn't wanted Leo to get involved, although it was Bob who had pushed him into taking unilateral action. He was on his way to meet Lizzie – for the first time, as it happened. He supposed it was a bit of luck she was out of prison.

'Your ticket's not valid, sir.'

A loud male voice spoke in his ear; he'd been pushing at the ticket barrier as if it would let him through. He hadn't even bought a ticket. He should have driven but he'd wanted a drink when he arrived. MPs don't drink and drive. Funny how he still thought of himself as an ordinary MP, obeying the usual rules.

There was no doubt that sleeping in Charlie's polluted flat and wearing Conor's too-tight suit hadn't helped his mental state. On a brief visit to the Commons to pick up his post (which he'd then abandoned to Denver's mercies), he'd noticed his hands were shaking as MPs and lobby correspondents competed to get his story. He should have stayed in Portcullis House. Even those he counted as friends seemed more salacious than supportive. He supposed it was the ordinary human pleasure in watching someone go through the mill. The only thing they all admired was his 'daring'. He was a bachelor, of course, not ticking the 'responsible' box that marriage conferred. He'd remained cool, repeating, 'Nothing to add at the moment.' At least the press attributed the absence of the home secretary to funk based on guilt. He'd never thought he'd line up with *them*.

Leo left the tube at Notting Hill Gate and started the walk to Portobello. Although it was after four and drizzling, a procession of visitors, almost entirely foreign, was still heading that way. He wondered at their confidence, attacking an unknown city with their Tower of Babel voices. It was cover for him, however, a moving world where no one would identify the eye of a merely British political storm.

He began to watch for numbers, knowing Portia's stall was inside a building. He'd never seen her at work and the thought amused him – little Porsh among this hubbub, pursuing her charitable goals. Not very seriously, he considered whether she was the best of the lot of them – the family, that is.

'Hi, Leo!' There she was, standing on the street, waving, her red and blue shawl flourishing. He felt a surge of affection and went forward quickly to give her a hug.

'I wanted to catch you,' she began at once. 'I really don't think you can pursue Lizzie. She's hardly functional. She began like the clappers, energetic, efficient, and then she collapsed.'

Leo drew Portia to a slightly less noisy and crowded corner. He didn't want irritation to take over from affection. 'Look, Porsh, I wouldn't do it if it wasn't important – very important. You've got to trust me.'

'Is it to do with this home secretary business?'

'Yes.'

'And it all leads back to Charlie?'

'Yes.'

'Oh, I wish life was simple!' She raised her arms so that her shawl spread like a pennant.

'But it's not. All I need from her is a contact. I know she knows.'

She went, then, and brought out Lizzie.

Despite Portia's warnings, Leo was shocked by Lizzie's

appearance. Her legs, in black jeans, were the size of normal arms and the expression on her drawn face reminded him of children he'd once seen on a parliamentary trip to a Yugoslavian war zone. Like them, she immediately asked for a fag. Her voice was husky. As they walked to find a shop where he could buy some, he was surprised by the obedient way she followed him, without any show of curiosity. He decided it must be behaviour learned in Holloway; he didn't much like being cast in the role of prison officer.

'Here.' He handed her the cigarettes and she lit up the moment she reached the street.

'Stupid to try and give up.' She gave him a first swift, assessing glance, then returned to concentrating on deep drags.

Her fingers with their bitten nails were trembling. Leo wondered if she was still in detox but he thought she'd been in prison long enough to get over that. 'Shall we go in here?' He indicated a coffee bar. 'Then we can talk.'

'About Charlie?'

'What?' She'd mumbled, but now he understood. So she thought he'd come to tell her about Charlie. Well, his story was in there somewhere.

He followed her and they found a table. She ordered the sort of pastry a fat girl dreams about and a *latte*. The café was busy but again with foreign tourists who were unlikely to know who he was. Now that he was faced with the reality of Lizzie, the conversation he'd planned didn't seem quite so straightforward. He'd seen some pretty desperate people in his MP surgeries, a handful out of prison, but none had seemed quite so vulnerable. Besides, he'd had a couple of 'good' women (Eloise included) to support him then, to mouth the anodyne phrases that seemed appropriate in the sort of cases where nothing would actually help.

'Is that all right?'

'Yup.'

She wasn't eating the pastry, just pushing it round her plate – as an excuse to keep her head down, he thought. Perhaps it was best to start by mentioning Charlie. Leo reminded himself that he'd never been a bully and disliked upsetting women. Why else had he stayed so long with Suzanne?

'How is he, then?' She'd started it off.

'He's had a relapse, I'm afraid. Under heavy sedation. Back in hospital.'

'Back?' Just a mutter.

So she didn't know he'd been out. Wanted by the police and who knows who else? 'Had you known him long?' That was a good, leading question. But she didn't seem to hear it.

'When they told me he was dead I thought I'd die.'

Leo saw she meant it. Why did Charlie think he could play about with lives like hers? Why couldn't he behave like the rest of society who left it to the professionals? Vaguely, Leo pictured a cohort of strong, sensible women who had something of Maggie's rosy healthiness, if not her beauty. Then he saw that Charlie had drawn him in, too, taking him across to the other side.

'You mustn't talk like that,' he said, more sternly than he meant. 'Neither must you rely on Charlie. Charlie has his own agenda.'

'I *love* Charlie!'

It was the first time she'd spoken up and it startled Leo. Why did people place so much emphasis on love? He'd managed to do without it. 'Yes. Of course.' He took a breath. 'I need to ask you some questions.'

Her head went down again. Leo reminded himself that he was dealing with a major issue here: corruption at the heart of government. The phrase sounded hollow in the face of Lizzie's obvious suffering. Weren't all governments corrupt to some extent? People hardly bothered to disguise cronyism and nepotism, although they gave them the more modern-sounding name of 'networking'. The home secretary was within his rights to pick the chief of the Met. How could blackmail ever be proved? On the other hand, maybe it could be proved that he had had sex with illegal immigrants. Everyone knew he was a sleazy bugger.

Leo stiffened his sinews. Perhaps it wasn't an accident that Griff had told him the name. 'I'm trying to track down a girl called Ileana.'

'Don't know her.' Lizzie's answer was unconvincingly speedy.

'I'm not going to hurt her.' Strictly, that wasn't true. Uncovering Ileana, producing her for even a limited audience, might be devastating for the girl in many different ways. The Higher Good, he told himself, adding, as if for greater reassurance, 'I'm serving my country.'

'What?' mumbled Lizzie. She'd now given up all pretence of

eating or drinking and wore the rat-in-a-trap look of a guilty pupil who daren't ask the headmaster for permission to escape.

'I want to help Ileana,' said Leo, going for broke.

Lizzie said nothing. Curiously, her face was not reactive – perhaps because of its heavy layer of anxiety. All news was equally bad news.

'Do you know how to get hold of her? It's important.'

'Don't know who you mean.'

Leo sat back. 'Where are you staying tonight?'

She shifted in her chair anxiously. 'With your sister. Charlie's sister.' A bit of life and colour came back into her face.

'Good. Maybe I'll pop in.'

Her head dropped again. At last a useful thought struck him. 'I'm staying in Charlie's flat. Just temporarily.'

'Charlie's.' She put her hand to her mouth.

'I expect you know it.'

'A bit.' She was already sensing a trap.

'I'll tell you what. We'll talk more about it – whether you want to go there, whatever – when I come by tonight.'

'Oh,' said Lizzie. Not an outright denial, although Leo suspected that she'd never been in a position to issue one. 'You know Charlie got me a place.'

'What?' Why did she have to mutter unintelligibly?

Behind him, footsteps approached. Portia stood at his elbow. 'Hey, you two.' She stared at Lizzie, then at the cigarette packet on the table. 'I didn't know you smoked.'

'Can't in here, can I?'

Portia's expression reminded Leo that she had a thing about smoking – and smokers. 'I'm pushing off.' He stood up. Kissed his sister. Looked at Lizzie. 'Might see you later.'

'You're still wearing Conor's suit!'

Leo saw his second chance. 'That's why I'm coming round later. With any luck I'll be able to get into my flat and pick up my own clothes by then.'

'Do you want a meal?'

With Charlie's squalor and the public nature of a restaurant as the alternatives? 'Great. I'd like that.'

'Around eight. Now, Lizzie, time to clear up and head for home.'

'Home?' queried Lizzie, as if it was a foreign word.

*

Lizzie curled on the sofabed, pretending she was asleep. She'd smoked so many fags that her throat felt rough and sore. It was a relief, though, in a way to be back to being herself. Cigarettes would be the last thing to kill her. She'd only given them up because a screw during an open day in the gym had chatted her up. She'd been pretty too, shiny dark hair, healthy-looking. She'd had this huge plastic dummy cigarette, twice her height, she could hardly control it, and she'd said she wanted just one recruit to the no-smoking brigade to make her day. So Lizzie made her day.

Turned out she was full of shit. She saw Lizzie a week or so later and started joking about it, said she'd been roped in at the last minute because someone had dropped out – 'Probably got lung cancer.' She joked. 'Of course we all smoke; she was laughing fit to burst. Can't do without our ciggies, can we?'

And Lizzie had felt a real polehead because she'd believed her and given up. With so much detox going on it hadn't been so hard, not really, with all the drugs they gave her. Then she'd got obstinate, done it to show that woman she was doing it for herself.

But today had been a step too far. Lizzie rolled over, but did it quietly. Portia was next door, wasn't she, although that boyfriend of hers hadn't stopped – 'Thank Old Cloven Feet', as her mother used to say. But she didn't want to think about her, among all the other things she didn't want to think about. Not going to Probation, for example. Ileana.

Too much had happened today, that was the trouble. Like a week's worth. Like coming out of that door – big enough for a tank – and seeing Father Bill standing there. Wet through and stinking a bit in the café, like men who don't look after themselves too well. But he'd been there, that was the thing. The good thing. And her too shocked to say, 'Ta', or even 'Thank you, Father.'

Then the market. For a couple of hours she'd been filled with all the go in the world, like the best days when she was eight or nine, before what went on went on. She used to love that market, skipped school to get behind the stall. Well, it was an education, wasn't it? She'd surprised that Portia until she'd crashed. Portia was all right.

Then he came, Charlie's brother, like him too, though not so fair and no blue eyes and not the thing that made Charlie Charlie . . .

Lizzie rolled over yet again and thought about lighting a cigarette, even though Portia had asked her not to.

Perhaps it was these weird hangings everywhere that made Portia against fags. Leo and her boyfriend didn't smoke either. Conor. He was all right too. Irish. Looked at her directly, like she existed.

Leo didn't do that, not even when he'd said about Charlie. She embarrassed him, probably. Funny sister-in-law. On the game. In prison. All he wanted was Ileana. When he went off again, he said, 'Write her address down, if you like. Give it to Portia.' Why did he say that? Why would that be different? He was in a state himself.

That Conor had said, 'Shall we see if you're on television tonight, Leo, wearing my suit?'

And Leo had got pissed off, although he'd tried to cover it. 'I'm here to avoid television and suchlike,' he'd said, or something pompous.

So Conor said, 'Sorry. I know it's serious. I'm on your side.' They hadn't watched TV.

At one point Leo got out his mobile. Then he said there were far too many messages on it and put it away without listening to any of them. Of course, Charlie didn't even carry a mobile so perhaps it ran in the family. Not many now didn't have mobiles. Even inside some of the girls had them – illegally, of course. But why should the screws care?

It was after the mobile came out and went back in again that Leo took her aside and asked her about Ileana again. 'It's important,' he said, like he'd said before. And she felt like saying, 'Important to who?' She didn't because she was scared of him. He gave her his home number. 'That's privilege,' he'd said, smiling like a crocodile. She was never scared of Charlie. Ileana had a mobile. Clung to it like life itself.

With sudden determination, Lizzie swung both legs off the sofabed. She'd have a fag in the bathroom, flush it down the toilet. What did she have to lose anyway? Portia would throw her out soon enough. She didn't even much want to stay. It wasn't as if she was doing anything illegal.

Stealthily, Lizzie reached for her bag and started to creep towards the door. Two months of sharing a cell had taught her how to move quietly in the dark. Halfway across the room, she caught the gleam of the telephone standing in its bracket. Not surprising she could remember Ileana's number when they'd been so close. She'd told Charlie that, hadn't she.

CHAPTER TWENTY-EIGHT

Murky Waters

Charlie and Imogen swam through murky waters at almost the same pace, although they didn't know it. For a second, Charlie seemed about to surface, but even his bull-like strength wasn't equal to the drugs pumped into him. His mother, on the other hand, sank lower, one circuit nearer to Davey Jones's locker.

'Land to starboard!' shouted Esmond. It was always best to note important information for yourself.

Maggie's eyes blinked open in the darkness. She guessed it was three or four in the morning but she knew she wouldn't sleep again. She put out her hand and felt Roland's naked shoulder. He had come back late last night – he always came back on Fridays – in one of his wretched moods. She hated it when he was wretched because it was such an effort to give him the love and understanding he deserved. She didn't love him enough and she didn't understand him at all.

The big house was quiet. The two boys, on the edge of puberty, had already entered that sleep-hungry zone, which if uninterrupted could last till midday. Esmond scarcely knew the difference between night and day, but over the weekends a nurse had arrived to lighten Maggie's load and, she'd begun to suspect, had given him something to make sure he didn't disturb her beauty sleep. Actually, the nurse had no pretensions to beauty and Maggie knew she should do something about it. Too many drugs weakened the heart.

Roland slept quietly too. Very quietly for a man, no snoring or wheezing, no heavy limbs splayed against her. He was secret even in his sleep. She assumed his distress last night, obvious but undeclared, was partly about Imogen but also about Leo. Just as he disapproved of Charlie for what he termed attention-seeking behaviour, thus disallowing any excuse of justification arising from his illness, he disliked any family head appearing above the parapet. The success parapet, as she thought of it. Hetty had long ago given up confiding in him her youthful escapades, innocent though they were. Two years ago Hetty had slid off a roof after drinking too much beer and broken her ankle. She'd insisted that Maggie attribute her injury to a fall from her horse. Guiltily, Maggie had agreed.

Now she couldn't help Roland because she admired Leo and didn't want to listen to his brother's fury. If the boys hadn't been there, going on about their needs – technical equipment, expensive – they'd have eaten supper in silence. Afterwards Roland had gone quickly to his study without even making a token effort at helping her clear up. She had left him to it, left them all to it, and gone to bed early. Tomorrow Hetty was coming home for the Easter vac and on Sunday they had friends for lunch. She needed to catch up on some sleep.

But now, of course, she was awake. Although a large woman, Maggie was used to getting up in the night without waking others. She slipped out of the wide double bed and went downstairs. In the kitchen Mungo raised enough energy to thump his tail in his bed by the Aga. Sitting in her armchair, Maggie considered the night before when, first, Charlie had come, then Leo. It was no wonder that once her body had enjoyed a few hours' sleep it snapped back on duty. Generally she considered herself a practical woman, non-intellectual, but tonight there was so much to think about.

Above all, she wanted to telephone Leo, as she had the night before. Galvanised by this recognition of why she'd come downstairs, Maggie stood, lifted the heavy Aga cover and pushed on the kettle. Because she'd gone to bed early, it was not full, as she usually left it, and she felt momentary irritation, followed by a hollow sense of fear. Would everything fall apart if she took her eye off it? Maggie seldom thought about her parents as, she could safely assume, they seldom thought about her – one in Perth, the other in a graveyard in Essex – but now she recalled the break-up of their marriage, the day after her tenth birthday, when her mother had said they were leaving her father, leaving England and she was leaving school. The last had been the worst. She had been an only child.

Maggie sat in her armchair drinking a cup of tea and thinking of Leo. Their kiss, which earlier had induced such euphoria, now seemed ambiguous. Was it a statement of love, as she'd assumed in starstruck schoolgirl mode? Or was it merely the instinctive behaviour of an unencumbered man when faced with a partly clothed woman, not without her charms, at six in the morning? She needed to talk to him. Even the sound of his voice would give her the answer.

Telling herself that it was ridiculous to disturb a man with so much on his plate when she didn't have anything to say to him, Maggie moved nevertheless towards the telephone.

Halfway across the room, she stopped at a sound from the doorway. She turned and saw Roland standing there. He seemed only half awake. He'd put on a dressing-gown but not tied it so that it hung open round his naked body. She looked at him as if at a stranger, his lean, slightly stooping frame, with the dark hair on his chest and pubis, his strong, well-planted legs. He seemed for a moment like the last-stage ape before it turned into man.

'I was worried,' she said.

Without asking what she'd been worried about (which would have required a lie), he came and sat at the table.

'It's too much.' This was almost a revolutionary statement from Roland, who loathed and despised any imprecise complaint. He slapped his hand on the table. 'How can I work?'

'I'm sorry,' said Maggie, humbly. He slumped forward, head in hands. A sugar bowl was dangerously near but she didn't dare remove it. A sudden wave of hysteria made her stop a giggle with her hand. 'Shall I make you some tea?' She was so awake now that she could have cooked him a whole dinner, if he'd asked. Was it at all possible that he was talking about them, that she came into the equation of what was 'too much'? No, she decided quickly, he was talking about Imogen, Charlie, Leo.

'No. No, thank you,' he conceded.

He had raised his head and his sharp, greenish eyes were looking directly at her. He never looked directly at her. Her hysteria was replaced by foreboding. Had he been sacked? But he was too grand to be sacked. He'd run his chambers for five or six years now. He sacked other people. 'Oh dear,' said Maggie, wishing she'd never left the bed. She went over to the chair and curled into it.

'I wonder if there's something wrong with our family.'

Did he want a serious answer? It was unlikely. He had a powerful voice, deep and vibrating, like all the brothers. After her parents' divorce, she hadn't had any kind of family. The only one she knew about was the one she'd created here in this house. She'd even managed to include a grandfather, Esmond, although, given his state of mind, the post was purely honorary.

'You're all very different,' she said, not fully believing it but fairly sure it was something he'd like to hear. They shared a competitive intensity – even Father Bill. On one of the two occasions she'd met him, he'd looked Imogen in the eye and said, 'Faith lessens the burden of self.' She hadn't forgotten because it took a brave man to confront her mother-in-law.

'Are you happy with me, Maggie?'

Roland's words, although softly spoken, were perfectly audible. Maggie felt a weakening in her body, a cowardly terror, followed by a determination to say nothing she might regret. 'You're upset.' Even to state that was daring. 'Of course I'm happy.'

He sighed. She stared at him, transfixed. He was looking down again. He hadn't brushed up his hair and she noticed that his bald patch spread further than she'd imagined. Even his strong will couldn't control age and nature.

'We should go to bed,' she said.

'I'm afraid I should never have married you.'

'What? *What?*' All Maggie's own regrets at their marriage were lost in vehement denial. 'How can you *say* that – when so much has come from it? The children, the house, your work – they're all part of our marriage!' Maggie felt a wave of burning anguish rush through her body. *She* had created these things! It was for her to point out where the deficiencies lay. She had given him everything. Was he saying that everything wasn't enough?

Roland got up from the table and moved further from her. He was still reflective, unaware, it seemed, of her burning passion. He was now holding his dressing-gown tightly round him, outlining his angular hips and prominent buttocks.

Maggie looked down. She'd never really *loved* his body. Yet she had never refused him, would not now, if he asked. An intimation that this scene was about something other than children and houses and work slowly took hold of her. It fell like a chill over her hot body. She sensed that he was on the verge of telling her something she didn't want to hear. She didn't try to guess what it was. She just hoped he'd draw back. His reticence, which had so often saddened her, now seemed an important part of the stability of their life. And stability was happiness. Happiness for all of them, including him.

In her distress, Maggie didn't allow herself to consider the obvious misery of the man in front of her. Nor did her feelings for Leo enter her mind, except as a vague sense of something cut off and out of bounds. Instinctively, she fought for the status quo.

'You're very good, Maggie. A good, loving woman.'

To Maggie's ears, these words, pronounced in a low voice, had a valedictory tone, which terrified her even more. She wanted to cry, 'What do you mean!' but because she didn't want to know what he meant, she merely denied what he'd said, although he was right. She was 'a good, loving woman'.

'No, Roland. I'm your wife.'

'Yes. Yes.' He walked even further from her. His face was very pale.

'I wish you'd have some tea.'

'Yes. Yes,' he repeated.

She assumed he referred to the tea and got up to put the kettle on. He came back and sat once more at the table. His long fingers tapped the top. He held his head higher and Maggie saw that he'd made up his mind.

'I want you to know,' said Roland, and his voice had resumed its distant, lawyer carapace, 'that I have had an affair with a male prostitute.'

The words sang in the night, reached Maggie's ears slowly and her brain even more slowly. Normally, she might have repeated his words to help them sink in. But this was not normal. Instead she was thrown back to childhood, when the headmistress of her school had announced, 'I'm sorry to tell you that Miss Melbury-Bright passed away in the night,' and she, alone among the five hundred girls, had burst into hysterical laughter, so prolonged that eventually she'd been led in shame, laughing till she cried, from the hall.

'Oh, Roland.' After all, she wasn't going to laugh. The anguish in his face was too great. 'I'm so sorry. I didn't know . . .' She stopped.

This was foolish. Of course she hadn't known. Her head flooded with questions. Did he expect her to be angry? What did his expectations matter? Was he telling her he was gay? That their marriage was a fake? Over? Who was the male prostitute? Did anyone else know? Why was he telling her now? 'How long has it been going on?' she asked.

'A few months.'

His pale face with its anguish tried to look calmly at her but she could see at once that he was lying. The 'it' that she'd asked about was undefined, as was 'a few months'. 'Why are you telling me?' she asked, a better question. Her earlier terror had left her now. She'd always been good in emergencies. She remembered that on Hetty's third birthday her face had swollen like a football, the skin shiny and taut, she could hardly take a breath, and when the ambulance didn't arrive, Maggie had driven her to hospital, crossing red lights, exceeding speed limits, and got her there just in time for the doctors to save her life. It had been a wasp sting in her mouth.

'I wanted you to know.' She saw he'd begun to shake all over, not just his bony fingers laid on the table as if he were about to play the piano but his whole body. When they made love, he showed less emotion. So, was he handing to her his inner self, a craven being? Did he want a mother? She thought of Imogen, apparently dying. Was he looking for a substitute? Imogen had never been the tender, caring sort. Nor did she have much time for homosexuals. Although many of her friends and admirers had been gay, men in the theatre, writers, designers, that had never curtailed her scathing diatribes against what she described as 'men without balls'. She'd always had a foul mouth. She wouldn't have enjoyed a gay son.

'Is it over?' There was the 'it' again.

'Oh, yes.'

Maggie noticed the air had become cloudy, as if conjured up by swirling emotions.

'The kettle's boiling,' said Roland. He must have been staring at the steam for some time. She'd make him tea. Perhaps he'd explain more. Did she want him to explain more? Probably he wanted her to hold him but she couldn't do that. A male prostitute! Suddenly she felt revolted. Images of their coupling made her feel sick. He was the father of her children. How could he use his body in such a way?

She rammed the teacup on to the table so that hot brown liquid rolled towards his fingers. 'You're disgusting! Corrupt!'

He said nothing.

'I don't want you here! Go away! Go back to your flat in London. I don't want you in my house near my children. Everything is over. You've chosen. You make me feel sick!' And, in fact, she went to the sink and was sick, pouring out the contents of her stomach in a flow of misery. She found a cloth, wiped her mouth and turned back to Roland. 'I don't want you near me ever again.' She stood over him, holding the dishcloth like a weapon.

'I understand.' His frozen face nodded on his trembling shoulders.

Maggie wanted to attack him but her passion and the vomiting had weakened her. She also was shaking, and very cold. She went back to the armchair, curled her legs under her and shut her eyes. She needed to gain some strength.

The room became quiet.

At five o'clock the electric clock moved forward with a little click. Roland looked up, dazed. He couldn't believe he had told anyone, let alone Maggie, about Didi. His tragic sense of mounting disaster had begun to cool. The physicality of Maggie's response, her vomiting and withdrawal, her utter disgust were not what he would have expected. Would she have responded in the same way if he had confessed to an affair with a female prostitute?

She was massed now, in an amoebic way, in that armchair she always sat in. He thought about the hard beauty of men, the straight legs, square shoulders and muscled buttocks. He pictured Didi in what he trusted was the spirit of nostalgia. It would not suit him to be openly gay. It would not suit him to abandon his marriage. He had told Maggie in order to shut the door to that other self. He supposed he'd expected her to forgive and enfold him in her ever-ready maternal embrace. Why was she so angry? After all, nothing had changed, except that he had been honest. Surely she must have guessed something. Or had she been so bound up in household affairs? A sense of injury was joining Roland's cooling emotions. He had a big case on Monday. It was five in the morning, admittedly on a Saturday but he couldn't afford to be exhausted at any time. Didn't she understand the huge pressures of his work? The strain of standing up in court? What had he done but cracked a little, shown a little human weakness? And now he'd confessed and asked for forgiveness. Implicitly, anyway. Why did she sit there with her eyes closed, like some great lump of suffering? Well, he was the one who was making the sacrifices.

'Maggie.'

Her eyes opened slowly as if she'd been aroused from a deep sleep. He wondered whether she would speak to him without shouting. It was extraordinary. She had ordered him from his own home, the home of his father.

'Maggie. I'm sorry.' He was sorry. But not abject.

She stared at him with a more knowing look in her eyes. 'You want it to be forgotten, do you?'

Of course that was what he wanted. It was in both their interests. 'I know it's very difficult. A shock.'

'Yes. Shocking,' said Maggie. She put her feet on the floor. 'We'd better go upstairs. Get some sleep. You can go in the blue spare room. I think the bed's made up.' She stood up, started for the door, then turned. 'I hope you've been truthful with me.' She left the room.

Roland was stunned. Maggie had never spoken to him like that before. No one had – except in court where he was highly paid to withstand the brickbats of opposing counsel. Furthermore, he'd given up the idea of objective truthfulness by the age of ten. Imogen used to say, 'Lies are the nearest we have to truth, darling.' Doubtless she'd still say it, if she were capable of speech.

It was essential not to think of Imogen since it was the idea of her death, on top of all the other worries, that had kicked off his ridiculous panic. Already he was regretting his confession to Maggie. He also felt extremely hungry. Breakfast, such as had been provided after balls he'd attended in his late teens and early twenties, seemed the answer: eggs, bacon, sausages, tomatoes, mushrooms, fried bread.

Roland crossed the room and headed for the pantry. In passing, he noticed there was light outside the windows, a thick whiteness as if the house was surrounded by fog.

CHAPTER TWENTY-NINE

Maybe, Maybe Not

Leo had managed to get back into his flat where the joy of a clean, comfortable bed, coupled with exhaustion, had sent him into a profound sleep. Eventually the telephone woke him. He answered it in darkness. 'Yes?'

The voice at the other end of the line was muffled, the syllables hardly English.

He sat up and turned on the light. 'Is that Ileana?'

'Is Ileana. But I not. I sorry. Maybe. Maybe tomorrow. Maybe next day.'

'I would very much like to meet you, Ileana. My brother, Charlie . . .'

'Charlie good.'

Was it a statement or a question? Leo didn't know. 'Charlie's in hospital but he told me about you,' which wasn't quite the truth but near enough. 'I need your help.'

'Is difficult.'

'I understand. Tomorrow. Could we meet tomorrow?'

'Maybe. I call. You have mobile?'

Leo gave his number, reminding himself that he must clear off all the messages received over the last few days. 'Goodbye, Ileana. I'll await your call.'

'Maybe. Maybe not.'

'Please, maybe.'

Surprisingly, after this call, Leo fell once more into a heavy sleep, waking only at eight o'clock when Bob rang him. 'Any news?'

'I got a night's sleep,' said Leo.

'Let's not be facetious. The House may well decide to ban you for anything up to six weeks. How do you think this plays with your constituents?'

'The non-facetious answer is maybe,' said Leo, sitting up. He pressed on the radio. 'I can't tell you more than that now. I'll keep in touch.' He put down the phone. He'd missed the Radio 4 news headlines but something told him he hadn't been on them. Unless the story moved forward, he would be viewed as one of those MPs who went a little crazy, got bees in their bonnets. Even in his time, he could think of half a dozen. Sometimes they were sacked, sometimes they resigned, sometimes they stood as independents, sometimes they joined lucrative companies, which, it turned out, had been on the cards from the beginning. The causes they'd espoused or their criticisms were soon overlaid by the present imperative and forgotten.

But the story would move on. Griff was on the job and now he'd got a line out to Ileana. And when Charlie was better, there'd be more information. Charlie was the one with the contacts.

Languidly Leo rose, on the way to a cup of coffee and a stronger start to the day. Behind him, he heard the voice of the radio presenter quicken and deepen, the tone of someone about to announce bad news. He stopped to listen.

'A report is coming in of two ships colliding in the Channel. Their names have not been released but one appears to have been a tanker and the other a hydrofoil ferry heading for Felixstowe. There was thick fog at the time. The ferry is reported sunk and fatalities are expected. We will bring you more information as it comes in.'

Leo walked to the window. The buildings on the other side of the road were partially obscured by a cotton-wool whiteness. It looked innocuous, and was probably the reason he'd slept so late. Fog muffles sound. In cities, benignly. Out at sea, fog is one of the enemies for safe voyaging. He remembered a Channel crossing he'd once made, fog and the news that a Yugoslavian fishing-boat had been sunk. His ship had changed course. Later, bodies had been brought on board.

What had the newsreader said? 'Fatalities are expected.' This could well be the tragedy to kick his political drama out of the headlines. It felt as if he was playing a game, thinking like that, but more and more he was tempted to believe that politics *was* some kind of game. If one home secretary fell from grace, another would appear to replace him, no better or worse. More than likely, the first would pop up in another guise and the merry-go-round would whirl on.

For these minutes, while Leo showered, dressed and, finally, made his coffee, he regretted making contact with Ileana. Griff had never supposed it was his job. Bob had pushed him into it. If she rang, he would have to start the difficult process of assessing her experiences. Soon lawyers would become involved. A moral failing would become a *cause célèbre*, a court case in which there would be winners and losers. Another kind of game and almost certainly a far bigger one than he knew about. He pictured the corpse in Charlie's hospital, the bloated face in which he'd searched for Charlie's features. The name escaped him – a musician's name – but he would never forget the face. Did the police still suspect Charlie? Somehow he didn't think so.

Sitting in his clean, orderly kitchen, eating stale cereal because he'd not yet been shopping, dread grew until he put down his spoon and stood up in the hope of breaking the spell. Although he'd not been listening to it, he'd left the radio on in the bedroom. He walked through.

The mobile was on the chest of drawers, and the moment he picked it up he was informed that there was no room for further messages. He imagined the calls from Bob, Denver, his constituents, journalists, Downing Street lackeys, fellow MPs. Methodically, he began to delete them one by one. Occasionally a few words not banished quickly enough told him that he'd been right about his callers. He didn't remember giving out his mobile number to so many people.

He'd reached the last few calls when the ten o'clock news began. The collision in the Channel was still reported as serious but 'the concerted reaction by French and UK emergency services was expected to keep loss of life to a minimum'.

A *minimum*. How many was a minimum? Leo sat down on a chair by the window. The foggy whiteness was clearing. Once more he could see the grandiose stone building opposite. He still held his mobile. Absently he pressed a button and heard a voice, heavily accented, 'Mr Leo, I try you again. No good. This Ileana.'

She had rung so early! Six o'clock. He'd never predicted this. The dread returned as he tried the next two messages but both had come in since nine, one from Bob, neither from her.

In the background the newsreader finally stopped making uninformed noises about the tragedy in the Channel by promising further bulletins. He moved to other items. As in a nightmare Leo heard, 'The body of a female prostitute, probably of East European origin, has been found this morning outside St Pancras Church in Northwest London. She had been severely mutilated but her identity is believed to be known to the police, although they are not yet giving it out.'

Leo rang Portia. When there was no answer, he remembered it was Saturday, obviously a big day at Portobello. He rang again. A hammer had started pounding at his right temple. This time the phone went directly to answering-machine. He left an urgent plea, more a command, for her to call him. But would Lizzie be with her? Maybe it was worth going round to the flat. Most likely she knew nothing anyway.

He rubbed his forehead, too late forgetting his bruised eye. Why was he so sure this murdered prostitute was Ileana? Answer: because he felt guilty. He pictured once more the face of the hanged man, whose name he now recalled: Horace Silver.

He guessed Ileana would have his telephone number on her. He could expect a call from the police – his friends the police. Unless her murderers had taken it from her. Dread and guilt were joined by a shaming fear for his own safety. Discounting this quickly, Leo stood up. Most of all he needed what was probably impossible: to speak to Charlie.

CHAPTER THIRTY

Purple Days

Portia didn't want to leave Lizzie alone in the flat. For one thing she might burn it down. Despite Portia's attempts to ban smoking, Lizzie was never now without a cigarette in her mouth.

'Why don't you come with me? Just for the company. You don't have to help.' It was seven o'clock. She was late already. Lizzie looked dreadful, ashen with huge dark circles, as if she hadn't slept. Perhaps she hadn't. Portia had certainly heard her wandering about in what was probably the middle of the night.

Portia herself felt disgustingly well. Conor had already rung, as he lay in bed, telling her she was his princess and how about a bit of telephone sex. Mindful of Lizzie's proximity, she'd declined the offer so he'd said she must take a lunch break and he'd rent a hotel room. He was joking, but the idea made her blush and laugh.

Through the veil of her own happiness, Lizzie's miserable situation didn't elicit as much sympathy as she knew it should. Portia handed over money to pay for a minicab to take her to see her probation officer – better late than never, she assumed – and suggested a visit to Charlie's flat that evening.

Only this got any kind of response. 'We can, can we?'

'Yes,' said Portia, firmly, sounding to her own ears like a schoolmistress to a child. 'We can. I'll be back about seven thirty.' A slight feeling of virtuousness prevailed as she considered how tired she'd be and how little in the mood for Charlie's flat. She must also fit in a visit to her mother.

'Thanks,' said Lizzie, following her to the door. 'I won't let you down.'

Portia wondered how she could do this. Inviting druggies to her flat? Or friends on the game? 'Just get some rest,' she said, 'and don't miss going to your probation officer.'

'Oh, no.' Lizzie's woeful eyes promised. She cupped a cigarette in her hand. She hadn't had any breakfast.

Once Portia was outside, walking briskly through a white mist to the underground, a sense of release increased her happiness. The contrast between her life and Lizzie's was so great it was like harbouring an alien. Yet she was used to thinking of herself as an outsider.

Lizzie sat on the edge of the unmade sofabed. She felt exhausted and further dispirited by her inability to go with Portia to the stall and do something she was good at. She had allowed the probation appointment to become an excuse when she knew perfectly well the office wasn't open on Saturdays. She might ring and leave a message. Shirley, her probation officer over many years, was all right but too busy to listen or understand. She'd go on Monday, to collect her money and to avoid going back to prison. Some of the girls didn't try. Straight back on their drug of choice and recalled in days.

She wasn't like that. She had Charlie. Lizzie tried to cheer herself, find a bit of energy to wash her hair, eat a bite of something. Tonight she'd go to Charlie's flat. Soon he'd be out of hospital.

Lizzie stood, walked a few paces, and there was the telephone. That was what was dragging her down: her conversation with Ileana. Being clean herself, she could hear all the drugs in Ileana's voice. She remembered her when she first came over. Oh, shit. Shit. She'd never expected to get through but Ileana was allowed a mobile when her pimps were expecting a big job. Some men liked to think they were getting direct access. Usually she was kept so close no one could get at her. Like a prisoner. Lizzie thought of her own weeks in Holloway. Ileana's situation was far worse than a prisoner's. She'd once shown Lizzie bruises all the way up her thighs. It was Jo who did it, not the clients. The clients were the least of her problems.

Lizzie gave up the effort of movement and sank back on her bed. Perhaps she shouldn't have rung her. But it was for Charlie's brother. Charlie knew about everything anyway. Those pimps hated him, called him 'that nosy fat pig Englishman'. That hurt her.

She looked at the small clock Portia had put on a table. Maybe she could manage a couple of hours' sleep.

Maggie looked out of her bedroom window. She was proud of the garden, three acres of lawns, shrubs, trees and long herbaceous borders, the plants there still predominantly green. Her favourite time would arrive soon when colour came through on the flower heads as if water had been brushed over one of those magic painting books she'd loved as a child.

Is my pleasure in everyday things childish? wondered Maggie. Do I fail to look for meanings, as an adult should? In fact, her garden was not as usual. Trails of mist wound in and out of the trees, lay like soft blankets over borders, dimmed the brightness of the daffodils clumped in the lawns. The mist was helping her to understand that things had changed. Roland had felt moved to make a confession. Even before they had parted, she could see he was regretting it. Once she had failed to open her arms and welcome him home to Mamma, forgiven, cleansed and reconciled, he had wanted to wipe out the whole episode. She had read it from his words, his look.

So, how should she react? Apart from disgust, that is. And she hadn't even dared be practical and think about AIDS. She had an explanation now for the coldness of his love-making, for his sec- retiveness. Should she tell him to bugger off and find himself a boyfriend? The idea almost made her laugh. The truth was that nothing fundamental had changed. She had an excuse now to banish him from her bed – but their love-making, in its own low-key way, had been satisfying. The real point was that they'd never been passionately in love – or even in love at all.

There, now, she must face up to her own part in this. In other words, Leo. Perhaps it had been the moment for a confession from her. But how could she do that without Leo's involvement? Two kisses in twenty years hardly added up to an avowal of love. Perhaps she was too level-headed. Was that the problem? A level-headed woman who enjoyed a bit of fantasy on the side. The picture was not appealing.

Instead she imagined how Roland would have reacted if she had made her confession: furious anger because it was Leo, then dis- believing laughter because it was her.

The garden became blurred as tears gathered unshed in Maggie's eyes. Even they knew their undramatic place. She went back to the bed and looked at her watch: still only just after seven. No one to look after, although Esmond might be awake.

She opened her wardrobe and chose a big furry dressing-gown and warm slippers. She padded along the corridors.

'Good morning, Maggie.' His small dark eyes gleamed knowingly beneath their heavy lids. This was a good morning then. It happened every few months, as if a fog had been lifted from him, revealing the shrewd, sardonic character beneath. Strange it should happen on the day when the fog had closed around her.

'Are you hungry yet?'

'Never hungry.'

Again, Maggie felt that he understood what he was saying or, rather, that he was saying something more important than the words. If you're never hungry, you don't want to live. It struck her that she should tell him of Imogen's situation. When she'd tried previously, he'd appeared not to take it in. It worried her. They'd been married nearly fifty years. He should know when his wife was dying. She settled like a kindly bear on the small chair by his bed. 'I have some sad news for you.'

'Ah, yes.' An indrawn breath as if he could expect nothing else.

'Imogen is not well.'

'A great beauty.'

Maggie watched him closely as he pronounced these words with pride. She'd never understood his marriage to Imogen, him so clever, her so consistently selfish and unfaithful. Maybe she would learn something at this last stage, even something useful to her. 'A great beauty'. Well, that would never be of any help to her.

'The doctor thinks she will scarcely last more than a day or two.'

'The ability to surprise.' The words were blurred. Esmond still had the majority of his own teeth but his lips were a little rubbery. 'The ability to surprise'. She looked round the room. It was small and functional, an old dressing-room with a washbasin recently installed in the corner. He'd chosen it when he was still capable of choosing. Surprisingly, the curtains were closed. Esmond liked them open. Maggie remembered the nurse. Still asleep.

'You like surprise, then, do you?'

'Free.' His claw-like right hand emerged from under the covers and waved in a gesture of celebration.

Imogen had felt free, all right, free to do what she felt like, thought Maggie. In other words, selfish. Yet he clearly admired her for it. She herself could never be free from ties of duty, responsibility, obligation, love. 'Yes. It must be nice to be free.'

'I believe in liberty.' He slobbered a little and winked at her. Or maybe it was just one of his lids weakening.

'Liberty' was a grander concept than freedom. Freedom spoke for the individual, liberty for the state. Maggie thought of some of the high-profile cases Esmond had fought, and mostly won, in his heyday. As a libel lawyer, he had, it was true, defended liberty or freedom, even if right was not always on his side. There was the famous case when he'd defended a national newspaper's right to publish the details of a young actress's life, which included heavy drug use, multiple sex partners – Maggie could remember the headlines now – and a heartless disregard both for her mother who suffered from Alzheimer's and her son, who had Down's syndrome. Esmond had won the case. The actress had a breakdown, went into rehab, abandoned her career and became an active president of a Down's syndrome charity. A happy ending.

'Would you like to see Imogen? To say goodbye?' She regretted the suggestion instantly. He would have to be taken up by ambulance. It would probably kill him too. Almost certainly, on the day he would not know who she was or even why he was there.

'Ah,' responded Esmond, his lips moving warily. He reached out his right hand to her.

She took it, felt the old dry skin and bones. Nothing but skin and bones.

He gripped her with surprising strength. His face, like that of an ancient tortoise, poked in her direction. The grimace around his mouth was supposed to represent a smile. He was reassuring her.

'Oh, Esmond!' The tears she'd managed to hold back till then came pouring out. She wept, as women always have, at the sorrows of the world, at the faithlessness of men, the disappointments she could do nothing to change. 'I'm getting old,' she sobbed, among other things. And somewhere Roland's name was spoken, and somewhere Leo's.

Later she thought it was an unforgivable indulgence, to lay the worst of her life on this antique, scarcely human man, who could do nothing to deflect its miserable weight. Yet she had felt curiously consoled, his great age calming her childish outpourings as if she had cried out to a mountain or some ancient monument. Life was fleeting. Nothing mattered as much as all that.

She had dried her eyes and was about to leave when the nurse came in, bustling about energetically to assuage her guilt at being late.

Maggie felt indulgent towards her. She was young, doubtless more able to oversleep. Good luck to her. There was a little kitchen near Esmond's room but she didn't want the nurse to feel cut off from the rest of the household.

'Come down when you've finished with Lord Shillingstone. We'll have a coffee together.'

The nurse turned to her suspiciously, if expecting a ticking off. Then, seeing Maggie's smile, she relaxed. 'That'd be nice.' She smiled too.

Pleased, Maggie thought, Life goes on. She would take the boys into town again, this time for a haircut. By the time they got back, Hetty might have arrived. She would think about her marriage later.

Leo had turned off his mobile, again, but not before the police had rung him. As he'd feared, they'd found his number on the phone of the murdered Ileana. They were aggressive. They wanted to search his flat, take his computer.

'I'll leave the door open,' he said. From this they might have guessed he wouldn't be there. But they didn't seem to. They wanted, of course, to interview Charlie. Clearly they were not the same detectives he'd met at the hospital. They seemed less controlled, angrier, perhaps more stupid. Perhaps more dangerous.

Leo had told them that Charlie was under heavy sedation, in the care of a consultant psychiatrist, Dr Cass Heilbrand. Then he turned off his phone and fled the flat, leaving the door unlocked. Frankly, he didn't give a fuck who came in.

Lizzie woke up and put out her hand for her cigarettes. Then she remembered she was in prison and didn't smoke any more. Then she remembered where she actually was, and grasped the packet. For a bad moment she thought it was empty. She drew out the last cigarette with shaking fingers and found the matches. Only then she sat up.

The violently red hangings made her feel ill. She drew deeply on the cigarette to calm herself. The clock said five to one. She felt sweaty, although the room wasn't warm. Tentatively, she put her feet on the floor.

The kitchen was very small. She went to the window, then retreated from the light, although there was no sun. Before opening the fridge, she turned on a radio. It had been creepily quiet before. The news had just started, some horrible accident. The world was filled with horrible accidents.

The fridge was almost empty, just a bit of wine left over from the night before, some milk and curling pieces of ham. She pulled out a shelf at the bottom and found tomatoes, cucumber and lettuce, healthy stuff. Perhaps she'd have more luck in the cupboards.

She'd just found a packet of chocolate biscuits when she heard the radio report that the mutilated body of a prostitute had been found in the King's Cross area of London.

Leo would have liked to drive out to Maggie again, to wander in the garden she kept so beautifully. They might kiss. He would feel her soft breasts. He began to imagine making love to her but his libido refused to play the game. They'd have lunch together in the warm bright kitchen and he'd explain to her all the complications of his present position – not that he understood them himself. It seemed that the moment he'd accepted the information and accused the home secretary he'd lost control of his life.

Sadly, a pleasant interlude with Maggie was impossible on a Saturday when Roland would be there. Now and again Leo tried to think about Roland dispassionately but it never worked. They had fought too much in boyhood. Their dislike for each other was moulded hard.

Once Roland had thrown him downstairs. He was still bigger then. They must have been seven and eight, just before boarding-school – and when Leo had got to the bottom he'd found he was bleeding quite a lot from his face. He could still remember the triumph. Now he could go to Imogen as a righteous victim. But, of course, she'd scorned him, 'What a cry-baby!' 'Settle your own disputes.' 'Learn to win.' Her reaction had been quite clear, if muddling to a child: she took the victor's side, not the victim's. Later the same day Roland had been promised a new set of points for his railway set.

Leo was driving through London in a southward direction. Maybe he would look at paintings in the Tate, try to avoid imagining the face of a young woman murdered because she knew too much and was prepared to talk. What would she have told him? That she had been brought to England on the promise of a better life, that she was held forcibly, raped, prostituted? That her clients had included the rich and powerful?

He'd read recently that one in ten men between the ages of twenty and thirty used prostitutes. The figure had amazed him. In his experience, women were crying out for sex and most were prepared to perform any acts either partner could think up. Perversion was an old-fashioned idea. So why did men need prostitutes? Were they so ugly or isolated? Surely not ten per cent.

Charlie went to prostitutes. He liked to boast about it, knowing it made Leo uncomfortable. Leo thought about Lizzie. He couldn't imagine ever wanting to have sex with her and, indeed, Charlie had announced that, although holy in the eyes of God, their marriage was unconsummated, *'un mariage blanc'* so that Mary Magdalene could be reborn as the Virgin Mary. Charlie's Catholicism always verged on the edge of sacrilege, thought Leo, and smiled at the idea. He himself, although confirmed at school, had become agnostic soon after.

Religion in their family was another source of division, inspired initially by Imogen, whose sudden conversion to Catholicism had been followed immediately by her decision to give away her third son to a childless Catholic couple. To Leo, only two years old at the time, the disappearance of a baby meant almost nothing, a mystery in his head, an instinctive belief in something lost. But the priests in the house, Imogen's excitement, his father's disapproval had been unsettling in the years that followed.

Inexorably wilful, she'd dropped Catholicism eventually. By then Leo had been eight or nine and old enough to wonder. Being good, even doing good, seemed easier than following rules of engagement that might be changed or withdrawn at any time.

Around the same time he'd learned it was best to be answerable to no one but yourself.

Despite the arguments that had taken place during his growing years, he thought they were all too selfish to be religious. Only Charlie, burdened by his illness, looked to the mystical. Of course, that was why he was driving south – he was going to visit Charlie.

Father Bill, walking out of church after saying Mass, would have been saddened, if philosophical, to know that Leo, in considering his family's religious tendencies, had not included his priestly brother. Bill had offered up the Mass for the poor people lost in the Channel collision. He imagined their cries, their struggles as icy water filled their lungs. He hoped that at least some had had the consolation of faith. It was hard, he thought, when faced by a tragic, meaningless event, to hold off the waves of despair and cling to the glory of an all-loving God.

It was Lent, of course, a time of suffering. It happened also to be the feast of St Margaret Clitherow, a cheerful butcher's wife who had refused to deny her faith and was pressed to death, a sharp rock below and a door laden with weights above. The story had given him nightmares as a child.

'Oh, Bill, there's been a call for you.' Aloysius, overcoat on, passed him in the hall of the presbytery. 'Lizzie. She promised to call again. A distraught young lady, I'd say.'

'Thanks.' That was the point, thought Bill, entering the kitchen. One must concentrate on individual tragedies, like Lizzie's, where there was the possibility of doing good, rather than indulge in voyeuristic misery for people he would never know. Christ had been a practical, hands-on man.

The phone rang under his elbow.

'Oh, Father . . .' It was Lizzie, all right, unable to find words for whatever was troubling her.

'Yes, Lizzie. Can I help?' Anything was possible with a lost soul like her. She might even have got herself back into prison.

'I need to see Charlie! Oh, Father . . . Something . . .' She gave up again. 'I've got to find Charlie! Please, Father.'

People in dire straits called him 'Father', a word of authority and strength.

'What is it, Lizzie? You know Charlie's unwell. Perhaps I can help.'

Now she began to cry so that he only picked up odd words, a friend called 'Leana', or something like, 'Leo' and 'death'. Or was that his imagination, with death so much on his mind? 'Where are you?' he asked. At Portia's, he gathered. That, at least, was good news. He wondered whether he should go to her but soon he must drive to South London for a mini retreat (he hoped Aloysius had remembered to leave the car) with a group of nuns, and nuns were rare enough these days to be nurtured, not abandoned.

'Please tell me where he is.' She'd got herself together for a further appeal.

It struck Bill that the hospital where Charlie lay was not far from the convent he was due to visit, if Lizzie could get herself to an underground station on his route. A sensible man might not have made the decision to help her in this way but Bill answered to a different call. Besides, he had married Lizzie and Charlie. He would pick her up outside South Kensington station, which she could reach directly on the Piccadilly line.

Many times Roland decided to leave for London. Even if it was Saturday, he could go to his office, sit at his desk, pretend everything was as usual. But Didi was in London, exerting a dangerous pull, particularly in his own unloved state. He couldn't even eat the magnificent breakfast he'd cooked for himself. With a touch of spite he gave it to Maggie's overweight Labrador, who was on a strict no-fat diet.

He decided to visit his sleeping sons. As he stared at their sprawled limbs, he wondered why, quite unnecessarily in such a large house, they'd elected to share a room. In truth, they were good friends, mates, muckers, so near in age as almost to be twins. It was ironic that he and Leo, who'd always been competitors for any boy's greatest prize, a mother's love, had been forced for lack of space to sleep in the same room. Then Charlie, without making any effort and without valuing it, had won the prize.

Restlessly, Roland prowled down another corridor. Esmond

might be awake, or what passed for awake, in the twilight zone he inhabited. Murmured voices stopped him. Maggie's sounded perfectly normal, as if she was conducting a reasonable conversation, which was impossible. He would have liked to get closer and listen but fear of discovery – an excluded schoolboy listening pathetically at keyholes – made him turn round. He could shave and dress while Maggie was otherwise engaged, then hide in his study while he made up his mind what to do. Again, he thought of driving to London.

This time he pictured himself visiting Imogen. Soon the nursing-home would telephone with their report. It seemed extraordinary that she was still alive. Her transparent skin already had the parchment colour of death. Suddenly overwhelmed by a passion of loss and misery, Roland bowed over where he stood outside the bathroom. She had been so beautiful. Great beauty exalts. Slim, tall, usually dressed in pale colours with a string of pearls that reflected her creamy skin. When she'd kissed him, he'd shivered as if touched by a spirit.

Portia received a text from Conor. He would pick her up at twelve thirty for 'a pure lunch'. It was ridiculous. She never left her stall for a moment on Saturdays. 'Certainly not,' she texted back. '2morrow.'

'2morrow 2 late,' came the reply.

What had happened to make them so close after two years? 'Quite right,' she agreed, with a French tourist. 'They're from Mexico, made in a women's commune. Half the money goes back to them.'

'Is that so?' The tourist was polite but didn't buy. Perhaps the idea of charity put her off. Not that Portia cared. For the second day running, her stall was emptying as fast as she filled it. Perhaps it was the early mist, now dissipated, that made the brilliant colours of her blouses and shawls so attractive. Several people had asked for children's sizes. She must make a note. Smaller garments would mean less material, less work and not much less money.

'I'm coming,' Conor texted.

Now and again a flush of unease pierced Portia's happiness. Everybody in the market was talking about the collision in the Channel. Two deaths confirmed, more expected.

She'd always found it difficult to be happy because of her

empathy with the suffering of others. Now she was determined to be selfish. She did, however, ring Lizzie to check she was all right. When there was no answer, she assumed she'd gone to her probation meeting. Too late it occurred to her that the office might not be open on a Saturday.

'Here 4 u,' she texted Conor. The strangeness of yesterday evening had drawn her closer to him. Leo had been edgy – to be expected, she supposed, with all he was going through, although she had never found it easy to believe in the reality of public life. Leo had seemed the least weird of her brothers – a straightforward man with straightforward objectives, like that programme he'd run in his constituency for cutting down on school truancy in seven-to-eight-year-olds. He'd told her they were mostly boys who could scarcely read or write. No wonder school didn't appeal to them. He'd always been serious about his work. Last night, however, he'd talked disjointedly or fallen suddenly silent, often looking at Lizzie either with surprise or with something else that Portia couldn't define.

Of course it was surprising to find Lizzie in their family, particularly with Charlie out of action. These were purple days, thought Portia, watching a woman holding up a shawl of that colour.

CHAPTER THIRTY-ONE

Mere Nothings

Bill was shocked by the sight of Lizzie. She stood outside the underground station, hunched in her skimpy jacket, with a cigarette pressed against her mouth. He didn't recall such very high heels. It was hard not to be reminded of her previous profession.

He stopped the car, which jumped and stalled. It was not very reliable. Behind him, a man hooted, which attracted Lizzie's attention.

Bill wound down the window and waved. She hurried over, tottering on her pin-thin legs.

'Cheers.' She slid in beside him.

He noticed her cheeks were flushed and her eyes darkened with makeup. 'You look well.' A lie, although for the first time he could see she might be attractive to some kinds of men.

'I bought some shoes, didn't I? I know I shouldn't have but Charlie is my husband, isn't he?'

She was giving herself courage. 'With your probation money, I suppose.' He smiled tolerantly. She said nothing.

The traffic was heavy and he had to concentrate to stop the engine cutting out every time they hit a red light. He needed time to think himself into the proper state of mind to meet the nuns. He would start with a short address based on Jesus's words from Matthew 11:28–30. He recited them to himself. *Come to me, all you who labour and are overburdened, and I will give you rest. Shoulder my yoke and learn from me, for I am gentle and humble in heart, and you will find rest for your souls. Yes, my yoke is easy and my burden light.* It was an indulgence to choose this text, which he knew so well and used so often to cheer his soul, but he thought the little group of women – there were only five, two already old and on the verge of retirement – might also find it helpful. The ministry of priests and nuns turned so much towards the sad, the sick and the dying that it was only too easy to lose heart. He often thought that the forced jollity noted among clerics stemmed from a desperate need to rise above the gloom of their daily work.

'Will he know me, do you think?'

Bill glanced sideways at Lizzie. He'd explained Charlie's situation several times. Once again, patiently, he explained that, no, Charlie wouldn't recognise her or anyone else because he was drugged, out of it. The shoes had been unnecessary. But he didn't say so because it would have been cruel. She was also wearing a garish lipstick.

There was a pause. 'I'll be with him. That's the main thing.'

'Yes,' agreed Bill, wearily. There was another text he knew by heart from I Corinthians 1:25–29. He had the same good memory as his brothers.

To shame what is strong, God has chosen what the world calls weakness. He has chosen things low and contemptible, mere nothings, to overthrow the existing order. And so there is no place for human pride in the presence of God. You are in Christ Jesus by God's act, for God has made him our wisdom. He is our righteousness; in him we are consecrated and set free.

Both he and Lizzie qualified easily as 'mere nothings'.

Lizzie, having lit a cigarette, now began to press the buttons that controlled the radio. Raucous pop music burst into life: not Aloysius's taste, surely. Would it be uncharitable to ask her to turn it down – or off?

'Rubbish.' She pressed the button and looked to Bill for approval. 'Not my taste.'

'I expect you like hymns and things. We had a priest really great on the guitar.'

He saw she was trying to make conversation and was touched. He'd got used to her prison self, too depressed to utter more than the odd word. Of course she was excited about seeing Charlie. He hoped the reality wouldn't be too lowering.

'I'll pick you up later, if you like.' As he spoke, the car died in a serious, shuddering way. Also, he was in the middle of slow-moving traffic. He turned the starter key with mounting desperation. A chorus of hoots came from behind.

Lizzie rose in her seat. 'Bastards! Can't they see you're a priest?'

Bill decided not to tell her that this information would probably make them hoot louder. The engine caught, then died.

Lizzie wound down her window and screamed out a string of insults and profanities. Bill thought that anyone identifying him as a priest now would get a shock. But he didn't try to stop her. In fact, he admired her spirit, although worried that some road-rage sufferer might move from hooting to violence.

At last the car fired and they started again.

Lizzie wound up the window and pronounced, with satisfaction, 'Surprised myself, didn't I? Like my mother. A real terror once she got going.'

Was she expecting thanks? The nuns would be looking to him for leadership and inspiration. In some moods, this pleased him more than it should.

'Mind stopping a mo?'

Bill looked at her with dismay. 'The trouble is, as you've already seen, the car's on its last legs. If I stop, we might never start.'

'I've run out of cigarettes, see.' Her voice had changed pitch to a querulous, panicky note.

Bill did see. He dealt with a lot of addictive personalities. 'I'll try to keep the engine running.'

Puffing frantically on her cigarette, Lizzie walked up the driveway to the hospital. Father Bill had cut and run. She didn't blame him. That car was worse than bad. They'd spent half an hour outside the newsagent. He'd have phoned the AA if he'd had his card. Then he told her as a joke that a prayer to St Christopher would be just as good and, sure enough, it did the trick. Best moment, really. God given. At times like that, she felt she could really get into religion, like some of them inside, although they weren't Catholics. Or perhaps they were. There were so many different sorts of God around these days, it was hard to tell.

Stumbling on the uneven ground, Lizzie stopped for a moment, one arm outstretched. She felt like a diver poised for descent. Above her, great trees arched like a church roof; ahead were the square blocks of the hospital. She was glad she was wearing such lovely shoes – only cost ten quid – even if they did make her progress difficult. After all, when had things been easy? As a child, she used to blame herself for all the things that went wrong, little and big – toast burning, Danny grabbing her from behind when her mum wasn't looking – but now she knew that was life, wasn't it? Her life, anyway.

That's what she wasn't thinking of: Ileana. Ileana used to cross herself now and again. Please, God, let it not be her on the news. Not Ileana. Please not. Charlie would set her right. But Charlie wasn't speaking. So Father said. Maybe he was wrong.

Lizzie ground out her cigarette, too anxious to worry whether it was burning the sole of her new shoe, and immediately lit another with clumsy fingers.

Just to be near Charlie will be enough, she told herself. She began to walk again. Above her head, a remaining tendril of mist broke free from high branches and trailed along behind her.

Leo sat in the hospital's waiting room. He tried to count how many days had passed since he was last there. Then he had been treated as an MP, arriving with the weight of power, greeted by the police as a privileged member of society. They had deferred to him, not just because his mission was tragic, the identification of his dead brother, but because they knew their place and respected his. It was surely not just his own paranoia (a new sensation) that made him find the policeman who'd stopped him at the gates of the hospital the very opposite of deferential. What was it the man had said? 'Mr Barr, is it?' Not a hint of 'sir'. 'I'll tell the super you're here.'

'I'm not here to see the super. I'm here to see my brother.' He had managed not to add, 'My brother who is, contrary to police information, alive.'

'Understood.' Still no 'sir'.

Leo shifted on his plastic-coated chair. A small amount of stuffing escaped from a hole. Although the day was no longer misty, the light had hardly brightened. Hopefully having thrown off the police, he was now waiting for a doctor to take him to Charlie. He wondered how much he minded about his new status. Was a thirst for self-immolation a desirable part of the successful campaigner's make-up? He feared he was too straightforward for that. He was fair-minded, certainly. But there had been little risk to him in his various battles to help his constituents. A new youth centre here, better traffic signals there, a programme to help persistent truants, a forum for discussion across the racial divide. Everybody had agreed these made a good agenda, even when they were on the opposition side. All his life he'd been popular and popularist, supported, as he understood so clearly now, by a body of opinion that might be called society. He'd been born and bred to it.

Leo stood, then walked to the window. It looked over the front drive and, beyond, to the large garden with its mature trees, on one of which Horace Silver had been found hanging. It took him a moment to see the wispy figure approaching. In her dark clothes, she seem insubstantial, only just held to the ground by a pair of brilliant white stilettos. Like a ballet dancer on points. In another moment, he'd recognised Lizzie.

At once his uneasy feelings of self-pity were put into place. Tottering along towards him, hesitating, bending to adjust her shoe, puffing on a cigarette, running her fingers through her hair, stubbing out the cigarette, pausing, proceeding, here came the real thing. Did she already know about Ileana?

Instinctively Leo moved away from the window. Ileana, so the police had said, came from the Ukraine. A further ring of darkness. Why had she not stayed within her society? Leo knew he was protesting with the secure man's tools. Why can't the poor, the mistreated, the abused stay hidden? The answer was one he knew perfectly well from his work in South London. The unfortunate need help from the fortunate. That was why he'd become an MP, not, like some, to enjoy a comfortable, prestigious job. He was a good man, Leo reassured himself.

Even so, he pulled back further from the window and sat down. She would find him, of course. She would watch with him at Charlie's bedside. The apparition on the driveway had been frail but filled with determination.

Maggie, brushing her hair in front of the mirror, gave her face a kindly look. It wasn't its fault that things had become difficult. She peered closer. She looked pretty, not even very tired. They would have to talk, she supposed.

Maggie's place was the large, airy kitchen; Roland's the small, dark study. He'd chosen it, saying it made his work easier on the computer, although from what she'd glimpsed he only read the papers there.

Maggie managed not to knock before she entered. Mungo had followed her, pushing his nose at her legs. She shoved him out. Her first thought was how handsome Roland looked, how distinguished. The room was cooler than the rest of the house and he wore a russet-coloured sweater under a soft tweed jacket. He stared at her. Coldly, she thought, the mask firmly in place. If he was afraid that she'd reveal his secret to the world, he certainly wasn't showing it.

She pushed some folders off an armchair and enjoyed the noise as they hit the wooden floor. She sat down.

'So?'

She'd made him speak first. Only one word but a triumph. She'd planned nothing in response. Just this spark of aggression. As always, practicalities came to help her. 'We have twelve people coming to lunch tomorrow. Sally and Sue are booked to cook and serve. There's your old friend the chairman of Covent Garden and your new friend the Australian businessman who you think might be useful – unless there's some other reason for liking such a boorish, conceited oaf.'

This speech pleased her and so did Roland's bewildered face. The mask had slipped. As he said nothing, she continued, 'We could give your mother's illness as an excuse to cancel it. Have you spoken with the nursing-home this morning?' This was a master stroke. Any mention of Imogen pierced Roland's heart. Here was the opportunity to become a different woman, one who stirred up pain rather than soothed it. Perhaps Roland would appreciate her more if she were like his mother, who'd excelled in the rapier thrust, or perhaps such behaviour had to be underpinned by beauty.

Today she was dressed in brown suede boots, a wide skirt and a hand-knitted cardigan. She was unashamedly large and powerful. But not beautiful.

'Yes,' replied Roland. 'There's no change.'

'They must be surprised.'

'They *are* surprised.'

Maggie crossed her legs to divert herself from issuing natural words of sympathy. 'So, what about the lunch?'

'What about it?'

What about us? That, of course, was the real question. After all, she was a coward. 'You want to continue with it?' Subtext: you want to continue with our marriage?

'You seem to have it all under control.'

'Do I?' No, I don't. I want love, warmth, companionship. I can't get everything I need from giving. I want something back, something more than my children can give me, than my playthings, the property I rent, this new project of a gallery. The way I feel now I shan't go on with that. What's the point? *What's the point?*

'I'm sorry.'

Maggie looked up blearily. All she wasn't saying out loud filled her head and made her uncertain whether he'd really spoken.

'I'm sorry, Maggie. I can't be what I'm not. I can't promise anything.'

'Oh.' She felt breathless. It wasn't like in the night when he'd been so full of misery. Now his voice was stiff and controlled – more difficult for him. She'd done him an injustice. He was willing to engage. On his terms. So, was it for her to take the decision? 'Hetty's coming home.'

Hetty looked like her father, tall and dark and slim. Quite unlike him in character. On her last visit, she'd romped about with the boys as if she were nine instead of nineteen. Then she'd made Maggie read the other part in a two-hander play she was acting in, before throwing herself into the chair and bursting into tears. She was leaving Stanislav, her latest boyfriend, because he'd slept with her best friend – well, a friend, anyway. But she had met someone called Johnny Wayward-Jones, or maybe Maynard-Jones, who had the longest eyelashes she'd ever seen. Stanislav's eyelashes had been negligible. Negligible! The tears were gone and she was up again, protesting she must give her mother a manicure. 'I can't have a mother with workman's nails!' she'd cried.

Maggie caught bewilderment on Roland's face. Could she have been smiling? Hetty always made her smile. 'I think we should go on with tomorrow's lunch,' she said. *Go on with the marriage.*

'You must decide.' He fiddled with a pen on his desk. 'I'll be spending much of the time in London.' And what was the subtext to that? Probably she didn't want to know.

'You always do.' She mustn't seem like too much of a pushover.

Were they in the process of arranging a marriage of convenience? Is that what they were doing? With so little said. Would they never sleep together again? Never the comfort of a physical presence, however remote. She was a physical woman. One step at a time, she told herself. We're both in shock. She didn't really believe in the idea of being 'in shock' but she said it to herself all the same, trying it out in the new situation in which she found herself. 'Shock' was an excuse in her book but perhaps she needed one. 'I should put on the spaghetti.' She stood up. He was gay, she reminded herself. Everything had changed. It must have been agony for him to have sex with a woman. And one who could never be confused with a boy.

Roland came over and put his hand on her shoulder. It was the touch of a kindly stranger. She flinched. AIDS, she repeated to herself. Sex with a rent-boy. He didn't normally touch her during the day.

'I expect we'll survive,' he said, not very humbly. 'But I think we should cancel the lunch tomorrow.'

Even though he was using his ironic tone, she gave a little nod of agreement. One step at a time. Separate bedrooms, she thought. Many wives would envy her.

A second policeman came into the hospital waiting room. He seemed senior to the first. Leo looked at his tabs: a sergeant. It was possible his antipathy to the police arose out of too much identification with his black constituents. But this man was black.

'My chief would like to interview you.' He was burly, the sort of chap who could pin a man to the ground. More of a bouncer than a guardian of the peace.

'I'm visiting my brother.'

There was a jangle of words from the policeman's earpiece. 'At whichever station you like, sir.'

Now he was called 'sir'.

'My chief says he's been trying to get messages to you.'

Leo sighed. 'I spoke to your chief earlier today.' There was no point in talking to this brawny mouthpiece. With the habit of fairness, he thought he'd be the right man to have on your side in a dark alley.

They both turned at a noise at the door. Lizzie stood, leaning against the frame. Her large eyes were fixed despairingly on the bouncer or, rather, on his uniform.

'Hi, Lizzie,' said Leo, trying to lighten things up. 'Have a seat. You look smart.' Her lips were painted a shiny pink. He hadn't noticed her full mouth before.

Ignoring this kindly meant invitation, Lizzie stared wildly towards the window, then swayed backwards. It was obvious she was searching for an escape route.

The policeman's earpiece spluttered again and he raised his eyes enquiringly at Leo.

'She's my sister-in-law. My brother's wife.' He moved a little in Lizzie's direction. 'The sergeant's here because of an incident last week. Nothing to do with us.' This had only slightly more falsehood than truth to it.

'I saw the orange strips,' whispered Lizzie. 'In the garden.'

'Last week,' repeated Leo, heartily. If no one had told her of the intricacies of Charlie's aborted death, he wasn't going to start now. Lizzie was still clinging to the frame of the door, like a drowning swimmer to a plank.

Behind her, another figure appeared, tall and female, wearing a white coat. 'Mr Barr, I can take you up to your brother now.'

In all the confusion of the policeman, his unseen but noisy confederates and Lizzie's tragic presence, the idea of Charlie, silently confined to bed, was soothing. 'May I bring his wife?'

The white coat with the kindly face above it came closer. She peered at Lizzie, who seemed unsure whether to be visible or invisible. 'Have you visited before?'

'No,' murmured Lizzie, and gulped audibly, either because she'd been holding her breath or because she was near tears or both.

As they mounted one staircase after another, waiting while doors were unlocked and locked, Lizzie began to regret her shoes, not because of how they looked – their elegant height and brightness – but because of their noise. It was hard to seem unassuming when every step you made rang out like cymbals, echoing upstairs and down. She gripped the iron banisters, hoping to lift off some of their weight and lessen the sound.

'Can I help?' Leo stopped and offered her his arm.

'I'm fine.' Clack. Clack. Clack. She was beginning to think he wasn't such a bad thing. When she'd first seen the policeman, she'd thought it was all up. No probation visit so back to gaol. That was how it worked. Although they didn't usually send you a personal escort quite like this one. He was big. But Charlie was bigger, she reminded herself. And this Leo, thumping along ahead of her, talking now to the Paki doctor, not much smaller.

Clack. Clack. Clack. Nearer to Charlie. Oh, Ileana! She'd have to ask Leo. But not now. She couldn't think about Ileana now.

Charlie's room was bright. They all blinked, a little dazed. It was on the third floor with a view of grass and trees. It was hard to believe they were still in London, even if it was the suburbs. Lizzie had expected respectful darkness, a kind of church atmosphere with, perhaps, a candle flickering in a corner.

Worse, it revealed Charlie to be a crumpled pink face half covered by a neat white sheet. He was at the mercy of others, she saw, hardly hero material. Nevertheless, she fell to her knees by the bed. 'Oh, Charlie!' She wept, buried her face in the pale blue covering. In this way, out of the strength of emotion, her faith resurrected.

'Dr Heilbrand has lessened the sedatives considerably,' said the doctor to Leo. 'As you've already seen, we have other issues to deal with.'

'The police, for example.'

'There has been a murder, so they say. Poor Horace Silver. Of course, we're more used to suicides. He has no known relatives. No one to accuse us of negligence.'

'How sad.'

'He'd been on the streets for years. Although he's not old. Your brother befriended him. They sang together.'

'Sang?'

'Hymns mostly. Horace had an Irish background. His real name was Bertie Flannagan. We did our best whenever the police picked him up, dumped him here. Your brother cheered him up. He'd never . . .' She hesitated, as if amazed by her next words '. . . have killed him.'

'Of course not!' Leo stared at the bedside scene of *pietà*. 'Charlie's the most non-violent man in the world. He looks threatening because he's so big and sometimes behaves eccentrically. People are frightened by the unexpected.'

'I'll get you some chairs,' said the doctor, without commenting. Before leaving she turned to Charlie. She took his pulse and raised the lids to look at his eyes. 'It won't be long now.'

'But doesn't he ever get up?' Lizzie, despite her tears, had been listening to their conversation with the attention she reserved for anything to do with Charlie.

'He has a catheter,' answered the doctor, briskly.

Lizzie put her head down again. Now she couldn't avoid noticing the bag of urine at the side of the bed.

In her own way she was praying. She was also dying for a smoke. Or, failing that, a coffee. Strong with plenty of sugar. She peered up at Leo, standing with his arms folded. He was wearing corduroy trousers such as Charlie favoured, although much cleaner, and a smart jacket.

When a nurse came back with two stacking chairs, she grabbed his arm – he was a scruffy-looking young man, not nurselike at all, although his badge read, 'Nurse George Jones'. 'Can I catch a smoke somewhere?' she asked.

'Sure. There's a room. Fancy Staff or Patients?'

Lizzie felt unable to answer this. Both seemed equally terrifying. 'What about the garden?'

'Ah, the garden. You'd need an escort for the unlocking and locking.' They both knew about being locked in, then, her and Charlie. Doors slammed shut. Keys turned. It was a bond, wasn't it?

'Here. I'll take you. The patients' room's closer. They're all drugged up to the eyeballs. You don't have to worry.'

He was right. When they arrived, the only sign of life from the four huddled figures sitting round the walls was the mechanical movement of cigarette from hand to mouth. Nobody even glanced at her.

'You'll make your own way back,' said George, not waiting for an answer.

Lizzie found a chair and joined the group. She thought she'd hit rock bottom in Holloway but now she realised there was plenty further to fall. The women in Holloway, most of them anyway, had been quite lively – too lively for her. They got involved with each other, worried about their kids and their men, usually in that order, and tried to swing things with the screws. Not like these zombies. All men, save one woman with the greasiest hair she'd ever seen. They wouldn't argue about things like the right to wash your own undies. Truthfully, she hadn't been concerned with such things herself but she'd always been able to speak, hadn't she? Well, truth to tell, not always.

How about Charlie, then? Perhaps even now he was sitting up, opening his eyes. She puffed harder till she'd finished the cigarette, flung it into an overflowing tin box, and dashed out into the corridor.

Charlie could hear voices. He liked the sound. They were not the voices he sometimes heard when his mind was out of his control. One was Leo's. He drifted a little, thinking of mornings at home when he was a child. Roland and Leo had had a room above his. Sometimes they played football, the noise rolling round like thunder above his head, like the balls Rip van Winkle had used to knock down his ninepins. Often they argued, Roland's voice bitter with accusation, Leo's straight and strong. Like his batting. Cricket was Leo's game and sometimes he needed a bowler or a batsman and then little brother was called in. That was in the country. He was put once more into a room on his own. Next to Imogen's, of course. He'd never asked to be her favourite. He'd never asked to be handsome and clever and good at all sports. Although he'd enjoyed girls falling for him. Once in the space of six months he'd had two sisters and their mother. Stunning, all three of them. He'd never asked to be tortured by drugs and doctors and hospitals.

Charlie rolled in his bed and flung out his arms.

'We'll take out the catheter now,' said a voice behind Leo, so he left the room, bumping into Lizzie who had raced along the corridor, bringing with her an aura of cigarette smoke.

'He's coming round,' explained Leo.

At the end of the corridor, he caught a glimpse of the burly policeman. Then a white coat shepherded him away.

CHAPTER THIRTY-TWO

A Hero

Portia held her mobile close to her ear. The misty weather had brought people inside to her stall for a second day. At lunchtime, Conor had appeared with hot pies and beer. Now she felt distracted, too happy.

'What? Could you speak up? Who is speaking?'

She moved backwards and crouched against the wall behind her stall. The female voice had a West Indian accent. At last she was beginning to understand it.

'The nursing-home.' That was what she was saying.

'Yes, Matron. Is it Lady Shillingstone?'

Now there were words to make her heart lurch: 'dead' or was it 'dying'? She must get out of this crowded, noisy place and listen properly.

She'd told Conor earlier that she was too old to feel for him the way she did. Yet her mother had been forty-five when she gave birth to Portia. Once Imogen had told her what she'd rather not have known, that she'd tried to have an abortion, that she'd thought herself too old for another baby. She couldn't because she'd been far advanced before she understood the unwelcome reason for her less willowy middle section. But perhaps she'd tried all the same. Perhaps that was the reason she, Portia, was so much smaller than her siblings. Or perhaps she'd had a dwarf father, an unidentified lover of her mother's, although Imogen had usually favoured the tall and handsome.

It was weird that she loved such a reprehensible mother as deeply as her still lurching heart confirmed. She'd always been a willing acolyte, humbly grateful for any little show of affection or attention.

Maybe it was longing not love. Once Imogen had given her a Victorian pendant, made out of a turquoise butterfly's wing. How she had worshipped it! She'd even worn it to school under her uniform until a teacher had noticed and banned it.

'I'm going somewhere quieter,' she said into the phone, and asked Brian to mind her stall for a moment.

A mother dying or dead. Memories of a childhood. A lover. A true lover. She had given up thinking about herself as a potential mother.

The mist was gathering lower over Portobello. The old lady with the three little dogs in the pram was out there, quite a group of admirers as the dogs yapped and spun. Further up the road she could hear the strains of the 'Singing Handyman' who bellowed an amplified Elvis from his van. 'You aint nothing but a Hound Dog.'

She walked further into a side-street. 'Yes, I can hear now.'

'We think she has an hour or two at the most.' It was an Irish accent, not West Indian at all, 'think' pronounced 'tink'. 'Your brother Roland is on his way from the country. Perhaps you could let the rest of the family know.'

'Are you . . . ?' Portia hesitated. They had been here before. She recalled Leo's distraction, Charlie's flying departure, their visit to the police station.

'We're as sure as you can ever be.'

'I'm sorry.' Portia promised to come immediately. She'd just finished the call when the phone rang again.

'You're on your way, are you, Portia?' It was Roland, sounding hyper.

'I've only just heard. Where are you?'

'Maggie's driving us up from the country. I'm using the phone. I'd like there to be an obituary. But it's difficult to arrange anything on Saturday afternoon.'

Portia was taken aback. 'But, Roland, what did Imogen do?' She wanted to add, 'She's not even dead yet.'

Anyway he ignored her. 'Have you called the others?'

'I've only just heard,' she said again.

'I might not get there in time. We might be too slow.'

Portia heard Maggie saying something in the background about trying her best and speed limits. Then Roland rang off.

I can't just abandon my stall, thought Portia, perplexed in this

199

moment of crisis before she recalled her new luxury, now a necessity. 'Conor. Oh, darling!' Of course, he would mind her stall, she knew he would, and there were plenty of taxis looking for customers round the market.

Leo had seen Charlie coming back from these induced sleeps before. It would take a little time but not much. Dr Heilbrand had suggested he could protect Charlie from the police but where was the doctor as they circled like vultures? Certainly, it was not only the police he needed to be protected from.

Treading gently, almost guiltily, Leo left Lizzie to sit at Charlie's bedside and went to find help. At a nursing station a young man, casually unkempt, was listening to another identically unkempt young man. The listener's badge proclaimed him a nurse.

'In the land of the blind, the one-eyed man is king.' This sentence took a very long time to complete as the man stuttered and stumbled. He then began the same sentence all over again. Leo was reminded of his father and tried to be patient. The nurse glanced at him and carried on listening.

They were at one end of a large room. At the other end stood a pool table. Leo had played a game on it with Charlie in recovery mode. Charlie had accused him of cheating, then of wanting to win. Leo had defended himself by potting five of his balls in a row. Charlie, hands shaking from the drugs, then went out in a single run. The black ball nearly bounced out of the pocket he hit it so hard. 'And you pretend not to be competitive,' Leo had commented with satisfaction.

'Did you want me?' the nurse asked him.

'I need to contact Dr Heilbrand urgently.'

'In connection with?'

Leo took against the nurse whose badged name was George Jones and who was staring at him intently. Perhaps he thought he was a patient. 'Is he in the hospital?'

'I'm far too junior to know a thing like that.'

Leo shut his eyes. When he opened them again, the nurse was still staring at him.

'You're that MP.' It was a statement. Leo turned his back and started to walk away. 'You can't unlock the doors without me.' Leo continued walking, 'I'm on your side, you know. Our government's crap.'

Leo considered. Was this why he'd put his career on the line? So that a young man who should command respect in an honourable profession could shout 'crap' across a hospital room? He turned reluctantly. 'I need an escort.'

'At your service. I don't often meet real live heroes.'

'I just passed on some information.' They proceeded side by side. Leo smiled wearily. He should be glad to have a fan. They were in South London. Maybe George was one of his constituents.

'One day I'd like to have a go at politics. It's our duty to be involved.'

Another nurse, female, accosted George. 'Is it you they're looking for at the pill dispensary? What's happened to your pager?'

'I guess it was driving me mad and I turned it off. But I suspect it isn't me you're looking for.'

Leo stepped aside from this altercation. It seemed his admirer was unreliable. Par for the course. In a minute or two, the female nurse led him briskly downstairs. She hardly glanced his way, as if he was included in her disapproval of George – 'I don't know where they find them and a new one each day.' She left him in the reception area.

In order to regain his equilibrium and escape briefly the atmosphere of disordered lives, Leo stepped outside. The fresh air reminded him that he'd had no lunch and was hungry. He looked at the murky sky, at the impressive trees nearest to him and tried to avoid seeing the orange tapes waving gently in the distance. He supposed he should listen to his mobile. Seven new voicemails, the first two from Bob, which he passed over, three from unknown numbers and two from Portia.

'Where are you, Leo?' Women always asked that question. He rang her back.

'Bad news, I'm afraid. Where are you Leo?'

Again. 'There can't be more bad news.'

'You mean those poor people drowning. The cold water. The cries. The fog.' She sounded jerkily distraught. Perhaps she was walking. He wanted to ask her where she was.

'It's not that sort of bad,' she continued. 'It's Mother. I'm on my way there now. You should come. It's the end this time. I'm trying and failing to get hold of Bill.'

Leo felt vaguely surprised. He supposed he'd never quite got the hang of Bill being part of the family. 'I'm sorry. I'm at Charlie's hospital.'

'Oh dear. Miles away.'

'It's still London. Charlie's coming round.'

'How ironic.'

She was right: Imogen sinking, Charlie rising. They rang off.

Leo thought of Charlie coming round to find Lizzie weeping over him. It didn't seem his style somehow. He heard a footfall behind him.

'Good afternoon, Leo. So you've come to join the welcome-back party.'

Leo had forgotten Dr Heilbrand's enthusiastic manner. It did him credit in a place of such foreboding. Leo also remembered he talked a good deal. 'Hello, Doctor.'

The doctor took his arm. 'The truth is, I wasn't planning such a brief escape for our dear Charlie from this world of turmoil and trouble. He's a strong lad, your brother, built like a bull, with the will of a fakir. The drugs I prescribed should have knocked him out for days but what do I find on my return from delivering yet another lecture? The price of fame but well received, I may boast. He's coming back to us! Yes, he is a man among millions. We should celebrate. Yet there is the matter of the police and poor Horace.' He drew breath to give a pitying sigh. 'They are ill-educated buffoons but we must deal with them all the same. Guardians of democracy, would you say?' He looked up at Leo suddenly, taking him by surprise. Sharp eyes glinted under bushy eyebrows. 'The world can and does provide worse.'

Leo pulled himself together. 'I have to leave.'

'So soon.'

'My mother's dying.'

'Today?'

'At this point in time,' said Leo, sadly, although pretty certain his sadness was only partly for his mother.

'Death takes precedence over life. I am used to the individual tragedies of the human mind. The mind is an extraordinarily complex mechanism. It is amazing that the percentage of certifiable, insurance-deserving breakdowns is so small. You must be off. As I described to you before – or was it your sister? – the men in blue cannot interview your righteous brother without his consultant's permission. As for the others, whoever they may be, let us hope that God may prove merciful.'

'You should know Charlie's wife is with him.'

'Wife?' It was the first time Leo had seen the doctor rattled.

'In name.' He felt weariness descend on him. Let Dr Heilbrand use his abundant energy on discovering the meaning of Lizzie. He scarcely knew it himself. 'Thank you. I'll keep in touch.'

They parted.

Leo paced reflectively to the car park. As he arrived, a car drew in. He wouldn't have noticed except that as the driver turned off the engine it gave a noisy shudder, like a horse sometimes does when a saddle is removed.

He watched and saw Bill, with a disgruntled expression, open the door. He stood outside for a minute, calming himself, looking at the trees. Leo was struck by how much he resembled the rest of the family, the height, the width of the shoulders, the thinning, curly hair, the square, well-featured face. How could he ever have doubted he was one of them? Of course he'd never really taken the trouble to think about it. Two brothers had seemed enough.

'Bill!'

CHAPTER THIRTY-THREE

The Brotherhood of Man

Bill was not very startled to see Leo; he imagined this hospital was filled with relatives. As he'd stood outside the car, he'd been thinking yet again – it was becoming a theme – about the nature of communities. The nuns to whom he'd given a talk lived in a small modern block on a noisy main road. The basement was used as a recreation area for any of those they helped who were capable of recreating. The ground floor held a reception area, an office and a cloakroom, the next three floors identical cube-like bedrooms with a shared bathroom. The nuns had insisted on showing him round, filled with pride at this newish acquisition, grateful to the Catholic philanthropist who had provided for it, happy at all the good it helped them effect.

'Oh, Father,' the mother superior had said to him, when he apologised for his lateness and explained the reason for his delay, 'we prayed for you as a community this morning. Your work is so hard, your day so full, yet you come to us.'

In truth, the afternoon had proved inspiring for him. More so, he suspected, than his talk had for them. He'd not been at his best, diverted by his difficult journey, by anxieties about Lizzie and Charlie. Yet the nuns, one of whom was Polish and another from New Zealand, had drawn him into their circle, to which he might have appended the word 'healing', and sent him away restored – not only in mind but in body, thanks to a plate of exceptionally large scones, served with liberal helpings of strawberry jam – a cheap, bought sort but none the worse for that. In their oasis of sanity (or so it seemed to him) it was hard to remember that they worked every day with the most recalcitrant human cases: the addicts, the mentally ill, the ill-wishing, the physically sick, the lonely, the despairing.

Before he left, they asked him to bless an old woman who'd come in looking for food and whom they'd permitted to stay. She lay in one of the cube bedrooms, leather-skinned, toothless, bundled in layers of odoriferous clothes, mumbling imprecations. In the old days she'd have been burned as a witch. The nuns had deduced she was Irish, probably Catholic, hence the blessing. They had produced a Tupperware pot of water, for him to make holy, handling it, after he'd obliged, as carefully as if it were a silver chalice. Such virtuous women put him to shame and, conversely, made him proud to be a priest.

'Bill! This is brother Leo trying to catch your attention.'

How unlike Leo to come out with the word 'brother'. He must be more upset by this home secretary business – which in fact was hardly on Bill's radar screen – than he'd appreciated. *Brother* – brotherhood of man, a band of brothers, a monastery of brothers.

'I've come to collect Lizzie, if she needs collecting and if my car obliges.'

'So that's how she got here. Have you been contacted by any of the family?'

First, 'brother', now 'family'. 'Not today. Of course, I haven't had my mobile on.'

'You may have said your farewells already.'

'Excuse me. Farewells?'

'Imogen is said to be dying. Finally dying. I'm driving to her, if you want a lift.'

Bill thought about this. To be with your mother at her last breath was a human obligation. Or was it? Leo was right. He had bidden her farewell. 'Oh dear.'

'I should be off.' He was back to the old Leo, commanding, impatient, perfectly able to take or leave this humble not-exactly-brother.

'You're very kind.'

It was reassuring to be cross with Roland about something as ordinary as backseat driving. Maggie was behind the wheel because Roland had given himself a huge shot of whisky a few moments before the nursing-home called. She understood his tension on just about every level one could imagine, but now they were off the motorway and entering the London sprawl, she felt ready to give him a hard time. Hard-ish, anyway.

'Do you *want* me to drive?' He didn't answer this, instead stared out of the window with a look of doom. She persevered: 'Your mother had no time for me. I didn't tick one of her boxes. Money, fame, beauty, breeding or wit.'

'She had no time for any of us.'

'Well . . .' It was easy to be cruel, just a question of lifting the foot from the brake of good behaviour. Ever so slightly. 'Well . . .' was a show of dissent, a reminder of Charlie.

Roland muttered something miserable she didn't catch, and she felt ashamed enough of herself to shut up. What was the point of suffering twenty years of Imogen's sneering patronage if she blew it at the home stretch? But what had been the point if Roland had never cared for her or their marriage and found his satisfaction with a 'bum-boy'? *Bum-boy.* She repeated the word to herself and found, instead of making her angry, it had brought tears to her eyes.

She had married the wrong brother. That was the long and short of it. With a little trickle of warmth in her desolation, she realised she would be seeing Leo very soon. The prospect made her want to behave more kindly to Roland. 'We're nearly there,' she said. 'I'm sure you won't be too late.'

'They'd have called.' He was clutching his mobile as he had throughout the journey. 'Portia thought it was ridiculous of me to try to arrange an obituary for Imogen.'

'She doesn't know about that sort of thing. Neither do I.'

'The *Daily Telegraph*'s our best bet.' Clearly Roland was talking to himself, clinging to a task. 'I can catch Jack Sims on Monday. He's good friends with the obituary editor. Imogen was a patron of more charities than anyone.'

Maggie resisted commenting that that was because Imogen liked going to smart parties wearing smart clothes. 'Wasn't she a model once?'

'Quite right. Just after the war, before she married. She worked for Dior in Paris for a couple of years.' He sounded excited. 'That's really clever, Maggie.' Against her will, Maggie found herself cheered by this compliment. 'A good photograph counts for more than anything. That's why they feature all those uniformed old soldiers. They'd love the photo of her in that Dior dress.'

'It was called the "New Look", wasn't it? It had a pleated skirt flared round her tiny waist.' Maggie had never had a tiny waist, not even as a child.

'That's the one. Can you remember where it is?'

It amazed Maggie that Roland hadn't tracked this famous photograph. Wherever Imogen went, it followed soon after, settling somewhere in her eye line. 'It's in the nursing-home.' She supposed this conversation was displacement therapy for Roland. He'd never been the slightest bit visual, allowing her to do over their entire house, except his study, when they'd first bought it.

'Good. Good.' Roland sat higher in his seat.

What was this fatal tolerance in her? She suspected that his night-time confession and her anger might gradually take the status of a nightmare, buried under Imogen's death, the funeral, the obituary. It would be up to her to resurrect it. Tolerance was a cowardly shadow of forgiveness, a virtue for those who didn't have the courage to confront. Lacking full-blooded conviction, she would reward herself with her love for Leo, unspoken, quite possibly unreal.

'That's a red!'

'Oh, God.' She didn't usually drive through red lights. Apart from the famous bee sting episode, her careful observance of traffic signals drove the children wild. 'Sorry.' She pulled herself together. 'Shouldn't you cancel tomorrow's guests?'

'I'd forgotten.' He was sitting close to the windscreen now, ticking off the last few streets before they reached the nursing-home. She'd never doubted his love for his mother. The sun had scarcely risen through the mists and the light was greenish, tinged by the young leaves growing on the trees at either side of them. 'Would you mind ringing round?'

She would do it, of course. 'Is it an important case on Monday?' Mostly he didn't talk about his work, unless to convey a sense of busyness and success.

'At least six weeks.'

'I suppose you can't postpone it?' She waited for him to respond, but he didn't, remaining silent until they drew up in front of the nursing-home. 'You go in,' she said. 'I'll find a parking space.'

*

Bill didn't feel comfortable being driven by Leo. It wasn't the driving, although it was faster than he liked, but the sense of Leo's remoteness, as if he hardly rated Bill as a passenger. The announcement of himself as 'your brother Leo' had clearly been an aberration. Or perhaps he was being over-sensitive. Or suspected he'd made the wrong decision in attending for the second time his birth-mother's dying. He reminded himself of an anonymous precept he'd once read: 'Always go where you are needed and modestly turn away from the places of glory.' Was he breaking that rule? Did Lizzie, in his mind's eye a sliver of hopelessness propped up on her ridiculous shoes, need him more?

After a while Leo switched on the radio. The news was just beginning and he turned up the sound. At once they were in the middle of the shipping disaster, the incomplete reporting. 'We still don't know whether anyone was trapped inside the smaller ship . . .', the human-interest stories, 'I had a ticket but got held up in traffic near Marseille . . .', the ministerial comment, 'Our hearts are with the families . . .'. Bill, while saying a prayer for all concerned and clocking that far fewer had died than originally feared – the death count had not risen beyond three – wondered why Leo wanted to listen to this and, indeed, the few items of news that followed: a double murder, the rumour of a future visit by the president of Pakistan, another of the marriage break-ups between two film stars he'd never heard of.

Leo snapped off the radio. 'That's a relief.' Bill looked at him with surprise, until he added, 'Not a word about the whistle-blowing rebel MP.'

Bill told himself to get a grip. Leo was a public figure, a representative of the people, who spent his time in Parliament helping to run the country. 'Did you want to be forgotten?'

'I was just being cowardly.' Leo glanced at him. 'Once an MP always an MP until the next election. Although they can throw me out of the parliamentary party like they did George Galloway. Or remove the whip for a period of time so I can't go to the House. I guess they'll prefer that, if they think I've shot my bolt. It'll cause less of a stir.'

'Have you?'

'What?' Leo cut in front of a lorry from the left.

'Shot your bolt.'

'I don't know the full story. I believe the home secretary got embroiled in some illegal goings-on and the police commissioner saw his chance for a bit of preferment but I don't know the details. I do know it's a bigger story, which will come out. Sooner rather than later.' He slowed down, allowing the lorry he'd just cut up to pass him with a blast of his horn and the V sign. He seemed unaware of it. 'Charlie's colleague warned me off getting further involved. He said he'd handle it in his own time. I tried to find out more but all I achieved was the death of a young woman.' He paused. 'Once a priest, always a confessor. Isn't that true, Father?' His tone was a little mocking.

'I listen if someone wants to talk.'

'Responsibility. That's what I thought about becoming a Member of Parliament. You know, we're pretty well paid now. As a bachelor I can live in comfort, even without a consultancy to boost my income. I bet you don't get seventy thousand pounds in expenses.'

'I certainly don't . . .' began Bill, but Leo was already on another line of thought.

'I'm frighteningly well educated, you know. My father saw to that. I was targeted at success. We all were. He put us in a cannon and fired us. Boom, boom, boom!'

'There's nothing wrong with success,' said Bill.

'You don't believe in the needle's eye?'

'There's also the parable of the talents.'

Leo had begun to drive faster again, taking lights on the amber, squeezing into gaps, braking too sharply. 'We're both bachelors. Both leading solitary lives.'

Bill's spirits sank a little. This declaration of common ground was unconvincing and suggested Leo was searching for a way into serious confessional mode. He tried to imagine what secrets might be hidden under Leo's confident exterior.

'You know the family now. It can hardly be a surprise we're so tangled up.'

'No more than most.'

Leo continued, as if Bill hadn't spoken, 'I sometimes think Charlie's breakdowns are for all of us.'

'I don't quite—'

'He takes the rap. He takes the risks too. Roland's a control freak. He knows what would happen if he cracked. That's why he hates

Charlie, although he doesn't acknowledge it. Charlie's his dysfunctional side. At least Portia and I love Charlie.' He became aware of Bill again. 'You do, too, don't you?'

'He brought me to the family.' Yes. He did love Charlie but he was embarrassed to say so.

'Typical. You see, that's why when this journalist fellow came and spun me a line about our home secretary I believed it. It came with Charlie's signature. Charlie was in hospital. It was my turn to take a bit of the responsibility. It's frightening when you stop to think that our bright lives are built on seams of black wickedness. Horace Silver's death made me even more convinced it was my duty to act.'

So, after all, it was a confession. Not the usual sort – about sin and repentance – but about choices.

'And then, of course,' said Leo, with a sudden mad, joyful look, 'I've been in love with Maggie for ages.'

CHAPTER THIRTY-FOUR

Last Gasps

'She's not so old after all.' Portia, Leo, Roland and Bill sat watching their mother take her last whispering breaths. There had been wonderment in Portia's voice. What she'd meant was that Imogen had regained her beauty at the end, her fine-boned face as smooth as marble, her eyelids perfectly carved, her mouth in a gentle arc. Although admiring, Portia also had a disturbing sense that those huge, pale blue eyes would open and stare at her, probably with disapproval. But she was dying, the doctor had said so. Her lungs were beyond repair. What would life be like without her? Any future Conor and she made together would be without Imogen's presence in the world.

Roland held his mother's hand. It was spotlessly white, one of the features of which she'd been proud. When they'd sat out in the garden, she'd not only worn a hat but also white cotton gloves. Someone had cut her nails short. That was odd.

He tried to remember his happiest times with her. They had been mostly in public. She'd had more time for him in public than in private. Once she had come down to Eton and watched him row in the winning team. She'd stood on the bank among the other parents; he could pick her out easily and not just because of her straw hat with lilac-coloured flowers dipping over the brim. He retained almost no pictorial images but this was one he'd never forget. Mostly she had appeared to celebrate his successes: on his graduation with a first at Oxford when she'd been attended by a handsome French diplomat (whom he'd tried not to identify as her current lover), on his reaching the bar, where she could hardly avoid the company of Esmond – a more distinguished lawyer than her son would ever be. She'd loved him on those occasions. Despite the current courtier, she'd given him her full attention, putting her white hand on his arm, kissing his cheek and whispering wickedly about others present: 'Does your housemaster usually have onions for breakfast, darling?' She had been a clever, witty woman, and he had been proud to be her first-born. He was still proud.

How he longed to press his lips against her delicate fingers. Instead, he put his head in his hands.

Sitting at the other side of the bed, Leo had been watching Roland's suffering face. He'd always known he and his brothers looked alike and had assumed, in their height and width of shoulders, they took after their father. Now he was struck by the similarity between Imogen and Roland, even though their colouring was so different. Perhaps Roland was right to claim a special relationship between them, one that could have lasted a lifetime but had been undermined so quickly by a younger brother's birth, then given the fatal blow by Charlie's. Mothers are not supposed to have favourites but Imogen had never played by the rules.

On the top of the wardrobe, he could see the famous photograph of Imogen at her most glamorous. Years ago she had tried to give him a copy. At first he'd been flattered, but soon discovered that Charlie had forcefully rejected the same copy. Later he'd boasted to Leo about how he'd seen her off: 'You're my mother, dearest Umbilical, not a pin-up.' Charlie must have been in his last year at school and Leo finishing university. He could still remember his shock that Charlie could be so rude to their amazing mother but he'd also admitted to himself the truth. Of course Charlie had been very into pin-ups at the time, the sort with huge boobs and legs straddled over chairs. He'd been shocked by them too.

At least Imogen wouldn't ever know that Charlie hadn't bowed her out. He was probably the only person to cause her real suffering; his breakdowns, which had started soon after he left school, had shattered his golden-boy image. At first she denied the diagnosis, railed against doctors, 'the new dictators', 'the new torturers', and refused to visit 'their charnel-houses'. When the reality became inescapable, she built up a new picture of Charlie as 'too talented for this world'. Maybe she even hoped he would die. She left the difficult practicalities of committing and sectioning to Esmond and only visited Charlie on special occasions – her birthday, for example.

Nevertheless, she persevered with her love, almost adoration, for Charlie, and even in his most destructive periods – calamitous love affairs with sixteen-year-olds, gambling with other people's money – she would never allow a word of criticism. Sometimes Leo had thought she did it to spite the rest of them but lately he'd decided she couldn't help it. She could have spared herself a lot of pain by giving up on him. But it was that sort of love.

Roland raised his head again and sighed.

Beside Leo, Portia held Imogen's left hand. Leo could see how his sister's fingers were clasped over the large sapphire ring that his mother had worn as long as he could remember. Over the last few years it had been his job to get the band made smaller as Imogen's fingers became ever more slender. On his most recent visit, the jeweller had said the width of the stone made it impossible to reduce the band further and, instead, put a bar across the back. Imogen had been petulant, making him the child who had failed again – she had always given out jobs with the opportunity for praise or blame.

Naturally Charlie had refused to play. Once when he was about sixteen, already strikingly handsome and surrounded by besotted girlfriends, Imogen had asked him – no, *commanded* him – to mark out the lawn tennis court at their then country house. She had departed for a weekend house party elsewhere. When she returned, she found the smooth green grass desecrated with thick white splodges, lines, dots, dashes, drips. Charlie was summoned and, very obviously the worse for a weekend-long binge, admitted he'd had a few friends over to help but expressed himself amazed by her horror. 'Surely you can see it's a homage to Jackson Pollock.' Leo had listened admiringly as he went on to point out the lawn's likeness, executed with 'sticks, trowels or knives' in the famous 'drip and splash' style, to Pollock's *Shimmering Substance*. He continued to point out, with an expression of injured innocence, that they had omitted any use of 'sand, broken glass or other foreign matter, often components of Pollock's work, out of consideration for the rights of the soil'.

The grass had grown through the white painting, at each stage creating new patterns so that visitors, not party to its origins, admired it as a work of art. It was a triumph for Charlie. To rub it home, he took up history of art as an A level, dropping Greek and thus causing both his parents pain. 'One must run with one's talent,' he announced. As far as Leo knew, Imogen had never given him another task.

Leo couldn't help smiling a little and unfortunately caught Roland's eye; his brother frowned grimly in return. Had they always been such enemies? He hoped not. At least, not on his side. They had had sport in common, a shared school life, the ambition to succeed. Maybe Imogen's death would make a difference.

Of course, it was ridiculous to think of Roland without thinking of Maggie. Yet he'd trained himself to do so. Maggie belonged to Roland, whether he appreciated her or not. Even now she was outside this room, doing some sort of social-secretary work for Roland.

Leo looked at his mother's face again. He was glad she was dying peacefully. He had feared some final ructions, perhaps the dramatic uncovering of ghastly secrets, or spectacular natural displays such as had accompanied Caesar's passing. But it seemed that this was it. Her life, for good or ill, had come to this moment: an old lady, still beautiful, faltering through her last breaths. She'd left no great works, no books, paintings, no great achievements in business or scholarship. He supposed that, since she had led a determinedly selfish life, they, her children, would be her memorial. Her troubled children.

Behind him, a chair shifted, accompanied by a heavy sigh. That was Bill. The son she'd given away. On hardly more than a whim. A religious whim, certainly. What must he be thinking? Did Christianity have an answer for that one?

The room was thick with emotion. It was the same with all deathbed scenes even when the persons attending had no real sympathy for the person dying. At the back of everybody's minds was the knowledge that they, too, would die and would have to put their lives on the line in just the same way. Mourning over the dying merged with mourning for the living.

As far as Bill knew, none of his siblings here present believed in an afterlife. It made him a little sad but he'd been born into an age when even a priest wasn't expected to preach to the unconverted so he didn't feel the urge for action. Portia ostensibly had a concern for the poor, which meant she was following one of Christ's most important precepts.

Reluctantly, he remembered what Leo had told him on their journey. Loving your sister-in-law was classic in a dysfunctional family. Not that they were dysfunctional in any obvious way. Outwardly they were successful activists, Leo, as he had shown, a daring man of principle.

Bill sighed again and looked at Imogen. She was still drawing tiny, fluttering breaths. A nurse appeared and bent over her. Bill knew he should be praying for her soul. Instead, he found himself wondering whether she had suffered when she gave him away to that childless couple. It seemed impossible that any mother should feel nothing for her child. Had she regretted it, maybe even poured out extra love on Charlie, the next son, because of the loss of the one before? If that was so, her strange donation had hugely affected the whole family. As far as he could make out, she'd never talked about it. She'd certainly shown no sign of welcoming his return to the fold.

He'd always known he was adopted, but his parents insisted his birth-mother wanted nothing to do with him, had requested no information. They never mentioned a father. They had instilled this view into him at an early age so that when he was old enough to search it seemed out of the question. As several of his seminary friends who knew his story liked to say, 'So then you found Mother Church!' They thought it good for a laugh, and he laughed with them. Why not? It was true in a way.

On the other hand, one could say that Imogen's approach to her children had something in common with the Church's. She was distant, dictatorial and expected a huge amount. Was *that* true? Again, in a way. The difference was that the Church allowed you to put down roots in her. He might twist and turn in disagreement but he still felt firmly rooted, secure. It was a blessing. To continue the analogy rather absurdly, he felt able to branch out and grow. He didn't think Imogen was capable of providing that. The only child she loved, Charlie, probably sensed that her loving was about possession and rejected it. Vaguely, he wondered whether there had been something in her past to make her so incapable of ordinary human warmth. Charlie had once intimated, in his fantastical way, that Lady Shillingstone had only married her husband because of a disastrous love affair in Paris.

It was strange to be analysing his family when he knew them so little. All the same he felt he was right about the children: rootless, growing tall and strong in the world's eyes but not in their own.

Of course, he'd only met Lord Shillingstone once. Roland had never shown any interest in him and their father lived in his house. He'd no regrets. The distinguished lawyer suffering from dementia seemed even less like his father than Imogen was like his mother, although it was true he'd always had a special sympathy for those who'd lost control of minds. He had spent two satisfying years as chaplain to a special hospital – that is, a prison for the insane. Perhaps that was why he felt close to Charlie.

Would Charlie be sad to have missed his mother's dying? Bill didn't think he was a man for events. He had too many in his own life. The dying was important for those present, but for those absent, it was the death that mattered. Charlie would manage.

Portia longed to lay her cheek on her mother's hand. She felt like a little girl again, allowed into Imogen's bedroom at breakfast time – perhaps before she went to school or, at weekends and during holidays, before she went riding. She would be dressed in the hard clothes of the outside world, her hands chapped if it was winter. Imogen lay among pillows, exquisitely pale like a princess in a fairytale. Hardly mortal. If Portia dared to kiss her cheek, Imogen smelled of her own special perfume: Arpège by Lanvin. Portia sniffed. Could she smell it now?

By then her brothers had left home or perhaps Charlie was still at university. Usually Imogen had a command for her: 'Fetch me my hairbrush, would you, darling?' or 'Find me a hankie from the second drawer.' How glad she had been to oblige. Was it all so very wrong? She supposed she should think so. It made Conor cross. At the thought of Conor, her tension softened. She wished he was here. Maybe she would ring him.

As Portia stood, the nurse came forward blocking her path; she bent over Imogen, then stood again. She folded her arms across her large bosom. Her face was portentous. Portia sat down. Everybody in the room, except Imogen, of course, looked at the nurse.

'You should say your farewells.'

Nobody spoke. Frozen, they stared at their mother. The breath stuttered, stopped, stuttered again, increased slightly in volume. Her children seemed unable to grasp that this really was the end, except Bill, who half opened his mouth as if to say a prayer or possibly obey the nurse.

The breath was silent, invisible. The breath stopped.

Portia found the room blurring. She thought of all those poor people dying in ice-cold water. Tears ran from her eyes.

Roland let go of Imogen's hand and stood up. Clearly he wanted to mark the event. Everybody looked at him. He was, after all, head of the family – unless you counted Esmond.

'Goodbye, Mother.' He had never called her 'Mother' to her face. Everybody noticed the change. Then he went out of the room. They could hear him in conversation with Maggie.

Maggie came in. She bent over and kissed Imogen's forehead. No one had dared to do that before. Then she went and put an arm round Portia's trembling shoulders.

Leo turned to Bill. 'Why don't you say one of your prayers? It would be nice.'

Bill thought for a moment, then knelt. Portia followed his example. '*Requiem aeternam dona eis domine, et lux perpetua luceat eis. Requiescat in pace.*'

As he finished Leo intoned, 'Amen', rather loudly. He turned to Bill, 'Didn't you ever resent her giving you away?'

'No,' said Bill, firmly, without adding anything further.

Leo took a step forward and, like Maggie, kissed Imogen's forehead. 'I never resented anything you did to me either. You taught me to be independent. I respected you for never pretending to be what you weren't. Sleep peacefully, Mother.' Then he, too, left the room. Maggie watched him go.

Outside the room, Roland and Leo had already begun to discuss the funeral. They were deliberately unsentimental and avoiding meeting each other's eyes so that the usual antagonism could go unacknowledged.

It struck Leo that at their last *tête-à-tête*, which had led to physical struggle, it was Charlie they had been mourning – or, rather, he had been mourning. On this occasion it was Roland who was suffering. As a second child, Leo had escaped some of Imogen's emotional pressure, if not the competitiveness.

'Most of her friends are dead,' he said, adding hopefully, 'Could we not have a small funeral? And what about Esmond?'

'He will attend, naturally.'

'I mean what about *his* funeral? He played an important role in English public life. People will expect either a grand funeral or a memorial.'

There was a pause. They were standing in a corridor that led directly to the nursing-home's reception area and front door. Leo heard a bell ring and the door opened. A policeman appeared with two men in overcoats behind him. Even at a distance, he could pick out the bewigged detective.

'What? Did you say something?' He turned his back and faced Roland. For a moment he felt embarrassed by his brother's obvious grief – he was near to tears.

'Mother drew up plans for her funeral. She made me promise to carry them out.'

'Ah, well, then. I'll leave you to it.' He didn't mean to be sharp. He meant that, if it gave Roland satisfaction to serve Imogen's wishes at the end (was he always to call her 'Mother' now?), he wouldn't interfere. To show more interest, he asked, 'Will it be Catholic?'

'She left Catholicism behind her years ago.'

'It was only a phase,' agreed Leo, although he thought it had left its mark on Bill and Charlie. 'I suppose Bill could always play a supporting role.'

'Bill wasn't around when she did the planning.'

'There you are. I'm sure he won't mind.' The conversation was beginning to depress Leo or maybe it was the presence of the policemen. Imogen's end had been calm, even what was known as 'dignified', in the sense that her body had not put forth any disgusting signs of death.

'She planned her funeral with Angus Streatham-Clark,' said Roland, his face swapping bitter rigidity for a more troubled expressiveness.

'Bad luck.' Angus Streatham-Clark had been one of Imogen's last lovers – or maybe merely a swain as she'd been in her late seventies. 'Didn't he organise parties? Perhaps you could get him involved.'

'Certainly not.'
'You're right. I'm here for any help you need.'
'Thank you.'
One should never underrate common politeness.

CHAPTER THIRTY-FIVE

Just For the Hell of It

Lizzie sat very upright on the chair, her legs crossed under it so that the bright shoes were invisible. She'd forgotten about them. The hours of being alone with Charlie had given her strength. She felt like a mother watching over her sleeping child. She hadn't even taken a second fag break, remembering, with wonderment, the shredded addict who had thought no further than her next fix. She was aware of her hunger but food had never held much interest for her and she enjoyed the spaces its absence created in her head. Sometimes she felt like she was floating over the bed.

Occasionally she shut her eyes and allowed herself to imagine Charlie up, dressed, filled with directive energy, his loud voice mocking and reassuring. But mostly she watched. In a way she didn't want this peaceful interval to end.

Charlie lifted his eyelids. It was quite an effort and possibly not worth it when all he saw was a grey ceiling. He knew where he was. He'd done this before, pushing through a weight of drugs to assert his presence in the world once more. It was always a difficult moment. His body sat over him like a depression in the weather, thick dark clouds, apparently immovable.

How was it this time? Not so bad, perhaps. He issued a command to a leg and it obeyed, turning under the bedclothes. The mind should always be in control of the body. Of course, there was the opposite danger when the mind swung back into action like a hurricane and the poor old body had a fucking dreadful time trying to follow it. Like hanging on to the end of a kite, rising higher and higher, exhilaration from the far-out-of-sight mind, terror from the body.

He didn't want to be there. He was too tired to be there. That was OK. The clouds were not too thick. Slowly, Charlie turned his head.

A raving maniac can expect all sorts of people to keep vigil over his bedside. His eyes, still not functioning with clarity, told him that a very thin, anxious nurse was doing the job. Poor girl, he thought. She must be a trainee. Not much of a bodyguard.

Lizzie's heart beat like a lover's as Charlie's blue eyes turned upon her. He gazed, and she sat perfectly still, holding her breath. He was coming back to her. 'Charlie,' she whispered reverently.

She thought he acknowledged his name. At least, there was a look of understanding. In her modesty, she didn't continue by supplying her own. He was the only one who mattered. She would have liked some sign, however, that he recognised her.

Bill had joined Roland and Leo in the nursing-home corridor. He noticed the atmosphere of tension between them. Even though he was only a brother in brackets or quotes, he took the lead. 'Shall we go into the waiting room? The nurse just told us the doctor was on his way to certify death.'

Roland gave him a look of surprise but followed him. Leo put his arm round Portia, who had come out too, and they followed.

In the cosy little room, dimly lit by a single lamp, Maggie was speaking on her mobile. She seemed disconcerted by their entrance. Her fair hair was bunched round her face and her cheeks were flushed, making her look younger than her age.

Bill, who scarcely knew Maggie, was struck by the disparity between her and her husband. He remembered what Leo had told him.

Portia also got on her phone, talking softly. Then Roland flicked open his BlackBerry.

Leo and Bill looked at each other. 'I'm trying to avoid all means of communication at the moment.' Leo smiled wryly.

'I can imagine.' Bill then remembered that he was due to say the six thirty p.m. vigil Mass. Tomorrow was the fifth Sunday of Lent.

As Easter neared, he found more people came to church. He looked at his watch. He could just make it if he hurried. No one needed him here. He felt a twinge of pain at this truth.

To his surprise, Leo took his arm urgently. 'What about Charlie? Someone's got to tell Charlie.'

Bill had forgotten about Charlie and, perhaps more important because she was one of his lost sheep, about Lizzie, left behind in the hospital. 'Can you go? We've only two priests at the moment. There'll be a biggish congregation. A priest's first duty is to say Mass.'

'Oh, really?' Leo seemed taken aback by this little lecture. 'Have you seen the police?'

'What?' Bill's eyes were on his watch again.

'The police. The place is crawling with them. I just spotted three here and they're at the hospital too.'

'I'm so sorry. I do have to go.' Bill would not let himself be sucked into Leo's problems and drawn away from his duty.

'Don't you see? They're longing to pounce. More questioning for me. No opportunity to see Charlie.'

Bill had reached the door. 'Couldn't Portia go?'

He caught Leo's mutter before he hurried away: 'Portia? I never thought of her.'

Once Bill was *en route* he became calmer and soon felt some penitence for his impatience with Leo. It was a product of their position in society, he thought gravely. He, Father Bill, brought up in Warrington of humble parents, working among the disadvantaged on the less salubrious fringes of Stoke Newington, found it hard to believe that Leo, product of Eton, Oxford and Westminster, could ever need his help.

He supposed it was a failing, although Christ concentrated most of his energies on the poor. He recalled the gospel of Christ the King – 'My kingdom is not of this world.' Leo had chosen to work in ways that could be seen and counted. He, Bill, had hoped to be a guardian of souls – the kingdom of God. Yet in the process, just like those good nuns, he had become involved in what must be called social work. In Holloway he often found himself making contact with partners or parents, filling in gaps where Probation failed.

That must be why saying Mass became such a joyful and important occasion. Mass was the time when he became most nearly the representative of Christ on earth. At Mass he was speaking directly to *souls*.

Bill went down the steps to the underground station, feeling satisfied with this explanation of his panic at Leo's plea for help. After all, their social differences were irrelevant; it was their vocations that counted.

The tube train was full and very hot. He stood beside two young women, both reading books held close to their faces. He admired their concentration. One of the sadnesses of his life was that he had no close women friends. His mother had been too old, he had no sisters or cousins and, when he was a young man, already thinking about the priesthood, he'd been nervous of women for obvious reasons. There were, of course, the 'good women' of the parish, those, often of Irish or West Indian descent, who washed linen, cleaned and prettified the church. Then there were the more educated of various nationalities, who read at Mass, led the singing, helped with groups or prayer meetings or with the education of children not at Catholic schools. This kind sat on the parish council. At the start of his ministry, the priest had always had the final say but more recently a new, argumentative sort of woman seemed to have taken over. He supposed this lessened his responsibility for practicalities but he wasn't drawn to those women. They were too sure of themselves.

He'd always felt attracted to the needy – women or men. An image of Lizzie as she'd swayed away from the car came to support this theory. It was immediately followed by the horrid memory that the car, damn its untrustworthy heart, was still sitting outside the hospital. Aloysius would be justifiably furious. On Sundays he used it to transport communion to the bedridden of their parish.

Now the peaceful prospect of Mass and its quiet aftermath was broken. He'd just have to take a million buses and tubes and collect the car later in the evening.

'Excuse me.' Taller than most in the carriage but without the confident air that usually goes with height and broad shoulders, Father Bill passed between the two young women, still deep in their stories of love and sorrow.

Portia watched Leo driven off with the three policemen; the siren began to wail as they turned the corner. Why would they want another interview?

'Are you sure you'll manage?' Maggie opened her bag. 'Do you need money?' They stood together on the pavement outside the nursing-home. The broad trunk of a plane tree, mottled like a snake, rose up behind them. 'Maybe I should take you part of the way.'

Portia was not used to being in the front line where family affairs were concerned. Suddenly there didn't seem so many of them, Roland staying around to organise post-death matters with the nursing-home, Maggie going back to the country to give Esmond the news, Bill (if he was to be counted) off on God's work and Leo whisked away in a police car. 'Of course I'm happy to tell Charlie,' she said.

'I know that. It's the mechanics of your journey I'm worried about.'

Portia thought Maggie lacked her usual calm. It was only South London, not the wilds of Mexico. She was still fidgeting with her bag or folding and unfolding a scarf she held. 'Don't worry. Conor will come and get me once he's closed up my stall.' She took Maggie's arm. 'Will it be hard telling Esmond?'

'That depends. He's refused to get out of bed this week but his mind's not too bad, which could be considered a good or bad thing under the circumstances.'

'Poor Father. I'm afraid I never help you enough with him.'

'I like looking after people.'

Far from being reassuring, this was said with such an air of sadness and irony that Portia felt confirmed in her sense that something was wrong with her sister-in-law. 'Do you have any children at home?'

'The boys have just come back for the Easter holidays and Hetty should be there too by now. Plus a nurse.' She turned away a little. 'We were supposed to have a big lunch party tomorrow.'

'I don't know how you do it!' exclaimed Portia, picturing her own little flat, her single life, with affection. If she and Conor made a future together (she didn't think the word 'marriage'), would they have an establishment? And children? She wasn't so old. Yet she couldn't picture it. I'm used to being a waif and stray, she thought, and dropped Maggie's arm.

They kissed and separated.

Maggie walked towards her car. She was glad to have the journey on her own. She'd not liked seeing Leo bend to get into the back of the police car. She thought she should have told Portia that money kept her show on the road. Roland's hard work, high earnings. She wondered if, after all, she should have transported Esmond to say goodbye to his wife. A nasty feeling in the pit of her stomach made her suspect she'd failed him. Her mind had been on Roland – and that was bad news too.

I put too much emphasis on happiness, thought Maggie, as she drove out of London. Every high street was filled with energetic weekend shoppers. Perhaps she could go to bed when she arrived home. But things might seem different there. Hetty would need lots of attention. She always did. And Roland would stay in London.

She was heading west towards a setting sun that struggled against the mist, not like the morning's thick blanket but low, vaporous trails. She hoped the sun would make it through before it disappeared for the night.

Leo felt the roughness of the policemen, not that they touched him physically, but in the brusqueness of their manner, in their way of not looking him in the face as if he had become unimportant, a nobody they were taking in for questioning. 'Why do you want to talk to me again?' he asked.

At the same moment the driver, a uniformed policeman, turned on the roof siren. It was clearly unnecessary, an act of intimidation. Leo reminded himself of a study he'd instigated in his constituency that monitored the use (or overuse) of sirens and found that more than fifty per cent of the time they were turned on just for the hell of it. Young men, policemen or otherwise, enjoy loud noises.

'Is that thing really necessary?' His voice was too mild, almost pleading.

'Saves you time, guv,' answered the driver, cheerfully negotiating through a red light.

Leo turned to the bewigged detective beside him. 'I have come with you voluntarily but it had better be important. My mother's lying dead in that nursing-home. I've just watched her die.'

The detective shifted slightly in what Leo hoped was shame. The odour of some too-sweet aftershave lotion rose from him but he still looked ahead.

The more formidable detective in front, Chief Inspector Roger Burrows, spoke quietly: 'We won't keep you long.'

Leo allowed himself to believe this. He sat back. He needed time to think about his mother, his family, Maggie. His present gaolers were hardly important in the scale of things. Proportionality – that was the modern buzz word. He wondered if the commissioner had entertained the same ideas when he was balancing his wife's imminent death from cancer against the potential end of his career. Would private disaster always tip the scales over public? It must depend on the make-up of the man.

The make-up of a man, particularly his own, had not previously been the subject of Leo's thoughts. He'd been taught to judge by actions, without too much curiosity about motives. He supposed this was not a very contemporary approach, when motives were sometimes given as much credence as behaviour. He'd grown up with a tougher approach and despised the kind of watered-down Christianity that encouraged forgiveness before penitence. Moreover, the morality of right and wrong had become tangled in crass psycho-jargon, which undermined the whole idea of personal responsibility. In this view, his captors would probably concur.

Leo shut his eyes. He didn't want to think these muddled thoughts. They got him nowhere. Imogen was dead. Fact. Maggie was married to Roland. Fact. Charlie suffered from manic episodes. Fact. He had accused the home secretary of succumbing to blackmail. And worse. Fact. A young prostitute had been murdered. Fact. He was on his way to a police station. Fact.

The car stopped. The siren stopped. Leo saw they were outside Paddington Green police station. A low and filmy sun glinted on the roof. Behind them rush-hour cars raced along the flyover. He had never felt so alone.

CHAPTER THIRTY-SIX

Angel Cakes

The hospital was winding down. Lizzie felt more than heard the decrease in noise and activities from corridors and rooms. It had been like that in prison, lockdown time. Then the noises had started from the cells again, music, shouting, TV sets turned up high. The people in here weren't like that. They were like Charlie. Drugged.

One of her legs had gone to sleep and she stood up to stretch it, glancing at the bed as she did so. Since that first movement, Charlie had opened his eyes half a dozen times, each for a few minutes longer. She wished he'd speak. She half believed he was playing some sort of game, waiting her out, ready to spring up the moment she left the room. But why should he do that? She was also beginning to wonder why Leo and Bill hadn't returned.

An hour ago a doctor had appeared. He'd stared at her with weirdly bright eyes under too-bushy eyebrows – she'd have made him shape them if she'd had the looking-after. 'Who are you, my dear?'

She'd told him and he'd become kinder, except that 'Ah, yes. The wife,' wasn't altogether kind. She knew what he meant, though. She'd never been wife material.

She turned her head at a noise. Here he was again.

'Off, are you? Mind if I sit? So, how's our patient?' He sat on the chair she'd just left.

He seemed chattier, or perhaps it was the time of day. It was getting dark now. 'No. I was just stretching. I think he's awake now. If you know what I mean.' She stumbled over the words and blushed.

'You must be starving. Hungry places, hospitals, and the hardest place to get food unless you're too ill to eat it. Once I had an operation – yes, doctors do have operations – and I lost a stone. Good news for some.' He patted his stomach. 'Not for others.' He turned his weird eyes on her again. His meaning was clear. It unsettled Lizzie. She knew she wasn't normal round food, had found it threatening since she was young. Funny when everyone round her, twice or three times her size, found it hard to stop eating and she – a 'will o' the wisp' her mum used to call her – found it hard to start. Some of her friends made themselves vomit, with fingers down their throats. She could throw up too, no need for fingers.

'Now, I'm sending you out for a sandwich,' continued the doctor, inexorable. 'Nothing in here, of course, so you go out of the main gates, turn left and left again till you find a group of shops. One of them will still be open. Understood?'

'Yes,' said Lizzie. She was used to that tone in men, used to being obedient in whatever way they wanted. With an effort of will she avoided thinking about some of the less OK ways. Charlie expected obedience too. No more drugs. He hadn't cottoned on to the eating thing, though. This doctor was quick.

'Off you go, then.'

'I'll be back, won't I.'

'Do not be afeared. Charlie's not going anywhere.'

Lizzie wandered away down the corridors. Quite soon she met the dishevelled male nurse called George Jones. He took her arm in a friendly way and asked if she was off for another fag break.

'I need something to eat.'

'Don't we all?' He grinned casually, as if he'd made a joke. 'So where are you going to find some?'

She explained carefully the doctor's instructions as he locked and unlocked doors and they descended the noisy stairs. (There were her shoes again, clanging away.)

When they'd got all the way down, he turned to her. 'Tell you what. I'm due for a break. A bit of fresh air would do me good.'

They walked down the drive together. George had his white jacket rolled up under his arm. Once they were outside, it didn't seem so dark. Lizzie looked up at the sky and somewhere there was a bit of a lemony colour and somewhere else a bit of purple blue, with gauzy layers of white. The branches of the trees were black, though.

She didn't really like walking with this George. She didn't feel safe. He was too young, too open, with far too much hair. She remembered the doctor's eyebrows. Perhaps hairiness was in fashion at the hospital. Yet in George's case it didn't seem quite real. In fact, he wasn't quite convincing altogether.

'A lot of buzz round Charlie, you know. Sure to be, of course, until they clear up this Horace Silver business.'

Lizzie didn't know what he was talking about and had a pretty good idea that she didn't want to. She pretended to trip a little on the gravel.

'Are you OK?'

'Fine.'

But then he went back to it. 'Then there's this MP brother. Wow! Brave, I kid you not. Quite a family!'

He seemed to expect a response. That wasn't so difficult. 'Yes,' agreed Lizzie, primly.

'The police just don't get it, do they?'

Lizzie was beginning to feel sick, and they hadn't got out of the grounds yet. Probably he knew about her being in prison. And why. He'd start talking about that any minute.

'Are you OK?' George asked again.

With relief, Lizzie remembered her cigarettes. She pulled them out of her pocket. 'Can't think why I waited so long.' There was no wind but it still took her a moment to light up. She drew in deeply, just managing to control a long shudder.

They continued walking. This time George seemed thoughtful. At least he was silent. She wondered why he was so keen to be with her. Not just because he wanted a breath of air, that was for sure.

The shop was brightly lit and warm. A tall Asian man stood behind the counter. He looked at George suspiciously. It was the kind of place where Lizzie was used to shopping: rows of ciggies, rows of sweets, some sad vegetables and fruit, a freezer humming too loudly, cereals and tins, everything of the cheapest, although not necessarily cheap. Obedient to the doctor, she moved to the shelf optimistically labelled 'Fresh Goods'. The only sandwiches were shrimp or egg mayonnaise on white bread spotted with lethal black seeds.

'The pork pies are eatable.' The nurse stood beside her. She couldn't imagine digesting fatty pastry and pork jelly. She turned to a shelf behind her and randomly chose a packet of biscuits.

'Do you seriously like fig rolls?'

Turning back, she chose with more care a packet of angel-cake slices.

'Those look disgusting.'

She walked to the till where the owner also looked disgusted. What did they know about her digestion? She could imagine the soft pink and yellow sponge and white creamy bits going down her tubes. At one time she'd lived on nothing but angel cake.

They started the journey back. George was swigging at a can of Coke. She'd forgotten to buy anything to drink.

'What do you think of the hospital?' he asked suddenly.

Lizzie, nibbling the edge of a cake slice, felt panicked. She supposed he was mocking her. How could she have a view on the hospital and, if she did, which she didn't, why would he want to know it?

'My view,' he continued, as she failed to answer, 'is that it's essentially a good hospital for one simple reason: it's possible to bend the rules. When rules are put above common sense it's a sure sign of a failing institution. I'm not saying there should be no rules – working with mental patients puts you off anarchy – but they should be constantly assessed against the true needs of the patient. That's logic.'

There was a triumphant note in his final words and he peered at Lizzie through the gathering darkness as if expecting applause. 'So what's your view?'

'Uh-huh,' she said and then, trying harder, 'Difficult, isn't it.' Maybe he was one of those men she'd come across now and again who tried to work things out. It made them seem stupid, even if they were clever. In all honesty, Charlie was a bit like it and that had been to her advantage, hadn't it?

But George wasn't like Charlie. He had an agenda. She could feel it. On impulse, she turned to him. They had reached the hospital grounds, with the tall trees over their heads, the night black around them. 'You're not a nurse, are you?'

That's what he reminded her of: those plain-clothes police who hovered round the girls, checking out on the drugs or whatever.

They always overdid the hair too, either shaved right off or sprouting like a bush. They didn't talk so much usually.

George smiled, for a moment neither agreeing nor denying. Then he said softly, 'You wouldn't want your husband to go the way of Mr Silver, would you?'

'I don't know what you mean.'

He stared at her. 'I don't believe you do. Just think of me as on your side.'

'Oh!' Lizzie grabbed George's arm. She'd heard footsteps just behind them.

'Like Mr Plod, aren't I?' A cheerful voice spoke out of the darkness. 'Your shoes are quite a giveaway if you wanted to do anything you shouldn't. Persil white, I call them.'

Lizzie never talked to policemen. It was one of her rules. Had been for years. Some of the other girls gave them lip or a come-on, thought it kept them on side, but she'd known better. Police were the enemy and the worst of all were the jokey ones. They'd take everything, then stick you in a cell quick as you could pull down your skirt. And that included the ones out of the fancy dress.

'I'm a nurse,' said George firmly to the uniform.

'Just checking, aren't I? And her?'

'She's a visitor. May I ask who you are?'

Lizzie liked that. Even if they were playing games. Then undercover often didn't share with uniform.

'You're going back in, are you?' The policeman didn't answer George's question, but Lizzie thought he'd lost some of his cockiness. He was bored, probably, out in the dark. Nothing to do with her personally. Probation didn't bother much over a weekend.

They continued walking, the three of them. To show she didn't care, Lizzie took out her angel cake and ate a whole slice. She was glad to feel it sit quite comfortably in her stomach.

Charlie was aware of Dr Heilbrand right from the moment he came into the room. He tracked behind mostly (but not always) closed eyelids the exit of the girl, whose connection to him now lay on the edge of his memory. The doctor was at the forefront. They had known each other for more than twenty years, ever since Charlie's odiously regular visits to this hospital had begun. Dr Mengele, as he liked to call him, had been the commander of the enemy forces who had trapped him and held him for weeks or months forcibly turning his mind with drugs and, on several occasions, ECT. When over-excited he'd often told the doctor how he hated him. 'Sadist! Monster! Pervert!' he would cry. Plus some expletives, with a garnish of Latin.

When he came back to himself, shaky, memory temporarily shot to pieces, he'd see the hairy, clever face peering at him, not so much with sympathy but with a kind of bright curiosity as if to say, 'Well, here you are again. Let's see how you've turned out this time.' His insults became more friendly, although he still called him Mengele, mainly to shock the nursing staff; sadly, most of them were far too ill-educated to understand the reference.

This awakening, without the benefit of ECT (it did have benefits, although he didn't like to admit it), was no different. There the doctor was, peering curiously.

Charlie held up a hand. 'Hardly shaking,' he demonstrated. Neither was his speech too blurred.

'True. True. Your treatment was modified.'

'Losing your taste for torture?'

The doctor sat back on the chair. This was unusual. He was a brisk, busy man. Even during their formal interviews in his office, he looked at his watch, made notes to himself on his pad, more lately, on his BlackBerry. Charlie assumed they were not about him. He liked that. It was reassuring that the doctor felt it unnecessary to give him his whole attention. Sometimes lately he had stopped fighting him and thought they had an understanding.

'How are you, Charlie?'

That was a stupid question. The doctor controlled how he was. No psychiatrist stuff, 'head screwing', as he thought of it. 'I'm in bed. I'm awake. I can see you sitting on the chair. In a moment or two I'll be ready to rock and roll.'

'But can you talk to me?'

'*Domine non sum dignus.*'

'Quite. But can you talk to me?'

'*Ça dépend.*'

The room was very dark. Even the gleam of the doctor's eyes was dimmed.

'How did it happen?'

'Alas, poor Horace . . .'

'How did they get in?'

Charlie felt the doctor's shadow leaning closer. 'Same way I got out.'

'Oh, Charlie. Charlie.'

'Do you mean you didn't know? The all-seeing, all-knowing one. A key buried in the earth. Out through the door in the wall at the end of the garden. A man must have his vod and smoke.'

'And on the way out you met Horace?'

'God rest his soul. *Requiescat in pace*.' Charlie closed his eyes. The doctor said nothing. 'Let there be light. *Lux aeterna*.' He opened his eyes. It was still dark but now there was light from the corridor, against which he could see the silhouette of the doctor hunched in his chair. It wasn't done to close the door of a madman's room. Standard practice. Charlie sighed.

'I met Horace in the garden. He knew what I was up to. He said, "Bring me a tube of Rolos, mate." '

'You had both got out into the garden? Despite being locked in? Sectioned?'

Charlie thought the doctor was not very surprised by this.

'You might say we passed through doors. The air was fresh in the garden. The birds were all hopping and squeaking, the way birds do. Bullfinch, tit, cock robin, you know the type. The things that have happened in that garden. We felt bright. We sang a little ditty: "On Richmond Hill there lives a lass more bright than May-day morn . . ." '

Charlie began to sing but his voice was hoarse and his heart not in it. He stopped.

'Then?' encouraged the doctor.

'Then Horace began to shiver. He only had a T-shirt on – one of those hospital-issue jobs that smell of cheap soap and the decay of hopes. His arms were smooth and white, apart from blue veins and goose pimples. He shook all over.'

'So you gave him your jacket?'

'Just while I went to the shops. Wonderful shop. Wonderful people. Mr and Mrs Patel with three junior Patels. Salt of the earth. They'd get me anything, God knows what England has done to deserve such people.'

'So you came back with your buys?'

'Lingered. I lingered a little. Patel junior *numero due* wanted to tell me about this prize he expected to win: Young Scientist of the Year. Competitive little bugger. Nice, though. Remind me to have sons some time soon. I told him that virtue brings the truest reward. If he wasn't so polite, he'd have laughed in my face.'

'Yes?'

Charlie knew why these lapses in the story occurred. Probably the doctor did too. Guilt is a hard taskmaster. Besides that, he was very tired. 'I came back. The door in the wall was open. That surprised me.'

For the first time Charlie pulled himself up into a sitting position. He put on a light above his head. It glowed a blue white. Not a friendly light. The silver in the doctor's bushy hair sprang out like steel filaments.

'I saw my coat first, hanging like a scarecrow in a field of rooks. Fuck. Fuck. Fuck.'

'I'm sorry.' The doctor bowed his head.

'The things you've seen.'

'Never any easier, Charlie.'

'If I'd locked the fucking door, they couldn't have come in.' There was a long silence. Charlie knew what the next question would be. He tried to put it off. 'If I hadn't lent him my coat, they wouldn't have thought he was me. I had a letter from Leo in the pocket. Commons' notepaper.'

'They? They?'

'It was my fault. He was dead as a dodo. Ugly, too. So I ran. Out.'

'You weren't quite yourself.' The doctor leaned closer once more. 'So you know who they are?'

Charlie was beginning to feel sick. It was the ghostly light, the drugs sliding around his body, the lack of food, of drink, the ghastly sight of Horace Silver. He'd tried to bring him a fucking tube of Rolos, not death. 'I need a drink of water.'

'Of course you do.'

When the doctor had left the room, Charlie switched off the light and lay back. He could feel his hands jumping about to the tune of his brain. What did he know? What had he told Griff? Not everything. Where was Griff? Scared? Done a runner? On the job? He must be calm. *Soyez calme. Pax vobiscum. Pax aeterna* for poor Horace.

'Are you there?'

'Hail, O dearest Mengele. I hope my drink is flavoured with something suitable – a man of sorrows and acquainted with grief.'

Sitting up in bed drinking the water, he felt a little grace descend on his soul. It made him think of women and, in particular, the half spirit, half woman who had watched over him. He remembered her now. 'They are the better sex, you know.'

'What? What?' Perhaps the doctor had fallen into a doze. He jerked up his heavy head.

'Women. Take the girl who sat like a guardian angel by my bed. A prostitute – sorry, a working girl. A drug addict. Desperate to lick the hand that helped her out of the mire. Can you imagine why they sent her to prison? One good reason?'

'Can we have the light on again?' complained the doctor.

'They cross the boundary.' Obediently Charlie switched on the light. 'Over the river of darkness and into Hades. Only Orpheus to save them.'

'I see you're feeling better.'

'Have you ever fucked a prostitute?'

'Certainly not!'

'You're a man of iron virtue.'

'I'm a healer, not a destroyer.'

'Ha. Ha. You don't call them "punters", then?' Charlie wasn't surprised to receive no answer. He himself had been a punter many a time and oft. Picked them from the street or rang a number. Just a cunt. Sometimes two breasts staring at him. The eyes of God. He lay back. 'I'm not sure I'm so much better, dearest healer. My head is spinning.' He caught a glimpse of satisfaction on the doctor's face.

'We must cosset you.'

'Cosset. Yes. Cosset with a posset.'

'No visitors except close family. Sleep that knits up the ravelled sleeve of care.'

' 'Tis a consummation devoutly to be wished for.'

'You have been terribly shocked. Even a man of your constitution needs time to recover.'

To Charlie's horror, he felt tears well in his eyes. Was he as weak as this? A little sympathy from the voice of authority and he dissolved like a child. 'Who has come to see me?'

'A brother and a wife. I ask no questions about the wife.'

'Quite right. A second-rate Mary Magdalene. It's an old story.' He was beginning to feel drowsy, his tongue thickening so the words wouldn't stay distinct. 'Mary Magdalene.' He tried to repeat the name, and failed. Suddenly he was afraid – a child's terror as night falls. 'You won't leave me alone?'

'Don't worry. I will see you're safe. And there's always young Mr Jones. A determined character. He told me he has the reflexes of an Indian wicket keeper.'

'You're a good old torturer,' Charlie wanted to say but his head lolled backwards and the lids dropped over his eyes.

CHAPTER THIRTY-SEVEN

Things a Captain Doesn't Tell His Crew

Hetty was all over her mother. Like a puppy bounding up and wanting to kiss, impeding her progress. Maggie pushed her off, kindly.

'So Grandma's really dead!' Hetty cried, the boys and Mungo behind her, a welcoming party in the hall. 'Do you realise it's my first death?' she continued, more reflectively. 'My first personal death, I mean. It's probably a defining moment.'

From the open door of the kitchen, Maggie smelled bacon. They'd been cooking. That touched her and made her feel sad. They could do without her.

She hugged the boys. At least they were still a head shorter than her, their bony shoulder-blades hunched against the world. Probably against her hugs too. 'I need a drink.' A glass of strong Spanish red.

'Driving to London and back, with Grandma and all that in between. You must be exhausted.' The drama had made Hetty sympathetic. She led her mother into the kitchen.

Maggie hesitated. 'I think I should go to your grandfather first.'

All three children looked at her solemnly. Their sensitivity made her want to cry.

'Yes. Yes. I'll go to him.' She hurried away without taking off her coat. They couldn't know that her distraught air was as much about their father as the death of her mother-in-law.

Esmond was asleep. The room was neat and tidy and smelled fresh. She could hear the television from the nurse's room.

She pulled up a chair and sat by the bed. When Esmond slept, he looked dead already. It had often unnerved her. Sometimes she'd studied his distinguished cranium, still crowned by white hair, and wondered what had happened to all the cases he'd defended. Were they lined up inside there, all the successes and the few failures, packed away, like a history book with no access? He'd been called the cleverest man of his generation with a mind that, like a chess player's, could predict and forestall his opponent's every move. Surely he must have been prepared for Imogen's death. Outside, an owl – it lived with its family in the barn behind the house – flew slowly by, hooting mournfully.

The nurse put her head round the door. 'I thought I heard someone.'

Maggie noted the questioning air. 'Yes. Lady Shillingstone died.'

'Ah. I'm sorry.' The nurse bowed her head politely.

Maggie found herself bowing in reply 'I'll wait here till Lord Shillingstone wakes.'

The nurse withdrew. Time passed and Maggie became more tranquil. She was doing her duty. Her mother, before she died in middle age, had impressed on her daughter the imperative of duty, the effort and satisfaction of doing the right thing. Not that she had always followed her own advice, having left her husband for no obvious reason. Letting out a long breath, Maggie stood to remove her coat, which she folded on a second chair behind her.

When she returned, Esmond's eyes were upon her.

'Good evening, Esmond.' She kissed his cheek. She believed in physical contact. It struck her that the last face she'd bent to kiss had been his dead wife's although, in that case, she'd directed her kiss to the forehead, as more fitting.

'That owl is like a foghorn tonight,' pronounced Esmond. So he knows where he is, thought Maggie, and would have spoken if he hadn't continued. 'A bird associated with wisdom in classical literature but in other cultures considered to be a bird of ill omen.'

'I thought the albatross . . .' began Maggie, tentatively. Even in his dotage he could make her feel ill-educated.

'At sea.' Esmond was firm. 'The albatross is a sea bird. The owl flies over land.' He half closed one eye, 'While alive, the albatross is an honoured visitor. Last time I sailed round the Cape of Good Hope, the ship was followed by an albatross. Very fat it was. One could appreciate why sailors are tempted to shoot it. Better than sucking-pig. Fortunately my sailors were perfectly disciplined. I gave them an extra tot of rum and that was it.'

So he knows where he is, thought Maggie, but not who he is. He was entering his captain-of-the-high-seas adventures, which could ramble on for half an hour or more, till his voice grew too hoarse to continue. Perhaps he saw himself as Captain Aubrey. There'd certainly been rows of the O'Brian novels in his study. She supposed it might figure that he would choose for his *alter ego* a character as unlike himself as possible.

'Esmond.' She had raised her voice.

His eyes fixed on hers immediately. The intensity of appeal, the nebulous colour, reminded her of someone . . . Roland, as he told her of his affair. The idea made her unhappy. Best get the telling over as soon as possible.

'I'm sorry.' She took his hand, willed herself to look honestly into those faraway eyes. 'I've just come back from London. I went to the nursing-home. All your children were there.' This wasn't quite true but it sounded better and he was in no position to check up. 'I told you this morning that Imogen was very unwell. Today, at about four, she died. It was very peaceful, very dignified. I'm sorry,' she said again, and bowed her head.

The hand she held was withdrawn and she felt a struggling movement under the bedclothes. Oh, my God! Was the shock going to kill him? 'Jacky!'

The nurse came quickly. She must have been at the door. Together they tried to calm him. Gradually Maggie got the point. 'He's trying to get out.'

Of course he did get out of bed some days, sat in the second chair with a rug round him.

They helped him then, pulling the chair closer, the nurse using her professional technique. It took time, his breathing loud and strained. Finally, he'd made it. Maggie brushed smooth his hair.

'I never thought she'd go before me.' His gaze, returned from the high seas, was sober but not filled with as much pain as Maggie had feared. A large vein in his temple throbbed purple. She remembered how he'd received news of the deaths of friends and contemporaries. He'd expressed regret but had been unable to disguise a tinge of victory. Was it possible he'd felt himself equally in competition with his wife? It seemed an inhuman proposition.

'It was her lungs,' said Maggie. 'She couldn't breathe. She passed away very calmly.'

'They say pneumonia is the old man's friend.' His voice was steady. 'She was a very strong woman. Almost all her life. Beauty gives strength. When will the funeral be?' At that moment he seemed completely in control of himself; he didn't even look so very old, sitting upright in his chair.

'Roland's arranging it.'

'Yes. Yes.' He appeared impatient at the idea of Roland.

'Apparently Imogen left plans.' She forbore to mention that the planning had been in co-operation with her last lover – not that Esmond had ever shown any interest in what he described as 'Imogen's young admirers'. 'Perhaps we can take you there.'

'There was a time when I went to a funeral every week of the year. Far too lengthy most of them. People have a tendency to overdo things. They don't take into account that many of the mourners are getting on. It's not like a concert when you can carry in a cushion.' He gathered breath and frowned. 'Then there's the question of the ageing bladder. I did leave early from the attorney general's, but it was taken badly. His wife, his third wife, a silly woman, didn't speak to me for weeks. She came from South America but I don't remember which country. Ah, memory!' He lapsed into silence again, then added, 'I hope Roland will keep good control of Imogen's funeral. She wouldn't want her guests incommoded.'

Privately Maggie thought that Imogen would want her final accolades to last as long as possible, although it was true that she had been a wonderful hostess, orchestrating an event so that nothing, lunch, dinner, drinks, dragged into anticlimax. She had been easily bored, of course. Perhaps that was as good an explanation as any for her succession of lovers and her impatience with her children. She should have had a career. Maggie had a vague sense that Imogen's life had been disrupted by the Second World War. She had never spoken of it.

'I like this room best,' said Esmond, his old head directing itself round, like a tortoise's from its shell. 'I used to like my chambers and then the House of Lords, although my office was disappointing and there were far too many stairs. The division bell usually found me in the Archbishop's Robing Room – miles from the Chamber. I preferred the bells on board ship. Eight bells, seven bells, that sort of thing. Gave a sense of order to the crew, only boys some of them. Have to make sure they get an education. Education's the key . . .'

This seamless reversion to life on board an eighteenth-century sailing ship always took Maggie by surprise. She decided it was the cue to leave. She'd brought the news and Jacky would summon her, if needed. Maybe she would lie on her bed for a moment too. Maybe she would consider her position.

Roland got back to his flat to find a note pushed under his door. On the outside was a crude drawing of what he believed was called a 'smiley'. He opened it. 'Darling, I miss you!' The writing was almost illiterate and could be no one's but Didi's. He was filled with revulsion; the smiley, in particular, struck him as an insult of mammoth proportions. And how had Didi discovered where he lived and, more upsetting still, got himself inside the building?

Roland sat on his overstuffed leather sofa and looked at the scrap of paper again. One side of his mind mourned the marble effigy of his dead mother, the other responded to Didi's crass note with growing sexual excitement.

Two minutes later, he'd poured himself a whisky and reached for the telephone.

Portia looked up at the hospital. Tier after tier of lighted windows rose out of the darkness and mist. The building was like a great liner in the midst of an ocean of nothing, she thought, and was reminded of the real tragedy of the day – not her mother's expected death but the collision of two ships. It was not a propitious date.

'Come on, my darling dear, let's get this over and done.' Conor took her arm. Neither of them was wearing a heavy coat and she could feel his warmth.

'You're so kind to drive me here.' He had picked her up from the nursing-home.

'Why wouldn't I? Your own mother, cold but not yet in her grave.'

They walked briskly, the gravel scrunching and turning under their feet. When they reached the lighted entrance, the doors were locked. Conor rang the bell. After a longish wait, a man came towards them. He had bushy grey hair and wore an overcoat. He peered at them suspiciously before opening the door. 'Could it be Portia?'

Portia was confused and said nothing. She felt washed out by the ugly light. Even her many-layered, many-coloured clothes seemed defeated by this cold hallway.

'She's in shock,' said Conor. 'Her mother just passed away and she's come to give the news to her brother, Charlie Barr.'

'Potts,' murmured Portia. 'Charlie Potts.'

The doctor unbuttoned his coat and took it off. He eyed Portia but took Conor by the arm. 'My patient, you see. Your Portia and I are old friends. We will talk a little, I think, before you see him.'

Portia, slightly resentful that the doctor had Conor's arm when she needed it (for ever and always), followed the two men along the hallway and into the waiting room.

'I've been listening to Charlie,' began the doctor, as soon as they were sitting. 'The situation is serious.'

Portia heard herself gasp feebly. She sat straighter. 'He wasn't so bad,' she said quite firmly. 'And after all he turned himself in.'

'Yes. Yes.' The doctor waved his hands. 'You misunderstand. I will explain.'

Remembering the doctor's loquaciousness, Portia settled back, although she determined to keep her concentration. She glanced lovingly at Conor's pale, rather girlish face. He was her companion, her lover. He could be doing so many better things on a Saturday evening than being lectured in a suburban mental hospital.

'. . . such an extraordinary case.' The doctor was already two sentences in. 'Charlie's story, unfortunately, is very peculiar and therefore not very convincing. Which does not mean it is untrue. Absolutely not. An institution such as this bulges with examples of the unexpected, both in mind and body. Horror stories, tales of the unexpected, are a misnomer. The horror arises from the fact that we *do* expect torture, cruelty, madness and death. We are born in fear and sigh, almost with pleasure, when we see its enactment. Why do gruesome murders command such wide interest? Easy. Because they satisfy our instinctive sense that horror is the reality of existence. We dance on a crust of terror, the hell of our unconscious . . .'

At this point, despite her best intentions, Portia's mind wandered. Why couldn't Dr Heilbrand say the world was filled with evil as well as good and leave it at that? Conor, she noted, seemed to be hanging on his every word. She didn't know whether he had any religious beliefs, but as he was born in Dublin to Irish parents it seemed certain he had been brought up Catholic.

'We are faced, therefore, not just with Charlie's distorted mind but with his role as a witness to a murder at very least. You see now why I am concerned.' The doctor stood up and faced them, as if in a court of law.

'What *did* happen?' cried Portia, impulsively.

'As I said.' The doctor sat down again and looked at Conor, who took the hint.

'The doctor explained that the patient was murdered while Charlie was out on an illegal shopping expedition. He had given his jacket to the other patient. Both men are large and, although not old, have physically deteriorated. It was a case of mistaken identity.'

Trying to overlook the horrible idea of Charlie's physical deterioration – due as much to the hospital's drugs as drink or his own behaviour, she thought defensively – Portia burst out, 'Then there's no reason to suspect Charlie!'

'You would think so.' Conor smiled reassuringly, then added, 'But he himself is in danger.'

'I want to see him,' said Portia, excitedly. She wanted to see Charlie *alive*, not surrounded by all these murky suggestions and not *dead*, like her mother.

'Certainly.' The doctor stood again. 'I shall take you myself. I merely wanted to put you in the picture.'

'We understand,' agreed Conor.

But Portia, thrown back to childhood, felt she understood nothing. This time she took Conor's arm.

They had reached the second floor, following the doctor, who moved swiftly, sometimes taking two steps at a time, when Portia heard other loud footsteps ahead. Another few stairs and she saw white shoes clanking laboriously upwards, then a slim dark form.

Bill had hurried straight to church. He'd robed in the purple vestments of Lent and approached the altar. A single server, an old man in a grey suit, preceded him. When the congregation stood, he felt himself lifted on waves of faith. Today, he thought, my mother died, and tonight I can pray for her soul at the altar of the ever-living God, at the altar of his Son who died to save us all from eternal damnation. 'In the name of the Father, and of the Son, and of the Holy Spirit.'

When the Mass was over, he stayed talking to a woman who was worried about her son's choice of friends – he'd tried his best, inviting the boy to visit him, which was unlikely to happen. Then he went to the church house for a quick bite before setting off to retrieve the car.

Aloysius had already finished eating but still sat at the table. As so often, Bill wished he got on better with his fellow priest.

'Probation's been on to you. A Shirley. Don't you listen to your mobile?'

'I'm sorry.' He could have given his mother's death as an excuse but judged it was better to say nothing. Aloysius knew he'd mourned one mother already. If Shirley was on to him it must mean Lizzie had failed to show. It was nice of her to call on a Saturday. Probation officers liked their weekends off. The joy of Mass lessened. Why hadn't Portia seen to it? It was wrong to blame Portia. She probably didn't even understand the system. 'It'll have to wait till Monday now.'

Bill rang Portia. But there was no answer there either. How often as a priest he'd rung with no answer and terrible events had followed. This was not the case now, he reminded himself. The worst scenario was Lizzie returning to prison for a few more weeks. Not a tragedy in the hopeless scheme of her life – a philosophical acceptance of her fate immediately contradicted by remembrance of the white stilettos. Charlie had made her hope for better.

'I'm off to collect the car,' Bill told Aloysius, who'd just turned on the television news, making a cheery corner in the dim parlour.

'Yes. I'll need it in the morning.' He didn't ask any questions because his eyes were fixed on images of a sinking ship at sea, helicopters in a misty sky, ambulances queuing on the shore.

Perhaps not such a cheery corner, after all, thought Bill, as he left on his journey, and he hoped, with a habitual kind of gloomy optimism, that the tragedy portrayed on the television screen was a natural not a man-made disaster.

'Lizzie!' exclaimed Portia, surprise followed by guilt tinged with irritation, before she felt kindly again.

Lizzie, poised at the turn of the final run of stairs with her angel cakes clasped to her slight bosom, answered only with a gasp.

'Ah Mr Jones,' the doctor hailed the nurse who led Lizzie. 'You're looking after this young woman, I see.' It might have been question, criticism or merely a statement of fact.

'Yes, sir. I like to keep the demons at bay.'

Lizzie's thin shoulders twitched.

'Why's your house guest here?' whispered Conor in Portia's ear.

'You've forgotten she's Charlie's wife,' whispered Portia, although the noise made by their leaders was quite enough to drown any asides.

Soon they were in the corridor outside Charlie's room. A single light glowed on the bed. It was empty.

The doctor seemed agitated. 'Where is he?'

Portia caught his arm as they crowded into the little room. 'What do you mean? He's here, isn't he?'

Behind her, Conor laughed. 'He is, actually.'

'Make way. Make way.' Charlie stumbled into the room. His much greater height and girth than anyone else's made him dominant, although he was clearly not well and clung to the edge of the bed. 'And now out!' he ordered. 'While I become restored.'

It was true that his pyjamas – a type of attire that Portia had only ever seen him wear out of bed (even as a boy he'd preferred to sleep naked) – were badly fitted and unbecoming. She remembered why she had come, dragging out poor Conor.

'I've something to tell you, Charlie.' She came up close and took his arm.

He half-shut his eyes. 'It's not Christmas or New Year, is it?'

Portia glanced at the doctor. Perhaps Charlie wasn't well enough to hear of his mother's death. The doctor, apparently reading her thoughts, nodded. But she was still doubtful. Charlie's hugeness and his befuddled air made him seem a captive giant. She pictured Celeste – admittedly female and an elephant – pinned down by hostile natives.

'Ah, Lizzie,' announced Charlie, as Portia still hesitated. 'I'm glad to see you.'

This was too much for Lizzie, who burst into tears.

Charlie surveyed the rest of the room with less approval. 'I've never liked cocktail parties,' he said sourly, and sat on the edge of the bed.

'We'll wait outside,' The doctor exerted his strong personality so that in a matter of seconds Portia found herself alone with Charlie. She looked down at his exceptionally long feet, the big toes decorated with delicate blond hairs.

'I'm glad to see you,' said Charlie, seriously. 'I have worries but I'm not out of my mind.'

'What worries, Charlie?' cried Portia. 'Perhaps I can help.'

Charlie studied her face carefully, then pronounced weightily, 'There are some things a captain doesn't tell his crew.'

Portia remembered the first time he'd said that to her. She'd been about ten, crewing for him in his sailing boat (named *Chastity*), when she'd suddenly noticed the bottom was filled with water. When she'd asked him if anything was wrong, he'd looked at her in the same way and given the same answer.

Now he walked over to a small wardrobe and, opening the door, peered inside. 'No,' he said firmly, closed the door and approached the bed. 'Yes.' He climbed in.

Portia tried to decide if these were the actions of a madman. She'd looked up to him too long for any objective view.

'Yes?' he said again, this time with a question mark. He sat demurely in the bed, propped high against the pillows. His not very clean fair curls (thinning on the top, though less so than his brothers') rose around his head like a halo.

'I'm afraid Mother's dead. Imogen's dead. Died today.'

'Ah.' Charlie frowned.

Portia wondered if he was remembering his wild visit to the nursing-home, his canticles of religious Latin, his disappearance into the night. She'd never known how much he remembered of his manic episodes. This time the up and the down had been so speedy that it seemed more likely that one self could remember the other – which was not to imply he was schizophrenic, oh no, or ever violent, never that.

'You're upset, Pygmy?' It was ridiculous but she was surprised and gratified when he remembered who she was and concentrated on her. Even if he had returned to his unflattering childhood nickname.

'Yes, I am. Of course, Imogen was never a very usual mother.' Tears were still in Portia's eyes.

'You have a loving nature.' It was a pronouncement, not necessarily a compliment. Love had never been highly rated in their family. But it had been said with affection.

'Why did you marry Lizzie?' Where had this question sprung from?

Charlie remained serious. 'You mean I don't love her, so why did I marry her? Only a girl with a loving nature would ask that.'

'She's outside, waiting. In tears. Last night she stayed in my flat.'

Charlie sighed. 'Imogen knew how to look after herself. Millions could have benefited from her advice.'

'Not Lizzie,' said Portia.

'Not Lizzie,' conceded Charlie. 'That's where I come in. It's obvious, isn't it? Or are you too much of the Imogen world to see it?'

'I don't know what you mean.' Portia was still standing but suddenly felt immensely tired. Why couldn't things be simpler? She went over to a chair and sat down. It was darker in the corner, calmer.

'Rich and poor,' intoned Charlie, like an oracle, with just an edge of satire, 'weak and strong. I look two ways. I am the face of Janus.'

Portia wondered if he was losing it again. His large blue eyes, rather red-rimmed, stared into the distance. 'Will you be better soon?' she asked.

'Ask Dr Mengele. He's the one who thinks I'm ill. When is Imogen's funeral?'

So he had taken in the fact of her death. 'Roland's in charge.'

'Poor Roland.'

'Whatever do you mean?'

'Trapped for ever among the winners. I suppose it won't be a Requiem Mass either. Imogen only became Catholic long enough to donate poor old Bill and pass on the germ to me. Was he present at the deathbed?'

'Yes. I think so.' Portia felt confused. A dark cloud of unknowing descended. It only happened in relation to her family – and Bill's role was the most confusing of all. 'Do you really think Bill is our brother?' She put the question timidly, but with heartfelt emotion. She'd been longing to ask since Bill's first appearance.

Charlie laughed. Almost a guffaw. 'Bill an impostor? That's a cheery idea. Not a priest either, perhaps. I like it, Pygmy!'

'Don't make fun.' The tears Portia had been on the point of shedding for Imogen now gathered for herself. 'And don't call me Pygmy.' There was no way she could express her sense of being cut off from the truth about her family. As Charlie continued with odd little chuckles and exclamations, her attention was drawn to the open crack in the door and a portion of a figure she could see in the brightness of the corridor. It was Conor – the man she loved and who loved her. She took out a tissue and wiped the tears from her cheeks. She stood up. 'I'll get the others.'

As she passed on her way to the door, Charlie reached and caught hold of her hand. His fingers felt soft and unhealthy. 'I'm sorry, Portia. I'm an oaf. You're too good for the rest of us.'

Portia tried to smile. 'What's the point of being good if you're ineffectual? All of you make things happen.'

'Men of action,' Charlie murmured, and lay back in his bed. 'Worldly men. Ah, well. Well.' He closed his eyes.

When the others came back, Lizzie once more composed, he opened them only briefly.

'Good,' said the doctor. 'What I most appreciate is a comatose patient. Now I shall make my way home. I have total confidence in Mr Jones.'

George came close to Lizzie and whispered in her ear, but loud enough for everyone to hear, 'You know that, don't you, Mrs Potts?'

Portia saw that Lizzie didn't know what to believe and felt sympathetic. It occurred to her that she was not the only one who moved in clouds of unknowing. Seeing what Lizzie was carrying close to her heart, Portia asked kindly, 'Do let's share your angel cake.'

Lizzie handed over a slice willingly enough but without any friendly bonding. Her attention was entirely fixed on Charlie.

Bill walked dispiritedly up the driveway to the hospital. He tried not to see himself as the lone pilgrim on an unending dark path. He reminded himself that when he was a young man studying in Rome a fellow seminarian who dabbled in painting had told him that a path or road or driveway was the most saleable of any contemporary painting. Everybody, however uninterested in or uncomprehending of their trajectory through the world, knew they were on a journey. The most popular pictures of all had light at the end of the road.

As Bill reached the car park, another figure approached from the direction of the hospital. At the same moment as he spotted it, another appeared from behind a car.

'Good evening, sir.'

Bill saw it was a policeman, parading his authority. He himself, who represented the authority of the Church and became Christ, Son of God, one part of the Trinity, when saying Mass, strove to retain his modesty. Of course, there was always the possibility he overdid it. Many people enjoyed reposing their souls on a higher authority.

'Good evening. Keeping a watch, are you?'

'That's it. After what happened last week . . .'

Bill saw the man was bored and lonely. He was a burly fellow but there was something childlike in his voice. 'There's someone else for you to watch.' He indicated the other man approaching.

The policeman turned. 'That's the doctor.' He sounded disappointed. He took a step forward until they were both standing under a light. He stared at Bill's neck. 'You're a vicar, are you?'

'Priest,' Bill corrected him mildly. He was very ecumenical but the word 'vicar' had always seemed unfortunate. Many of his Anglican friends called themselves priests now.

'I tell you, this place doesn't suit me.' The policeman was confiding, again childlike. 'All those crazies. You never know what they'll do, do you?'

'I suppose not. Are you on duty much longer?'

'Should've been off hours ago.' As if on cue, the phone on his chest buzzed into life.

Bill stepped back a few paces.

'Never known the place so busy.'

Bill turned to face the doctor. 'I'm collecting my car. I dropped a girl here earlier. Lizzie Potts. I don't expect you know if she's still inside. Unlikely, since it was hours ago. You probably throw out visitors . . .' He stopped as the doctor waved a commanding hand.

'They are all gathered round Charlie's bed. A tribute to the strength of family ties.'

Bill found himself surprised by this. 'All?' he queried.

'Don't let's quibble. A sister. A wife. That sort of thing. I must be

off. Ring the night bell. You never know, someone might let you in.'
He swept away, halting again as he reached the policeman. 'Good
evening, Officer. Don't forget, there's a bed ready for you any time
you need a rest.'

The policeman recoiled. 'I'm off, guv. Thanks for the thought.'

Bill smiled as he set off for the hospital. Clearly the policeman
thought madness was catching.

CHAPTER THIRTY-EIGHT

Men of Power

Leo was sitting in a neon-lit waiting room. It was overheated and his head was starting to ache. Near enough to a prison cell, it had a heavy door and a small square window through which he could see the sky, dark but with the orange sheen of city lights. Eerily, because he knew he was very close to the Marylebone flyover, he couldn't hear any traffic noise. At his feet were two polystyrene cups with the dregs of coffee, doubtless contributing to his headache.

Before he succumbed entirely to prison mentality (made up, he decided, of claustrophobia, self-pity and a strong sense of isolation), he must remind himself that he was a voluntary inmate, assisting with police enquiries, as the saying goes, which meant he didn't have a lawyer. He'd already been interviewed three times, quite briefly.

The questions were about Horace Silver whom, as he'd pointed out, he'd met for the first time in the hospital's mortuary, and Ileana, whom he'd never met at all. His two interrogators, the sombre chief inspector and his bewigged sidekick, allowed long pauses to develop during which they all drank the revolting coffee and the sidekick wiped his sweating forehead with a surprising red-spotted hand-kerchief. Clearly he sustained a flamboyant self-image.

If a capacity to adapt to circumstances is a human rather than an animal strength, then Leo had to admit he was failing. By now, surely, he should have accepted his surroundings and be nurturing righteous anger, a man of power held like a criminal, a Member of Parliament (still – just) treated like an ordinary citizen.

The truth, as always, was more complicated. Although his accusation in the House had not been mentioned, it had to be the real agenda. He'd forced their boss to resign (him with the dying wife), he'd pointed a finger at corruption within the force. He was hated. All the men and women in this fortress-like building hated him. Somewhere among them were the bad apples, but they all hated him equally. To continue the metaphor, which gave him a certain light relief, he had upset the applecart – or, to be more accurate, he'd tried to upset it. So far only the chief had gone and not admitting the true reason. The home secretary was supported by the prime minister. Parliament didn't want to know.

Only two people had been punished and they were both innocent victims: Horace Silver and Ileana. When he had pointed out that Charlie must be in extreme danger of the same fate since he knew more than anyone, there had been yet another silence. At least it seemed clear that they no longer suspected Charlie of being the murderer.

Standing up, Leo went to the door and opened it. He'd become so demoralised that it was a surprise to find it unlocked. Gaining energy, he strode along corridors until he reached a reception desk.

The officer on duty, an attractive woman, looked at him without any particular interest. He began to tell her that he needed to leave when it struck him that, since he was here voluntarily, there was no need to tell anyone anything.

Expecting a loud voice, a heavy hand on his shoulder, he made for the doors, passed through them and walked briskly towards Edgware Road. Never had London street life seemed more harmonious and welcoming. It was eight o'clock on a Saturday evening. The shops were all open and as many cafés, restaurants and bars. Lights shone from their glass fronts, from signs, from traffic signals, from car headlights and overhead lamps. The damp, misty weather gave each its own aureole, increasing the spread of light. Escaping from the dim neon of his captivity, Leo felt dazzled and rejuvenated. The noise, too, was exhilarating: buses, cars, lorries, motorbikes and, not least, the chatter of passers-by, using a Babel of language. Their movement, men, women, babies in pushchairs, plus the continual stopping and starting of traffic, added to his sense of release. He was back in the world.

He decided to walk home. The lulling cadence of walking, the anonymity of being one of many on busy streets, softened the experience of the previous couple of hours and made him feel in charge again. Even so, although he pulled out his mobile phone, he decided against making any calls. Imprecisely, he feared the police might be bugging it. Imprecisely, because under the Wilson agreement Members of Parliament may not be bugged.

Maggie rang Roland's flat to report on Esmond's reaction to his wife's death. There was no answer. Then she tried his mobile but it was turned off.

The children were watching television. She could hear them barracking some programme or other. She liked their youthful joking. There! It sounded as if one of them had thrown a cushion. Hetty shouted something. Jake laughed. This sort of horseplay always irritated Roland dreadfully. Poor Roland, suffering so much after his mother's death. Why shouldn't she feel sorry for him? He just wasn't born with the gift of happiness. Or, more likely, Imogen had snuffed it out.

Roland sighed, a long sigh of satisfaction. A *je m'en fou* sigh to all the cares in the world.

'You're so rich,' Didi whispered in his ear.

Roland rolled over. How could Didi look so incredibly beautiful even after sex? He tried to distance himself a little, search for imperfections. But the face was too seductive with the full red lips, small straight nose, bewitchingly curling lashes narrowing the black eyes. The body, limbs golden and lightly oiled (Didi believed in what he called 'products', pronounced 'produx'), was proportioned like a Greek statue, except that one point was significantly larger.

Roland swung himself into a sitting position. It was time to get a grip.

Didi draped over him. 'So rich. I saw it.' He ran his hands down Roland's chest.

'How did you get in?'

'The man at the door. He love me.'

Roland didn't doubt it. The porter had arrived recently from some unfortunate country and gave out uncoded signals of lovability. He'd even been slightly tempted himself. 'How did you know where I lived?'

'I have card.'

Which meant he'd stolen a card from Roland's wallet. It had been foolish of him to have one there. Yet he couldn't bring himself to care so much. 'You must never come again. Never. Understand?'

'Oh, yes, sir.'

'I will come to you.'

Maggie picked up the telephone receiver to ring Leo. Even that gave her a warm feeling. She'd caught him looking at her as she'd bent over to kiss Imogen. Surely she hadn't imagined a special attentiveness on his face. The kiss. They really had kissed. After an interval of twenty years.

The phone rang for a long time. Clearly there was no answering-machine. Just as she was giving up hope (although she wasn't hopeless because even hearing the phone ring in his flat was a consolation) Leo's rather breathless voice picked up. 'Hello. Who is it?'

Maggie sighed and sat down on her comfy chair in the kitchen. An awareness of being ridiculous didn't diminish her contentment. 'It's me. Maggie.'

'Oh. Maggie.' She thought she heard him also settling down. 'I've only just got back from the police.'

'You must be starving.' What a stupid thing to say! But she didn't care about that either.

'I think the last time I ate was that huge breakfast you cooked for me.'

'It's been quite a week!' If she was destined to make inane remarks, then that was the way it was.

'Not even a week.' He paused, as if reflecting on the previous days. 'The only people who want to see me now are the police. Even the press have given up on me. On Mondays I expect a vote of no confidence from my constituents and on Tuesday a banning order from the House. You're talking to a pariah, Maggie.'

He spoke with conviction and tinged with irony but no bitterness, rather a kind of wonder that such a thing could happen to him. Neither did he seem to be asking for sympathy. 'But you still think you're right to have asked that question?'

'Of course. It'll all come out eventually.'

Maggie managed to refrain from saying. 'Well, that's all right, then.' Instead she looked round her comfortable kitchen and took a breath. 'Why don't you come and stay here?' As he didn't answer immediately, she rattled on, 'Hetty's here and the boys. They'd love it. We've got so much food. We had to cancel one of Roland's grand networking lunch parties because of Imogen . . .'

'Is Roland there?'

That was the point, and the reason Leo came to stay so seldom. She'd known that for ever. 'He's not here now. But he'll probably arrive some time.' At her and Roland's wedding dinner the brothers had had a furious argument over seating arrangements. How Imogen had laughed!

'Esmond would love to see you too. That's why I rang.' A small lie. 'I told him about Imogen and he seemed to understand. Took it well.'

'When would I come?'

'Whenever.'

'Tonight?'

'I'll keep something on the Aga.' Maggie thought she heard a sigh.

'And there won't be a lunch party?'

'Just the food.'

'Maybe you could ask Portia too.'

Was he suggesting a family get-together after their mother's death? Precedence was not good in that area. At the last Christmas family party (some years back) Charlie had stripped naked during charades, insisting he was the spirit of Christmas, then poured brandy over his feet before setting light to them. Roland had been justifiably angry – Charlie hadn't appeared to be suffering from a manic episode – and tried to wrestle him out of the house. Since Charlie was bigger and stronger, he only managed to get him out of the drawing room, being humiliated and bruised on the way.

Eventually Leo had persuaded Charlie to dress and he'd headed for his car, not returning till breakfast – a formal meal when Imogen stayed – at which he'd entertained the company with stories of Winchester's red-light district. Luckily Roland had already left for a day's shooting. 'Farmyard girls, most of them. Brought up to bulls' balls and pigs' anuses,' he'd told a blushing Hetty. 'Winchester rutting could teach those namby-pamby Londoners a trick or two.'

Again Leo had led him away and this time he'd gone, which didn't stop Roland having an almighty row with Leo on his return.

'I suppose Charlie's still in hospital?' said Maggie, into the telephone.

'So I believe. Portia went to tell him about Imogen. You might think of inviting Portia's boyfriend too. A practical man. Lent me his suit.'

The family party grew. At least Bill would be too busy saying Sunday prayers. She hoped that Leo came tonight and Roland didn't. All things considered, it didn't seem such an indulgence.

Charlie was holding forth from his bed. Bill was surprised that the drugs hadn't brought him lower, although every so often he slumped back and shut his eyes. Perhaps he was showing off to Lizzie, who dangled on his every word.

In one of Charlie's rest moments, Bill took her arm and led her into the corridor. She came obediently, although he felt her attention still directed towards Charlie.

'You haven't been in touch with Probation, Lizzie.'

Immediately her eyes filled with tears, as if she could picture only too easily all the miseries that would follow from this oversight. She bowed her head, and mumbled something that sounded like 'What's the use?'

Bill fought against the irritation that arose now and again as he tried to help the 'damaged' and 'inadequate'. He pronounced the words to himself as an antidote. 'You could telephone now.' He felt for his mobile.

'We must go too,' said Conor, misreading Bill's intentions.

Bill remembered he'd come to fetch the car, not Lizzie. 'You'll be taking Lizzie, won't you?' She'd left a message with Probation, delivered in a whining, lacklustre voice. There was something wrong with that relationship, thought Bill. A good probation officer should be a support, not an enemy. Maybe he'd see if he could get her on the books of one of those post-release charities.

Through half-closed eyes Charlie watched the room clear. He feared the long night ahead, yet knew it was important not to speak and to let them go. He would have liked a blessing – at length and in Latin – from dear old Brother Bill. Or they could have recited the *Credo* together. *Credo in unum Deum, Patrem omnipotentem, factorem caeli et terrae, visibilium omnium et invisibilium.* That would have scared away any of Satan's emissaries straying down the corridors.

Charlie turned off the light over his head. Animals and humans rested in darkness. He needed to rest. He could feel his mind still on the edge. Badgers and owls and foxes and probably lots of other lovable and unlovable animals came out at night. But they had murdered Horace in broad daylight. They had no shame. Griff's reaction when he'd first told him had been spot on: there was enough pitch to blacken a cartload of saints and they weren't dealing with saints. Must look up the derivation of the word 'pimp'. Pimple, maybe. Far too charming for today's brand.

He'd worried about Griff but he knew what he was up to. He'd get the photograph, get the story. Keep out of trouble. There was not much more an old crazy like him could do – except stay alive. His info would be important later. Good old Leo. You needed to shake the tree if you wanted the bad apples to fall – and sometimes they clung like limpets. That was what Griff had said. Old-school journalism. No frills, plenty of grit.

Charlie turned restlessly in his bed. Each day he'd expected that photograph. What was the girl called? Ileana? That was a bad story. But it didn't mean Griff wasn't getting there. Quite the contrary. Probably meant they were in a panic. Fucking pimples. Warts, more like. Ileana. A pretty name. *Domine non sum dignus.* He had a good memory for names, drugs or no drugs, and he was certain he'd never been with her.

From down the corridor, he heard footsteps approaching. Heavy. A man's. One of the nurses bringing him sleeping pills.

Charlie opened his eyes. A tall man stood over him. Not wearing a white coat. He switched on the light and angled it so that it drilled into Charlie's eyes. He shut them quickly.

'Open.'

It was a trick from a cheap thriller. Under the bedclothes, Charlie felt his hands and feet go cold with fear but his poor fuddled mind remained defiant.

'What do you want?' The words were only a little slurred.

'No photograph.'

So Griff had got his pic. End of home secretary. But he wouldn't go round knocking people off or even threatening. He'd been un-lucky. Slept with the wrong girl.

'I don't have a photograph. You've come to the wrong man.' He felt tears rolling out of his eyes. It was just the effect of the bright light but it felt unmanly. If he wiped them, his visitor would see his shaking hands. 'I'm sick. In hospital.'

'Crazy fellow.' The man was behind the light but Charlie could imagine his grimace. He probably came from a country where the insane were shoved into homes and beaten till the devil flew out. A sharp pain was stabbing the left side of his forehead. Who had let his visitor in?

'You tell. You boss.'

If that's what they wanted him to do, they'd hardly give him the Horace treatment. The knife to his forehead made him want to cry out. The water pouring from his eyes contained real tears now, a mix of two rivers, the Amazon and the Negro. Fuck. He must steady his mind.

Down the corridor came new footsteps, almost in time with the throb in his head. His visitor heard them too. He straightened and walked towards the door. Charlie pushed away the light. He heard himself sobbing with relief and pain. He curled up and held his head in his hand.

Above his own noises, he heard scuffling and thumps, a cry, then those footsteps banging in his head. He squeezed his eyes tightly shut. Fuck. Fuck.

'Charlie. Charlie. Are you hurt?'

Hurting, that's what he was. Bloody so-called nurse. Bloody life. Pulling back the bedclothes. What a nerve! Glad he came when he did, though.

'Say something, Charlie.'

He opened his eyes. 'Forgot to breathe, that's all.'

'You don't want to do that.'

As George took a step back, Charlie saw that he had a tear in his white coat and his usually cocky hair was dragged about his face. 'Saw him off, did you?'

'Hadn't taken his medication recently, I guess.'

The pain was receding. He put up his arm and the word 'Extasie' danced in front of his eyes. It seemed too complicated to work out what George believed about his visitor. Was he seriously suggesting he was a fellow patient? It did happen. 'Don't let him come near me again,' he said wearily, 'and hand over whatever pills you've got in your hot little paws.'

As he tossed them back – long practice had taught him how to do it without water – he thought that the sooner Griff got that photograph published the better. The moment that happened, according to his plan, the bad boys – the murdering sort from foreign places – would know the game was up and get out of the country before they found themselves facing twenty years in prison. That left the fall-out for the home-grown variety – the 'bad-luck boys', Griff called them, who made one mistake and found their whole life torn apart. You could almost feel sorry for them.

Griff was cool, thought Charlie, as the drugs took hold, and hard. They'd worked together before but never on something as big as this. The paper would be pleased as long as its stupid proprietor didn't lose his nerve. Big mouth. Small cock.

'George.'

'Yeah.'

'Don't go.'

'I'm just flexing my muscles, aren't I? Let the weirdos of the world beware . . .'

His voice receded and disappeared.

CHAPTER THIRTY-NINE

Lies and Loyalties

Bright sunlight poured into Maggie's kitchen. After the mists and darkness of the day before – the deaths – it was bewildering. She'd been about to turn on the radio to hear the news but instead she went to the window and flung it open.

Spring was here. Why hadn't she noticed before? Without waiting to put on shoes, she unlocked the side door, stepped over the stack of newspapers and out into the garden. The grass was cold and wet, not yet warmed by the sun, so she danced across it, feeling the tickle between her toes, taking deep breaths of sharp air. The lawn merged into rough grass, clusters of white narcissi shining out from under the trees and shrubs, the evergreens dark, spiky with new green leaves.

She stopped and looked back. It was a charming and substantial house, bought with Roland's earnings and embellished with a gift from Esmond when they had given him a home. She thought of those inside – sleeping presumably, since none had descended. Leo had arrived just before midnight. He'd been too tired to eat the soup she'd prepared and she'd shown him straight to his room. He'd thanked her almost impersonally so she hadn't told him Roland was still away. He'd needed sleep, beyond words, beyond feelings. She'd left him at once.

He must be still asleep, too. That made her happy. The boys would certainly be out cold, probably not rising for another couple of hours. Esmond might be awake. She looked for his window. The curtains were still closed. But that might mean the nurse hadn't got up. The old had a different attitude to sleep, except those who were still hanging on to the world, determined to keep up their energy.

Esmond wasn't like that. Besides, he had Imogen's death to consider. Or perhaps he was on the deck of his ship, cresting the great waves of the South Atlantic.

Maggie swivelled round again to face the sun. It was still only just above the trees. A bird was singing very beautifully directly in front of her. She wondered if it was the same thrush that had entertained her last summer when she'd spent many afternoons gardening and thinking about Leo. The sun made her feel calm and relaxed and filled with love. Just now, although her face was warm, her feet were cold. Time to put the kettle on.

Slowly, her feet drawing dark stripes on the dewy lawn, she walked back to the house. When she reached the doorstep, she picked up the stack of newspapers, awkwardly cradling their weight. A few leaflets dropped out, but she ignored them, dumping her load on the table. Without even glancing at the headlines, she went towards the Aga. Mungo wagged his tail from his bed, too old and lazy to get out. Usually, she would have put on the radio, but this morning she was enjoying the silence, broken only by the song of the birds.

Sighing, she went once more to the window and leaned there, waiting for the kettle to boil.

Leo woke with a sensation of peace. He felt physically well – for the first time in days. As he became more aware, he questioned a peace that depended entirely on good health. Nothing had changed. He'd fired off an explosion which would continue to ricochet round him for some time yet. Perhaps for ever. A particularly sharp piece of shrapnel might be his personal sword of Damocles.

But because he felt so well, this seemed like playing games. He pushed off the bedclothes and got up. Naked, he stood by the window. The cool air and morning sun combined in a stimulating cocktail. He was still a young man, some might say in the prime of life. He smiled at himself and flexed his muscles. Since this whole affair had started, he hadn't worked out once. What did his trainer say? A month to gain a muscle, a day to lose it. Something like that. Well, there was no reason why he shouldn't go for a run.

Roland was a fitness freak so there was probably exercise equipment somewhere around but that didn't appeal. He needed to feel the ground under his feet, needed to move forward. The last few days had felt as if a quagmire was trying very hard to suck him under.

A sword of Damocles above and a quagmire below, thought Leo, as he pulled on jeans, a sweatshirt, trainers. It was no wonder he'd become disoriented. The way he felt now, he might throw up his job, whichever way the sword fell, make a new life abroad. With mother dead, father out of his mind, no wife, no children, there was nothing to hold him. Think Sydney.

At the stairs, which were rather grand and swept round into a hallway at the bottom, Leo hesitated. His good humour had over-looked the fact that he was about to spend a day in Roland's company. That was the point about good humour: it rolled over insoluble problems. Slightly sobered, he continued down into the kitchen.

'Hi!' Maggie turned round from the open window. She seemed taken by surprise. The kettle spouted steam on the Aga as if it had been boiling for some time. There was no sign of Roland. Maggie came towards him. She was wearing some sort of patterned wrap with a shawl draped round her shoulders. 'You look more alive.' For a moment he thought she was going to kiss him. Instead she pulled off the kettle.

'I thought I'd go for a run before breakfast.' He hesitated. 'Isn't Roland down yet?'

'He's still in London.' She turned her back on him to take mugs from a cupboard. 'He might not come at all. He needs to do work for a big case tomorrow.'

Leo watched her put five mugs on the table. He wondered if his relief and delight were obvious and whether she was feeling some-thing similar.

'I'd better get running.' He patted the papers, still face down on the table. 'A good idea to avoid these a little longer. Want to come too?'

'I don't do running.' She smiled, looking at him directly for the first time. 'Wrong shape.'

She was quite right. Her thin wraps showed the outlines of her full breasts, the swell of her stomach and hips. Sometimes he'd run with Suzanne. She'd been like an arrow, sharp and hard. ' "You are stately as a palm tree, and your breasts are the clusters of dates." Song of Songs, seven seven.'

'Thanks. I'll come out with you and point the way.'

They stood close together at the end of the garden. The dew had dried in the sunnier parts and the birds were singing less loudly. A red squirrel dashed out from the trees, then, seeing them, ran back again.

'A good omen,' said Leo. 'Did you know red squirrels have taken the place of black cats?'

'We're lucky, then. We've quite a few. Roland shoots the grey ones.'

'So, which way?'

As Maggie gave him directions, Leo began his stretching exercises, bending, raising his arms, touching his toes. He could feel Maggie watching him and it was a kind of showing off: OK, Roland can shoot grey squirrels but just look how strong and virile I am! Without waving goodbye, he set off down the driveway.

Conor had stayed the night. They'd made love as quietly as possible, given that Lizzie was on the sofa next door. Portia had protested, but only for a moment.

She watched the light suffuse the red curtain with a warm glow. Conor was no longer beside her. As she woke further, she heard voices next door: Conor and Lizzie. What could they have to say to each other? The trouble was, try as she might, she couldn't get close to understanding Lizzie. Take her behaviour yesterday: surely she should have prioritised signing up with her probation officer. Charlie wasn't going anywhere – not for a while, anyway. It was almost as if Lizzie didn't care what happened to her, whether she returned to prison, slept on Portia's sofa, went to a hostel or Charlie's flat – that was an option forgotten during yesterday's drama.

For example, when Maggie had rung late last night, inviting them to the country for the day, and Portia had asked if Lizzie would like to be included, she'd answered, in that maddening mumble, 'I don't mind, do I.'

That was not the question. And the continual smoking! Usually good-tempered, Portia didn't enjoy feeling irritated. Then there was Lizzie's ridiculous hero-worship of Charlie, her absurd status as 'wife', those ludicrous white high heels. Portia had noticed she was hobbling by the time they'd left the hospital. She put people out, too, as if it were her right. Look at poor old Bill, driving her all the way there. Would she put Portia in the position of kicking her out? Again, she thought of Charlie's flat. It was a pretty unpleasant place to live, certainly, but why should she take root there? Someone Charlie had married on a whim, probably when he was out of his mind. Bill should never have allowed it to happen.

And there she was, next door, still chuntering away with Conor. Well, that was an exaggeration: their voices were sporadic at most.

Portia got out of bed, reached for her Mexican smock, exuberantly embroidered with birds and leaves. It put her in a slightly better mood and she went through into the other room.

'Hi.' Conor looked up from the floor where he had all the papers spread round him. 'I was just going to bring you the morning's headline news.'

'Hi.' He was so lovely, the bumps and curves of his vertebrae showing through his T-shirt. Lizzie sat cross-legged on the sofa-bed, also wearing a T-shirt. She was smoking. But that didn't strike Portia as much as her extreme thinness. Her arms had as little flesh as the stick Hansel and Gretel had put through the bars of their cage to fool the greedy witch. She felt a bit like a witch herself, full of ill-will. 'Shall I make some coffee?'

'Coffee before or after the news?'

Portia turned to Conor again. Why all this keenness about the news? He was perfectly aware it was an unusual day when she read a newspaper.

'Look at this.' He turned round the front page.

Portia was enough out of the political loop for it to take her a moment to take in what she was looking at: a large photograph of the home secretary with his face pressed against the breast of a young woman. It had probably been taken on a mobile phone. Her face was more blurred than his, whose jowly features were usually seen above a tie and beside some important official.

'It's Leo's story.' Conor picked up the paper and waved it at her. 'It's wiped the shipping collision off the front page. Now they've got a pic, Leo's off the hook.'

Portia sat down on a chair. 'It can't be as simple as that.' She was back in her usual role of not understanding the big world of her brothers.

'No, of course not, but it justifies his question. I'm wondering if there's a drama-doc in it: the Home Secretary, the prostitute and the gang who brought her into the country then pimped for her. Well, there is, and I'd like to be part of it from its juicily corrupt beginnings. I'll call it *Wolves of the Night*.'

'What does the paper say?' Portia glanced at Lizzie. She'd lit another cigarette and sat smoking it, shoulders hunched, eyes half shut. This was her world.

'Not that much. Waiting for the home secretary to resign probably. I can't believe we didn't listen to the news last night.'

'It only happened this morning.'

'Things always come out the night before. I can't wait to see Leo.'

Portia thought about this. 'I suppose the press will be on to him again.'

'Probably. Although the story suggests he was given a tip-off to stir things up in the House. The story's written by an investigative journalist, Griff Banks. Read it for yourself.'

Portia took the paper with a certain reluctance. She was glad if this made things better for Leo but she couldn't match Conor's enthusiasm for convulsions in the system. Most women valued order, she thought. Men preferred destruction. Lizzie caught her eye: she had been staring fixedly at the front page of the paper, which Portia had laid back on the floor.

'No wonder she bought it.' Her usual mumble made it hard to pick up the words.

'What?' Then Portia saw she was crying. Crying and smoking at the same time. 'What is it?' she repeated.

Lizzie, head resolutely down, got up and went to the bathroom. Again, Portia was shocked by her thinness. It reminded her of something. 'I'll make some coffee,' she called after her.

Conor put his arm round her. 'I don't think she's going to much appreciate a jolly family outing to the country.'

'It was that photograph.' They looked again.

'Perhaps she knows the girl.' Portia didn't want to be saying this. The Mexican women she helped were dignified. They lived in mountain villages where the ground was rocky and infertile. When storms came the rain fell in torrents, dragging off what little topsoil there was. They worked all the daylight hours and in every spare moment they embroidered the cloth she brought them, creating beautiful things like the smock she was wearing.

'I was wondering about that.' Conor smiled at her. 'You're exquisite. Do you know that?'

Portia was glad he said things like that even when it seemed the wrong moment. 'I don't feel very strong this morning.' Her Mexican women also liked to use skulls as a decorative feature. Usually she managed to steer them away, although lately she'd noticed they were becoming a fashion on the sarongs hanging along Portobello.

'Your mother died yesterday.'

That's what Lizzie's lack of flesh recalled: her mother's arms raised so that the wide sleeve of her nightdress fell back. Not yesterday. Yesterday she had lain straight and still.

'I'm so tired.' Portia rubbed her forehead between her eyes.

'It's a beautiful day. The first day of spring.'

'I'll feel better after a mug of coffee.'

Sweat ran down Leo's temples, some trickling into his eyes, trickled down his back and legs into his socks. He was still running at a good speed as he turned into Roland and Maggie's garden.

Maggie watched him approach, pounding across the lawn, past where Tom and Jake had their goalposts. As he came nearer, she withdrew from the window in case he saw her. She pulled the kettle back on to the hotplate and waited for him to come in. The table was laid now, the papers bundled on to a chair, but no one had appeared.

'God, I needed that!' Leo thumped through the door, panting. 'How long was I out?'

Maggie looked at the clock. 'Twenty minutes.'

'It felt longer.' He seemed disappointed.

'Did you run fast?'

'Enormously fast. Like the proverbial wind.' He laughed.

Maggie turned away. She didn't want him to see how she longed to touch him. He'd brought in the smell of dewy mornings and sweat. 'You should have a shower.'

'I feel so good!' He stretched his arms over his head.

'You'll get cold and stiffen up.' She hesitated. Her voice was trembling. 'There isn't a shower in your bathroom. I'll show you where there is one.'

'No hurry.' He came towards her and leaned near her. 'I'm warm enough here.'

Maggie couldn't resist turning to him. He caught her hand. 'Maggie.'

'Yes. I . . .' She could think of nothing to say and felt her face redden.

He put up his hand to her hair and pushed it away from her face. 'I'll have a shower if you have one too.' He smoothed his fingers over her face and ran them down her neck. Slowly, he bent and kissed the swell of her breast. He whispered, 'I want you, Maggie.'

She felt the sweat on his face. She imagined his lips were salty. She wanted to feel him all over her body. How easily she would open for him! Did she really have to resist? After what Roland had told her, did she still have to resist? 'The children,' she murmured.

'Show me where the shower is.'

They went up the stairs together, stumbling with the weight of their desire.

The shower was next to Roland's dressing room. It was strictly forbidden to anyone but him.

Leo took off his clothes. His cock was already hard. 'I want to undress you.' Slowly, he pulled off Maggie's shawl and, opening her robe, let it fall to the ground. Underneath she wore a thin nightdress. 'You can keep that on for now.' He started the shower, checked the temperature and led her into the glass box.

Under the bright spray of water, they came together, as if whatever was wrong would be purified. They kissed until neither could bear any more. Then he lifted her nightdress and entered her.

Afterwards they still clung together and the water still ran.

'I love you,' said Leo.

'I love you,' agreed Maggie. She felt a huge sense of relief and joy. She was crying although the tears were washed away as soon as they came. Nothing mattered any more. She could bear whatever should follow. If she never saw Leo again, this would be enough.

Leo turned off the shower and they stepped out, saying nothing. Maggie found him a towel. She didn't care that it was Roland's.

'I'll go to my bathroom.' She smiled at him. He was already rubbing himself dry.

'You're the most beautiful woman in the world.'

She started away but stopped at the door. It was hard to leave him. 'I'll see you in the kitchen.'

He came to her, tying the towel round his waist, and whispered in her ear, 'You know what? It's lucky I didn't have a heart-attack.'

She laughed and went to her room.

Leo was soon down in the kitchen, but instead of Maggie, there was Hetty, spread over the table, papers in disarray around her and on the floor. She wore tracksuit bottoms and trainers and looked as if she, too, was on her way out for a run.

'Hi,' said Leo, unsuccessfully denying to himself her striking resemblance to Roland.

'Hi. I didn't know you were here.'

'I came late last night.'

'I thought you were Dad.'

'He's in London.' Please, God.

Hetty moved back on to her chair, uncovering more of the paper. 'I suppose you know all about this.' She was casual, vaguely indicating some already crumpled pages. 'It's your thing, isn't it.'

Warily, Leo came closer. For a second his eyes flicked to the sunshine, still pouring into the room, although through a different window. 'Let's see.'

Hetty got off her chair to give him space.

Leo knew as he looked at the photograph, front page on all three papers, that he should feel immense relief. The home secretary would be lucky to avoid prison.

Then why, as he scanned the pages – principal story by Griff Banks – did he feel deflated, even depressed? Two innocents had died, which was reason enough to be sad, yet it wasn't that. He'd been standing over the table but now he sat down. It wasn't either that these events interrupted the sudden happiness of his time with Maggie. It was more that this whole story brutally exposed the nature of the men he worked with, the world that he'd chosen as a profession. When he'd asked his question, he'd assumed that someone, preferably the prime minister, would take him seriously. At very least, interview him. After all, even if he failed to toe the line on occasions, he had a good reputation as an honourable man who

268

worked hard for his constituents. Did they believe that he put their interests above the party's? Probably. And probably it was true. His constituents and the truth. Truth. Morals. That was what he believed in – even if he'd just finished fucking his brother's wife.

'Uncle Leo?'

'What is it?' Hetty was staring at him. 'Sorry.'

'I said, do you want tea or coffee?'

'Coffee. Thanks.'

'It is your story, isn't it? I never really followed it but my boyfriend said something about you speaking out against corruption – he was awfully admiring. He's brilliant. Despises politicians.' She rethought. 'Except you.'

'It's a bad story.' He looked at Hetty's smooth young face. 'What are you reading?'

'Media studies.'

'So you believe in the press?'

'Well, look at it.' She came over quickly, pulled the paper round. Her energy confounded Leo. He leaned away. 'They winkle out the truth, don't they?'

'In this case,' said Leo. He remembered how young he'd felt that morning; Hetty was making him feel cynical, sullied by too much knowledge. It came to him that he was at a turning-point in his life. He'd thought something like it earlier but then it had been a light-hearted sense of potential freedom, new roads, a new future. 'I may resign,' he said.

'What?' Hetty hadn't heard him. She was making a pot of coffee. He could smell the fresh grounds. 'Where's Mum, anyway? She hasn't even fed Mungo.' She glanced over her shoulder, as if Maggie might be hiding under the table. Her tone was slightly aggrieved.

'She was down earlier.' Leo pushed away the papers.

Hetty plonked the pot on the table. 'She might be with Grandpa. She often sits with him.' Suddenly seeming embarrassed, she muttered, 'Sorry about Grandma.'

'Thank you. She was old and ill.'

They sat at the table then, opposite each other, reading the papers. Gradually Leo's good cheer returned. He caught Hetty's eye. 'I gather there's a family lunch on the way.'

'Shit. I'd forgotten. Portia's OK but she's coming with her

boyfriend and Charlie's wife – at least, his kind-of-wife. I've never met her. Can't think what got into Mum.'

'I'm afraid I suggested it.'

'Oh, sorry.'

He could see he'd gone down in her estimation. With a funny little thrill, he realised he wanted to please her because she was Maggie's daughter. They both looked up as Maggie's steps crossed the hallway.

'Where have you been, Mum?' cried Hetty, as the door opened. She sounded about ten.

'Washing my hair, darling.' Not facing either of them, Maggie removed a still damp strand from her face.

CHAPTER FORTY

Whatever the Consequences

Conor had put Lizzie in the front seat of his car. It was a precautionary measure. He was afraid she might throw herself out of the door if she was alone. He'd whispered this to Portia but she hadn't offered to sit with her in the back so now Lizzie huddled beside him where he could grab her, and Portia, a little sulkily, which was unlike her, sat in the back.

Conor glanced at her now and again in the rear-view mirror. It almost seemed she was jealous of the pathetic Lizzie. It was true Lizzie gave off a certain waif-like sexiness, remnant perhaps of her past profession, but nothing any sensible man would want to follow up.

He'd understood quite soon after they'd met that Portia had problems with her family. Being an only child himself, with a mother who expected him home for tea every day till he was fourteen, he hadn't taken it too seriously. The last two days had taught him differently: first, the MP who had made front-page news by snitching on his own party leader – well, home secretary. That had been a wild scene in the flat, Conor's offer of a suit exchange accepted, much to his surprise. Then, yesterday, that visit to her other brother whom she'd spoken of in hushed tones as if he was a saint or something, and there he was, mostly out of his mind, in a mental hospital. Now, as if those two weren't enough, they seemed to have inherited Lizzie, ex-prisoner, ex-junkie, ex-prostitute, if that was the PC word, which he remembered it wasn't. Ex-working girl.

The point about all this – Conor continued thinking as neither woman seemed keen on a conversation – was that Portia had given him quite the wrong impression. Everything she'd said about her brothers – or, more accurately, 'let drop', because she never talked about them directly, as if she didn't dare – had emphasised their brilliance, their success, as against her own inadequacy and failure. Sure, Leo was an MP and Roland, the one he'd meet today, was a top barrister, but so far what he had seen was recklessness and the determination to do things their own way, whatever the consequences. In fact, they reminded him of Portia, who had made her own path disregarding what the rest of the world might think appropriate.

The first time he'd met her she was trying to persuade an uncooperative taxi driver that her Mexican boxes, piled on the pavement outside her flat, would fit into his cab. Somehow he had taken the man's place.

'I really need to stop.' Lizzie was speaking suddenly, clearly. 'I just need them. Sorry.'

Cigarettes, she meant, of course. Portia would go mad. Or perhaps she was asleep. He could see her head, with its thick dark curls, against the window.

At the next newsagent Conor pulled up, and Lizzie was out and back in a flash. As they started off again she lit up and puffed energetically. Conor saw Portia stirring. Perhaps Lizzie had sensed it too because she turned round and leaned her arms on the top of her seat.

'Sorry about this.' She waved the cigarette. 'It's an addiction, isn't it.' Portia opened her eyes. A curling stream of smoke headed for her nostrils. 'I've kicked the worst,' continued Lizzie, 'but not this, not yet. Not civilised, puffing smoke in and out of your head. It runs in the family, though. My mum's smoked fifty a day since she was ten. I wouldn't take life insurance on her.'

'You have a mother?' Portia suspected she'd sounded amazed.

'Course I have a mother. Not that she does me much good.'

'You mean you don't see her?'

'More like she doesn't see me.' The smoke curled round the car. 'But at least she's there, kind of.'

Portia saw her mood had darkened. Had Lizzie remembered whose mother had just died? It seemed more personal. She waited.

'That's where Ileana went wrong, didn't she. Coming over here. Didn't stand a chance. Thought she knew a thing or two, the bright one at home, learnt a bit of English, pretty, brave, you know.'

'She was a friend of yours, then?'

'I told her, "Run for it." But it was too late. They'd got her on the stuff. Half the time she didn't know where she was. Better that way. She was pretty, though. Suppose you couldn't tell in that photo. With that big lout.'

'I'm sorry.'

'That's life, isn't it.' Lizzie snorted abruptly, 'Death, more like.'

'She was unlucky,' said Portia.

'Unlucky?' Lizzie frowned. 'One name for it.' She turned back to face the front, stubbed out her cigarette and lit another.

Portia opened her window wide. The air was fresh and warmed by the sun. They were in the country now. She could almost see the spring buds unfurling on the trees. She thought that the story of Ileana and girls like her was just about unbearable. No wonder most people gawped at the drama, then did their best to forget.

'Portia's a funny name, isn't it?'

Lizzie was facing her again, as if the tobacco intake had given her energy.

'Comes from a Shakespeare play. A heroic lady barrister.'

'Heroic what?'

'She defended a man against a Jew who wanted a pound of his flesh.'

'Weird.'

'It was a long time ago.'

Lizzie sighed. 'Heroism runs in your family, doesn't it?'

'I'm not sure . . .'

'Charlie's a hero. Saved me, didn't he. One night. I was on the street. Not usual for me, but there I was. Sometimes it seemed the best place. He picked me up. Walking he was, not in a car. He said, "You're coming with me." Well, of course I was if he paid me. But he didn't mean that. He marched me to one of those all-night coffee places. He made me laugh – not easy I can tell you. He said I reminded him of his mother so he'd decided to save me. He said his mother had a wasp waist and a sting to her tongue to match. He said he hoped I had the waist without the sting. I thought he was drunk or high, didn't I? I didn't know he was always like that.' She paused. 'Except yesterday. He'll be all right, won't he? He's my hero, see, like your Portia lady.'

'Yes. I do see.'

Lizzie turned back to swap cigarettes once more. This time she talked facing the front as if she wanted Conor to hear too.

'Thing is, I'll make his flat nice for him. Not the one he got for me. That's a room, isn't it. I'll clean his up so it sparkles, paint it, sort out his things, and when he gets out of hospital, I'll look after him. You know, like a housekeeper. This wife bit is pretend, I know that. Charlie doesn't follow rules. But I can be useful. I learned how to do a professional painting job inside. You saw how I sorted out your stall, didn't you, Portia? Once I get a bit more strength to me. Eat a bite or two.' As if to prove her point, Lizzie used her free hand to pull out the squashed remains of the angel cake from her pocket and waved it with see-what-I-mean triumph.

'That's great,' said Conor.

Portia nodded. She did remember Lizzie's burst of energy on her stall but she also remembered how she'd faded. On the other hand, Charlie's flat could do with any kind of attention, although she doubted he'd welcome Lizzie sorting out his things.

'Is it right or left here?' asked Conor.

'Left, then right at a T junction.'

'So now tell me who'll be there.'

As Portia explained, she noticed Lizzie shrinking into her seat, as if the sound of these names, Maggie, Roland, Leo, Esmond, Tom, Jake and Hetty put the lid on her previous volubility. For the first time she felt some fellow feeling. She tried to remember what Maggie's attitude was to smoking.

The kitchen was filled with bodies. Maggie, fuelled with love, ordered them around confidently. Even the nurse had come down from her room and stirred white sauce in a heavy pan. Hetty was laying the table with as much noise as possible. Tom and Jake lay on the floor playing some portable computer game. Above them, Leo and Conor, holding beers, discussed the next stage in the political saga. They'd just heard on the news that the home secretary's resignation had been accepted by the prime minister.

'Funny about politics,' Leo meditated. 'Everything seems so fixed – then, snap, the whole picture changes.'

'You're a hero,' said Conor, possibly echoing Lizzie earlier.

'I just did what Charlie asked.' He smiled. 'It's almost a principle with me now.'

They were interrupted by Hetty instructing them that lunch was ready. '*À table!*' she cried, with an exaggerated French accent.

Lizzie, curled into what she couldn't know to be Maggie's arm-chair, watched all this. When Portia had gone off to see her father, she'd wanted to follow her, tag along like a toddler, hold on to her hand. Now she was calmer. No one took any notice of her, except that Maggie had put a glass of wine into her hand. She'd drunk it quickly, feeling the alcohol churn through her body like a hot spring. It took the place of cigarettes. She hadn't dared smoke – not with those kids and food and everything.

Portia stopped for a moment at the doorway to the kitchen. The scene of homogeneous good fellowship was startling. Everybody was sitting at the table and even Lizzie appeared to be having a playful conversation with Jake, Portia's younger nephew, still pink-cheeked and blond like his mother. Leo was making an effort with Tom, who bore the weight of being the elder brother. Leo seemed extraordinarily relaxed for someone at the centre of a storm who, presumably, would face the press once more if he returned to his flat.

It was Maggie, Portia supposed, who had created this country-life dream. Telling Jacky, the nurse, that her charge was sleeping comfortably, Portia slipped into her place between Conor and Hetty. 'Perhaps we *are* a regular family,' she whispered to Conor.

'Families can be fun,' intoned Connor, and smiled sweetly.

Roland's concentration on his papers was nil. He decided to see if leaving his flat and going to his chambers helped. He was soothed by his walk through the mostly empty courtyards, past the walls, ancient trees and fountain. He stood in a long line of lawyers who had trodden this same path, including, of course, his father. That was not such a calming idea, considering Esmond's present mental health. The line moved on continuously, leaving behind, then disregarding, those who could no longer keep up. Roland remembered the DPP, one of his mentors and a clever, kindly man, who had been caught kerb-crawling. End of upwardly mobile career.

He would never manage to work if he allowed his thoughts to become uncontrolled.

Noticing for the first time that it was a sunny day, he found a wooden bench and sat down. On the other side of the courtyard a tramp (or, at least, an old man tied about with coats and scarves, wearing a beard and surrounded by plastic bags) was just coming to the same conclusion. He yawned and blinked and shifted a little so that the sun struck his shoulders. He performed a heaving motion, something like a stretch. Roland imagined the smell arising from his filthy clothes. As he continued to watch, the man (perhaps not always a tramp but once a civil servant or even barrister) bent down, selected one of the bags and extracted, with some difficulty, a large can of what looked like cider.

On an impulse driven more by a wish to avoid his desk than charity, Roland felt in his pocket, found a note and began to cross the courtyard. The man was drinking, not indelicately but with breaks for obvious enjoyment. He seemed unaware of Roland's approach.

With a sensitivity that surprised him, Roland wondered whether it was such a kind act to bring a reminder of the old fellow's undignified poverty. As he swigged at the can, he was a happy man.

Roland returned to his bench. He should think the unthinkable: his mother's death had provided an honourable reason for retiring from the case for which he was failing to prepare. He wanted to convince himself that Didi didn't come into it, just as he didn't come into anything important in his life. A colleague in his chambers had just become free after his case had been postponed. He could be rebriefed. There would be a delay, of course. It was not impossible. If he'd had a car crash it would have to happen. If the judge agreed. If the defendant agreed. If the solicitors agreed and the clerks fixed it. There were a lot of ifs. His colleague never came off the golf course on Sundays.

Nevertheless, he knew there was no way he could stand up in court the following day and fight a case. He got up and started to walk back to his office; he would begin by calling Mike. A good clerk, and Mike was the best, was never more than a heartbeat from his BlackBerry. He would know the lowdown on the cast of characters that needed to be brought on side.

Roland frowned and stood still. Did Mike know about his sexuality? They'd worked together for twenty years. He assumed his absolute knowledge of everyone else's private life, so why not his? And if he knew, did everybody in chambers down to the most callow junior clerk? He pictured the one with the lacquered quiff and tight pinstripe suit. Wayne.

Roland went back to his bench. The tramp was sucking at his can with the desperation of a baby at an empty bottle.

He couldn't fight this case. Not tomorrow. He imagined himself gibbering and jabbering nonsense, shouting in his confusion, 'My Lord, I'm queer!' The jury astonished, eyes popping, sniggering, the clerk of the court stabbing his pen, the judge, a woman, eventually adjourning the court until the learned prosecutor had recovered himself. He would be taken out, a madman, between two keepers, like Charlie . . . Where had that thought come from?

Finally, he'd yell as he was dragged away, 'My Lord, have mercy! Have mercy! On Saturday my mother died!'

CHAPTER FORTY-ONE

Home, Sweet Home

Lizzie saw the car on the drive. After a good start with the posh kid, whose attempts to be cool had made her smile, the lunch hadn't been much fun. Not terrible. Just too much food for her to push around the plate. And she didn't want to drink. Mustn't drink. In the end she'd slipped out for a smoke. So she saw the shiny black car, driving too fast in her view, swish up to the house.

Instinctively she took a step behind a bush. A man got out. Tall, like the other brothers. This must be the one she hadn't met. There was something different about him, though, not just that he was better groomed than Charlie and Leo – after all, that Leo was smart enough. She watched as he parked by Leo and Conor's cars. It was pretty clear from his expression that he hadn't expected them and wasn't too pleased neither. Funny how men could never hide their feelings like women could – even when they thought they were. That was it. She could see it now, quite obvious. He was gay, wasn't he? Nothing wrong in that. But what about that plump wife in there and all those kids? Not that anything could surprise Lizzie with men and their you-know-whats. She'd had gays come to her for sex, crying like babies. Odd in this day and age. That's what she thought. Well, there he went, into 'the bosom of his family'. She'd read that somewhere and it'd stuck. 'Bosom', wasn't it? Not chest, as in man. Not that any of it meant a fucking thing to her. That man was going in the door like he was spoiling for a fight. Maybe she'd stay out a bit longer. Lovely day, wasn't it.

*

Leo, at the far end of the table, looked up as Roland entered the kitchen. The expression on his brother's face reminded him of their childhood when, for a couple of years around the age of ten or eleven, Roland had been subject to terrifying nightmares that led him to sleepwalk from his bed and sometimes out of their room. Imogen had seemed fascinated by this strange sight – Roland's greenish eyes wide open but blind to the normal world. 'He is seeing horrors, horrors,' she would say, almost with glee. They were instructed not to wake him – apparently this would induce terrible trauma – but to try to lead him back to his bed.

Strangely, this memory made Leo feel sympathetic to his brother for the first time in a long while; strange, not only because they'd seemed locked into a struggle to the death but because he'd just committed the unpardonable act of fucking his brother's wife. Or perhaps that was the reason he felt sympathetic.

'Hi, Roland.' He raised his hand in salute.

It was clear at once that Roland was having none of it. His staring eyes narrowed. 'What the hell . . .'

Maggie blinked. 'You came, after all. What can I get you?' At least she didn't say 'darling'.

Roland seemed unable to speak. The fury turned his face dark red but he walked through the kitchen into the hall.

'I'll send some food into your study, if that's where you're going,' Maggie called after his retreating back, and her voice held a hint of triumph.

Didi prowled about Roland's flat. The weekend porter was a push-over. They even had a friend in common, a good guy, very beautiful. He came from Somalia and worked in a bar. A gay bar. Upmarket. Mostly.

The trouble was now that he was inside the apartment he wasn't sure what to do. If he took stuff that made him a thief, and Roland might dump him. He wasn't a thief anyway. Poor, that was all, because he sent so much money home. He didn't do drugs like most of them either. A bit of crack but that was . . . What was it called? 'Recreational'. He liked that.

Didi sat down in a soft armchair. At his elbow was a heavy silver ashtray, clearly never used. It reminded him of a hotel, this place. He didn't like it much. No character. Probably Roland wouldn't notice if he took the ashtray. More silver glinted on a side table. Photograph frames. Now, that was interesting.

He got up and brought them to the chair. He was a family man himself. He had a mother, a father, who hadn't been seen for a while, and six brothers and sisters, excluding the brother who was in London with him. If he had his way he'd bring them all over here. It would stop his mother spreading his money through his village. Through half of Morocco. She liked showing off to the cousins, that was the trouble.

Didi sighed and yawned. Lack of sleep was a problem in his line of business. If he got home this summer he'd sleep for a week, make his sisters wait on him hand and foot. Have a boy in now and again to keep him in practice.

Dreaming of home, Didi wandered into Roland's bedroom. An hour or two sleeping here would do no one any harm.

Roland sat at his desk. For some reason the curtains were drawn, which suited his mood. He was still angry and knew he was ridiculous, which made it worse. Maggie had every right to hold a lunch party in his absence. The guests were mostly his children or his family anyway. He put his head into his hands.

There was a knock at the door.

'Who is it?'

'Hetty. With your lunch.'

She couldn't see him like this. He grabbed the phone and, because he had to dial somewhere, rang his own London number.

'Hi, darling.'

To Roland, Didi's voice, half asleep, languorous was unmistakable. Only too conscious of Hetty at his elbow as she placed a plate of food on the desk, he panicked. 'Who are you? What are you doing in my flat?'

'What is it?' Hetty leaned over him, excited and curious.

'It's an intruder. In my flat in London.'

'An intruder!'

'How did you get in?' He was shouting, not listening to anything Didi might have to say. Suddenly it struck him that he could put down the phone.

'Why did you do that?' said Hetty. 'You should have kept him talking. Called the police.'

It was obvious she watched TV thrillers, or so Roland thought before he answered firmly, 'I can't ring the police when I'm already on the telephone.'

'Mobile. I could have used your mobile,' She was undeterred, filled with enthusiasm. 'Aren't you worried? A burglar in your flat! Why don't you ring the police now?'

'I'm going to. Hetty, I need to be calm. It might have been the porter.'

'But you'd know his voice, wouldn't you?'

'Some of the weekend porters . . .' began Roland, then decided that enough was enough. He shouted, 'Go now, Hetty. I can manage it without your help. Understand?'

She went.

Hetty, returning to the kitchen, carried her story with her. 'Dad's been burgled. He's in a foul mood. I dumped his food and ran.'

But no one seemed very interested. They were planning a game of football on the lawn. Tom and Jake were already bouncing a ball outside the door while Maggie was trying to insist that the adults had coffee and a sit-down first. 'It's not good to dash about straight after a meal.'

Leo went up to her and held her close for a moment. Nobody noticed, not even Hetty. 'You can't be such a spoilsport,' he said, and she agreed, smiling. There was today first, then tomorrow.

In his study, Roland had rung back Didi. There was no point in asking how he'd got in. 'Why are you there?'

'Because it's you.'

'It's not me. It's my flat. Are you planning to steal?'

'Why I do this?' His voice was reproachful.

'Then why?'

'No reason.'

Roland thought this was probably true. Didi didn't follow pre-conceived plans. How could he, when his main occupation was waiting to be wanted? Roland wanted him at that moment.

'If you tell me, "Leave", I leave. Go. Depart.'

Roland remembered when Didi had known only four English words in total. Hi. Fucking. Yes. No. Now he knew three different words for getting out. It was progress. Even success.

'Good. Go. Leave. Depart. I'll ring tomorrow.'

'Darling. I suck your cock.'

Oh, God. Roland put down the phone. What if someone had listened in? Once more he put his head into his hands.

Gradually he became aware of shouting from the direction of the main garden. In his present state of mind anything seemed possible: a fight, police, burglars, a maniac (possibly Charlie), hitmen. Trying to subdue his agitation, he walked slowly out of his room and into the hallway. There, he hesitated for a moment. No sound came from the kitchen. The best and most unseen view of the garden would be from upstairs. Again, he moved hesitantly, as if this wasn't a house he'd owned and lived in for fifteen years. He took a corridor to the right and another right turn to a bedroom.

Esmond sat up in bed. His hair was ruffled, his eyes bright. He looked birdlike, perhaps an eagle or a white parakeet. 'What's going on out there?' he asked, showing no surprise at his son's appearance.

Roland walked across to the window and stood staring.

The sun was still out, making a brightly lit stage of the lawn. The goalposts, white and netless, marked either end. In one goal crouched the nurse, having dispensed with her white uniform, a solid figure in jeans and sweater. In the other, Portia's boyfriend, gangly but surprisingly dextrous, was in the process of saving a ball struck by Hetty who was following it in, escorted by a rejuvenated Mungo, barking furiously, and a shrieking trio of Tom, Jake and Lizzie. On the wing, Leo bellowed to Jake, 'Get the ball out,' while Maggie, a whistle swinging and glinting round her neck, waved an orange card at Hetty, who had now forced the boyfriend to the ground, and raised her whistle to her lips. 'Foul!' shouted Portia, out on the other wing.

Roland turned to his father. 'They're playing football.'

'Aha,' said Esmond, in a tone of great satisfaction, as if that explained everything, not just the noise but everything, the whole damn caboodle.

Roland took a chair. 'I'm sorry about Mother.' He noticed, as his siblings had earlier, that he no longer called her Imogen.

'Ah, indeed.' Esmond looked as if he might say more, then merely nodded, repeating, 'Indeed.'

'I'm arranging the funeral.'

Esmond smiled encouragingly.

Roland couldn't be sure that he was taking anything in but he persevered all the same. He needed someone to talk to. 'I'm trying to get out of a case. First time I've ever done that. Did you ever do that? I suspect not. I wonder why you chose libel. Was it chance? Or your respect for the power of words? I sometimes regret I chose criminal work. It teaches you to dehumanise yourself – or go mad.' Roland smiled wryly. 'Can't risk that with our family history.' He paused. 'But you're past all that, aren't you? Somewhere calmer, I hope. Just now, today, I wouldn't mind being past it. What do you say to that, Father? Surprises you, doesn't it, that your clever, eldest son in the prime of life could say that?' As Roland leaned closer, the two men were face to face. Esmond's unblinking eyes seemed filled with knowledge, at first beneficent, a father's understanding, then challenging.

It was his own face, ancient, incapable. Wicked. Still wicked. Roland controlled a terrifying urge to smash in the old skull, with its winking, deep-set eyes. But it wasn't his father who was the wicked one. He must get a grip. He stood up and went back to the window. The game was still in progress. Leo was running, Maggie laughing, Jake rolling on the ground.

'Dear boy.' The words had come from behind him. But his father never called him 'dear boy'. Now he was imagining things. What would Didi do next? Had he left the flat, as directed? Perhaps he'd led his friends there. A Sunday-afternoon orgy in progress.

'Dear boy.' There it was again. 'Ah. Ah.'

His father had lain back. Closed his eyes. Roland sat down beside him once more. His father had become a judge eventually. Imogen had been an expensive wife, so he'd needed to amass a fair fortune before he could take the cut in salary. Perhaps she'd thought the loss of money was an appropriate trade-in for the title. Maggie had never shown any interest in being Lady Norrington Barr. He'd toyed with the idea a year ago. There'd been overtures. But that was before Didi.

Roland shut his eyes. It had been ages since he'd had a good night's sleep. The shouts and laughter from the garden became louder, Leo's voice stronger than anyone's. How could he sound so light-hearted? Roland allowed his ever-simmering resentment against his brother to bubble a little higher. He'd heard the news on the drive here. He'd been so concerned with his own anxieties that he hadn't considered what it all meant to Leo: the photograph in the newspapers, the speedy resignation of the home secretary, accepted by his mate the prime minister. Westminster in flames. The political journalists running round like headless chickens. For once there was so much news there was no need for invention. And all this mayhem kicked off by Leo. Roland disapproved of so much destruction, almost anarchy. It might even bring down the government. All because one (note: divorced) minister, a human being like everyone else, had picked up a prostitute who just happened to be an illegal immigrant. Bad luck, surely, not bad judgement. The other part of the story, the blackmailing Met chief, hardly seemed convincing. No one had seemed too interested in it anyway since he had taken compassionate leave. Maybe they'd get back on to it if and when his wife died.

'Run, Tom, run!' How dare Leo bellow like that at his son? *His* son. *His* garden. *His* house. Leo should have supported *his* government. *His* party. It was Charlie, of course. The bad apple in the pack. Once again, Roland felt a rising tide of rage. How good it would feel to smash something, someone – anything!

'Late. Late.' Esmond was struggling to sit up, his eyes open and unfocused, his speech scarcely intelligible. 'Rocking. Feet out. Feet first. Late. Oh. Oh. Just listen to that wind in the rigging. From the south, is it?'

At first bemused, Roland remembered that Maggie had told him his father's delusion: that he was the captain of a warship *circa* 1800. He'd hardly believed the story and didn't visit him enough to check. A crazy old man was woman's work. They employed a nurse, didn't they? At great expense, incidentally, she was now spending Roland's money as a goalie on his lawn.

Roland flung open the window and yelled, 'Nurse! You're needed! At once!'

The cheerful scene in front of him froze and all faces turned upward. He felt like the pantomime devil who appears in a puff of green smoke and stops the action dead. It didn't displease him. The nurse recovered first and, flinging to the grass a pair of striped gloves she'd acquired, came running towards the house.

Roland withdrew his head from the window and slid it down carefully. Esmond was still muttering but had stopped his fretful tossing. Only one hand, outside the bedclothes, clawed at the air.

The nurse appeared. She was red in the face, panting and sweating, with a twig in her hair.

'Ah, Nurse . . .' He couldn't remember her name, although he'd seen her face at other weekends.

'I'm so sorry. He was asleep. But that's no excuse.'

Perhaps she expected to be sacked but he bore no malice. In fact, after her speedy answer to his summons, he felt favourable towards her.

'He seems better. I'm sorry I shouted.' He was surprised to find himself apologising. She was at his mercy. But that didn't usually deter him.

'I shouldn't have gone.'

'Nonsense. I overreacted.' He left her then, went to the kitchen and made himself a cup of tea before returning to his study. There, he listened to a message from Mike: 'You're in luck, sir. Had it on the grapevine. Your opposite number, Timothy Holder QC's got a new bird who's giving him stick for never being free. A week's postponement of the case and he'll drift her off to the Gazelle d'Or. You know the place, turbans in the restaurant and camels in the garden – or the other way round, if you fancy them. So he'll be on your side. That's a postponement, mind. You're still in the hot spot. Can't hand it over. The solicitor's not playing. Can you make it Monday week? Then we'll get on to the judge. Not easy, sir, this one.'

Roland put down the telephone. A huge surge of relief made him feel like weeping. Mike was a gladiator. Earned half a million and deserved every penny. He'd still have to go to court in the morning and do his stuff with the judge, but with the defendant on his side he was halfway there. OK, there'd be talk. A day off for a mother's funeral was acceptable, a whole week extraordinary. And could he even carry on the following Monday? He wouldn't think about that now.

Now he was calm. He picked up the phone to ring back Mike, then hesitated. Was Didi still in his flat? Didi respected him. Or, at least, his money. Didi could be sorted when he returned to London.

CHAPTER FORTY-TWO

Two Somnolent Men

A priest had come to give Charlie communion. Not Bill, a small man with spectacular bags under his eyes. It was already two in the afternoon.

'Do you want to stay in bed?' he asked Charlie wearily. He opened a battered case and took out a chasuble to wear round his neck and a little velvet pouch, which contained the Host.

'It looks like you need bed more than me.' Charlie swung out his legs.

'There's only me today.' The priest didn't even look up.

'My brother's a priest.'

'That makes two of us.'

'As bad as that, is it?' Charlie stood up and the priest became even smaller. Charlie laughed. 'Don't worry. I'll kneel.' He felt gentle with this poor man of God who laboured to bring Christ to believers. With some difficulty, he lowered himself to the floor. Co-ordination bad, muscle tone worse. He held out his hands but they shook so much that he changed his mind.

'Body of Christ.'

'Amen.' He opened his mouth.

Afterwards he felt the expected surge of virtue. 'Let's have a coffee together.'

The priest looked at his watch.

'Come on,' urged Charlie.

'I've missed lunch anyway,' the priest conceded, and sat down while Charlie clambered back into bed. He rang the bell.

'With any luck, young George will come. He's at my beck and call at the moment. I much prefer the young, don't you?'

The priest sighed. 'I see so few, unless they're in big trouble. Occasionally I get called in then.'

'I suppose you think you're part of a dying profession,' said Charlie meditatively.

The priest seemed startled and sat up straighter. 'No, I don't. I'm just tired. Sorry.'

Charlie saw that newspaper bulged from his jacket pocket. 'Mind if I have a look? I've missed it this morning.'

'Take it. It doesn't help. Seeing that sort of thing. On Sunday.'

Charlie looked down at the paper. He stared, read the commentary, but didn't turn to the following page. He pushed it away. Griff had done his work. It was good news. If the police did their work properly Ileana's death would not be in vain. One more victim. Many less victims. Sadness and tragedy. Now he would tell the police everything he knew. Those men. What they did to the girls they brought into the country and marketed to sleazebags like the home secretary. He had been there once. He felt his mind blur and vibrate like a car about to race. He mustn't go there. He lay against the pillows.

'There's so much evil about us,' said the priest, as if he couldn't pretend otherwise for another moment. He sighed heavily, sat back and shut his eyes. In a second or two there was the sound of modest snoring.

'What is it?' A nurse, not George, put her head round the door.

'Two coffees, queen of my heart, biscuits to match.'

The nurse left, smiling.

Charlie drew the newspaper back to him. Who would be after him now? The photograph was everything. He'd always tried to tell himself that. Murdering Ileana had been too late. They may not have known, of course. Or it might have been revenge. He put his trembling hand to his head, pressed his temples. He knew so much. He was a witness. They would know that.

The priest slept more heavily, his head dropped to his chest. Did he dream of gilded clouds, like sofas, held up by choirs of heavenly angels, God in all his glory, somewhere above? Alleluia. Alleluia. Ileana probably dreamed the same and even poor mad Bertie Flannagan (alias Horace Silver), fled from the wilds of County Clare but still Irish at his core.

The story would soon be over. He must sleep. Mourn. *Courage, mon brave!* Where was George? He was lucky to have such a watchdog.

The nurse returned with the coffee. She gazed for a moment at the somnolent men. It struck her as weird, not quite laughable. She put the tray on the table and, since neither man woke, left the room, carefully leaving the door ajar.

CHAPTER FORTY-THREE

Monuments Don't Talk

Monday was Bill's quietest day. He tried to keep it like that, reading his breviary, saying the first Mass. It was still early when a call came from the Probation Service. 'You know Lizzie didn't keep her appointment? We've tried her contact number, the one you gave us, but there's no answer.'

'Good morning, Shirley. She left a message, didn't she? Can you give her a little longer?'

'You understand as well as I do what a little longer means. A little longer to score, a little longer to steal, to sell her body. Lizzie's been here before, and she's a not a bad girl.'

'What girls are?' Bill sighed. 'Till lunchtime? I'll bring her in myself.'

'Better you than the police.'

The same springlike weather as the day before made the air soft, the sky bright. Maggie flung open her bedroom window and felt her heart beating like a young girl's. It was still only six thirty but she needed time to be on her own. To think. Instead she smiled, and remembered, and listened to the birds.

Everybody she loved and looked after was in the house. Quite a thought. After that absurd football match, they had all kind of collapsed. There had been tea and high tea and supper and somehow nobody, except Conor, eventually, had left. Portia and Lizzie were in one spare room and Leo in another. Roland was in the dressing room.

Roland had been tolerant, almost good-humoured, then gone to bed early. He'd said he'd be leaving at six a.m. to be in court but then he'd be free, whatever that might mean. Maybe his outburst from Esmond's window had shamed him. If he had been anyone else, you'd think he was cracking up.

Maggie wasn't prepared to think of him that way. She serviced him, that was all. That was how he wanted it. No intimacy. A good working relationship, honed to a fine art over twenty-three years. She closed the window with a snap. She didn't like the way her thoughts were going. Did this 'working relationship' make them equal? Could she not consider herself misused? Was there moral equivalence between his male prostitute and her love (now consummated) for Leo? Did Roland's high earnings cancel out his bad temper?

Maggie decided to dress. The springlike air was cooler and damper than she had expected. Then she had a better idea.

Leo lay in bed, half awake. Half asleep. When Maggie's smooth, cool body slid in beside him, he didn't open his eyes but rolled heavily towards her. He felt the weight of their limbs and torsos, like statues combining in arousal. Yes, they were monumental, he thought, feeling her breasts, her hips and knees. They were meant to be together. Monuments don't talk.

'Darling,' he whispered.

'Yes. Yes.'

The kitchen was empty when Maggie came down but someone had made themselves tea. Roland. The word 'adultery' repeated in her ears but she felt too happy to take it up.

'Isn't life a turmoil?' said Leo, cheerfully. 'Now I'll have to go back and face the music. What are the odds that being proved right makes me no more popular than before? Do you get the papers delivered?'

'Any minute now.' Maggie, standing by the Aga, glanced at her watch, then at Leo. He was so handsome, smooth-shaven, clean shirt – he must have brought it with him. He looked at her warmly, true, but he was thinking of what lay in wait for him, not of what had happened this morning and yesterday. She brought over coffee and a pile of toast as he'd asked.

'Now I feel ready for anything.' She hoped he meant more than a good breakfast. He smiled at her. She was grateful.

Lizzie gazed up at the smooth white ceiling. As she watched, grey blobs formed and marched across, then shivered and broke up. It was the sun through the curtain, a light breeze. She was in the country. The silence had woken her all through the night.

She reached for her ciggies on the bedside table. Her throat was sore from smoking so much, but that wouldn't stop her. She eyed Portia's still sleeping figure. No. Perhaps she'd dress, not that she was fully undressed in her pants and T-shirt, and go into the garden.

Lizzie peered through the curtains. Who was out there? Two figures as tall as giants. No, it was their shadows, stretching out black into the sunshine. It was Maggie, all right, in some kind of robe, her pretty hair, glinting golden. Natural, too. They kissed. Must be that Roland, then. He was in his car and off, narrowly missing a van coming in much too fast. A fat woman jumped out, dumped some papers and drove away again, just as fast.

Life in the country, thought Lizzie, trees and birds and cars whizzing up and down with everything you could want. Time for a fag. She'd be more herself then.

Portia watched her go through half-open eyes. She'd been waiting to put on her mobile and catch Conor, with any luck, before he went to work. Before she did anything.

Only one message. An unknown number. 'Portia, I'm so sorry to bother you but Lizzie's gone missing. Or at least her probation officer, followed by police in a matter of hours, is on her tail. She isn't still with you? Because . . .'

At this point her machine cut off Father Bill's anxious voice.

Now she'd have to get Lizzie to where she should be. Lizzie herself clearly didn't think about it at all, as if the prospect of a return to prison was in the hands of Fate, not her own. In fact, the only time she ever showed any interest in anything was when she talked about Charlie. Although that wasn't quite true either. Look at her wild enthusiasm for the crazed football match.

Irritated that she was thinking about Lizzie when she could be talking to Conor, Portia scrolled down her mobile for his name. There, she hesitated, enjoying the sense of well-being even his name produced. She sniffed. Someone not too far away was smoking. She got out of bed and opened the curtains. There Lizzie was, huddled outside the kitchen door, puffing like a chimney. Her pale face was bleached entirely by the sun. Her legs were the same size as the drainpipes that ran down the wall.

As Portia watched, the door opened and Maggie appeared, put an arm round Lizzie and drew her inside.

Maggie was glad Leo had left. She could act her role of mother and wife without conflict. At the moment she even felt free of the expected guilt. She cooked poor Lizzie scrambled egg on toast and was glad when she ate a bite or two. She told her newly arrived cleaner where to start in the house and checked with the nurse that Esmond had passed a reasonable night. She rang the gallery and told her assistant, an aspiring painter, that she'd be in a couple of hours later than planned. Then, as an afterthought, she booked a hair appointment. Maybe Leo would return some time soon. When Portia arrived downstairs she was watering her plants from a pretty painted can with a usefully long spout.

'And I expect you've done all the weeding too.' Portia seemed to be in a bad mood.

'Cooked breakfast?'

'No time. I've got to get Lizzie back to London.' Accusingly, she looked at Lizzie, who kept her head down and said nothing.

'Oh dear.' Absentmindedly, Maggie collected Lizzie's plate and began to finish off the scrambled eggs.

'You haven't a spare car, have you?' Portia said, in the tone of someone asking for the salt.

Maggie licked her fingers. Of course they did. 'Hetty uses it but she could do without for a day or two. It's pretty battered. Goes all right, though.'

'Probation, is it?' Lizzie's voice somehow surprised both women. They stared at her without speaking. 'In prison, you see, you get out of the habit of doing things for yourself. It's like you're a child again. Go here, go there, do this, do that. They lead you from one place to another. Then they chuck you out and say, go here, go there, but there's no one to help you, see. I had a mate, she'd been inside four years and more when they let her out, told her to catch a train here and cross London on two undergrounds, then another train back home where her probation was. All by midday. Well, she couldn't do that, could she. She was back inside two days later. Never got further than London. Back on everything she could get hold of. Too much hard work on the outside, she told me. She had kids too.'

'That's dreadful!' exclaimed Maggie.

'*You* have us to help you. And Father Bill.' Portia brushed her curly hair off her face. Her cheeks were pinker than usual.

'I had to see Charlie, didn't I.' Lizzie was defensive. 'You never know, do you.'

Maggie thought about this. Until the last few days she was sure she knew. Even with Roland being such an enigma, she'd assumed she knew the picture. She pushed the coffee pot towards Portia. 'At least have a coffee before you go. I'll find the car key.'

As soon as Maggie left the room, Portia seemed to make up her mind. 'I'm sorry.'

'What's that for?' Lizzie drummed her fingers on the table. She'd finished her last pack of cigarettes. Then she began to chew her nails. She wanted to say, 'Let's get on with it, then,' but it wasn't her place. She was just a transport. If she'd had her way, she'd go straight back to Charlie. Charlie needed her. He was the only person who did. Or if he didn't, she needed him, loved him. That was the truth. It was a good feeling, saying that, even to herself. Like yesterday. His family. Playing silly buggers with his family. She'd sometimes wondered how the rich got off. Never thought it'd be football. It was fun, though. 'Where's the kids, then?'

Portia looked surprised. 'In bed. So, what's the address of this probation place?'

'She's Shirley. She's nice. Kind and that.'

Portia looked surprised again. 'So why didn't you go and see her?'

'It wasn't her fault. I told you just now. I needed to find Charlie.' Lizzie wondered why Portia couldn't get it. You did what was most important. That stood to reason. Only two days before she'd been told Charlie was dead. She had to see him, touch him. Like that Thomas, doubting Thomas, in the Bible. She'd always been on his side – as a kid, that is, not read the Bible since school.

'Have you got the address?'

'It's written down.' Here's hoping she could find the bit of paper. 'It's Chalk Farm tube, I know that. It's not as if I haven't been there often enough.'

'OK. That'll do for now.'

They went with Maggie to find the car. It was still sunny, although clouds were gathering in hefty grey clumps to their left. Might be the west, thought Lizzie. One day she'd buy one of those little pointers, told you east, west, north, south. It'd be nice to have a bit more idea where she was.

Maggie hugged her. Warm and soft. 'Good luck,' she said. A lot of people had said that to her, most not meaning it. But maybe Maggie did.

'It was nice being here.' She meant it too. She didn't dare add, 'being part of Charlie's family'. They could feel sorry for her and help her but she shouldn't try to be part of anything. Lower down the ladder than that smelly old dog of theirs. Trailing along behind Maggie now. He *was* part of the family. That's life. Nothing to complain of.

They drove off down the driveway, Maggie waving at them all the way.

Dr Heilbrand came into Charlie's room first thing.

'Morning, Mengele.' Charlie was sitting up in bed, the papers spread round him.

'I wish you'd stop calling me that.' The doctor tugged at his beard.

'You never minded before.' Charlie smiled goadingly.

'I gave you leeway.'

'As a member of the insane class. I understand. You're not going to tell me that Dr Mengele committed the worst atrocities that one man could invent to torture another. Or remind me that he enjoyed injecting chemicals into children's eyes to see if they changed colour. Or that your family are Jewish and your mother and aunt disappeared in the Holocaust.'

Charlie watched the doctor's face as he spoke. Probably he was a child looking for boundaries. Anyway, it seemed important how the guardian of his life reacted. The tugging of the beard (never performed in his presence before) stopped and irritation changed to anger, his face flushed, then a few deep breaths, and calm descended.

'You can shock me, Charlie, but not with Mengele. His name is nothing. It's his deeds that live and should be remembered. Clearly you are feeling better this morning.'

'Yes. I've decided to grow up. Mengele is banished for ever to the reddest flames of hell. You are my saviour. From now on I shall call you Christ – that is, if you don't object? You have much in common.'

Heilbrand sighed. 'I see you've read the papers.'

'Ah, yes. Griff's done his stuff. Yesterday, today. The government blasted apart. With any luck, the crapulous pimping perverts too. There's no point me staying here.'

'You're sure of that? And you feel well enough?'

'Sit down, Doctor! Sit down. You're the one qualified to assess my mental health. For the rest, I am in God's hands. In hospital, I am a mere victim, pulled this way and that, filled with dangerous chemicals . . . How should I know how I am? I might as well tell you, though, that I have not taken a pill since yesterday.'

The doctor sat down. 'And you slept?'

'Sleep is relative. There's the sleep of death, the sleep of a baby, the sleep of an adolescent, the sleep of a labourer, the sleep of an intellectual, the sleep of a dreamer . . .' He paused as the doctor looked at his watch.

'And which kind of sleep did you have?'

'The sleep of the newly sane. It is a tentative kind of sleep, unsure of itself but hoping to please.'

'So did you sleep at all?'

'An hour or two.'

'If I let you out, you'll need someone to look after you. There'll be all kinds of over-stimulants. The police will interview you. Maybe look after you. Maybe not. Ditto the press. Here I can stop them. Once you're outside, you'll be on your own. I presume the threatening elements will have run for cover, but how can one be sure? Poor Horace Silver is still dead and the orange bands still round the tree where he died – or didn't die, as it turned out. There is much to be uncovered still and, from what you've told me, you can hardly avoid your part in it. This poor young woman. She, too, is dead. The responsibility for that may spread further than is comfortable for you. Your journalist friend will eventually name his sources. All this needs a strong mind to cope with. Is your mind so strong?'

'What bollocks you do talk! Action, Doctor. In the end, one must move forward or die. The picture is dark but we must see beyond. You are a religious man, even if your faith doesn't cater for a future of life everlasting. Let us agree, my mind is like the maladjusted workings of a beautiful, many-cogged timepiece. Sometimes it runs too fast, sometimes too slow, but it runs, it works! Is the answer to stop its movement for ever? No, there must be life until there is death.' Charlie smiled. 'See? I can talk bollocks too.'

The two men looked at each other. Eventually the doctor stood up. 'I've never been able to control you, Charlie. You just tell me when you want to leave and I'll sign the papers.'

'Crikey! With one bound he was free!' Charlie imitated an old-fashioned schoolboy chortling as the doctor went to the door. But afterwards he lay back passively, although his hands were shaking under the bedclothes.

CHAPTER FORTY-FOUR

On the Quarter Deck

Imogen's funeral was to be held in All Saints Church, Margaret Street, W1. Her last escort, who had been something between an interior decorator and a party-planner – perhaps more nothing than something – had fallen in love with the church.

On Monday afternoon Roland went to see it and make arrangements. He had spent his morning at a meeting room inside the courts where he eventually managed to persuade the judge that he was not fit to fight the case that should have been starting as they spoke. He left feeling humiliated and cowardly. The judge's more sympathetic comment, 'Your family has been in the news, Mr Norrington Barr,' only added to his sense of failure and chaos.

The church surprised him by being located a stone's throw from Oxford Street, then shocked him by being built of an elaborate patterning of red and black bricks, the kind of style he associated with Victorian factories in Manchester. What had this to do with his light and elegant mother?

'If you're not grabbed by this,' said the priest (ostentatiously robed), who had met him at the courtyard in front of the church, 'you'll be horrified by the interior.'

'The spire's very fine,' said Roland, feebly.

Inside, an organ was playing. That was all Roland could take in because the darkness was overwhelming.

'Sixty-nine stops,' meditated the priest, 'ivory with names painted on them. That's our student practising. He might play at the funeral.'

'How do you light the church?' asked Roland, trying not to sound brusque.

'Butterfield – the architect – liked it dim.' The priest laughed. 'Wait a moment and you'll see better. We do have illumination on the altar.'

As the priest walked off down the nave, Roland peered around him without much enthusiasm and soon found patterns and carvings in rich colours and designs, while faces peered back at him from every window and wall. He went closer and saw marbles in kaleidoscopic fantasy, tiles painted with friezes of a biblical kind and, above, the jewel ruby and emerald of stained glass leading to elaborately soaring roof beams. In his state of emotional intensity, and instability, it seemed like a nightmare of religious verbosity.

'You will have guessed we're Anglo-Catholic,' said the priest, returning. Behind him, gold-framed paintings of saints glowed above the high altar. 'I hope that fits in with your family's beliefs.'

'Beliefs!' Roland heard his voice more high-pitched than usual. 'One brother's a priest – a Catholic priest – another possibly Anglican, I'm a non-believer . . .'

'And your mother?'

'Our mother.' It was impossible to summarise Imogen's view on the meaning of life. In later years, she dressed for her evening engagements at midday. There she sat, exquisitely beautiful in silk or brocade, garlanded with pearls or diamonds. The first time he'd dropped in at lunchtime, he'd questioned her, concerned that she'd lost her grip on time. She'd given him her 'silly boy' look. 'At my age, darling, it's far too much effort to dress twice in one day. Besides, I like to sparkle.' 'She liked to sparkle' hardly seemed an appropriate answer to the priest's question so he said nothing.

He found, however, that the image of his mother, as he'd seen her on Saturday evening, had taken the place of the confident woman dressed up in her finery. His knees weakened, his heart beat too fast. He looked for a place to sit, but in this central part of the nave there were only acres of marble flooring.

'Are you all right?' The priest put out a hand as if to support him.

'Yes. Yes.' But he wasn't all right and the concern he felt from this robed stranger was making him feel worse.

'Perhaps a coffee. In my office. Some people find the church oppressive. Even those who worship here.'

*

Once in the functional office, Roland felt physically more himself, but also found a growing desire to use the man opposite him as a confidant. When had he last had one? Or had he ever?

The priest, Father Edward Fairfax, was explaining arrangements and Roland noticed that a leaflet setting out ways of contributing to a newly launched appeal had been placed prominently. The sight restored him slightly, reminding him that he was a man of means, to be courted by the big world.

'Friday would be possible,' said Father Edward.

'Friday would be good,' replied Roland, but his concentration was not on the funeral. Could it be that the good priest in front of him was gay? Many priests were, Catholics, Anglicans and Anglo-Catholics. But, then, he didn't think of himself as gay – just as a man with sexual needs that were most aroused and satisfied by another man.

'I suppose you get a great variety of people visiting your church. Off Oxford Street, on the edge of Soho.'

'Certainly not quite like a country parish,' the priest conceded, although Roland, perhaps over-sensitive to his own preoccupations, thought he looked as if the idea was not altogether a comfortable one.

'Do you offer confession?'

'We do, as a matter of fact. Very high church.'

'Many come?' These questions were a game, of course. As a barrister, questioning was his most natural form of dialogue.

Father Edward, who had thin fair hair and pale blue eyes, began to look restive. He said, 'I have a printed list of the questions that need to be answered regarding the service. Incidentally, I assume your priestly brother may want to concelebrate?'

'They planned it all – my mother and her friend.' Roland took several typed sheets and handed them over. 'Before my brother re-entered the family.'

The priest didn't question this but looked at the papers. Roland watched his hands, which were slim and white. 'Everything's here. We can talk further on the phone.'

Roland noted that he seemed keen to bring the interview to an end as if he'd noticed something in Roland's manner that made him anxious. Roland liked the feeling. It gave him the upper hand. Yet he still sat there, fighting the urge, more an itch really, to confide.

'Can I help you with anything else?' said the priest.

Roland knew he meant anything else to do with the funeral but his heart raced all the same, as if he'd been asked a quite different question. 'I have become entangled,' he said.

'Entangled!'

Poor Father Edward's eyes widened in such horror that Roland nearly smiled. More that that, it showed him the absurdity of his situation. He stood up and held out his hand. 'Thank you. We'll finalise the details tomorrow.'

Outside in the street, he breathed deeply and found his hands were damp with sweat. He walked away briskly, hardly noticing where he was going until he passed a familiar building. It was a hotel where he and Didi had met more than once.

Portia sat in her car outside the probation office. It was on the corner of two very busy streets but she'd found a meter and the traffic passed her by. She'd bought a paper, but on seeing that the front page was all about the home secretary and the prostitute, she put it aside. These political disturbances were like the volcanoes and storms that periodically attacked the lives of her Mexican women. Yet that wasn't true. Politics was man-made, with man-made disasters. Reluctantly, she pulled back the paper. Perhaps it was her duty as a citizen to read the sordid tale of corrupt power and powerless victims. Her brothers, naturally, at the vortex.

This time she dropped the paper on the floor and leaned back against the seat. The sun came in and warmed one side of her face. She felt drowsy, not displeased with her situation. She'd achieved Lizzie's return to the straight and narrow. This afternoon she'd do her accounts, as she always did on Monday afternoons. This evening she and Conor would meet and make love. Before that she'd try to transfer Lizzie to Charlie's flat. If she wanted to clean it, she was very welcome to.

Portia's content diminished a little. How had it happened that Lizzie had become her responsibility? She sat up straighter and took out her mobile. It rang for some time before it was answered.

'Father Bill, how can I help?'

This was her *brother*. 'It's Portia. I'm waiting for Lizzie to come out from her meeting with Probation . . .'

'Well done, Portia.'

'I wondered who's in *charge* of her. I mean, she seems quite incapable of doing anything without a minder . . .' As Portia spoke, feelings of disloyalty surfaced. Lizzie was her *sister-in-law*. What was it about her family? She remembered Lizzie's passionate plea to be allowed to look after Charlie.

'She takes care of herself,' said Bill, sounding weary, 'with the help of her probation officer, who's a nice, conscientious woman, and anyone else who's prepared to get involved. She might do well to sign up with NA, even if she is off drugs at the moment.'

'NA?' enquired Portia. 'And what about her mother?'

'Narcotics Anonymous. I don't know about the mother. Is there a problem, Portia?'

Portia thought that his whole life was dedicated to looking after other people. It was his vocation. His job. Admittedly, she raised money for her Mexican women but that was her choice and she enjoyed doing it. Her real aim, like that of ninety-nine per cent of sane people, was to be happy, ordinarily happy. Lizzie threatened that at just the moment when it seemed, for the first time ever, within her grasp.

'She's so hopeless!'

'You've done too much already.' Bill sounded alarmed. 'You're probably still in shock after your . . .' he hesitated '. . . our mother's death.'

'I do feel a bit unbalanced.' She'd just spotted Lizzie emerging. She was with an older woman, glasses, streaky grey hair, a blue blazer. Lizzie pointed her way. 'I just had a text from Roland,' Portia said absentmindedly. 'The funeral's Friday. Eleven a.m. At some church off Oxford Street.'

'Is that so?' Portia guessed Bill hadn't been told. 'I'll have to cancel my New Testament study group.' He was trying not to sound hurt.

'Anyway, Lizzie's here now. Don't worry. I'll sort her.'

The blazer with glinting brass buttons was approaching. Portia got out of the car. They stood together on the pavement. The noise of traffic was almost overpowering. Lizzie stayed at a little distance, smoking. The probation woman, Shirley, also smelled of smoke, of hot offices, of tense situations.

'Lizzie says you're her sister-in-law.'

'That's right.'

'Excellent. I'm so used to her lies. I've been trying to sort her out for years. She shouldn't have gone to prison but the magistrates had tried everything else. I've lost count of how many times she's been fined – she doesn't pay, of course – or been given community sentences when she doesn't turn up. Even so, she wouldn't have got it this time if she hadn't had a whacking great knife in her bag, "bladed instrument", as it's called in the jargon.'

'A knife!' exclaimed Portia. They'd been sharing a bedroom.

'Doubtless for self-defence. She'd been in a fight with another of the girls before. Got off that time. And the time after.'

'Lizzie in a fight!' Portia glanced to where she stood, arms wrapped round her chest. 'You could blow her over.'

'Drugs change people. At least prison worked on that front. And she's still clean.' Shirley looked enquiringly at Portia, then carried on. 'With the help of her new family. You should pat yourself on the back, dear.'

Portia was struggling to sort out this new light on Lizzie; up to this moment she hadn't given a thought as to why she'd been put in prison. She'd just seemed a rather sad victim who, rather annoyingly and possibly for dubious reasons, brought out chivalrous instincts in men. 'So she wasn't picked up for prostitution.'

'Picked up, yes. Rounded up, in fact, now and again. Haringey-style, it's called, because Haringey Council likes that sort of action. Most of the women don't even bother to go to court so they're given an eighty- or ninety-pound fine. They have to be "known prostitutes", another piece of jargon.' Shirley laughed. She seemed to be enjoying educating the ignoramus in front of her.

'But not prison?'

'Certainly not. Needs years of it. Thieving too.'

'Thieving!'

'Shoplifting. Even that wouldn't get her inside. But the fighting and the knife make her look dangerous. Anyway, some magistrate thought so, or just got fed up and decided he'd give prison a chance. Turned out well. So far. Look, must go. She's got to report weekly for the next seven weeks till her sentence is complete.' The woman, her face bright and kindly, peered at Portia. 'You look shell-shocked. You should see some of my clients.'

With this she left, giving Lizzie a few encouraging words as she passed. Lizzie trod on her cigarette and came over to Portia. 'What's she been going on about? I could've turned into a lamppost.'

'You. She was telling me about you.'

'I thought so.' Lizzie seemed pleased at the idea. 'Been bad, haven't I?'

'Well.' Portia got into the car and Lizzie slipped beside her. 'I never thought what you'd done. I mean, apart from . . .'

'Being a working girl. Your sort don't want to know. They might not find it so easy to help.'

'I don't know.' Portia didn't. Was it cowardice, lack of interest or a wish to look to the future? 'I suppose I want to think whatever you've done is in the past. Not relevant to the future.' She began to drive, heading to her flat.

'Isn't, though. The past kills. That was written on a wall in the showers. Prison showers. I didn't quite know what it meant, did I. But I know how the girl felt who wrote it. You can't never get away from it. It's who you are. It's on my face. On my body. All those years. Every punter. Every needle. Not that I was ever much of a needle woman. Joke. I preferred a sniff or a smoke. It's like they said in that rehab place. You're always an addict. Even when you're clean.'

'I'm sorry.'

'Just thought what else it's like.'

'What's that?'

'A priest. Once a priest, always a priest. Isn't that the saying?'

'I don't know.'

'You're in a very don't-know mood.'

Lizzie was right. Whenever Lizzie got into one of her voluble moods, Portia felt completely flummoxed. There seemed no point of entry between their two worlds.

'Any news of Charlie today?'

Of course, Charlie was the point of entry. 'Not so far.'

'But we can ring him, can't we?'

'When we get back.'

From then on Lizzie was silent until they got out of the car. Then she took Portia's arm. 'Shirley said I'm doing great. Can't say fairer than that. Right?'

'Right,' agreed Portia. She was pleased that Lizzie had wanted to give her this information.

Hetty was bad-tempered about the absence of the second car. 'You know I'm not insured for yours. So what am I supposed to do all day?'

'I'm sorry.' Maggie was on to her fourth breakfast and there was still the boys' to go. Apparently they'd sneaked off and watched *Batman II* till three a.m. and probably planned to spend the morning in bed. She fought against a feeling that things were out of order and that it was linked to, if not exactly the outcome of, her illicit hours (actually, more like minutes) with Leo. She had purposely not put on the radio in case he should be interviewed and she should give herself away to Hetty. Not that Hetty, in her present mood, would notice anyone outside herself. 'I could drive you,' Maggie offered, taking yet another piece of toast. No wonder she was so fat.

'It's not the same. That car's mine. You should at least have asked me.'

'Strictly speaking, that's not true. You use it most but—'

'Oh, I'm not staying here arguing.' Hetty flounced out.

Maggie sat on. She could hear Agnes, the new Polish cleaner, hoovering next door. That was soothing. And the sun still shone. Just the day to do some gardening. She'd been meaning to cut back the Potentilla for two years but it was always too quick for her, budding up before she got there. Maybe she'd cut it anyway.

Calmer now, she wondered if she and Leo could ever make a pair. The secret of her marriage to Roland was that he left her alone. And she left him alone. Could it be different with Leo? He'd been a bachelor for a very long time. Even when he'd had a girlfriend, they didn't seem to live together. Charlie was the same. Perhaps what she had with Leo was as good as it could get. She wasn't sure if this was reassuring but she got up, placed cereal bowls for the boys and went out to find her gardening things. She was pretty certain that Hetty would appear soonish, apologise, and ask to be driven somewhere.

CHAPTER FORTY-FIVE

The Importance of Cover

Charlie surveyed Griff. He always forgot what an insignificant little wanker he was. He even wore a suit, cheap-looking but definitely a suit. 'Congratulations, my old fruit. You'll be on the staff yet.'

'How are you, then?' Griff sat down by the bed. He clearly didn't expect an answer to his question. 'Bad news about that girl, Ileana.'

'The Almighty will look after her.'

'Still taking His name in vain.' Griff turned his head, shaved since Charlie had last seen him, to look at their surroundings. 'Get this luxury out of our taxes, do you?'

'Everything a man could want. Doctors, police escort, plenty of interesting company.'

'I'd enjoy it a bit longer if I were you.'

'That's what you came to say, is it? I thought you were just being friendly.' Charlie swung his long legs out of bed and stood in front of Griff. He flexed his muscles. The writing on his arms danced. Is this a man to be kept out of the action?'

'I got a bit of a warning, that's all.' Griff punched Charlie's arm. 'Go on, get back into bed.'

Obediently, Charlie climbed in. 'You're the boss.'

'Just give the police time to do a bit of sorting.'

'The police!' Charlie burped loudly.

'I know. I know, Ileana's inquest's tomorrow at St Pancras. Let that happen. A couple more days.'

'You know, Griff, you're a very caring chap. I should say mate, mucker, old cheese. So, how are you looking out for yourself?'

'Carefully. Let's leave it at that. And I won't say another thing about you either.'

'That's the ticket. So what are we on to next?'

'Get well, Charlie.'

Bill didn't receive many letters that caused him excitement. Mostly they were circulars about retreats or pilgrimages or cut-price offers on candles. This letter had been placed on top of the small pile by either Aloysius or Mary. Obviously they had seen the Westminster Cathedral stamp. Instead of opening it in the kitchen as usual, he took it to the parlour.

He opened it carefully. Strictly speaking, it hadn't come from Westminster Cathedral but from Archbishop's House where the cardinal, head of the Catholic Church in England, lived with some of his staff. It was written by one of the secretaries, Father Mark, whom Bill knew from his days in the seminary and whom he still saw occasionally.

Bill read the letter twice, although it was not long and very clear. A new job was being created, and his name had been put up for it. What was his reaction? A date for a meeting was proposed. The letter had been posted last week and the proposed meeting was the following day. They wanted to move quickly, otherwise the money – from a sponsor – might move elsewhere.

Bill's first instinct was to pray. So he did. Then he began to think. The words 'preferment', 'obedience' and 'the will of God' surfaced. The last he had always found very comforting. Finally 'power'. However humble the priests who ran it, Archbishop's House was the centre of power. The very fact that they could summon him from his modest role as an ordinary parish priest attested to that. Any earthly organisation wielded power. He was no fool, knew the gossip about the ambitious bishops and their networking secretaries. It was not a world he'd ever wanted to inhabit, not in any way the reason he'd been drawn to the Church. He admired those who liked to administer and was uncritical if it brought them enjoyment of their power, but had always assumed it was not for him.

Now, it seemed, it was. 'The will of God'. Of course, he would be a small cog in the machine but he knew, from Mark, that the machine was not large. Only half a dozen men at the centre, excluding the nuns and voluntary workers. There would be committees, squabbles, reports. The cardinal, his boss, was not appreciated by all in the hierarchy. There were those who coveted his position. He would have to deal with this and, quite possibly, although the letter didn't suggest he had any duties in this area (it would be absurd, given his lack of experience, if he should), he would have at least to take into account the press.

Bill began to pray again but his prayer, a psalm he particularly liked, *God is for us a refuge and strength, a helper close at hand, in time of distress* . . . was interrupted by the word 'Westminster'.

He thought of what it meant to most people and, in particular, to Leo: Westminster, the centre of government, of temporal power. Leo's recent experiences hadn't made as much impression on him as perhaps they should. On the whole he tried to avoid the constant stream of news, as if, he now thought self-critically, by avoiding it he could absolve himself of responsibility for the cankers and boils of society. He tackled the problems within his immediate grasp – the Lizzies, for example, whom he met in his prison work – but he was glad to exclude from his thinking the *reasons* for such sad people's existence. Now he would have to think about these things, about contraception in an AIDS-decimated Africa, about homosexuality among priests, about the causes of poverty and homelessness in London. He would be forced to acknowledge – even, possibly, have an opinion on – the wider picture. *So we shall not fear though the earth should rock, though the mountains fall into the depths of the sea.*

Of course he had no choice but to go to the meeting and accept the post, if it were offered him.

Lizzie was shocked by Charlie's flat. Such squalor when there was no shortage of space or, probably, money. Silverfish slithered round the kitchen, moths flew about the bedroom, mouse droppings (could they really be?) decorated the sofa. If it were a council flat, Pest Control, or whatever they were called, would have been in months ago, kicked out the owner more than likely.

However, since Lizzie wanted to serve Charlie, the sight wasn't altogether unwelcome. Here was need indeed. On the other hand, if she saw a mouse, she'd scream blue murder and run like hell. Gingerly, she opened a cupboard to look for bleach, bathroom cleaner, brushes, rubber gloves. Nothing, of course. Or nothing she'd want to touch. But she'd got her forty-six quid from Shirley and there was a shop on the corner.

With a sense of purpose she'd not felt for months – or years, more like – Lizzie set out for the shops. She'd throw out all those stacks of newspapers first thing. She'd need to get the porter on side for that. He'd given her quite a look as she went in but she was used to worse than that.

'Afternoon!' She nodded breezily as he popped out of his little cubicle. 'Giving Mr Potts's flat a clear-out, aren't I?'

'About time he got it done,' replied the porter, friendly enough.

So what if he thought her the cleaner? Although it hurt a little all the same.

'May need a pair of strong arms later.'

'I'll get out the Stallone growth hormone.' He winked.

Satisfied, Lizzie walked out. Men believed anything you told them. But that weasel-faced twerp was just the help she needed.

Roland put down the phone yet again. His friends were either not in their offices or were too busy to talk to him. It made him see how seldom he made this sort of call, a call for help. *I want an obituary for my mother. Just one will do.* It was pathetic. He had lost the art of asking for favours. Maybe he'd do better at e-mails. The trouble was that his contacts were on the chambers' computer. He certainly couldn't ask for help from there. He looked at his watch. Still only four o'clock. He'd never known a day so long.

He stood up and sat down again. His study struck him as immensely gloomy. Perhaps he'd be better in the country. But the country was Maggie's province. Sometimes he felt like a visitor. A visitor who paid the bills, of course.

He got up again and moved restlessly round the room. If he had a day off, he went early to the golf course or, during the season, out shooting, or occasionally stayed with friends. The country was used for entertaining – the kind of networking lunch that they had been due to host yesterday. But those people weren't friends.

Yesterday, after that football match, everybody had come in and sprawled round him in the kitchen. They were red-cheeked, smelling of damp grass and earth, steaming. They talked of the game in loud voices: the cheating, the foul tackling. They were filled with good humour and were kindly towards him, with a slightly surprised air, as if he were an alien landed in their midst. They were 'bonded', that ridiculous word, a fairly peculiar collection of people, including an Irishman, who seemed to be Portia's boyfriend (he hadn't even known she had a boyfriend), and Charlie's so-called wife, who looked like the kind of dead beat he saw hanging round the courts. Leo was on a high, with this home secretary business bursting on to the papers. He obviously didn't understand how it could rebound back on him. Lawyers understood the importance of cover.

Naturally this made him think of Didi. Not that, if he were truthful with himself, he ever didn't think about Didi. He reached up to a shelf and, at random, chose a CD. Tchaikovsky. Yes. That figured. Not at random, then. This was the joyous violin concerto that the composer had written after, at last, moving to live with his boyfriend.

Roland put away the CD. He'd never rated happiness highly and he wasn't going to start now.

Portia assumed she hated doing her accounts but, oddly enough for a woman who wore tasselled shawls and believed in making the world a happier place, she was rather good at them. Numbers bounded in and out of her head with surprising ease, leaving her pleased with the order she created. She didn't like to admit it was in her genes, but it certainly wasn't her schooling.

On this afternoon, with the sun streaking the rich colours of her walls and hangings, she sat down quite cheerfully. Lizzie was taken care of, Conor would come later and she knew Friday and Saturday's takings had been excellent. The first piece of paper she opened undid all this positive news: the owner of the arcade in which she rented a stall had decided to triple his charges on the basis that, with the increase in tourism leading to many more people in Portobello every day of the week, they could open their stalls for six days instead of just Friday and Saturday. Of course, he was a new guy who'd inherited the arcade from his father. He didn't know or care about the effect of the extended congestion charge. In fact, he was quite simply out of date. Numbers were down every day except Friday and Saturday.

Portia put down her pen and turned to her computer. She Googled the man and found thousands of entries. He was a successful businessman, owning a chain of electrical-goods' shops. The arcade could only be a pinhead in his accounts, a leftover from his father's retirement. An idea was forming. She picked up the phone and dialled Conor's office. 'The rent on my stall has trebled so I'm thinking of getting a mortgage on my flat and putting in an offer for the whole arcade.'

Annoyingly, she heard Conor laugh. 'I thought you were a charity worker, not a property developer.'

'That's the whole point. Of course I wouldn't be in it for the profit. Well, only enough for me to live on. I thought you might be interested in coming in too.'

'That's one of the more unlikely invitations. A non-profit investment.'

'There're rooms above. Fairly squalid. Could make a flat or two.'

'Now you're talking like a property *mogul*. So what makes you think the present owner might sell?'

Portia explained how it seemed to her the owner wouldn't want the bother of fighting the stall-holders when he already had a big business to run. She heard her confident words with some surprise. All the same, she couldn't resist imagining herself and Conor living in a newly done-up flat above the arcade. It would be light and airy with pale blinds and limewashed wooden floors.

Charlie had very few belongings. He didn't believe in underpants, and police Forensics still had his jacket, or so he assumed. Before he left that afternoon, Dr Heilbrand had lent him a copy of Dante's *Paradiso*, saying he needed a brighter outlook on life, but that could be stuffed into his pyjama-jacket pocket. His shaving kit could go in the other. Griff should never have told him about Ileana's inquest if he'd wanted him to stay in hospital. When had a warning been anything but a challenge?

He stood by his bed, annoyed by his shaking hand. Wanking

drugs. Only one more night in this white-out prison. He climbed into bed and a slew of newspapers that George had bought him earlier from Mr Patel cascaded to the floor.

CHAPTER FORTY-SIX

Turning and Turning

The coroner's court was in an area Charlie knew well, not far behind St Pancras station; it was actually in the graveyard of St Pancras Old Church, near the old Hospital for Tropical Diseases and the Grand Union Canal. In the last few years the rebuilding of the lines and station to receive European trains had made large areas into construction sites. The great new line was emerging high above roads, wasteland and the water basin.

Charlie got out of his underground train from South London at King's Cross. It was after the morning rush-hour but he still felt harassed by the amount of people pushing up the escalator, hurrying to bus stops, crowding round newspaper kiosks or thrusting free papers into his face.

It was sunny, but a blustery wind made the air feel cold. Nevertheless he decided to walk, keen to throw off the clinging warmth of the hospital, unwilling to push his way on to a bus. Construction barriers stopped him taking the usual route. Instead he set off along York Way, one of the busy thoroughfares north. It was a relief when he turned off, even though he was under concrete pillars below shining electrical pylons that decorated the new railway line like steel tinsel.

He reached the church and graveyard first. He was shivering. He thought of Ileana working out here on bitter nights, although the construction would have disrupted her trade as much as anyone else's. She'd moved northwards.

The graveyard had been turned into a kind of gloomy public garden, ineffectively cheered by pots of yellow polyanthus. At the far side was the coroner's court, more like a Victorian village school than an official building, with pointed tiled roofs and Gothic windows. Charlie hesitated, suspecting he was early. Somewhere over the last few days he'd lost his watch.

He was standing near a tree, partly shielded by a hedge. With a start, he noticed that the lower trunk was entirely surrounded by a hundred or more closely packed headstones. Weirdly, it had grown over the stones closest to it, flowing heavily in greyish waves, obliterating most of the inscriptions. One remained: 'In memory of . . .' Nothing more.

Charlie dug his hands deep in his pockets. He was cold through and through. The sun had gone in where he stood, although it still shone on the spires of St Pancras station, away to his right. He would have to go into the court for warmth.

A man appeared suddenly beside him. He'd come from behind the church. Tall, wearing a black baseball cap and a leather jacket. He said nothing. Neither did Charlie. He felt ill. He walked quickly towards the court house. The tree had unnerved him, but that wasn't it. He felt the presence of evil. Surreptitiously he crossed himself.

No one stood outside the court. There were two signs, to the right indicating the Coroner's Court, to the left Pest Control and Dog Warden, Laundry and Mortuary. The man in the baseball cap didn't follow him through the boundary railings.

Charlie was about to enter the court when he spotted a third sign pointing to a gate at some steps heading down to a road. On impulse, he passed the court and hurried through the gate. His departure would be hidden from the man in the graveyard by the court building.

Half running, he reached the road, which almost immediately passed under the new railway line, before he saw the sign again, Camley Street Natural Park, this time incorporated into an archway above open gates.

Charlie had no interest in wildlife but this seemed like an invitation to a freer, happier life. He turned in, stumbling rather as he reached a rough path. It led among half-cleared undergrowth to a wooden hut, plastered with childish paintings of frogs and minnows. He glimpsed the canal, wide and gleaming an oily brown, between the shrubs.

He continued walking and found himself among a gathering of parents and small children. They leaned over a pond with nets and buckets. Behind them was a bench. He sat down. The sun had come again lighting the scene in front of him. Mostly they had their backs to him, concentrating on whatever task was in hand but now and again a toddler broke ranks. One, possibly a girl, came to stare at him, her face as smoothly pink and white as that of a doll.

Gripped by tension, he couldn't manage a smile, but their eyes met for a second or two before she became bored and went back to her mother. Of course, the man in the peaked cap would eventually guess that he'd escaped but not, perhaps, until the court adjourned. Therefore he shouldn't be sitting here in the sun but on his way while he had the chance.

Where to? The flat he'd got for Lizzie where he'd gone before? He might as well be buried alive. Why shouldn't he keep the date he'd made with Leo at the House of Commons? There were enough policemen, some with Heckler Koch carbines, stun guns, mace, who knew what? It was probably the safest place in London.

Charlie stood up abruptly, lurched, regained his balance – his muscle tone was pathetic – and started back down the path.

A young woman, come out from the hut to offer the large man a leaflet, watched his receding back.

The sun made the ornate gilding glitter on Big Ben and the Houses of Parliament. Leo, standing at the window of his office in Portcullis House, could just see them to the right. Westminster Bridge was more directly in his line of vision. He thought of Wordsworth's poem and Whistler's paintings and was happy to be in this beautiful place. On the other side of the river the skyline was broken by the London Eye, a giant bicycle wheel, with the pods hanging below like glass succubae. Further right and opposite the Houses of Parliament was the modern block of St Thomas's hospital. He'd once visited a minister there, cut down by a stroke, yet able to see his place of work from his hospital bed. A kind of torture, Leo had rather daringly proposed, and the man, unable to speak, had nodded. Still, it was a fine location for death.

The bridge led south to his constituents. For him it was the actual and symbolic crossing-point between his life at the coal face and his life as part of the executive. He'd crossed the same bridge with Maggie. He always thought of her in the country, in the pretty house, with pretty garden, lively children.

Now they were lovers. Another outcome of the past week. It was impossible to concentrate on her without his mind switching quickly to the urgent matter of his career. Maggie wasn't going anywhere. Maggie loved him. Always had, he supposed. They were drawn to each other, that much was clear. Leo smiled to himself.

Behind him, Denver sat at his desk, opening an ever-growing pile of correspondence. He didn't disguise his enjoyment of the drama. He'd just passed over a request from the chief whip to attend her office at three p.m. 'She's giving you a medal for service beyond the call of duty,' he joked.

Leo continued to gaze out of the window. The bridge bore its usual load of red buses, taxis and pedestrians. Nothing was resolved. Some things defined. The prime minister would announce the new home secretary in a press conference at midday. Everybody knew who he was already. The police commissioner, on compassionate leave of absence from the Met, was expected to make a statement at much the same time, announcing that his wife's illness was likely to be more prolonged than first estimated; as a consequence, he was offering his resignation. The collision of the two ships in the Channel was almost certainly due to human error. Everybody knew that too.

Roland had called yesterday afternoon and, in his most clipped tones, given details of Imogen's funeral. When Leo suggested Bill should be on the altar somewhere, Roland had answered stiffly that it hadn't been their mother's wish. Maybe it hadn't, but that wasn't the point. Leo didn't argue the case.

Portia had called, asking whether he'd be interested in a business venture. He'd been unable to take her seriously. She got the message and rang off. He'd call her back some time.

Bill had called, deferentially and modestly, informing him that he was being considered for a new job at Westminster Cathedral and could he pop in for tea or something.

Charlie had called, sounding relatively calm, and asked if he could drop in for a booze-up after Ileana's inquest. That had stopped Leo on several counts. 'You're leaving the hospital and going to that murdered prostitute's inquest?'

'I knew her.'

'That doesn't mean you have to go to the inquest. You've done enough already. It will only be opened and adjourned anyway.'

'Ah, the cynicism of the man! Where's your humanity? Ileana had a mother, sister, aunt.'

'And how about the men in her life?'

'They were bastards.'

'Including you?'

'Including you and me. Worst of all. We killed her.'

'I thought you were a Catholic. What about free will? She *chose* to become involved.'

'Some people's wills are freer than others.'

Leo had given up. Now he stared at the London Eye turning so slowly as to seem immobile. Charlie was a force of nature. No one had ever deflected him from his purpose, however ill-conceived or self-destructive. It was perfectly possible he'd make a scene at the inquest and end up in a police cell. That was not the worst thing for him.

'I'll expect you round twelve thirty to one, then.'

'Chin-chin.'

The police had also rung several times but he hadn't taken the calls.

So had the press: four newspaper journalists, three from radio and three from television. He hadn't taken their calls either. Denver had been most disappointed. He'd left his flat at five a.m. to avoid them. He'd never been in this for self-publicity.

Maggie hadn't called. Nor had he called her. What was that line in *Macbeth*? 'She should have died hereafter.' Macbeth on hearing of Lady Macbeth's suicide. But he was no murderer. This evening he would be in his constituency, first with Bob, then with his core workers, finally at yet another open meeting. He expected this one to be different from the last. He might even be hailed as a hero. Perhaps it would help him make up his mind.

Maggie was buying Easter eggs in her local town. The dramatic events of the last week had diverted her from the usual preparations for a festival she particularly enjoyed. The shop windows were filled with daffodils, chocolate eggs, decorative chicks and ducks and other farmyard animals. She stuck to the eggs but, as a country-bred girl, she was glad of this celebration of animal life.

Picturing the comforting rotundity and trusting eyes of Mungo, she thought that animals knew about love as she understood it.

Changing her mind, she swapped two of her eggs for cheerful chocolate rabbits, clad in gold and red paper.

Perhaps Leo would never acknowledge what had happened between them. Perhaps Roland would continue to place his trust in her.

CHAPTER FORTY-SEVEN

Pinnacles of Power

Charlie reached King's Cross station. He hoped he was still on his own. There were not so many people as before but he could see no leather-jacketed, peak-capped man. He felt very tired and, with relief, allowed the escalator to carry him downwards. When the train came in, he sank into his seat and closed his eyes, causing him to pass through Embankment where he'd planned to change, and arrive at Waterloo. Instead of changing there, he decided to get off and walk back across Westminster Bridge. Despite his exhaustion, he felt that the sight of the river, of Big Ben and the ridiculous pinnacles of power, would invigorate him.

Bill's interview at Archbishop's House had reassured him. In fact, he was fighting against excitement that a new world was being opened to him. In the first place, the splendours of high government, of which he'd been ready to disapprove, were not in evidence. The office where he'd been interviewed was small, badly lit and badly furnished. The computer's age suggested lack of funds. All this made him feel at home.

He'd not expected this as he'd approached from Victoria station via the wide piazza in front of Westminster Cathedral. In his nervousness, he'd arrived half an hour early, so he'd decided to say a prayer, offering himself to God for whatever purpose He chose. He entered the cathedral past an old man rolled in layers of coats, held together with string. A sign advised him not to give money to beggars as they were looked after by a Catholic organisation.

The soaring brick vaulting didn't lessen his nervousness but nervousness was close to humility and humility was a virtue he understood better than most. The cathedral, this morning clothed in its Lenten purple, was built a mere hundred years ago and remained uncompleted. Gradually his awe changed for pride at being a small part of such an exalted place.

It seemed that he was being interviewed to play a new role. A wealthy Catholic businessman, whose family had emigrated from Poland many years ago, had had the idea of sponsoring a priest to look after the immigrants of all nationalities now entering Britain. The cardinal was concerned about the spiritual and temporal needs of those, legal or illegal, who were flooding London. Bill's friend, Mark, knew about Bill's work in Holloway, where a third of the prisoners were foreign nationals, and thought he might be the man for the job. He would live and work in Clergy House, adjoining Archbishop's House, and would probably have various other local duties, such as covering for Mass in the chapel of St Mary Under-croft.

'What chapel is that?' asked Bill.

'Otherwise known as the Crypt. An ornate little place under the Houses of Parliament. All denominations use it, but you'd be surprised how many Catholic MPs and peers there are.'

Bill *was* surprised.

'Oh, yes,' continued Mark. 'There're prayer groups and all sorts in there. It's not just the Americans who put God into government.'

Bill studied his friend's face. This was more what he'd feared and expected. Here, at very least, was a hint that souls were to be counted according to their position in the world. On the other hand perhaps it was priggish of him to think this way. It was certainly naïve.

He smiled. 'One of my brothers is an MP.'

'Really? Then you can have the pleasure of saying Mass for him.'

'Sadly, he's not a Catholic.'

'Not ever?'

'Never.'

'Would I know him?'

Bill saw that Mark was trying to think of an MP with his surname and failing. Surely he knew he'd been adopted. It was not, he thought, the moment to introduce Leo's name with all its present reverberations. 'He's a backbencher,' he said, which wasn't a lie.

They moved on to other subjects. He would not generally be expected to deal with the press – they had a spokesman for that. This was a relief. On the other hand, he might need to attend press briefings on occasion.

It was after midday when Bill left, walking down Ambrosden Avenue briskly. A cool wind snaked out of the courtyard that led to the playground of Westminster Choir School. A small boy in a cherry blazer ran to collect a ball. Someone shouted at him. On the other side of the road the sun lit up the flame-coloured bricks of the row of tall, elegant apartment blocks. They were the same colour as the cathedral and all the buildings around. Not hellish flames, Bill decided, the red of religious celebration. It seemed he would be appointed.

Soon he was on Victoria Street, looking hungrily at a Pizza Hut and a McDonald's. He'd never had good taste in food. Maybe he could swap his invitation to Leo from tea to lunch. Certainly it would be wrong to hang about for hours when he always had so much to do. Normally this was his afternoon for visiting Holloway.

He took out his mobile indecisively. He knew it was ridiculous to be afraid of his own brother. Or, at least, what he represented. He'd have to get over such cowardice if he was to succeed in his new job.

He took a small notebook from his pocket, found Leo's name and carefully pressed in the numbers.

Roland sat on an upright chair in his flat. He was dressed in a dark suit as if for chambers or court. He had nothing else to wear in London. The buzzer rang in the corridor.

'Yes?'

The porter – the regular, not the flirtatious one – spoke. 'There's a Mr Smith Dunbar for you.'

'Fine.'

When he came in, Roland was struck by his visitor's dramatic good looks: very fair, very sunburned, very blue-eyed. He wore a cream cashmere jacket and jeans. His figure was good too.

'All these years,' Smith said, his friendly voice tinged with a tight South African accent. 'I'd decided I was off your list.'

'Want a drink?'

They drank beers. Roland thought, This is the first time I've solicited a meeting with a gay man who is not a prostitute. He felt exhilarated.

'Not in court today?'

'No. My mother died.'

'I'm sorry. I remember your mother. She made me wish I fancied women. Didn't have much time for pervs, I assume.' He paused. 'So, you married?'

'I'm still married.'

Smith Dunbar sat back in his chair. He seemed a little bewildered. 'Frankly, I never thought you'd want to see me. I just rang for old times' sake. To niggle you a bit, if I'm honest. I don't come to London often.'

'Do you have a partner?'

'Not at the moment. You know me. Faithful to myself at all times. So, why *do* you want to see me?'

Roland didn't answer at once. Unless he'd changed considerably in the twenty-five years since they'd met, Smith was as trustworthy as an elephant on heat. Not someone in whom to confide your secrets. 'I'm still gay.'

Smith laughed, showing slightly crossed teeth, his only imperfection. In the past, Roland had found that appealing. 'I guessed that. What do you want me to do? Procure boys for you or something naughty?'

'No.' Roland was shocked, making his visitor smile again. 'I just wanted to say hello.'

'Well, hello, sailor! Incidentally, what has your brother been up to?'

Roland remembered that, even when they'd been lovers, he'd never actually liked Dunbar, as he'd called him then. He was clever enough, but in a facile way. 'You're still working as a journalist?' he asked stiffly. 'No trouble with the government?'

'Trouble for what reason? All right. Change of subject. Actually, the ANC have done a lot of good things. It's sad that only the murders get reported over here.'

As Smith talked intelligently about the problems facing South Africa, Roland decided that the experiment of meeting him had failed or, at least, it had taught him that he wasn't ready to change his future. He felt uncomfortable with him, embarrassed by his attractiveness.

Yet suddenly, impulsively, he found himself saying, 'My mother's funeral's on Friday. Come along if you like.'

Dunbar gazed at him with his sky-blue eyes. 'That's a very kind invitation but would your mother approve?'

'It's her funeral.'

Leo had booked a table for his lunch with Charlie in Portcullis House. He knew Charlie wouldn't be pleased, preferring the grander restaurants in the House of Commons, probably as a backcloth to whatever eccentricity he was planning. Flouting convention was more fun against stone-mullioned windows, Pugin wallpaper and sombre oil paintings of Victorian statesmen, thought Leo, tolerantly. Today Charlie would have to make do with the modern. In his present circumstances, he felt calmer the nearer he was to his own office.

'There's a call for you.' Denver sounded suspicious. 'He says he's your brother.'

'He *is* my brother.' Assuming it was Charlie, Leo took the call. It was a moment before he gathered it was in fact Bill. Was he free at lunchtime? Well, yes and no. He'd been looking forward to *à deux* with Charlie, now that he was out of hospital. He glanced at his watch. He didn't expect Charlie till one fifteen. 'How about a quick drink?' That didn't sound very friendly. 'The bar has a great view of the river. Go through St Stephen's entrance, giving my name, and I'll meet you in Central Lobby. How soon can you be there?'

'It didn't sound like your brother,' commented Denver, when Leo put down the phone.

Leo knew what he meant. Bill's northern accent always surprised him too. He'd go down in fifteen minutes, give Bill half an hour in the bar, then race back to meet Charlie. It was only then that he realised he'd just arranged to do exactly what he'd determined to avoid: enter the lion's den of Central Lobby where he was sure to be nobbled by someone he didn't want to speak to.

'Fuck!'

'*Excusez-moi.*'

'Hey, Denver, could you make a little trip for me to the Central Lobby?'

'Sure thing, boss. To collect your brother, I presume.'

'Bring him up here.'

'Funny, isn't it? Most MPs spend their whole time trying to catch the attention of the press and here are you trying to avoid it. Haven't you noticed they're on your side, man?'

'Yes?' Leo was fond of Denver. His cheeky manner disguised a sharp brain. 'My Denver's a good boy,' his mother had said, when she appeared with him in his surgery, like something out of an American movie, but she'd been right. 'Bare your teeth at anyone who asks questions.'

'Call me Tiger. That bruise on your face has gone the coolest shade of green. Almost *eau-de-Nil*, pardon my second attempt at French.'

'Thanks.'

When he'd gone, Leo began reluctantly to read some of the letters from his constituents. He'd already seen a lot of the email ones and knew that they'd be mostly congratulatory. The home secretary had become unpopular in the last few years, gaining a reputation as a bully and a womaniser. So why did he find it a disagreeable experience? It was the same old story, he supposed, disenchantment with the political scene.

Perhaps he'd lost his self-importance or perhaps he'd never had enough. When he was first elected, he'd picked up order papers, read his name on them or in Hansard with real pride and excitement. He'd worked hard to get on select committees, eventually becoming junior minister in the Home Office. Ironic that now. He'd been dropped in a reshuffle after he'd voted against the presentation of the Freedom of Information Bill. He'd worked on it too – the prime minister had never forgiven him for that. Of course he'd voted against the war in Iraq too.

Leo got up and went to the window. The bridge was nearly as busy at lunchtime as at rush hour. Small figures, their features blackened by distance and the mystery cast by the river, hurried along the pavement. One, far away, stood out in his brightly striped jacket. The sort of garb Charlie favoured.

Leo turned back to his desk and this time opened his laptop. He hoped Bill would get a move on and not stay too long.

Lizzie was sitting down for a moment. She peeled the rubber gloves off her fingers. The kitchen was nearly done. She'd found an old radio to keep her company and now it was telling her it was twelve thirty. Nothing would be as bad as the kitchen, she thought, all that filthy china and sticky pots. At least the water had been hot.

She lit a cigarette and dragged deeply. Bottles and bottles of booze too. Empty bottles. Vodka mostly. The serious drinker's choice. Charlie was certainly not ashamed of it. Or perhaps he didn't let anyone into the flat. She'd talked to that porter about getting in Pest Control for real. There were some funny insects she didn't like the look of at all. Quite apart from the moths in the bedroom.

She'd be disgusted if it was anyone but Charlie. Wouldn't give it the time of day. Lizzie lit another cigarette from the stub of the old one. She imagined Charlie coming into the flat, his voice first, booming out crazy jokes she didn't really understand, then his presence filling the space, dressed like no one ever had before, hitching her life to his so she'd never be alone again. Pity she couldn't really believe it would ever work out like that.

Sighing just a little, Lizzie decided it would be the bathroom next, then another break while she got that chirpy porter to help her carry away some of the rubbish.

Bill approached the St Stephen's entrance to Parliament warily. He didn't like to see policemen with guns – never had – and these were big black submachine guns or Kalashnikovs. He'd never wanted to know anything about guns so he'd probably got it wrong. He was shocked, too, by the ugly blockades, spoiling the elegance of the buildings behind them. Why should security so dominate? Our lives are in the hands of the Lord, he thought, before correcting himself for too much piety. We needed our government to feel safe. He stepped up to the first tier of police.

'I've come to see Leo Barr.'

'Oh, have you just?' The policeman's tone was amusedly ironic. He pointed Bill to an outside security van.

Once through that, checked and searched, it seemed that he was free to pass the police with the guns, which didn't look so big now he was closer, proceed through Westminster Hall, St Stephen's Hall and into Central Lobby. The way was pointed to him and he passed a couple of groups of tourists, one of children, but he still felt overawed by the marble flooring, the statues, frescos, stained glass, fan vaulting and chandeliers. What a morning! From the central government of his church to the central government of the country.

He found a bench and sank on to it with relief. Beside him, he noticed yet another statue. He read the inscription: 'George Leveson-Gower, Granville'. A Liberal who had served under prime ministers Russell, Palmerston and Gladstone but never become PM himself. In other words, a failure.

Bill smiled to himself.

'Mr Barr?'

Bill didn't respond for a moment till he guessed that the snappily suited young black man in front of him had drawn a wrong conclusion.

'Yes.' He stood up. 'I'm Leo's brother, although my name is Bill Wright.'

'Life is full of surprises,' said the young man, chattily. 'You're a person of faith too, I see.'

They shook hands and Bill followed his companion across the marble floor.

CHAPTER FORTY-EIGHT

Alleluia

Charlie went up from the underground for a vod in the Waterloo station bar. And then had another. Small man, small shots. Big man, big shots. He looked round. The place, darkish and lit with red lamps, was surprisingly full for lunchtime. Men and women. Mostly with cases at their feet, but not all. There were people who just liked being there. Or preferred it to anywhere else.

A clock on the wall told him he was still early for his date with Leo. Outside, announcements were being made about train departures, security, delays and platform numbers. The muffled sounds were soothing. Combined with the warmth, low lighting and alcohol, they made him feel safe and unwilling to venture out. The girl behind the bar was foreign, pale face, pale hair. When he tried to chat her up a bit, she smiled without understanding.

After half an hour or so and a fourth vodka, he stood up. He would cross the station, take the walkway over the road and, that way, reach the Embankment. From there, he could get up on to Westminster Bridge.

He didn't feel so frightened any more, but wary. Out there someone was trying to kill him. *Soyez calme*, old boy.

The weather had turned colder again but the vodka provided insulation. It strengthened his legs too. This summer he might take Chastity out of mothballs. Do him good to get out on the ocean waves. Might take those nephews as crew, he thought rather vaguely. Although that funk Roland would probably put a stop to it. Perhaps he'd take the Patel boys instead; they were planning to go places. Leo might come too, and maybe even the saintly priest. Poor old Bill. All duty, no fun. Of course his fun came from celebrating the sacred mysteries. Lucky Bill.

'Alleluia! Alleluia!' His spirits were lifting nicely and he was already halfway across the walkway. Soon he'd be quaffing a spot of claret with the most famous MP of the decade. *Dearer yet the brotherhood that binds the brave of all the earth.* Quote, Sir Henry John Newbolt. He hoped Leo would duly thank him.

His manner sobered as he thought of Ileana. And he hadn't even been able to pay tribute by attending her inquest. Bastards. *Bastards*! Instinctively, he glanced round him but there was nothing or nobody even faintly sinister, unless you counted a couple of ferocious pigeons who looked as if they planned to dive-bomb a girl walking in front of him.

'Fuck off!' he shouted, waving his arms. The pigeons changed course and the girl turned, a sandwich halfway to her mouth. He bowed with a flourish and she turned back, increasing her pace.

That's gratitude, thought Charlie, but he didn't mind. The girl had been pretty with big blue eyes. *None but the brave deserves the fair.* I am born to be a girl's saviour, he boasted to himself, and for a moment pictured Lizzie. Not without her charms now she was off the drugs. He'd get rid of that depressing flat he'd rented for her. Must have been mad at the time. Actually, he was!

Charlie laughed out loud, causing another pedestrian, this time a young Japanese girl, to hasten her steps. He was on the Embankment now, the river, churned a little by the wind, on his right.

Slowing his pace, he looked up at Big Ben. He'd always liked its silly bong. One New Year when he was very young he'd been allowed to stay up late. At midnight the whole family had listened reverentially to the twelve bongs coming from their old-fashioned radio. He'd felt so filled with anticipation and excitement that his heart had bonged in time with the clock. When it finished there was a second's magic silence, broken by Imogen's complaining voice, 'Haven't you opened the champagne yet, Esmond?' How she hated not being the centre of attention – even when her rival was a clock. Poor Imogen! Her life spent on a fruitless quest for happiness. How she'd suffered! The Grim Reaper had got her in the end – as he does us all, good and bad. Strange how unwilling people were to recognise that fact.

Smiling, Charlie mounted the stone steps that took him on to the bridge. The sun glittered all around him, on the turrets of Parliament, on the tops of black taxis and silver cars, on the crisping waves behind a boat moving down the Thames. Heart beating with a kind of exultation, he halted a moment at the top and surveyed the scene. Then, crying, 'Alleluia!' he strode forward into the traffic of people and cars.

The walls were thick, the windows double-glazed. All the same, Leo heard the wail of the ambulance, the police car's siren. He was peering down when Bill came in with Denver.

'Hi, Bill.' He turned, then turned back. 'One more cyclist lost.' He tried to smile. 'Let's hope it's a cycling Conservative MP.' His joking covered a sickening fear.

Bill joined him. 'What a view.'

'Yes.' He added distractedly, 'I chose the office for the view. I could have had a bigger one.' He was still craning down.

Someone was being carried into the ambulance, he thought. No sign of a bicycle. No crashed car. It was all happening so quickly.

'I'm going down!' He was out of the office, running to the lift. Denver and Bill hesitated, then followed. They stood side by side in the bright lift. Leo, pale-faced, didn't feel the need to give explanation.

Together they raced out of Portcullis House, pushed through the crowds outside the underground, crossed the road and arrived at a police cordon keeping back an already biggish crowd.

But the ambulance had done a U-turn and headed off. Leo reached for his MP's identity card; the policeman knew him anyway. 'Afternoon, Mr Barr.'

'What was it? What happened?'

'Hit-and-run, sir. Funny that. Should be "hit and drive".'

'Who was it? Who was knocked down?'

'Can't tell you that, can I?'

'A man?'

'Yes. A man. A very big man. Not as big as a car. A big car, too, according to the witnesses.'

'Witnesses?'

'Oh, yes. Plenty of those. So far none of them had the sense to take the registration number. That's foreigners for you.'

'And how was he? The big man?'

'Not good.' The policeman acknowledged a signal from a colleague. One of the police cars had already left. He was wanted.

'How not good?'

'As bad as could be, sir. I'd say that.'

'Dead?'

'The car caught him, flung him in the air, knocked him down, smashed his head against the pavement or the wall.'

Leo stepped back. Bill caught hold of his arm, as if he thought he'd fall. Denver took the other and the policeman left them.

'I thought I saw Charlie,' Leo muttered, more to himself than to them, 'crossing the bridge. They'll have taken him to St Thomas's.' He swivelled round to look at the Houses of Parliament. He picked out the windows to the dining room where Charlie preferred to lunch.

The policeman, already in the car with siren blazing, turned to the driver. 'See what was scribbled on his arm? "Extasie". Gives you a clue, doesn't it.'

CHAPTER FORTY-NINE

The Value of Silence

'Thank you for coming here.' Roland stood in the living room of his flat with arm outstretched, as if he wanted to shake Leo's hand or even clasp him. Eventually, as Leo came no closer, he let it fall.

'I'm glad to get out of Westminster.' Without looking at his brother, Leo took a chair and sat down heavily. 'Strange, though. The same people who didn't want to know me over my unveiling of our unsaintly home secretary are being very kind now. Going out of their way to be kind. Little notes lighting up my pigeonhole like it was a pinball machine. Haven't seen such a thing since Thatcher's demise – political demise, I mean. Notes of condolence pinging on to my computer. Poor Denver can hardly cope. And this morning I had a letter of sympathy from my constituency with over a thousand signatures, all collected over a couple of days.'

Roland said nothing. He was surprised that Leo should tell him all these things. The words 'open his heart' sprang into his mind. He couldn't help remembering the last time – only ten days ago – when they were also facing the news of Charlie's death. Then they had fought, like children or animals. He had the remains of a cut on his cheekbone to remind him and the bruising round Leo's eye was still visible.

'I suppose it's partly the manner of his death. Everyone hates a hit-and-run driver, as if we all might be guilty one day. We're all cowardly. Every one of us would run given the chance.'

Surely Leo couldn't believe that Charlie's death had been accidental. It had to have been a second and successful attempt at murder, by the same forces of darkness that Leo had himself helped to uncover. Yet he didn't want to interrupt Leo's monologue. He was continuing to record the reaction in Parliament and in his constituency.

'Before this happened, I'd more or less decided to leave politics. I was disgusted by the lack of support. I felt out of tune with just about everybody. I knew there was a young party worker in my constituency who fancied standing in my place. She began by fancying me and moved on to fancy my job. She made me cups of tea but that didn't fool me.' He looked at Roland for the first time. 'You can't be kicked out at the bar. Isn't that right?'

'Not unless you do something truly terrible.' Roland thought that having a male prostitute as a lover just might come under that heading, but probably not. The bar was tolerant of its members' private foibles. It would be different if he was a judge.

'Dear old Bill's been helpful too,' said Leo. 'I can see why Charlie liked him. People with a secure belief are very comforting. He'll have to do Charlie's funeral.'

'Of course.' Again, Roland considered the manner of Charlie's death. The papers had already speculated. There would be an inquest and, if circumstances were thought to be suspicious, the police wouldn't release his body. But he still said nothing of this to Leo. Leo was in shock. 'You're an excellent MP.' How had these words come into his mouth? Why was Leo accepting them as if it was natural? It must be the first compliment he'd given him in their lifetimes. Perhaps they were both in shock. 'First we have to get through Imogen's funeral.'

'Yes,' Leo agreed, but he didn't look as if he was thinking of his mother. 'Bill told Lizzie the news. She's staying in Charlie's flat. She took it better than he expected. Apparently she said that he was too good for this world and when she'd seen him in hospital – she was there for hours apparently – she'd taken the precaution of saying farewell. Bill couldn't quite believe her because she spent a whole day cleaning out Charlie's revolting flat for his return. But if that's the way she could deal with it, then who was he to argue? He was particularly pleased that she consented to say a prayer with him.' He looked at Roland. 'I think we should give her the flat, don't you?'

'She is his wife, I understand,' said Roland who had difficulty taking the idea of Lizzie seriously. 'Which would make her the legal inheritor.' Once, about ten years ago, Charlie had picked up another stray – a teenage boy that time. His parents had claimed him eventually, making all kinds of ridiculous accusations. Charlie had always been resolutely heterosexual. He'd only known about the boy because at one point it seemed the family might go to law and Charlie had come for advice. Money had been the answer, of course. There'd been others he'd helped too, often ending in recriminations.

'Charlie liked to play God,' Roland said.

Leo stood up. He went to the window. 'Nice view. I can't bear to look out of my window at the moment. I might swap offices. I keep hearing the sirens, remembering the flash of colour that I'm sure was Charlie's jacket.' He swung round, eyes staring. 'Without knowing it, I very probably saw him walking to his death.'

He sat down abruptly and took out a handkerchief, which he pressed to his eyes. Roland looked away, embarrassed but also sympathetic.

After a moment or two, Leo blew his nose loudly and began to talk again in a lower tone. 'We were both educated for all this, weren't we? The nice views, offices, the good salaries – better than good in your case, I would imagine. I wonder if Charlie would have been the same.'

'Without his mental instability, you mean? They say all saints are madmen, if that's your point. But you know my view on that.' This was dangerous territory. Roland regretted speaking. But Leo was clearly in no mood for an argument, let alone a fight. As the silence lengthened, Roland spoke again. 'I'm glad you've decided to hang in there.'

'Have I? Yes, I suppose I have.' He reflected. 'So far I've only taken in the horror of Charlie's death. I don't have a real sense of loss.'

'No. After last week . . .' Roland decided not to continue.

'I want to tell you something.' Leo was looking straight at him. In his wide-spaced eyes, cropped hair, strong nose and mouth, Roland had a curious sense that he was seeing his own mirror image. They were brothers, born scarcely more than a year apart. When they were dead and skeletons, no one would be able to tell them apart. 'I don't want to know,' he said. He knew instinctively he didn't want to hear whatever Leo had to tell him. His words were more of a plea than a command. He wanted to say, 'Don't spoil things between us at the moment when I'm willing to acknowledge our similarity.'

Instead, he murmured, 'As a lawyer, I've learned the value of silence.'

'Yes.' Leo still seemed undecided.

'Already there's too much for one family to bear.'

'Family?' Leo queried the word, adding almost at once, 'It can wait. You're right. Later. When things are calmer.' He glanced at his watch. 'I should be going. I have yet another meeting. There's a great deal to be played out yet.'

Roland stood up. The two men, so alike, approached each other. Slowly, tentatively, they embraced.

After Leo had gone, Roland continued to sit in his chair. He allowed himself to consider Didi, not just as a beautiful body but as someone he cared about. He felt as if there was a long road of understanding ahead of him but that he'd started along that road. After Imogen's funeral, he would try to progress further. He would try to confront the anger and fear that had possessed him as long as he remembered. The prospect was difficult but brought with it a kind of resignation, which in its turn gave him a feeling of peace. Even of hope.

He would talk to Maggie again. Not yet. Not for quite a while. He still believed in the value of silence, as he'd told Leo. But some time they would talk. Charlie dead too. Imogen and Charlie both dead. How much love he'd expended on one and hatred on the other! He would have to see what was left of himself now they were gone.

Portia sat on a box in the middle of a dirty, dusty room, surrounded by other boxes. She was crying again. Exhaustion made her stop fairly soon.

Conor came up the stairs. He stood and looked at her. 'More tears.'

She squinted up at him. The hour had just changed and, although it was evening, he was backlit by a low sun piercing the streaky window. She rubbed her eyes. They felt hot and sticky. 'I don't like the idea of a future without Charlie. His death makes me more unhappy about Imogen. And Esmond.'

Conor smiled and came over to her. He crouched down and put his arm round her. 'Haven't you left out the bereaved Lizzie and that poor Ileana who was murdered and that other man in the mental hospital?'

'You're quite right. My mourning spreads and spreads, to the whole world, in fact, and whenever I feel happy, I feel guilty. Because I *am* happy, Conor.' She took his hand. 'I'm so happy I could cry.'

'Oh, no, please!' Conor protested mockingly.

'I can imagine us living in this flat, waking up together, loving each other even when we're cross. I can imagine it but I can't *believe* it.'

'Happiness is like that is for people like you, I think. Unreal. But it's still there.'

'What do you mean, people like me?' She stroked his cheek but she was suspicious all the same.

'You don't want me to start on your family, do you?'

'No. Definitely not.' She stood up hurriedly, as if to make further discussion impossible. She waved her hand. 'This will be our own living room. Two white sofas. One wall hanging I shall commission from Maria Carmen – she's the best embroiderer of my women. When we have a baby, Maria de la Luz will weave her a shawl. Skulls and skeletons strictly forbidden.'

'A baby?' said Conor, hugging Portia so close that she had to put her arms round his neck. 'There's a thought to get a man going.'

Slowly, tenderly, they kissed. Then they lay together on the dirty floor.

Lizzie looked up at Bill. 'You've come to see me again?'

'I'm worried about you.' He knew she'd slept in Charlie's flat since his death.

'Everybody's worried about me. Portia, who was never too keen, wants me to help out on her stall. She's on to something new.'

Bill, who'd been standing in the doorway of the flat, took a step forward. 'You've made this nice.'

'You saw it when you came to tell me.' She was sitting in a big chair, the only one remaining after her clear-out.

'I wasn't in the mood to notice. Are you really all right, Lizzie?'

'I'm not likely to be surprised by the worst, am I? Anyway, Charlie's still here.'

Bill, the priest, felt confused. 'Of course. The human spirit is eternal.' He looked round but there was definitely nowhere to sit down. 'I'm doing something new too. I thought it might interest you.'

'Charlie's here with me all the time. And now they say I can stay here so he'll never go. He'd be pleased how his flat looks, don't you think?'

'Oh, yes,' lied Bill, Charlie had never cared what his flat looked like, and found tears had come into his eyes. 'I'll pop in tomorrow with another chair and a few more bits and pieces. We can talk then.'

'We're not born to be happy, are we, Father?' She was looking at him earnestly but not tragically.

'Certainly not, my dear.' Bill turned his back, sniffed and moved towards the kitchen. 'A nice electric kettle, that's what you need.'

After Bill had gone, Lizzie knelt down and said a prayer. 'Please, God, look after Charlie and me and all his family.' That morning she'd been to that bridge, seen where Charlie had died. She didn't want to embarrass Bill with talk of heaven and hell, but in her view Charlie was already in heaven and whoever had killed him was well on his way to hell. Her job now was to keep his spirit alive in the world.

Maggie answered her mobile in the evening. In the garden. The wood-pigeons were calling so loudly that they interfered with her concentration or perhaps she was frightened to hear. Nevertheless, she'd had the phone with her as if she'd expected Leo to ring.

'I wanted to talk to you before Imogen's funeral tomorrow. I'm sorry I haven't been in touch before.'

She knew from his tone what he was going to tell her. But there was really no need. His silence over the last days had said everything. Even before Charlie's death, she'd suspected this was the most likely outcome. All he had to say was that he loved her. That would be more than enough. Enough for another twenty years anyway. You always had to hope for a future, however far away.

'I'm so terribly sorry about Charlie.' She would divert him to that.

Around her the twilight was deepening under the trees where she'd been walking – and the light shining brighter from the house.

'Yes. I still can't deal with it. And now it's in the hands of the police.' He paused, and this time she waited. 'That day – last Sunday was it? It seems weeks ago – was one of the happiest of my life. Even *the* happiest.'

This was good. But it wasn't love. It was a happy day out in the country, eating, drinking, playful football, being nice to the children. 'Yes. It was a wonderful day.'

'It was like a day off. Oh, Maggie . . .'

Would he not say those few words that would make the whole difference to her life? Her pride, although not strong, would not allow her to cue him in because how could she believe him then?

'Please, Leo.' She'd allow herself to weep after he'd rung off. Go under the trees and moan in tune with the pigeons. And when they'd gone to their nests, she'd creep back into the house and take the lasagne out of the oven and open a fresh bottle of Pinotage. 'What?' What was he saying? The dire nature of her thoughts, the birds' rising vibrations had actually deafened her.

'I love you, Maggie. You know that. We know that. And I'm sorry it can't be more than that. So sorry. Yesterday Roland and I met and we didn't row. We were both too tired, I think. And suddenly I understood he was my brother and there was absolutely nothing to be done about it. Do you see what I'm saying?'

'You didn't have to say anything.' But he did! He loved her. She wouldn't listen to anything else. She didn't want reasons. Just the love. The pigeons had gone entirely quiet as if at an order.

'I love you, Leo.'

'Yes. I'm glad. We'll get through tomorrow, then. And afterwards. Goodbye, Maggie.'

'Goodbye, Leo.' After he rang off, she stayed absolutely still and even held her breath.

Then she turned and went across the lawn towards the house. Hetty was standing at the door, with the boys behind her.

'We couldn't think what you were doing out there in the dark. You've got to realise we're all jumpy after what happened to Uncle Charlie.'

Maggie wanted to laugh, not about poor Charlie naturally, but out of happiness. Instead she put her arm round Hetty. 'You mustn't worry so much, darling. Remember, it's Easter in ten days' time.' She didn't know quite why she said that, except to disguise her happiness with something they could all celebrate together.

CHAPTER FIFTY

Going Below

Far out to sea Esmond, standing on the quarterdeck of his first-rate ship-of-the-line, struggled against a gale-force-eight wind. Beside him, seven sailors bent all their weight to control the wheel. There should have been one more but he'd fallen on the deck and now struggled to regain his feet.

Esmond had no interest in them. A captain trusted his sailors or flogged them if they failed. He looked out across the ocean, narrowing his eyes against the walls of spray thrown up across the deck. The air had become colder. They were heading to the southern hemisphere. Somewhere to port lay the long coast, not too close, he hoped. He glanced briefly at the officers to his right and left. He had sailed round the world with them and was doing it again. They were strong, taciturn men. He liked that.

Esmond spread his legs further. His feet in their tall black boots gripped the slippery deck. There were a hundred guns on this ship, all primed and ready to fire. But no enemy would appear in such weather.

Stay on course, that was the point. Steer further and further south till ice islands floated on glassy waters. He'd been here before. He'd been through the worst that man and nature could throw at him. He'd led his eight hundred sailors to safety, rounded the Cape and headed into the safe harbour.

From the fo'c'sle, seven bells rang, struck firm and true, a strong bass to the whine and shriek of the wind. Ships were noisy places but the bell was the best sound in the world. Half an hour to the change of watch. Sometimes half an hour could seem like an age; at others it passed in a flash.

In half an hour, he would join his lady wife in the cabin. She wasn't well. The doctor had shaken his head but prescribed nothing. She'd always been pale, with her Nordic hair and glacier eyes, but now she was ghostlike in her translucence – as beautiful as an icy wave. He would join her and open a bottle of the best champagne. She'd like that. He preferred a shot of whisky – always had – but he wanted her to be happy. He might ask along some of those officers, Harry and Aubrey and Ned. Those sort of names. She liked men like that.

Esmond swayed a little and even took a couple of steps back as a particularly strong gust hit him in the midriff. There had been a time when he wouldn't have budged an inch, however powerful the wind. He was weakening. There had been a time when he could direct the guns from this very deck, twelve twelve-pounders, watch the men bend to their task, keep his eye on the enemy, on the clouds, wind and sun. Then he was a man!

In truth he was happier then than at any other moment. Even Imogen couldn't compete. There was his guilt, because she knew it. Not at the beginning. But soon enough. She was his prize. He'd carried her off but she could never be the most important part of his life. How could any woman compete with the full-bodied feel of a ship under sail? He was a man in a lifelong battle with the great elements of wind, sea and sky.

You had to be strong, though. If not, you might as well go down, go right down below the waterline, find the surgeon in the orlop, safe from the gunfire up above.

There was no gunfire. Esmond shook himself a little and water flew off his hat and shoulders. The wind was lessening, the clouds drifting behind them. Ahead the sky was opening. A change at sea could come so quickly. At one moment you were steeped in inky clouds, draping themselves over the rigging spurs. At the next, you were surrounded by a blazing blue sky.

Watching is the most important activity on board any ship from the grandest ship-of-the-line to the humblest fishing vessel. Watching, waiting. Then acting decisively to make the right decision.

The ship's progress was smoother now, her bows less low, her risings less high. The wind was still blowing but the fountains of water had turned to garlands, brushing past him and disappearing

340

into the air. The sea was no longer an ugly, turbulent brown, but shot through with blues and greens.

Soon the wind would sing, not scream, through the rigging.

Then he would go below, join Imogen in the spacious cabin where the panelled walls curved outwards like the sides of a bell. There it was now, ringing more clearly in the greater calm.

The officers turned to him, big fellows, buffeted and wet through like him but not showing it. Their faces were ruddy, their eyes keen. The ship was safe enough in their hands. Yes, he would go below.

Acknowledgements

With thanks to Jane Wood, Bruce Hunter, Sara O'Keeffe, Hazel Orme, Belinda Wingfield Digby, Mark Fisher and Jo Higgs. In different ways, each was important in making this book possible.

Also, thanks to my wonderful family, particularly Rose, Chloe and Hannah, who were invaluable early readers.

Finally, to Kevin, whose support for my writing now spans forty years.